THE FUTURE'S SO BRIGHT

Published by Water Dragon Publishing
waterdragonpublishing.com

All rights reserved.

No part of this book may be reproduced or transmitted in any form or by any means, electronic or mechanical, except for the purpose of review and/or reference, without explicit permission in writing from the publishers.

Cover design artwork copyright © 2022 by Dany Rivera
danycomicsarts.com

Cover design copyright © 2022 by Niki Lenhart
nikilen-designs.com

ISBN 978-1-957146-64-5 (Trade Paperback)

10 9 8 7 6 5 4 3 2 1

FIRST EDITION

Foreword
copyright © 2022 by Elyse Russell

"Born in the Black"
copyright © 2022 by Brandon Ketchum

"The Comforting"
copyright © 2022 by Kevin David Anderson

"The Ear is a Vital Organ "
copyright © 2022 by Nels Challinor

"Emergence"
copyright © 2022 by A.M. Weald

"The Emperor's Proposition"
copyright © 2022 by David Wright

"The Faceless Enemy"
copyright © 2022 by Stephen C. Curro

"Hopfull Future"
copyright © 2022 by Alfred Smith

"Hydropolis"
copyright © 2022 by Julia LaFond

"Imaginary Friends"
copyright © 2022 by Steven D. Brewer

"Lady Jade"
copyright © 2022 by Maureen Bowden

"The Last Gift"
copyright © 2022 by Nestor Delfino

"Legacy"
copyright © 2022 by Syn McDonald

"Machine Intelligences Don't Care about the Fermi Paradox"
copyright © 2022 by Jetse de Vries

"Misty and the Windmills"
copyright © 2022 by Gail Ann Gibbs

"Night Circus"
copyright © 2022 by Regina Clarke

"The Repairwoman"
copyright © 2022 by Henry Herz

"The Salvage at the Selvage"
copyright © 2022 by Christopher Muscato

"Scars of Satyagraha"
copyright © 2022 by R. Jean Mathieu

"Xenoveterinarian"
copyright © 2022 by Gwen C. Katz

All rights reserved.

FOREWORD

"AND THEY LIVED HAPPILY EVER AFTER." How many times have we heard that phrase? The end of most every children's story is butterflies and rainbows.

Good triumphs over evil. Love prevails. Happiness is found. Now you can pull your covers up to your chin and go to sleep, snug in your bed and in the knowledge that all is right with the world.

That is, until we grow up. Then we see that all is not always right with the world. In fact, it sometimes feels as though we are stuck in a pit of sand from which we cannot escape. All of our struggles only cause us to sink down further amongst the grains. War. Disease. Loss. Despair.

Where are the butterflies and rainbows now, when we need them most?

It's sometimes so difficult to look to the future with any hope in the heart. What will this world look like for our great-grandchildren? What will become of humans? The questions spiral and the sand pulls us down.

Have you ever heard of the Baader-Meinhof Phenomenon? It explains how, after you learn of the existence of something, you start to see it everywhere. For instance, you are told about a certain celebrity and start seeing their face in every advertisement. It's like a strange moment of waking up to the world being just a little bit bigger than it was moments before.

Well, here's my hope: that this book sparks that phenomenon for you. Tuck into bed, pull the covers up snug, and read about how maybe the future could be bright after all. Then...maybe you'll start seeing bits and pieces of it here and there, all around you, in real life. Soak up some of that positivity. Perhaps it's a story in the news of a brilliant new

Foreword

breakthrough in medicine that saves lives. Or a video of an animal being rescued and adopted. People coming together and fighting back against injustices. Trees being planted. A parent playing with their children in the park.

Of course life isn't all butterflies and rainbows, but ... the story isn't over yet, is it? We're still here. There's still a chance.

This collection of stories runs the gamut of positive emotions. Some are bittersweet, others are steady lights of hope, and a few will even make you laugh out loud. Some are expansive views of what the future could hold for all of mankind, and others are microcosms of hopeful futures for just a single person.

But what they all have in common is that, perhaps despite some sadness, happiness is ultimately found. These authors have crafted tales for you to escape into, yes, but also to carry with you long after you put the book down. The creation of this collection is a story in and of itself: a story about people wanting to push some positivity out into the world and provide a respite for others.

All is not lost. The future really *can be* bright.

Elyse Russell
curator of *The Future's So Bright*

CONTENTS

The Ear is a Vital Organ 1
Xenoveterinarian 15
Born in the Black 33
Emergence 51
Misty and the Windmills 73
Hopfull Future 85
Hydropolis 95
Night Circus 117
The Comforting 139
The Salvage at the Selvage 159
Scars of Satyagraha 177
The Faceless Enemy 203
The Repairwoman 221
Machine Intelligences Don't Care About the Fermi Paradox 233
The Last Gift 245
The Emperor's Proposition 265
Lady Jade 277
Imaginary Friends 289
Legacy 297

Nels Challinor is a writer, musician, and teacher from the Pacific Northwest of the United States. His work has appeared in *The Wells Street Journal, Visual Verse,* and Brain Mill Press's *Ab Terra 2020 Collection.* Nels is also the co-founder and editor of Great Ape, a literary magazine for absurdist humor.

• • •

I wrote "The Ear is a Vital Organ" after reading Robin Wall Kimmerer's incomparable "Braiding Sweetgrass". I was inspired to create a positive vision of the future that does not involve humans gaining something we lack, but learning to appreciate and respect what we already have. Thank you to Dain Weisner for fact-checking the ecology in this story.

THE EAR IS A VITAL ORGAN

NELS CHALLINOR

THERE ARE SOME SOUNDS that cannot be heard. Trees speak to each other, sending messages through fungal networks belowground. Tadpoles wriggle through the murky waters of a still pond. The mountains crumble beneath the weight of themselves. Most of us are too busy listening to sound to sense these subtle changes in the world. But those of us who live with silence, like my Aunt Sadie, whisper along to the symphony of nature. And when she speaks, everyone stops talking so that they can listen.

Many years ago, when Sadie was a young woman who still had her hearing, and I wasn't yet an idea in my mother's head, no one cared to listen. Everyone spoke as loudly as they wanted, secure in the belief that it was only us, only people, who mattered. They told themselves that this made them healthy and happy, but really, nobody anywhere had ever been so miserable. When I ask Aunt Sadie why people lived like this, she explains that nearly the whole world forgot that the ear is a vital organ, even when it no longer works the way it's supposed to.

On days when I feel self-pity clawing at my gut, I wish that my own ears stopped working, or started working in the way that Aunt Sadie's and Rebecca's do. I know that my hearing is an asset when it comes time to hunt or greet strangers. I know that not everyone can be blessed. But I still envy Aunt Sadie, because I wish I could add my quiet voice to the forest. Instead, my whispers sound alien and harsh, all wrong, as though I am singing in a different key from the rest of the chorus. I have decided to speak only when absolutely necessary.

• • •

My mother tries to convince me to speak more often as we pick blueberries on the Northern face of Big Slide. We do this every three days: waking early to make the 10-mile hike out to the trailhead from our cabin. We walk in silence the whole way there, barefoot because it's summer and because that way we can hear if someone's coming. But once we reach the summit and arrive at the great open rock face for which the mountain is named, my mother asks me why I have given up speaking.

"You have such a beautiful voice," she says. "Why hide it from the world?"

"I don't," I sign back. "And I am training myself to hear. Like Aunt Sadie hears."

She shakes her head. "Aunt Sadie doesn't hear."

"You know what I mean."

"No," she says, "you don't know what I mean. Aunt Sadie herself will tell you that she doesn't hear. Hasn't heard since the bomb that took her husband."

"But," I argue, "she told me that the ear is a vital organ. I know hers don't work anymore to alert her to sound, but she still hears the world. She still hears so much more than you or I ever will. She hears the garter snakes molting, the birch back peeling, the waterfalls crashing. She hears it all, somehow."

My mother looks up at the dull gray sky, so close from this high up. Today it is cloudy, but the intensity of the sunlight, even with the clouds, feeds the hungry blueberries. They cluster in tight bunches spread across the rock face. We are not the only ones who graze here. These purplish pockets of sugar entice birds and squirrels, who will eventually deposit the seeds in digested form. And the blueberries will spread. The whole chain of communication from sunlight to blueberry to squirrel repeats itself year after year for no particular reason except that this is how the conversation has evolved.

My mother sighs. "I can't speak for Sadie. Wouldn't dare. But it seems to me that she might be implying that the ear is more than someone's ability to hear."

"No shit," I sign.

"Watch it," she says.

We drop the subject, concentrating instead on filling our two large wicker baskets with berries. By the time we return to camp, our backs are cricked, and our calloused fingers bear new cuts and scrapes. We give both baskets to Rebecca, who pours them into a pot over the fire with a small ration of granulated sugar.

"Where's Sadie?" I sign to Rebecca, but she just shrugs.

I'm too tired to go looking for her, so instead I head for my room with a small candle. I try to draw, to commit the view from the top of Big Slide to paper, but the horizon doesn't come out the way I want it to, so I tear it in half. Then I look at the pieces on the floor of my bedroom.

When my father and mother were young, people split the Earth itself in half, looking for precious stones. They unzipped the clouds with puffy white chem-trails. They diverted rivers, burned forests, dumped thousands of tons of plastic into the ocean. Is it any wonder then that the elements themselves turned on people? That tsunamis, earthquakes, wildfires, and hurricanes rose up to stem the flood of human intervention? The Earth is old and much stronger than anyone realized; it was not the one who needed saving.

My parents speak of a time when other people were inescapable. Wherever you went, you found them. When they talk about this, my parents assume the far-off reminiscent look of golden days gone by, but to me, it sounds awful. We see people from time to time, crossing near our camp, or when we're out scavenging, but sometimes a year or more will go by between these sightings, which is fine by me. After the "natural disasters" took away people's access to food and shelter, violence spread across the world. Those who couldn't live quietly without supermarkets and televisions and SUVs were killed, either by themselves or someone else.

"The only people you can trust," my parents once told me, "are us and Sadie and Luke and Rebecca."

That was ten years ago though, and my parents have started trusting again. I will occasionally see my father laughing with other men in town as we are scavenging. Or my mother will invite a passing stranger to share our fire and our food for a night. The lesson, I suppose, is that you can't trust everyone, but most people are harmless.

I fall asleep waiting to hear Aunt Sadie's heavy footsteps outside my door.

• • •

The next morning, I wake at dawn, ready to help gather firewood or water, whatever we need. Outside, by the smoldering firepit, the adults are arranged into a circle, discussing something.

"She's done this before," my father signs.

"Something feels different this time," my mother responds.

"Different how?" Luke asks.

"She's my sister. I know her better than you all do. And this is different. Something has happened to her. Otherwise, she would be back here, at home, where she belongs."

I feel my mother's worry creep underneath my skin. They haven't yet realized that I am eavesdropping.

My parents have told me that when they were young, they felt certain that they would live to see the end of the world, by which, they meant the end of human beings. Even before the violence and the death, they were told that the Earth would give up sustaining them. Nobody worries about this anymore. The abundance around us is so evident, you can sense it, or at least Aunt Sadie could. As I listen to the adults talk about where she could be, I feel a panic not unlike what they must have felt when they were young. I feel like I will live to see the end of the world.

"We can check in town," my father says. "Maybe she went scavenging."

My mother shakes her head, but says nothing.

"I'm coming with you," I sign to my father and he only nods, knowing that it would be futile to argue.

I don't go into town often, not because I'm not welcome, but because I have little interest. The shops and the cars and the consumer goods do not trigger the nostalgia my parents feel. I have never known a world with them. For this reason, I am terrible at scavenging. I prefer to spend time around camp and in the woods, where the knowledge that my mother and Sadie have poured into my head is readily accessible. But I would walk through the rubble of urban sprawl for years if it meant finding Aunt Sadie.

I lace up my boots. Barefoot is not an option in town, what with the broken glass and rusted metal. I fill my backpack with water, a bag of nuts and seeds, and a pocket knife.

My father and I set out, following a herd path for a mile or two, until it joins a two-lane highway. Walking on the concrete feels strange, as though my feet are being slapped with each footfall. I jog a bit to keep up with my father, whose stride is long, his eyes set straight ahead. We pass cars and trucks, abandoned along the road where they ran out of gas.

Eventually, we come to a metal bridge above a river. Turning my head downstream, I hear the roar of the river reduced to a swift burble. A young stand of alder sprouts from one of its banks. This is a new bank, created by gradual buildup of sediment brought by the rushing water. The skinny white trees will reinforce the ground, until another storm comes and redirects the river again. Tufts of elk fur still cling to the trunks and branches.

Sadie once told me how alder may as well be a feather bed to an elk. They love the feeling of the closely packed trees on their hides. While rubbing themselves, they graze on the shrubs and shoots sprouting in the underbrush and then they deposit manure, which fertilizes the soil. More nutrients, more trees. The river is the director of this pocket drama, determining who goes where and when.

"Keep up," my father says. He is a good twenty paces ahead of me, halfway across the bridge.

The air itself changes on the other side. It tastes like moldy upholstery and smoke. The moisture and fragrant spruce and pine have been masked by the stench of humans. As we draw closer to town, the houses get closer together, until one buts right up next to another. It never ceases to amaze me that people used to live so close to each other.

On Main Street, we come across a man carrying several bags. He looks exhausted, but still raises a hand in greeting to my father. "Howdy, Jim. This your boy?"

My father nods and places a hand on my shoulder. "We're looking for Sadie. Have you seen her?"

The man shakes his head. "Sorry, can't say I have. Been staying home most days though, what with the new baby."

My father smiles. "How is she?"

"Beautiful," the man says, beaming.

"And Portia?"

"Recovering well. I'll tell her you asked after her. She'll appreciate it."

"You do that," my father says.

As the two men continue talking about the man's family and the early summer rain and what it will mean for our respective gardens, I drift away, seething. I hate my father for not feeling the same urgency and panic that I feel. I don't understand how he can carry on about the weather at a time like this.

In the broken window of a ransacked pharmacy, I see an untouched greeting card display. The side closest to me has birthday cards. One of them sticks out to me. It features a cartoon bear with the words "Have a Grrrrrrr-eat Birthday!". My father gave me this card two years ago. He must have found it on this very rack.

I remember that birthday, the gooey sweetness of the nut bars my mother made, dipping into our precious flour supply. I remember the fire and the laughter. I remember smiling so much that my cheeks were sore, and I had to keep massaging them. Sadie hadn't spoken a word all day, to me or anyone. My father, drunk on sugar and protein, ribbed her for it, asking whether she'd forgotten that it was my birthday. Sadie ignored him, turning to me instead.

"Are you ready for your present?" she asked aloud. Sadie's voice is a harmony of rough stone and smooth water. When she speaks, she directs, as powerful as a river. The adults quieted down so that they could listen.

"Your present is a story. A lesson. It's the story of a birthday.

"Many, many years ago, all the world gathered for a birthday party. Everyone was so excited and nervous. Squirrel kept chittering from his treetop. River babbled incessantly to a silent moose. The pine trees shivered in anticipation, casting their prickly needles to the ground. They were all waiting for the guest of honor, a small hairless ape that they decided to call human.

"Human, it was known, would be born with a different kind of brain. There was much discussion about what this brain would do, but nobody knew for sure. Despite the discussion, which at times grew heated, the whole world agreed that they would treat the human as an equal.

"When the baby emerged from the womb of the world, tiny and pained, into the cold air, it arrived crying. This was not uncommon. Soft, gentle moss grew up around it. But the moss did not comfort human, who grabbed and tore and only screamed louder. Moss retreated and wolf moved in to swaddle the child with its soft fur. Human, though, threw its arms around wolf's neck, squeezing tighter and tighter and not even redwood, with all its power, could pry them loose. Thinking that human might just need a distraction, trout swam around it, flashing beautiful pinks, greens, and silvers. But human was not amused. Instead, it took a huge bite out of trout's back.

"Everything in the world tried to get this new creature to calm down, and everything failed, even the wind and the waves. The baby only grew more hysterical. And as they stood by watching the contagious pain and suffering of human, they wondered why it couldn't just calm down so that they could end the birthday. Because it had been going on for far too long. And even the mountains had grown tired of it."

For two years, I have tried not to cry or yell. I tread carefully so as not to crush snails or beetles underfoot. I do not want to take up space like human did on its birthday. But, standing here on the cracked asphalt in front of the pharmacy, I can feel a selfishness creeping up my throat. I let out a sob as I remember Aunt Sadie, the wiry wisps of her graying hair and the way they felt on my cheek when I hugged her. By the time my father finds me, my face is streaked with tears. He comforts me and we poke around a few more darkened buildings before heading home empty-handed.

• • •

A week goes by with no sign of Aunt Sadie. Then another. My mother cries herself to sleep every night. My father's and my feeble attempts to comfort her accomplish nothing. She has been hollowed out by the pain and worry. "This is normal," Rebecca signs to me over breakfast one day. "We have to let her grieve." My mother's grief is jagged. She will sob for hours and then her mouth will twist into a violent scream, sending the birds — crows and sparrows — flapping away. I cringe, ashamed of my mother for disrupting the world with her screams.

As summer turns towards fall, the rains begin. The damp earth is softer underfoot and the whole forest smells of decomposing leaf litter. Luke and Rebecca ask if I'd like to join them on the annual chanterelle hunt. I leap at the opportunity. Anything to get away from my mother for a few hours.

Rebecca and Luke were Sadie's friends in the city before they all moved here with my parents. Luke is stocky and strong, with a seemingly inexhaustible supply of energy. He maintains the house, turns dead trees into firewood, and still finds time to build snares and traps for small game. Rebecca is the opposite. Like Sadie, her contributions are mostly to our collective knowledge and understanding of the world. Born unable to hear, she doesn't speak to communicate, but when she signs, we give her the same quiet reverence we give to Sadie.

We find a small cache of the delicious mushrooms. As Luke kneels to harvest, Rebecca turns to me. "How are you?"

"Are you asking rhetorically or do you actually want to know?" I ask.

Instead of answering, she kneels beside a spruce tree. Surrounding the tree is a ring of small white mushrooms that have recently sprouted through the needles and dirt. "Fairy ring," she signs.

I nod. "Sadie told me how they sprout from threads of a single fungus, interwoven with the roots of a tree."

"Did she also tell you what they mean?" she asks, fixing me in her pale green eyes.

"What do you mean, what they mean?" I ask.

"People used to believe that you could get trapped in them. That they would turn you invisible if you stepped inside."

"The tree's still there," Luke observes, joining us.

"Only people could be cursed in this way," Rebecca explains. "Unable to communicate with everyone you left behind. It's tragic sure, but I never saw it as a curse. If our absence is felt, is it still an absence?"

• • •

After a month, I decide that I am going out to look for Aunt Sadie by myself. Nobody seems to notice me coming and going; Luke and Rebecca are too busy providing for us and my parents are too deep in their grief, too certain that she's gone for good. Somebody needs to figure out what happened to her.

Sadie and I used to take walks together, always following the old trails that people cut into the forest floor, since partially overgrown, so that we could easily find our way back. I follow the main trail from our cabin for a few miles, eventually stumbling upon the old dam, which has broken. With no one to repair it, the water streams through the gaping holes in the wood. One day, it will collapse, and the lumber used to construct it will become part of the riverbank.

Above the small pond created by the dam, I see Tahawus, forever keeping watch over our lives. This is the name that the people who first lived here gave the mountain. The people who came after them called it Marcy, but we prefer Tahawus, "Cloudsplitter". The peak grazes the clouds. It is a silly thought, childish even, but I wonder whether I could spot Sadie from that great distance. Without another idea, I set off on the trail to the summit.

After a few hundred yards, my path is blocked by a fallen tree. I begin snapping off branches, recklessly, until I pause, sensing something on the underside of the limb in my hand. Slowly, I turn it over to reveal a nursery web spider nest, the webbing thick and matted, like a tarp partially covering the spiderlings. Dozens of them are tucked away behind the intricately woven silk. I have always wondered how spiders learn how to weave these delicate homes. It occurs to me now, looking into this web, that they spend their formative moments ensconced in an example. I see through their miniature eyes, looking up and studying the sprawling patterns of glittering white thread, so that one day, I will know too. And I do this until these shapes and patterns are all I see, all I know.

Keep your eyes moving and your ears open, Sadie once told me, and the world will reveal all its secrets to you.

My gaze shifts to my feet, where I see the shiny arc of a broken bear claw, stuck between two rocks. This one is tiny, less than an inch long, and must have belonged to a cub. I feel adrenaline prickle across the skin of my neck. I have been taught since my infancy that bears are mostly harmless unless you come between a child and its mother. The claw is clearly old, but I still can't shake my fear.

I pause, standing in the middle of the trail, and scan the surrounding woods. I don't hear or see anything that would indicate a bear. Just before moving on, my eye catches on something that should not be there — a scrap of purple cloth snagged on a tree limb. My breath catches as I recognize it, immediately, as a piece of Aunt Sadie's favorite coat.

Suddenly, I can see it, the whole scene appearing before me. Sadie walks this trail to collect her thoughts and gather whatever she can. She comes across a bear cub, its claw broken where it caught between rocks. Maybe a bit of blood lays fresh on the ground. Sadie pauses. Perhaps she knows that this is it, that she has found herself in a dangerous situation without a way out. And then she takes her last deep breath, sucking in all the delicious air that this world generates, before the bear's mother is upon her.

I walk over and retrieve the scrap of cloth. Sadie is back there somewhere, but I don't dare look. Nor will we make any attempt to retrieve her body. She always said that however she died, she wanted to be dragged into the woods and left to be eaten and decompose like all the other dead things. There is something unspeakably beautiful to me in the fact that the world granted her this wish.

• • •

Before hiking back to camp, I take the scrap of cloth up to the top of the mountain, thinking all the while about the bear and my anger. Anger can only be satisfying when it has a target. But try as I might, I cannot attach it to the bear. I understand her actions. They were justified. She killed my aunt to protect her child, just as my mother would kill a bear to protect me. But I need some outlet for my anger. It cannot stay inside of me, or I will slowly devour myself.

A light rain begins to fall. I remove my pack from my back and insert the scrap of cloth. I have to show it to my mother. I have to be the one who tells her what happened. But not yet.

The summit is bare, a mound of stone capping the mountain. A large pile of rocks, half-scattered, sits at the peak. I asked my father about these once and he told me that people used to bring rocks to top of the mountain because they considered it a tragedy that the mountain was crumbling. They thought that the rocks would become part of the mountain. They thought that they could save it.

Nothing can be saved. That is the simple truth that Sadie taught me. Everything is temporary — our lives, the rivers, the mountains. All will end, but the ends have meaning, insofar as they make room for beginnings. I take a deep breath, connecting with my anger as I wonder what strange beginning will come from its end.

I live to see the end of the world. Each moment that this Earth survives is also a moment of death. Life and death overlapping and releasing a scream like hot iron in water. I thank Aunt Sadie for showing me how to sense the world, all its end and its beginnings. Tears fall from my eyes, joining the raindrops, and all this water tumbles down the mountaintop where it will run into streams and rivers and eventually, the ocean, which beats against the sand and stone along its shores. The wind whips through the Big Leaf Maples, showering the ground with their helicopter seeds. I can feel them turning in swift circles as they fall. The whole world and everything in it comes together to form a song, loud as life and quiet as death. I open my mouth to howl my pain to the clouds overhead and for the first time, I am on key. The scream that I produce is pitchy and uneven, but it is honest. It belongs. And so do I.

Gwen C. Katz is an author, artist, and game designer living in Pasadena, California with her husband and a revolving door of transient animals. Her novel, *Among the Red Stars*, tells the story of Russia's famous all-female bomber regiment known as the "Night Witches".

•   •   •

Back in 2020, I was suddenly inspired to write a whole spate of stories revolving around viruses and bacteria. Can't imagine why.

XENOVETERINARIAN

GWEN C. KATZ

T HE BIGGER THEY ARE, the harder they step on a nail. "Why was there a nail lying around in the first place?" demanded Vivian as she ducked a swinging tentacle. She couldn't blame the octophant for being cranky. She'd feel the same way if she had a two-inch piece of steel embedded in her foot. "Everything on the station is self-assembling!"

"My husband's wild about DIY," said the owner, and he had the decency to droop his gills apologetically.

Vivian added "home carpentry gone wrong" to her mental list of perils to domestic animals and tried to figure out how to get close to the octophant. It was eight feet long from nose to tail and the thrashing tentacles dangling from its face were thicker than her leg. There was no way that thing was going to let her pick up its foot.

"We're going to need to anesthetize it," she said.

"You will not!" the owner protested. "I'm taking her to the big show on Hephaestus 7 tomorrow and I won't have her all groggy from chemicals. Octophants are extremely sensitive creatures."

"I could put a liter of morphine in her bloodstream and she wouldn't even feel it," said Vivian. "She'll be fine. Unless you want to try pulling that nail out yourself?"

The owner scowled, but allowed Vivian to escort him out of the examination room. She sealed the room and flooded it with anesthetic gas. It took three doses before the massive beast finally swayed on its tree-trunk legs and went down.

She purged the anesthetic and opened the door, not without a hint of trepidation. Air hissed past the door's rubber seal, laden with the astringent smell of chemicals.

The beast twitched, making her flinch back, but she approached and lay a hand on its flank. It was out. At last she could get close and truly appreciate its beauty. Its eight tentacles splayed across the examination room's white plastic floor, each one strong enough to constrict a horse, yet delicate enough to pick a flower. Its skin was not gnarled like an elephant's, but smooth and velvety, spangled with an intricate pattern of russet-brown rings and zigzags that camouflaged it among the rocky canyons of its native habitat, for massive as it was, there were still creatures on its home planet that hunted it.

Luckily for Vivian, no one had yet tried to keep any of those creatures as a pet, or if they had, at least they hadn't brought it to Tau Station.

Removing the nail turned out to be a trivial affair. She pulled it out with pliers and injected the octophant's red, swollen foot with antimicrobial nanites.

"The nanite spray you got on the way in should have decontaminated everything, but I'm sending you home with another dose just to be safe," she explained. "I'm also giving her a nonsteroidal anti-inflammatory to bring the swelling down. She should know to stay off that foot on her own; just don't let her do anything strenuous. She'll be all right in a couple of days."

"I can't have her limping for the show," said the owner. "Give her a stronger local anesthetic so she'll be able to walk properly."

"I will not," said Vivian. "She'll hurt herself if she can't feel the pain. Her need to heal is more important than your need to win a medal."

The owner puffed up his throat sac and looked daggers at her. "Are you telling me how to care for my own animal? Do you know how difficult it was to even get the permits to transport her? If I miss this show —"

Vivian didn't hear the rest of the speech, because at that moment she felt a tentacle snaking around her leg.

The anesthetic was wearing off.

She held still, trying not to spook the octophant. It was groggy and disoriented and was just trying to get its bearings. Unfortunately, it also wrapped a tentacle around its owner's waist. He cried out, the startled octophant dragged him to the ground, and the room became a chaos of striped and spotted limbs.

Vivian slipped her leg free — octophant tentacles had no suckers, so a quick counterclockwise twist was enough — and rushed over to the beast.

"Forget about her! Help *me!*" protested the owner as he tried to pull off the tentacle threatening to bisect his abdomen.

She ignored him. Instead, she stroked the top of the octophant's head. "Shh, shh, it's all right. No one's going to hurt you. The procedure is already done."

The beast continued to struggle. It struck Vivian in the back of the shin with one knee, nearly knocking her off balance and promising to leave a nasty bruise.

Vivian remembered a trick she'd heard from another octophant owner and felt the crease along the creature's neck. There it was: a patch of smoother skin. She ran her hand along the crease, clicking her tongue. "There. That's a good octophant. Just lie still."

At last the creature relaxed. Its tentacle slid off the owner's waist.

"What was that you just did?" asked the owner once they were safely outside the examination room.

"Octophants are social," Vivian explained. "They bond with each other by rubbing their tentacles along that patch of skin. It's their version of a hug."

The owner looked at her blankly.

"You're not very experienced with octophants, are you?" she asked. "Do you have any experience at all working with large animals?"

He replied, "That's none of your business."

An hour later, the octophant was properly awake and her owner led her away, grumbling about bad service.

"Feel free to take her to the *other* large animal vet on Tau Station," Vivian couldn't resist calling after him.

Vivian's receptionist pinged her com box. "Are you ready for your next patient? There's a kid here with a hamster."

Vivian slumped against the wall. "Oh, thank goodness."

• • •

Back in her hab, Vivian made green tea in her lacquerware teapot and put a fresh bandage on her thumb. The hamster had gotten its fur tangled in its exercise wheel. It had bitten Vivian's thumb when she tried to extricate it. All in all, it had not been the best day.

While the tea steeped, she picked up her com box. "Station wardens? I need a check on Hab 2024. There's an exotic pet owner there who doesn't know a quagga from a quokka. Can you go make sure his permits and licenses are in order?"

That done, she sank into her armchair. Her pet greenling, May, left her spot under the grow light and jumped into Vivian's lap, the leaves on her back rustling contentedly. August the decapede curled around her stocking feet, his many legs sprawled out in every direction, while January occupied her usual spot in a glass bowl on top of the fridge, a rime of frost forming on the rim of the bowl as she slept.

Vivian poured the tea and took a sip, glancing regretfully at the three other cups sitting in their spots in the velvet-lined box. She put on a soap opera and watched it half-attentively, not bothering to push August down when he raised his serpentine body to get a peek. Her com box pinged. Vivian's face lit up when she saw her elder daughter.

"Cindy!" she cried, picking up the call. "What a nice surprise. It's been ... what, two months? Nothing's wrong, is it?"

"Everything's great! I just wanted to tell you that I got the gallery space."

"For the cardboard sculptures? That's great!"

"The opening's in a little over a year, and I was thinking ..." Cindy scratched her neck. "... Would you like to come out and see it?"

"What, to Brightsun Colony?" Vivian unwound August, who was trying to wrap his rough body around her arm.

"Why not? I haven't seen you in ages."

"No, no, it would be lovely to see you! But you haven't visited Tau Station in six years, and ..."

Cindy groaned. "This is why I don't call more often. It always comes back to your kids abandoned you and moved to *terra firma* and never even learned the family recipe for scallion pancakes."

"You don't have to be so defensive. I just think you girls could have learned a little about our own culture before you ran off to live with aliens."

"Well, you can take it up with Amy when you see her."

"Seeing Amy?" Vivian frowned. "What are you talking about?"

"Oh, hasn't she told you yet? She's coming out to Tau Station in July, and she's bringing Arykh and Ilykh. You'll finally get to meet your grandkid!"

"And she talked to you first? She hasn't said anything to me about ..." Another ping on her com box. It was Amy. Vivian hurriedly took the call.

"Hi Mom," said Amy, smiling brightly. "I've got great news! You know how you're always telling us we should take a vacation?"

• • •

Vivian watched through the curved window as the transport pulled its ungainly, sprawling bulk into the docking bay. She'd been begging Amy to visit for eleven years, yet now she felt a twinge of trepidation.

People poured out of the vessel and into the airlock, where misters sprayed them down with antimicrobial nanites. The first-time travelers twitched and wrinkled their noses at the unfamiliar sensation. Then they all came pouring out in the awkward half-walk, half-bounce of people unused to low gravity. A hubbub of excited voices filled the station.

And then there were the three of them, waving at her from across the terminal.

Amy had hardly changed: same bright smile, same sensibly bobbed black hair.

Next to her was Arykh, half a head above the rest of the crowd. As a species, Vivian had to concede, the Taroczi were striking, with four glossy horns, long, tapered faces, and skin fading from russet brown to creamy white. Yet there was something unsettling about their too-large hands and the way their mouths were slightly downturned at the corners, as though constantly disapproving.

Trailing a few steps behind them came Ilykh, who lacked horns (for which Vivian was secretly grateful), but shared Arykh's face shape and countershaded skin. The kid had one hand on their com and the other buried in an animal's shaggy brown fur. Their dzacta? They brought it along?

"Mom!" said Amy, setting down her luggage to give Vivian a hug. "It's so good to see you. It's been way too long!"

"It's so nice of you to finally come out to visit," said Vivian, and then wondered if that had come out meaner than she meant.

Arykh bowed and pressed the curved sides of their horns into Vivian's hands.

"Oh! That's ... so chivalrous," said Vivian, pulling away a little too fast.

"It is a traditional Taroczi greeting for elders," said Arykh.

Vivian laughed awkwardly. "I hope I'm not as old as all that."

"And here's Ilykh," said Amy, waving the child forward. "Come and meet your grandmother!"

Ilykh ambled forward, their eyes still on the com video they were watching, the dzacta trotting close by their side.

"Goodness, you're getting big!" said Vivian, realizing that she sounded like one of those dull adult relatives she'd always disliked as a child. When she was a little girl, she hated comments about how she kept growing, as if she had any option to do otherwise. But Ilykh really was quite tall and sturdy for an eleven-year-old, even considering that they were half Taroczi.

Ilykh turned to Amy and asked her something in a rapid-fire language full of consonants.

Vivian frowned. "You speak Taroczi together?"

"Well, of course," said Amy, but there was tenseness in her smile. "That's what all their friends at school speak."

"It's just ... I didn't know," said Vivian.

"Ilykh says they thought they'd be able to feel the nanites walking around on them," Amy translated.

"Oh, nanites are much too small for that," said Vivian, relieved to be back on familiar territory. "They're really quite amazing inventions. They can tell the difference between harmful bacteria and beneficial bacteria, and they hunt down and destroy the harmful kind."

"We wouldn't need that on Tarocz," said Ilykh. "Hardly anyone gets sick there." And then they turned back to Amy and said something else in Taroczi.

"Speak English," Amy scolded them. "It's rude to speak a language your grandmother can't understand."

The dzacta bumped Vivian with his broad, soft nose. Everyone laughed.

"What a handsome fellow!" said Vivian.

"His name's Ushk-Ushk," said Ilykh, still not looking up from their com.

At Vivian's blank look, Amy explained, "It's a noise they make with their noses."

"Like a snuffle," said Vivian. "And you brought him along? Even on vacation?"

"It's the custom," said Arykh. "Every Taroczi baby is given a dzacta when they're born, and it goes with them everywhere. Even at school, there's a pen where the dzactas graze while the children are in class."

But they're not a Taroczi, Vivian wanted to say. Not a full-blood Taroczi, anyway. Dzactas were fine — they were lovely animals, actually, shaggy mastiff-sized puffballs with wide-toed feet like geckos — but it hurt her how wholeheartedly Amy had embraced Taroczi customs. Did she really have to give her kid a Taroczi name? What was wrong with human names?

"Besides," said Amy, "We thought you'd like to meet him."

"You have me there," Vivian admitted, scratching the beast's ears. "Who's a good dzacta? I never see them at the clinic. Taroczis aren't big travelers, are they?"

That was a nice way of saying that Tarocz was a backwater. If Amy hadn't gone there on that interplanetary tree survey as an undergrad, surely she would never have ended up living there.

"If you'd seen the woods of Tarocz, you wouldn't want to travel either," said Arykh.

Vivian forced a smile. "I suppose everyone's home seems like paradise if you've never seen anything else. Well, perhaps Tau Station will change your mind. Come, let me show you around."

Touring the station didn't take long, and soon they retired to Vivian's hab for tea. The tiny living room was crammed full: Amy and Vivian sat on the loveseat, Arykh occupied the easy chair with their horns poking the upholstery, and Ilykh sat on the floor leaning against Ushk-Ushk, still absorbed by the show on their com box. May, August, and January crept around, trying to squeeze their way into any inch of available space.

"She's cold!" Ilykh exclaimed when January sets a delicate paw on their knee.

"She's a frost ferret," said Vivian. "She works just like the compressor in an air conditioner. See those long pipes coming out of her back? They vent the hot air. Hold your hand over them; you'll feel how warm it is."

Ilykh gave it a try and a look of surprise crossed their face. "That's so weird! What about that one?" They pointed to May.

"She's photosynthetic," Vivian explained. "Those things on her back aren't really leaves, they're flaps of skin filled with symbiotic algae. She can use them to convert light and carbon dioxide into sugars. As long as she spends enough time under the grow lights, she doesn't need to eat."

"Does that mean she doesn't poop, either?"

"That's right."

Ilykh snickered.

"That's why I love working with animals," said Vivian. "You're always learning something new."

She told a few stories about the curious animals she'd treated at the clinic, and Arykh and Amy talked about their encounters with Taroczi wildlife. With all four cups of the tea set in use, Vivian felt keenly that this was how her life should have been.

At last, Ilykh began to nod off with their head cradled in Ushk-Ushk's fur. Arykh took them back to their quarters. Amy stayed behind to keep catching up with Vivian.

"Are you happy?" Vivian asked her.

"What do you mean?" asked Amy, her fingers tracing the irises painted on the lacquer cup. "I couldn't be happier. Arykh is wonderful, and Ilykh ... they're a miracle."

Vivian had seen enough ectopic pregnancies and prolapsed uteruses that she'd decided to have both her babies artificially incubated, but Amy wanted to have a baby the old-fashioned way. It wasn't easy — the single-sex Taroczis were very biologically different from humans. Three pregnancies had failed. Ilykh was the fourth.

"They're a great kid," said Vivian. "But don't you ever want more from life? You were so bright in school. Your sister is off becoming a famous artist. And you ..."

Amy sighed and set down her cup. "See, this is why I left Tau Station. No matter what I do, it's never enough for you. I like my life. Can't you just accept that?"

"I only meant that you could —" began Vivian, but Amy was already heading for the door.

"Forget it," she said. "Just forget it."

• • •

At the clinic the next day, Vivian found herself having trouble focusing on the spine-covered felid anesthetized on the exam table.

"She's having a difficult pregnancy," said the owner.

"I'm surprised these things ever have an easy pregnancy," said Vivian, looking at the thorny protrusions that covered the catawampus.

She ran the ultrasound wand over the creature's belly, the only smooth spot on its skin.

"Yep. That's what I thought. The kittens have become entangled. We'll have to do a C-section."

But as she shaved the catawampus' swollen belly and marked where she was going to make the incision, her mind was on Amy, Ilykh, and Arykh. They were spending the day on an asteroid cruise. Amy had demurred when Vivian offered to take the day off from the clinic so she could go with them.

"No, no, I'm sure you've done these cruises lots of times," she'd said. "I'm sure they need you at the clinic."

Their first visit to the station, and Vivian had done her best to make it their last. Well. There was still dinner tonight.

The kittens came out as sharp and thorny as their mother, screaming their displeasure as Vivian untangled them. There were eight altogether, fat and feisty. She nestled them next to a heating pad while she sewed up the mother.

A ping on her com box interrupted her just as she finished stitching. She grabbed the box from the counter. There was a text from Amy. "Sorry — we won't be able to see you for dinner. Ushk-Ushk is sick."

• • •

"You didn't have to come over," said Amy. "I'm sure it's nothing. Just a little case of the blahs."

Vivian said, "Nonsense. I'm a vet and I'm here. Now let's have a look."

She had to give the Taroczis credit: The bonds they formed with their animals were incredible. Ushk-Ushk lolled listlessly on a cushion, his eyes dull. Ilykh knelt beside him, petting his fur and offering him dried sweetgrass, which he refused.

"He's never like this," said Ilykh, their brows furrowed anxiously.

"I'll get to the bottom of it," said Vivian.

But the examination was inconclusive. Ushk-Ushk's pulse was slow and his blood oxygen levels were low, but his temperature was normal and the rapid blood test didn't show any toxins or antibodies. There was no sign of injury. She swabbed his nose and throat, but in the end, she left, shaking her head.

"I'll culture these back at the lab," she told the others. "It must be a bug he brought from Tarocz. He couldn't have caught it on the station — the nanites would have taken care of it."

"Impossible," said Arykh. "Dzactas never get sick back on Tarocz. They're very rugged creatures."

"Well, it came from somewhere," said Vivian. "At least let me take blood samples from the three of you. If he picked something up from anywhere, one of you is the most likely."

Ilykh flinched as she pricked their finger. They asked, "Will this help you treat Ushk-Ushk?"

"I hope so," said Vivian. "But it's probably nothing serious anyway. He'll probably be fine in a day or two."

He was not fine.

By the next day, Ushk-Ushk couldn't stand. He lay on one side, huffing for breath, his thick black tongue hanging out of his mouth.

Vivian brought him into the clinic. His blood pressure was dropping. Five pounds had melted off him impossibly fast. She began a saline drip and began a full battery of tests. Scans showed no tumors or internal damage. The bacterial cultures she'd taken must have been contaminated; they grew into an indecipherable mass and she had to throw them away.

The blood tests from Amy, Arykh, and Ilykh were another matter. "Now this is strange," she said as she looked over the results. "Amy, your blood is normal. But Arykh and Ilykh — you two are swimming in antibodies. You can't possibly have been exposed to all these diseases."

Arykh took a look at the monitor. "Those numbers are normal for Taroczi. We have strong immune systems. It's why we have so few illnesses, especially as children."

"Interesting," said Vivian. Taroczi must have very unusual biology. But that didn't help her diagnose the dzacta.

"Who cares?" Ilykh said, raising their face from where they had pressed it into the thick brown fur. Tears stained the dark stripes across their cheekbones. "I just want to know what's wrong with Ushk-Ushk!"

"I don't know," Vivian had to admit. "But I promise, I'll give him the best treatment possible. He'll pull through. You'll see."

"Do you know that or are you just saying that?"

Perceptive kid. Vivian dodged the question. She ruffled Ilykh's hair and said, "I've treated thousands of animals with every possible condition. This isn't the worst I've seen. Let's go do something to take your mind off him. This is still a vacation, after all."

Ilykh shoved her away and clung tighter to the dzacta. "I'm not leaving him."

"Staying with him won't help him get better any faster," said Vivian. "Now come on. Your parents and I were going to get sodas. And Tau Station has a great VR space."

"Go without me," said Ilykh.

When even their parents couldn't convince them, Vivian had to give up and leave Ilykh by the sick beast's side. To occupy them, she left them in charge of the second set of cultures.

"If anything grows in those Petri dishes, you ping my com box," she instructed them.

They nodded solemnly.

The three adults went for drinks in the observation dome, which commanded a 180-degree view of the Milky Way. Amy and Arykh got purple Taroczi cocktails; Vivian had unfiltered sake. But the creamy, sweet wine didn't do much to brighten Vivian's mood. She cursed herself for not being able to help the one creature that belonged to someone she truly cared about. Why hadn't she studied dzacta biology? Why couldn't more Taroczis have traveled through Tau Station and given her more experience?

"I'm sorry," she finally said to break the lingering silence that had grown between the three of them. "This is not the vacation hoped for your first visit to Tau Station."

"It's not your fault," said Amy.

Vivian shook her head and studied the flecks in the terrazzo-patterned floor. "I've put pets to sleep lots of times. It's the worst part of my job. I've seen lots of heartbroken kids. But Ilykh ... I'm worried about whether they'll be okay. I've never seen anyone so attached to an animal. If Ushk-Ushk dies, I don't know if they'll get over it."

"They will," said Arykh. "Sooner or later, everyone has to experience the death of their dzacta. It's our first heartbreak. The dzacta is the first thing we learn to love and the first thing we must let go of."

"Pardon me if I don't want their pet to die as an object lesson," snapped Vivian. She didn't need a Taroczi to lecture her about the bonds between people and animals. "This is the only thing they're going to remember about this visit."

Her com box pinged. She checked it and saw Ilykh's face.

"Mrs. Yi?" they asked.

"You can call me Grandma," she said.

"I watched the Petri dishes like you said, and they're covered with blobs of fuzz."

"How much fuzz?"

Ilykh sent her a photo. Once again, the petri dishes were completely covered with bacterial colonies: white, orange, green, black.

Vivian made sure to mute her com before venting her frustration. "Don't tell me I contaminated the cultures again! Even if he's got an infection, there's no way there can be that much bacteria in his body. And yet ... no antibodies. Not low levels. None. Even if he were perfectly healthy, he should still have antibodies."

"What does that mean?" asked Amy.

"I have no idea," said Vivian. Turning her com back on, she told Ilykh, "I'm coming back to the clinic."

• • •

At a loss for what else to try, Vivian took a biopsy. Ushk-Ushk was too weak to do more than flinch. She prepared the slide while Amy and Arykh tried to calm Ilykh, who was barely keeping themself together.

"I have to be missing something," Vivian muttered to herself as she put the cover slip on the slide. She asked, "Arykh, your people have been living with dzactas for a long time, haven't they?"

"Since our prehistory," they replied. "We used to use them as pack animals, guard beasts — everything except for food. Dzacta meat is inedible; it turns to mush."

"So your two species have truly coevolved. Like humans and dogs, but even more so." That was interesting, but she didn't see how it helped. There had to be something else about dzacta biology she wasn't yet grasping.

As Vivian brought the slide into focus, her jaw dropped. Instead of the usual patchwork sheet of round, blobby cells, the dzacta's cells formed a spongy latticework. The empty spaces were full of some kind of pulpy mass.

"What? What is it?" asked Ilykh, grabbing her arm.

"It's like nothing I've ever seen," said Vivian. "I can't quite tell with this microscope — the magnification isn't high enough — but it almost looks like …"

"Like what?"

"Like a bacterial colony." Vivian grabbed her com box. "Get me the station wardens. You're the ones who administer the nanite spray? Is there any way to deactivate the nanites?"

• • •

Purple-blue water washed over the pebbles of the Taroczi shore. Away from the water, a feathery cushion of fungus covered the rocks until it vanished into the looping fractal trees. Arykh was right: Tarocz was gorgeous. Vivian sat on the fungus with Amy and Arykh, sipping a cold Taroczi cocktail. She should have visited long ago.

Ilykh raced alongside the sea, Ushk-Ushk by their side. The dzacta's eyes were bright and his coat glossy again, and thanks to all the extra sweetgrass Ilykh had fed him while he recovered, he'd put on a good ten pounds more than he'd started with.

"Well, are you glad you came out?" Amy asked Vivian.

Vivian sighed. "I needed a break! If I never have to talk to another news vulture, it'll be too soon."

"Imagine all that fuss over something the Taroczi have been doing for ages!" chuckled Arykh.

"There's more to your customs than I realized," Vivian admitted.

Dzactas, it turned out, were not single organisms at all, but complex colonies that played host to enormous colonies of virulent bacteria and viruses. Proteins in their blood entered the bacteria and altered their DNA, rendering them harmless. Dzactas built their entire bodies out of the very organisms that tried to kill them — but spraying them with antimicrobial nanites caused the whole system to collapse.

Ilykh shrieked with laughter as Ushk-Ushk licked their face. Vivian now saw that this was an age-old way that the Taroczi protected their children. As the child and the beast touched each other, Ushk-Ushk absorbed microorganisms from Ilykh's skin. Meanwhile, Ilykh was exposed to harmless versions of countless viruses and bacteria. No wonder the Taroczi got sick so rarely.

"So what now?" asked Amy. "I hear you've gotten a lot of offers to help develop new therapies based on dzacta biology. They're saying it could revolutionize medicine." She smiles to herself, as if she's remembering all the times Vivian asked her why she wanted to live in a place like Tarocz.

Vivian waved her off. "And spend six months holed up in a lab with racks of test tubes? Leave that to someone else. I'm a vet, not a researcher. I was thinking I'd like to stay here for another week or two, actually. The people on Tau Station can pull nails out of their own octophants' feet for a little while. Maybe we could get Cindy to join us. Look at this gorgeous landscape! Surely it could inspire an artist."

Ilykh ran up to Vivian, holding a squirming six-legged salamander by the tail. "Have you ever seen one of these? They eat rocks and they poop out mud."

"Neat!" said Vivian, taking the salamander. "Maybe I'll bring him home with me. I could call him September. You like animals, don't you?"

Ilykh nodded.

"Do you know we have internships on Tau Station? You could learn to be a vet."

Ilykh broke into a grin. "Really?"

"You can apply when you're fourteen. But be warned: An internship isn't a vacation. It's hard work, and they're very selective."

"I can work hard," said Ilykh.

"Show me," said Vivian. "There's a lot we still don't know about the animals of Tarocz. Help me collect and catalog them. Who knows what else we might discover?"

Ilykh didn't need any encouragement. They set off down the beach, turning over every rock and bit of driftwood and crouching to look underneath. Their brown-and-white skin stood out against the purple sea.

Vivian stretched out on the soft fungus and watched her grandchild with a smile.

Brandon Ketchum is a speculative fiction writer from Pittsburgh, Pennsylvania who enjoys putting a weird spin or strange vibe into every story, dark or light. He is a member of SFWA and the Horror Writers Association, and his work has been published with Air & Nothingness Press, *Perihelion*, *Mad Scientist Journal*, and many other publications, including the short story collection, *Legio Damnati*.

• • •

When I conceived of "Born in the Black", I wanted to combine the wonder of hopeful science fiction with the positive outlook of space travel and exploration. I wanted to capture the sense of humanity spreading to the stars. With this in mind, I cast about for the best plot concepts I could couple with this kind of a setting and story. I didn't have to think long to hit upon the most positive and joyous thing to pair with my concept: the birth of new life. Thus, "Born in the Black" was, well, born.

BORN IN THE BLACK

BRANDON KETCHUM

SUNDAY AUGUST 10, 2081

[REC][•]
Low Batt.

BLACK

"Is this thing on?" Mom snaps.
"It says it's recording," Dad replies.
"Then why can't you see anything?"
"I don't know," he says defensively. "Maybe I —"
"You left this on."

CLICK-CLACK
BLINDING LIGHT

"Hey, get it together," Dad says. "It's starting!"
"Hold it still, then."

[FOCUS]

Mom's beaming, freckled face squints at the vid screen. Her red hair's pulled back in a ponytail, and she's dressed in blue overalls covered in indistinguishable patches. In the background, the sun gleams on metal latticework climbing heavenward, supporting a spaceship.

"I got you, I got you," Dad cries.

"Okay, good," Mom says, slightly breathless. "Hi kiddo!" She waves. "It's me, Mom!"

A chuckle from behind the vid camera. "Not yet, you aren't!"

"That's Dad, by the way, videoing us. He's right — you haven't been born yet. C'mon, get over here."

The vid camera jostles, the spaceship shaking as if bouncing through an asteroid field. Dad's fresh-shaven, square-jawed face appears next to Mom's, his dark skin contrasting her pale complexion. His arm extends beyond the screen as he holds the vid camera selfie-style.

"You're not even a twinkle in my eye yet." He grins at the vid screen.

"You're not supposed to be," Mom says. "I'm not allowed off birth control — don't worry, we'll teach you all about that stuff, now that you're a teenager — until we're two weeks in the black. No use getting used to Earth standard anything when you'll be growing up on ship, or hopefully settling another planet."

Dad hugs her close. "We'll have plenty of time."

"We're making this vlog from beginning to end, kiddo," she says. "From now until you're born. Wanted to use a vid drone, except there's no way they'd let us operate a drone on the ship."

"And sorry about the impersonal *kiddo*, kiddo. We thought about coming up with names, one for a girl, another for a boy, but don't want to jinx it. Not before we even blast off. And what happens if you're twins or triplets?"

"Anyway, we decided on eight videos. Eight, because if you lay it sideways, it's the infinity symbol. And that's kind of where we're going, into the infinite black yonder; out to colonize the galaxy. See, there's our shuttle."

[REFOCUS]

Their faces disappear, replaced by a full-frame shot of the spaceship, *Seedling One* scrawled in bold black letters across the silver hull.

[REFOCUS]

Mom and Dad reappear on the vid screen.
"That's not the generation ship itself," Mom says.
Dad says, "They built *Seedling* in orbit, obviously."
"It's got everything needed to start a colony," she continues. "Weapons, for self-defense and hunting. Pre-fab sheeting to build with. Farm equipment, from tractors to, well, seeds."
"No terraforming on this expedition!"
"And a hull specially designed to block out harmful radiation, since we won't have an atmosphere to do it for us. We don't want to lower your white blood cell count and weaken your immune system before your first breath."

BEEP BEEP BEEP

"Oh, hey," Dad says, disappearing from view again. "Battery's dying."
"Alright, so that's all for now, kiddo," Mom says. "We'll be checking in with you again soon, though."
"When it's magic time," Dad says, chortling.
Mom blushes furiously.

CLICK
BLACK

[END REC][•]

Born in the Black

SUNDAY AUGUST 24, 2081

[REC][•]
[FOCUS]

A narrow door in a dull aluminum-composite corridor, centered on the vid screen, Mom and Dad floating in front of it, Dad clutching the vid camera before them.

Dad waggles the fingers of his free hand at the screen. "Hey kiddo. It's been exactly two weeks since launch."

"Seeing as us women spent months Earthside coordinating our cycles — I'll have to tell you all about monthlies, if you're a girl — it's go time."

"*Magic* time," Dad corrected. Mom sticks her tongue out at him. "We figured we'd show you our suite. Only the couples got suites, for, ahem, obvious reasons."

"C'mon," Mom says. "Check it out."

The door slides open, revealing a narrow room with a table bolted to the floor and two contour chairs layered with straps. Two other doors lead off to either side; potted plants sit behind plexiglass under a fluorescent bulb against the far wall.

"It's not much," Dad says, "but it's home. For a long time; maybe the rest of our lives; hopefully not *yours*."

"The tiny bathroom's through there —" Mom points to one door. "This one's the important one right now, though. The magic one, I guess you can say."

Dad gives another of his chortles. "There's only room for a bed and a crib," he says as they waft into the room, walking along the wall with their free hands. "At least the bed's big enough."

"It has to be, because we'll be spending a lot of time there." Mom's laugh is a mischievous counterpart to Dad's mirth. "We're heading to bed now, in fact."

"This room's special in one other important way: it has its own gravity function, separate from the ship's gravity, which is only on a few hours every day. It's available any time we ... 'need' it. Since it's impossible to fertilize an egg without gravity, it's kind of a must."

"Something to do with my *vestibular system*," Mom says. "We're just colonists, so we're not clear on the scientific mumbo jumbo. I'm sure you're a brilliant scientist by now, so you probably know all about the vestibular system."

"We could offer a whole sex ed lecture right now, but I'm sure we've freaked you out enough already."

"Bye, kiddo," Dad says. He turns and kisses Mom on the cheek. "Hellooo Mom."

CLICK
BLACK

[END REC][•]

OCTOBER 22, 2081

[REC][•]
[FOCUS]

Mom appears in the middle of a chamber full of exercise machines and monitors, a cross between a gym and doctor's office. Other women studiously ignore them, busy utilizing the equipment, while techs roam the chamber, observing everything.

"Hey, kiddo," Dad says from off-screen.

"Dad's not allowed 'in here,' we've decided."

"We? *You* decided."

Mom ignores him. "He can run the vid camera, that's all. This is *our* space, yours and mine alone." Dad clears his throat. "Well, and for all the other expectant moms, too. Guess what, though? You're the *first!*"

"That's right, we got pregnant — well, *I* got *Mom* pregnant — before anyone else. You're scheduled to be the first birth on this expedition! Plenty have been born in orbit around Earth, but you'll be the first interstellar baby ever. There'll be hundreds of studies about you."

"Okay," Mom says, "so this is one of the ship's gravity and exercise chambers, the one for expectant mothers." Dad moves the vid camera around, shows computers with complicated monitors, women using leg machines and exercise bikes, and techs monitoring them, lingers on the gravity engagement button, and finally returns to Mom.

[REFOCUS]

Mom says, "Gravity's not just for conception. Apparently you've got to have it to facilitate the flow of fluids to the embryo — from my body to you, kiddo. You'll need it to exercise and develop strong muscles, too."

"Oh, hey, tell her about the morning sickness!"

"Why'd you have to bring that up?" Mom shoots him an annoyed look and sighs. "I was hoping to be one of those mothers who never got morning sickness. Sure enough, I have to puke my guts out all the time. Every morning. Can you imagine projectile vomit in zero gravity?"

"It's not pretty."

"Flatterer. Now, that's the disgusting end of my digestion; the *cool* part is when I get cravings. Pregnant women have been known to eat everything from soap to coal because their body demands the nutrients in those substances, and somehow tells their mind the best way to get the highest concentration. Can't get hold of everything in outer space, can you?"

"Nope," Dad chimes in. "The scientists thought of everything, however."

"They've got all kinds of food processing gizmos and vitamin supplements and whatnot to craft a cocktail to satisfy every possible human craving."

"And not a few animal ones, I bet."

"I've never felt better fed in my life." Mom rubs her stomach, which hasn't changed since the last video. "You're not showing yet, kiddo — I'm only at eight weeks — but I can feel you growing inside me. The medical docs say I can't yet, of course, and they're technically right. The psych docs say it's a healthy thought process, imagining our connection, that I'm bonding with you already."

"So am I," Dad says. "I'm right here with you both."

Mom tears up a bit. "So long for now, kiddo. We'll be back soon."

CLICK
BLACK

[END REC][•]

DECEMBER 25, 2081

[REC] [•]
[FOCUS]

Red light dances in a clinic full of diagnostic equipment. Dad pans the vid camera around the room, passing a matronly woman who offers a kind-hearted smile, and settles it back on himself and Mom. She's laying back in a chair, bulging belly bared; Dad kneels next to her.

"Merry Christmas, kiddo," he cries. "We're here with the doc to get an ultrasound!"

"I'm only a tech, now," the woman says off-screen. She has a lilting, joyous quality to her voice. "A sonographer, if you will."

"'Only,' she says." Mom giggles. "She was 'only' one of Earth's best sonographers, or she wouldn't be up here."

"She's kind enough to let us film the procedure," Dad says, "and we asked her to describe what an ultrasound's all about, too."

[REFOCUS]

The sonographer smiles again at the vid screen. "What an ultrasound does is transmit high-frequency sound waves, inaudible to the human ear, through the abdomen via a transducer." She picks up a sleek white device that looks like a cross between a computer mouse and a ship transponder. "This transducer sends wireless data back to the monitor, which records and transforms echoes into video and photographic images of the baby — of you!"

"What all can you see with it?" Dad asks.

"Oh, all kinds of things. Images of the baby, of course, and the amniotic sac, placenta, ovaries ..." The sonographer winks at the vid screen. "I don't want to bore you with too much detail. It can pick up major anatomical abnormalities and birth defects. Let's hope we find none of those. Ready to get started?"

"Can't see you nodding," Mom says.

Dad clicks his tongue and nods the vid camera up and down. The sonographer sets the transducer down and picks up a long tube. "I'll be using this gel as a conductive medium to aid the image quality, applying it topically to the surface of the skin. That's the technical way of saying I'm going to spread a bunch of cold goop over your mother's tummy and roll the transducer around in it."

She takes off the cap and squeezes colorless gel out. Mom squeals as it contacts her skin, then giggles.

Dad says, "They assure us there's no evidence that a prenatal ultrasound will harm you or Mom. It doesn't use radiation, like X-rays."

The sonographer begins swirling the transducer slowly through the gel.

"The ultrasound can do one other nifty thing she didn't mention," Mom says. "It *could* tell us your sex already. Dad and I decided we don't want to know until you're born, though."

Images begin to appear on a monitor, one after another as the computer rapidly records each and moves on to the next.

"Yeah, people usually want to know so they can prep the house, buy baby clothes, and stuff like that." Dad plucks at his overalls. "Everything's unisex up here, and it's not like we brought supplies to paint our quarters with."

"The psych docs argued for stuff like that," Mom puts in. "They said it would aid the mother's nesting instincts in outer space. It just wasn't practical."

"Plus, we want you to surprise us like we're going to surprise you with this vlog."

"How we doing?" Mom asks. The sonographer, eyes glued to the monitor even as she works the transducer, offers a thumbs up.

"Looks like you're healthy at this stage, kiddo," Dad says, "which is all that really matters to us."

"Zoom in on the monitor," the sonographer says.

[REFOCUS]

A radar-shaped black-and-white image fills the screen, similar to an outline for wireless signal strength, but with a grainy sketch of a little human recumbent inside it rather than wave bars.

"If we wait a bit," the sonographer says, "we might be able to — yes, look there!"

A tiny arm moves apart from the body, then drifts down again.

"I felt that," Mom says. "You're pretty calm today though, kiddo. Last night you were kicking up a storm."

There's a crackly whooshing sound coming from the monitor's speakers, slow and steady.

"What's that?" Dad asks.

"Let's focus in and see." The sonographer presses a button on a keyboard, and the monitor zooms into a specific area of the picture, a kind of off-kilter circle with smaller, nebulous circles inside it. The sound continues as the circle throbs. "That's the baby's heart."

"Your heart, kiddo," Mom says, her voice catching. "Your heart."

The view jumbles and shakes.

[REFOCUS]

Mom's crying in her chair, Dad holding an arm snug around her shoulders. He's tearing up too.

"We're getting a little emotional here," Dad says. "Time to let the sonographer finish her job and let you escape this mushy stuff."

"Bye, baby," Mom whispers.

CLICK
BLACK

[END REC][•]

FEBRUARY 8, 2081

[REC][•]
[FOCUS]

Mom's sitting in a huge reclined chair cushioning every inch of her, arm extending off-screen to hold the vid camera. Gentle light filtered from hundreds of sources plays over her. Melodious music composed of string instruments and a mellow wind sweeps gently from the speakers.

"I hate to tell you, kiddo — we've got to do this one alone," Mom whispers. "As in Dad can't even run the vid camera. Honestly, he's driving me crazy, so I appreciate my daily alone time. Yet I'm never alone, am I? I've got *you* to talk to.

"This is the stim room, short for stimulation, used to provide enough light and sound for healthy fetal development. It helps form your sense of sight and hearing."

She lowers the vid camera to show how much her stomach has grown, then raises it again. "I could have shot this weeks ago. Seems like I spend half my days in this chamber.

"I'm kind of disappointed we decided to only do eight videos. I could have done fifty-two, one a week! In the end, it's probably for the best, otherwise these would all run so long together you wouldn't be interested in watching it all. Not with a teenager's attention span.

"Oops, I'm raising my voice a bit too much. I should probably shut up now and let the music do its work. Tomorrow it's going to be jungle sounds. Remind Dad to do his orangutan impression for your birthday."

CLICK
BLACK

[END REC][•]

APRIL 15, 2081

[REC][•]
[FOCUS]

Dad pans the vid camera around an exam room with charts and anatomical diagrams, interspersed with electrical equipment, buttons, and monitors embedded in the walls. A seemingly old-fashioned exam table is centered in the room. Mom's already in her gown, laying peacefully on the table. She waves to the vid camera.

"The doc's about to come in," Dad whispers off-screen. "We decided to spare you the actual exam —"

"— But still wanted to say hi, and show you the room."

"I'm going to turn this thing off, and come back online to hear from the doc afterward."

CLICK
BLACK

[END REC][•]

• • •

[REC][•]
[FOCUS]

Mom and Dad sit next to each other in waiting-room chairs. A middle-aged man with wavy salt-and-pepper hair and a genial smile sits across from them, chair angled so the vid camera can capture his features in a carefully staged manner. The screen is perfectly still, so it must be on a stand.

"Everything's perfect," the doc says. "Mother and baby each appear healthy. It's clear you're both getting plenty of nutrients."

"How's fetal responsiveness?" Mom asks. "You said before we might have issues in that regard."

Another genial smile. "Yes, there's so much we don't know — *can't* know, yet — about interstellar pregnancy. The stim room seems to have had the desired effect with you, however."

"That's great to hear." Dad releases a pent-up breath.

"In fact, all the babies-to-be are responding well to the light and sound therapy."

"What about radiation?" Mom wants to know. "The captain continually assures us the hull painting has held up ..."

"And so it has." The doc nods and spreads his hands. "Look, there are so many firsts on this voyage, they're too many to count. Everyone, from the captain to the medical crew to the pending parents, are doing a fabulous job bending all their energy toward making the entire process as smooth as possible, from conception through birth."

Mom and Dad share a glance and relax in their chairs.

"We're good for now, then?" Mom says.

The doc says, "Better than good; we're *textbook*. One last checkup to ensure all systems are *go*, so-to-speak, and then —"

"Magic time," Dad exclaims, causing laughter. He winks at the vid camera, pulls a tiny remote from his pocket, and —

CLICK
BLACK

[END REC][•]

MAY 28, 2081

[REC][•]
[FOCUS]

The exam room again, with Mom in her gown, pacing around.

"It looks like the same room as last time," Dad says from off-screen, "but it's not. They're all identical. We're in number three this time instead of four. Whoo-wee!"

"Anyway …" Mom stops and rests her hands on either side of her enormous stomach. "This is it, kiddo. Last stop before the big day. Next time you see me, I'll be all sweaty and disgusting, trying to push you out."

"You, disgusting? Impossible."

A smooth sliding sound, and the doc appears at the edge of the screen, forestalling her reply. "How're we doing?" he asks, gesturing to the table.

Mom frowns at him. "Actually, I just got a shooting pain in my lower back."

The doc moves swiftly, grasping her elbow and leading her to the table. "Nothing to worry about, I'm sure. Just hop on up."

"My belly," Mom cries as she settles on her back, clutching her swollen abdomen.

The doc grabs at a box of gloves. The screen jostles as the vid camera backs away.

[REFOCUS]

The doc presses a button on the table; stirrups spring from the sides. The doc guides Mom's feet onto them.

"What's happening, doctor?" Dad's voice cracks on the question.

Ignoring him, the doctor rolls a chair up, sits down, and thrusts his now-gloved hands beneath Mom's robe.

"Ooh, that's tender," Mom complains, wincing.

The doctor's hands reappear, coated in bloody slime. Dad makes a strangling noise from off-screen; Mom cries out incoherently. The doctor pushes at the table, rolling to the wall, and slaps a big red button. Nothing happens. He presses a smaller blue button next to it, holds it in, and says, "Likely placental abruption, room three. Prepare for immediate delivery."

CLICK
BLACK

[END REC][•]

MAY 28, 2081

[REC][•]
[FOCUS]

Dad in the waiting room, sagging in a chair and holding the vid camera to record himself, relief plastered across his face.

"Sorry to scare you, kiddo. I won't lie, it got a little hairy back there. They kicked me out and rolled Mom off to one of the birthing chambers quick as a flash. I'm not sure what all happened, but there was a *placental abruption*, whatever that is, and they had to induce birth right away. Wouldn't let me inside to film it like we'd planned, but that's okay. Probably would have embarrassed you. Then again, isn't that a parent's job?"

Dad attempts a chortle that comes out breathy and lame. "I'm told Mom's fine, that you're doing fine, and are due any minute now. I'm not sure we'll keep that last section in the vlog, or this bit, so I might be talking to nobody now. I'm rambling. Not much else for me to do anyway, apart from pacing and worrying, so, if it's all the same to you, I'll keep the vlog rolling and ramble away."

Static and crackling from off-screen.

"Wait, something's coming through ..."

[REFOCUS]

A boxy speaker nestled in the intersection of the wall and ceiling. The crackling sound issues from it.

"One last push," the doc's voice comes through, loud and clear.

A great scream of effort — Mom's straining voice. Then heavy breathing, and nothing else.

[REFOCUS]

Dad's tense face. "That ... is that ... ?" Sudden squalling: a baby's cry. "It is! That's you, kiddo. Oh my god, that is *you*!" More squalling and joyous cries. Tears spring from Dad's eyes, streaming down his cheeks. He swipes at them. "Got quite a set of pipes on you, I have to say. Oh, oh, they're letting me in!"

CLICK
BLACK

[END REC][•]

• • •

[REC][•]
[FOCUS]

Mom's propped up in a bed, blanketed and cushioned with pillows, holding a tiny human in the crook of her arm. The baby's covered in blood and mucous and white chunks of something, umbilicus still connected and leading underneath Mom's blanket. Dad zooms the vid camera in on the baby's face. A shock of hair's plastered to — his? her? — head; freckles stand out on a light brown cheek.

"We made it through," Dad says from off-screen. "You made it out, safe and sound."

Mom, from off-screen, says, "You're the bravest baby I've ever known, the *first* baby born on the expedition."

"All that fuss, and you're already sound asleep!" Dad says. The baby hiccups and whines, eyes opening. "Or not."

"Show her the display."

The vid camera jounces, flashing blurs of movement. Mom and Dad argue gently about how to do what with whom, and when to pass off baby and vid camera.

[REFOCUS]

Dad stands with her cradled in both arms before a black wall. He nudges a small button with his elbow, and the wall lights up, displaying the star-pocked black of outer space. He angles her face toward it. Her eyes widen; her umbilicus leads off-screen toward Mom. "That's the vast unknown, kiddo," Dad says.

"We can't keep calling her that," Mom says from off-screen.

"Well then, how about 'Star'?"

"— Astra," Mom says simultaneously.

"Astra." Dad rolls it around in his mouth. "It means the same as 'Star,' but says it so beautifully. You're right, of course."

"Better get used to me being right, Astra," Mom says.

"Oh yes, just ask her." Dad shifts her in his arms. He leans low, lips beside her ear. "You're going to be mother to one of the planets out there, Astra." She coos in response.

"A shining star around which the world will orbit," Mom says.

Dad chortles. "So, you know, no pressure or anything."

[REFOCUS]

Dad crouching down bedside with Mom, holding the baby together while she slumbers. In unison, they murmur, "Happy Thirteenth, Astra!"

CLICK
BLACK

[END REC][•]

A.M. Weald grew up in the United States but has lived and studied all over the world. While in grad school, as a mode of productive procrastination she started writing fiction as well as professionally editing academic manuscripts which, after obtaining a PhD in anthropology, she continues to this day. She also dabbles in multimedia projects and thinks about cats way too often.

• • •

When I saw the prompt for The Future's So Bright, *I dug deep into what I thought the future might hold for Earth and humanity. Space travel? Time travel? I couldn't make up my mind. For inspiration, I listened to my playlist titled "spaaaaaaace". Right away, M.I.A.'s "Space" bored into my brain, and I knew my lead character would be into the song, too. I imagined, at first, a* Mass Effect*-esque mini space opera taking place on an exoplanet. I saw my lead character bopping to this song while at work, whatever that work was. Botanist? Engineer? And then a phrase popped into my head, and wouldn't leave: "A duster bot was stuck again." So instead of space, I went underground, and I went with honesty: the Earth in the 21st century is in peril, and humans are to blame. What might happen if we ignore our mess for too long? How would humans adapt? Would it be too late to save the planet? Oh, and throw in some romance, because why not.*

EMERGENCE

A.M. WEALD

A DUSTER BOT WAS STUCK AGAIN.
It happened every so often, either from gear malfunction, clumps of leaves, or an errant branch. The bots dedicated to cleaning the solar panels needed a clear path up and down the columns, and, if they picked up too much debris or, worse, dragged malfunctioning parts behind them, they could damage multiple panels. And then everyone in Pod North would really be fucked.

Alone in her room, solar lights dimmed, Kelle grooved to her space jams, minimally dancing in her desk chair as she watched her monitor. The mix was her go-to when she was anxious, bored, or claustrophobic — something about listening to songs about floating in space made her feel rebellious and free. Probably because she, like every other survivor, lived underground, and most, like Kelle, were born in the pods, never knowing life under the Sun. Only a handful of founders who had lived on the surface were still alive, their grandchildren now adults.

Kelle longed to see the sky — the real sky, the blueness of it. Stories from elders about the wide expanse, the horizon, the infinite blue told her that photos, videos, and simulations on visi-screens didn't cut it. So, she downloaded classic songs from the Intranet, many with lyrics she and her friends couldn't relate to. Rainbows and bluebirds, cavemen on Mars, space cowboys — songs written by people who lived an unconstrained superterranean life.

"Come on, you little fucker," Kelle murmured as she guided the camera for a closer look.

There ... she had a visual. The bot's rear left gear was broken, dangling at an awkward angle. She flagged the bot for maintenance, then sat back and watched as the rest of the bots dust busted, as the maintenance bot retrieved the busted duster to be examined by a human.

It was summer now, no snow to worry about, only ash. And the ash was minimal, lately.

Kelle's line beeped. She reached for the handset, laid her thumb then a finger down for each beep until it reached the count of five. The audio crackled as she pressed the handset to her ear.

"Mother-Duster Kelle of Pod North, at your service." She grinned and wound the coiled cord around her forefinger.

"Guess. What."

Kelle rolled her eyes. Arjun, always the drama king, with a voice both deep and theatrical. Her best friend — if someone from a different pod she'd never met in person could be her best friend. He was assistant to the head solar engineer of Pod West, specializing in expanding the lifespan of solar panels.

"What now?" she asked.

"What do you mean '*What now?*'"

"You're always *guess what*-ing me. And it's always bunk. If it was something worth knowing, they'd blast it over the coms, or at least over the subcoms."

"Not if it's" — he paused — "secret."

"Why would anyone tell you a secret?"

"Cute."

To break the drawn-out silence, Kelle asked through a sigh, "*Ho*kay, I'm game. What's up?"

"This is gonna blow your nerd brain: They're. Connecting. The Pods."

"What do you mean? Like, physically?"

"Yes."

Oh ... oh shit. The various city-sized pods had never been connected — that was the whole *point* of the pods: quarantine, maintainability, civility. No possibility of interaction aside from interconnected landlines.

"Are ... are you sure?" she asked. "Why would you know this?"

"That question is hurtful," he said with a touch of sarcasm.

"I'm serious. Who told you? Did they say why? Who did they hear it from?"

"It doesn't matter who told me," Arjun said. "You don't know them. They're someone who knows. You're just going to have to trust me on this."

"Okay, fine. But ... how? How are they connecting pods? Tunnels? Or were there already tunnels? Are they ..." She exhaled sharply. "Are they *opening* the pods?"

"Not to the surface, not yet. Tests show the radiation is still too high."

"So, tunnels."

"I don't know the details. But, yeah, interpod travel, Kelle."

Arjun fell quiet. Kelle was speechless.

"Interpod travel," Arjun repeated. More silence. "Kelle?"

"Yeah." She looked at her monitor, watched as a replacement duster was placed upon the solar panel column by a robotic arm. "Yeah, I'm here." The replacement duster came online, and she set it to work.

"We could meet, Kelle," Arjun said, his voice soft.

Down the duster went, cleaning the panels of minimal debris.

Meet.

Kelle froze, all her faculties concentrated on the duster which had since powered down and tucked into rest position like all the others, its daily duties performed. *Her* daily duties performed. She tugged at her grey uniform sleeve and looked at the projected sundial. It was almost time for her Solar Meet.

"Kelle?"

"I'm here." She reclined into her chair, rested her feet on her small desk. The plastic phone cord coiled so tightly around her wrist that it cut off circulation. "Meet," she said.

"We could. If you wanted to. I thought, I mean, it's been so long …"

Four years. It started as conference calls, meetings of all engineers and people in related fields. Then chit-chatting after the meetings. Then private conversations.

Kelle wished for an old tech called the Internet that she'd learned about in history class — text messages sent instantly, documents shared across the world, video chat — but it required equipment and power they just didn't have. Each pod had the Intranet, but access hours were limited to save on power consumption. So she and Arjun, like anyone else in different pods, were limited to the telephone.

Four years. And she'd had a crush on Arjun for three.

Her heart fluttered. She put her fingertips to her throat, catching its pace. Fast, but okay. She breathed deep, slow, willing herself to calm.

Did she want to meet Arjun? *Should* she?

PODS WERE SEPARATE FOR A REASON. Cross-contamination could mean the spread of disease, errant plant-eating mites, or the toxin …

"It's fine," Arjun said. "It might not happen for a while, anyway. I just wanted to — it's fine."

"It's not fine, Arji!" Kelle threw her legs off her desk to sit up straight. "Ninety-nine percent!"

"What —?"

"Ninety-nine percent of us!" She shot to her feet. "We nearly destroyed ourselves, our planet! It's been generations, right? Is that enough to recover? What if it's not enough? Are we sure we can meet without finishing what the war started? THE PODS ARE MEANT TO BE SEPARATE!"

Kelle fell into her chair, spent. She rested her forehead in her palm, kept the handset pressed to her ear. "I'm sorry," she said softly. "I'm sorry, Arji. I want to. You know I do. And I know it's not my job to worry about the bigger picture beyond these bots, but what if I'm the *only* one worrying about the bigger picture?"

"You're not the only one," he said, voice so subdued Kelle wondered if he was crying.

Fuck. I'm a monster.

"Okay," he said. "Let's pretend it's safe. They've run the tests and all is perfect." He breathed deep in great huffs. "You'd meet me?"

Kelle's heart was pounding now. Maybe not from fear so much anymore. This adrenaline came from excitement.

"Of course I'd meet you, Arji." Why was she crying? She wiped her cheeks dry. "Even if we had to wear those bulky yellow suits."

"We probably would," he said through a laugh, "if it was early on."

A tingle ran up Kelle's right arm. She leaned back against the chair, closed her eyes, letting her psychosomatic reaction to Arjun's imagined touch overtake her.

Touch. She could *touch* someone, *like that*. There'd never been anyone she'd wanted to, aside from Arjun, and she didn't even know what he looked like beyond a description — brown skin, black hair, dark eyes, a beard now that he was older. The same as her. Minus the beard.

"Did they say when?" she asked him.

"Hm? Oh, no. No timeline. Not that my friend knows of, anyway."

A loud *BEEEEEP* echoed over the line.

"I gotta go," she said. "Solar Meet."

"Yeah. Me too. Call you tomorrow?"

"Okay." She couldn't move. She didn't want to move. "Arji?"

His line crackled. "Yeah?"

She felt that shiver again, this time traveling from elbow to neck. It passed, her body unclenched, and she finally said the words: "You're my person. You know that, right?"

Arjun made a sound that made Kelle think he was smiling. "You're my person, too."

• • •

Arjun sat in the middle of the broad, round, low-ceiling Solar Meet room, nude save for his plaincloth wrap, soaking up his daily dose of filtered sunlight. The ceiling above him glowed a translucent off-white. Today was violently sunny, if the brightness of the room was any indication.

There was a piece of apparel Arjun had learned of — sunglasses. Tinted plastic worn over the eyes. He wished for these, but the eyes were major absorbers of sunlight. And he needed a lot of sunlight.

"*Please remain seated and silent for the daily announcements,*" a pleasant, realistic robot voice sounded over the speaker system. Arjun mouthed along to the rest of the preprogrammed message: "*Once completed, you may mingle for the remaining hour.*"

The news neglected to mention anything about pod connections. Perhaps his friend Hodge, who lived in Pod South, had lied to him. Though Hodge had no reason to lie. Perhaps he did know something no one else was meant to know. Perhaps someone had lied to him.

"*There has been a reduction in average daily ashfall of 97%,*" the computer announcer said.

Arjun opened his eyes and shot his gaze to his colleague, Tink, who sat beside him, her dayglo pink hair alight from the illuminated ceiling. Her expression said exactly what he was thinking.

The nuclear winter was ending. It might have already ended, given there were more sunny days than not lately. And now the reduced ashfall.

If the air was safe to breathe again, if the radiation had faded, if the ozone layer had healed, if the toxins ejected by dirty bombs had also died out ... They would open the pods. Not just connect them, *open* them.

But Kelle was right, it was years too soon. No, they wouldn't open the pods, couldn't. The best they could hope for was interpod travel. If it was safe. And Hodge seemed to think it was safe. Or, whoever told Hodge. Or whoever told whoever told Hodge ...

"The remaining satellites have recorded images indicating a regrowth of polar ice caps by 200% beyond pre-crisis diameters."

"Oh wow," Tink said quietly, and Arjun had to hold in his excited laughter.

They did it. They fucking did it.

Well, global warming, the virus, the meteor, the war and nuclear fallout, and the bioweapons did it. Saving the planet from ecological disaster was an unintended aftereffect of unmitigated tragedy.

At least Pod South saved a handful of honeybee colonies and staple crops, and random animal species. Pod North saved some mammal species and fodder to support them. Pod West saved a mix of flora and fauna, and boasted the biggest underground greenhouse of all American pods.

Unfortunate, what happened to Pod East ...

"Our final announcement: there will be a graduation ceremony today during the evening meal. Please congratulate our future geneticists now."

The solarbathers' applause was interrupted by, *"This concludes our daily announcements. Please have fun. Goodday."*

"Two-hundred percent!" Tink squealed in Arjun's ear.

"Yes, I heard."

"As long as it doesn't grow too much beyond that, we'll remain in an interglacial, which would be better, to not always be cold enough to snow."

"Many glacial periods are drier than interglacials, so it might snow less often."

"It can still snow when it's dry," she chimed. "Just ask my — well, you can't, he's dead, but my grandad's dad lived in Wyoming and it was so dry people had to bathe in cream, but it snowed for like three-quarters of the entire year."

"That … doesn't sound right."

Tink shrugged. "That's what I heard. Anyway, what do you think? With the ashfall and ice caps all remedied …" Her lips quirked up, and she looked like she was about to hop in place. "Surface missions?"

"I'll leave the speculation up to those who know the details." He didn't mention the rumored tunnels. That was different from surface missions, anyway.

"I gotta go talk to my auntie," Tink said as she walked backward away from him. "See you."

"See you."

Arjun scanned the room, looking for people he knew. He wasn't supposed to do that, and he certainly wasn't supposed to talk to family. He was meant to meet new people. People he might want to share a room with. People he wasn't related to.

He wasn't *expected* to have children. That would be a constitutional violation. In fact, wanton conception was vehemently discouraged, even with the population of Pod West lingering at replacement-rate levels, which, given the diverse founding genetic pool, had been deemed healthy decades ago. Room sharing was encouraged because there were indeed children being born, and those children grew up, needing their own rooms. But there were only so many single rooms, and those were assigned under limited circumstances. Arjun very much needed to move out of his parent's room. And he very much wanted to have children.

And it hit him — gene flow. There wasn't much Arjun remembered from biology, but he remembered the very basics. Bottleneck, founder effect, gene pool, gene flow. Were they connecting the pods to allow for gene flow between bottlenecked populations?

He clenched his fists in the anticipation of — and deliberation about — telling Kelle.

Did Kelle want children? They were both in their twenties, but she never mentioned having any partners. Would she want to be his partner?

Could he *switch pods*? Could she?

Arjun began to sweat, and not from the Solar Meet room's dry heat.

"Hello?" came a deep voice behind him.

Arjun turned to see a handsome man with pale skin and stark white-blond hair, a scratch of golden stubble across his jaw. "I'm Jair, Tink's brother. We're usually on a different Solar Meet schedule, but this time ours aligned. She said I should talk to you ..." The man looked away at nothing, down at nothing, then at his toes, at Arjun's toes. "I'm in genetics," he said, finally looking at Arjun again. "You're in engineering?"

Arjun smiled. "Yeah. Solar engineering."

Despite his annoyance at Tink for very clearly setting him up, and nerves at the very raw reality of meeting someone new who was also wearing nothing but a cloth wrap, Arjun offered his arm, as was the custom, and he and Jair walked over to the area with floor cushions where they could chat.

• • •

"A roommate," Kelle said, tugging at the phone cord. A lump in her throat grew and swirled then snaked its way down to her stomach until she reminded herself that a roommate was *not* the same as a partner, but it could be a slippery slope if there was an attraction. And it had been a week since she'd last spoken to Arjun. A lot could happen in a week. "I'm sure your parents are ecstatic."

"You have *no* idea," Arjun said, laughing. "Jair's a nice guy. You'd like him. Genetics nerd."

But is he your PERSON? Kelle wanted to yell, but didn't, because that would be crazy, and selfish, and against everything that was expected of someone from society.

"What's he look like?" she asked instead. "Gimme the rundown."

"I wish I could send you a picture of his smile. It's like if you took both your fingers and hooked them into the corners of your mouth and pulled. Pretty lips."

Kelle didn't want to imagine Arjun pressing his lush lips — because that's what she imagined them to be — to another person's. Why was she being so possessive?

"As long as he treats you right," she said, "then I'm really happy for you. I, on the other hand, am still happily roomed with my platonic partner."

"How is Cyb?"

"Still snoring like a broken gear, but I trust her. She trusts me. It works."

"That's what matters."

Kelle hummed, examined her stubby fingernails, checked her monitor. Today was so boring. At least she had this phone call.

Arjun had a roommate ...

"So, you heard the announcements," Arjun said, a statement of fact stated excitedly.

"Ice caps and ashfall," she said.

"Yeah, and I had a thought about the pod connection rumor."

Kelle waited.

"Gene flow," he said.

"Gene flow?"

"I talked it over with Jair. He wasn't supposed to tell me, but it just came out. He says I'm right — that there are rumors of pod connections because there have been movements toward exactly that. They're doing it for gene flow, Kelle, to transfer genetics between pods. It makes sense. And maybe it won't be a totally open thing, more like a directed transfer. Just a few people to deepen the gene pool."

"I guess that makes more sense than a potential contaminant free fall. Is that the only thing they'd let people transfer for?"

"I don't think so. They probably want to trade supplies as well as people, either for their genes or their profession. Apparently the tunnels were there the whole time, just sealed off, secret. Do you think you would do it? Transfer? Or ..."

"Or what?"

Kelle heard the smallest sounds on Arjun's end, as if the man's mouth began various words without finishing them.

"I thought," he finally said, "maybe, if you wanted to, we could, you know, see if we get along, if we meet. And we could ... Well, I've always wanted children of my own. I'm not asking — fuck, sorry, this is so weird of me. Forget I said anything. I just got to thinking of gene flow and obsessed all night over it. I'm sorry."

Kelle's heart fluttered from a mix of different anxieties.

Arji wants to have children with me?

The Solar Meet alarm beeped, and Arjun spat an emphatic "Fuck," which relaxed Kelle into a smile.

"I'll think about it," she said. "I told you — you're my person. And if the opportunity to meet happens, if we can room together ..." If Jair wouldn't mind, or if they could get a larger room, or a suite ... "I'm not saying no, okay? I'm saying let's —"

"Circle back to it at a later date?" Arjun sputtered in laughter.

Ugh, that phrase.

Kelle pinched the bridge of her nose. "Ay, I hate you."

"Talk to you later, my dust buster from another cluster."

• • •

Kelle stared at the visi-ceiling as she lay in bed, fingers winding around the phone cord. A starscape video slowly rotated above her. Occasionally, a meteor would dart across the illusion.

"I can't believe you'll be here soon," she said to Arjun and Jair. "It doesn't seem real. How do your families feel about it?"

"Talking to your imaginary boyfriends?" Cyb asked as she walked on the treadmill that charged their room's auxiliary power.

"They're not imaginary," Kelle protested. "They live in another pod. And they're not my boyfriends, they're each other's boyfriend."

"Mhmm." Cyb put her earbuds back in and chuckled at whatever she was watching on the treadmill's little screen.

"How do you know we're not imaginary?" Jair teased. "We could be digitally constructed personalities."

"I think you mean AIs," Kelle said.

"I'm an AI," Arjun said. "Always Intelligent."

Kelle rolled her eyes.

"Always Interesting," he added, then laughed in the way one laughs when being tickled. "Always Impressive."

"Always Incorrigible," Jair said.

"You're both incorrigible," Kelle said.

Their conversation lulled, and she could hear the men share a kiss.

"They bled us dry for tests," Jair said, "so it better be real. And to answer your question, we're telling our families today. We didn't want to say anything earlier only to learn that our tests showed something that prevented us from leaving."

"What did they test for?"

"Communicable diseases," Arjun said, "and for the virus. I was wondering if they'd do genetics testing, but apparently that's illegal."

"It's not *illegal*," Jair said. "Eugenics is illegal, with good reason. But they still require testing to make sure people aren't closely related before having children."

Children. The more Kelle had thought about it, the more she wanted to be a mother. As crazy as it sounded, to want to bring a child into *this*, this underground world of filtered and artificial sunlight, of hydroponic gardens, water so heavily treated you could taste the chemicals and maybe-just-maybe a hint of the recycled urine, of cows and chickens living and breeding in bunker barns ... She wanted this, but only because of Arjun. She wanted to look down at an infant in her arms and see herself, see Arjun. And if anyone changed their mind, fine. She wouldn't wither and die without a child. But she might wither and die without Arjun, in her life, in any capacity that he wanted.

"We can worry about all that later," Kelle said, gripping her abdomen out of anticipation. She looked at beautiful dark Cyb, all curves, purple braids down to her waist that flicked with every step. "For all I know, you'll meet Cyb on her way to Pod South, become absolutely smitten, and follow her there."

"I don't do relationships!" Cyb hollered. Murmuring, she added, "Or children."

Kelle smirked, but her mood dimmed when the line went quiet. "You there?"

"We're here," Arjun said. "Just smiling."

"He's really excited," Jair said.

Heat rushed to Kelle's face.

"Pod South will be lucky to have Cyb," Arjun said.

"Maybe if we meet in the tunnels she'll autograph my uniform," Jair said. The Solar Meet alarm *beeeeeep*ed on his end of the line. Kelle's and Cyb's was earlier.

"Showtime," Jair said.

"Break it to them gently."

"That's the plan," Arjun said.

Kelle hung the handset on the wall and sat on the edge of her bed. She couldn't stop grinning.

The treadmill slowed to a stop, and Cyb stepped off. "Your turn," she said.

Kelle switched off the visi-ceiling, slid on her exercise boots, and climbed onto the machine.

"You know Arjun's in love with you, right?" Cyb said before shedding her clothes and slipping into the shower.

"I thought he was imaginary!" Kelle called back.

Cyb laughed, then started to sing one of her hit songs.

• • •

Jair squeezed Arjun's hand as they walked side by side, hand in hand, down the subterranean grey plastic tunnel dimly illuminated by the occasional solar light. Walked, because there was no other way to reach Pod North. The dim tunnels were narrow, creating a long line of the thirty transfers and four guards. The journey would take approximately three weeks, depending on how long the group rested and slept between episodes of walking.

They had to move as a group, as they all carried the group's burden. Some could carry more, others less. Water was heavy, so Arjun, being strong, carried quite a lot for the whole group. One woman, in a wheelchair, was able to attach a small cart behind her to tow bulky, but lightweight, supplies. Small children carried nothing but their favorite toy — heirlooms made of plastic or motley things newly forged from recycled heirlooms.

The guards, differentiated from the others only by a bright orange band sewn onto their grey uniform and the gear they carried, marched at the front and rear of the line. Only they knew the way, and they prevented any deviations down the various branching corridors.

Kelle was expecting them, of course. She hadn't applied for a large room yet — they would worry about that later. First, Arjun and Jair, and the other transfers, would have to live in quarantine for two weeks. During this time, they could meet Pod North inhabitants, but it would be through a barrier.

A child began to sing a children's song.

"It's the Solar Meet, meet
I see your feet, feet

Hold on to your sheet, sheet
Ew, what did you eat, eat!"

Jair snorted. "You want one of those?"
Arjun grinned. "Several, if that happens."
Jair patted his chiseled abdomen. "But, Arjun, my figure!"
"You would, wouldn't you. If you could."
Jair grinned, but then frowned and fell quiet for a few steps. "Do you really think Kelle will like me?" he asked, somehow looking worried and hopeful at the same time. Even after months of talking to Kelle on the phone, Jair still felt nervous.
Arjun smiled, and he hoped his confidence showed. "She already likes you," Arjun said. "I know what you mean. In person, it might be different. But Kelle and I are so alike we might as well be the same person. So I would assume she'll love you."
"Are you going to tell her that you love her?"
A minute, a mile, a sum of distances Arjun couldn't measure passed inside this infinite tunnel as he deliberated Jair's question. He'd had months between announcement and departure to figure out his answer.
Arjun was in love with Kelle. He was also in love with Jair. And Arjun was still Kelle's person, and she, his. Jair said he didn't mind, and truly didn't seem to mind. If Jair was at all jealous of the bond Arjun and Kelle had, he was good at pretending he wasn't. But none of this meant Kelle thought of Arjun as anything but a friend.
"Should I?" Arjun asked Jair. "I should. Of course I should. I have to. Maybe not immediately. In quarantine, that would be awkward."
Jair squeezed Arjun's hand. "Just say it when it feels right."
They shared a quick kiss, and a child behind them giggled before singing a rhyme about *k-i-s-s-i-n-g*.
A figure in the distance took form, dimmed, then shined again under a light. Two guards, followed by a handful of people, one of whom with bright purple hair, were heading toward them.

"Cyb?" Jair strained on his toes to look ahead of the line of transfers. "Hey, Arjun, look!"

• • •

Kelle recognized Arjun the instant she saw him. Tall, thick, dark. Black eyes. Luscious lips. He must have shaved his beard before the journey because it was shorter than he'd described. And beside him, a small thin man, pale and blonde, pretty. Jair.

She ran to the barrier at the same time Arjun did. They each pressed their hands, fingers splayed, against the clear plastic, mirroring. She felt that tingle again — that impossible tingle, because they weren't touching, couldn't even feel his warmth. Her heart was fluttering, but she didn't monitor her pulse. She breathed through the nerves, through the tingle, the excitement, and the dread.

Is she what he imagined? Did that even matter anymore? Who was she to him, beyond friend? Beyond potential coparent of his potential children?

Now that Arjun was here, right here, standing before her only a centimeter apart, Kelle couldn't bear the thought of never seeing him again and a sob burst out of her lips. Arjun's muffled voice rumbled the plastic barrier. When she looked up, he was holding a phone handset and pointing to hers. She slowly brought it to her ear.

Jair hung back in the shadows, selflessly giving them this moment.

"I'm here," Arjun said, voice unsteady. "I'm here."

Kelle looked up at him, so tall, and blinked because it was all so blurry from tears. She pressed her forehead to the plastic, then felt a dull thud when Arjun did the same.

"You're here," she said. "You're here, you're here." She felt it then, his fingers linking with hers, felt it in her mind, the barrier between them the thinnest it had ever been.

Others in the dim wide room greeted transfers from behind the plastic. Some sobbed heavily; some jumped with joy. Perhaps they, too, had met via telephone. Out of the corner of her eye, Kelle saw Arjun reach behind him for Jair. They clasped hands.

"This is Jair," Arjun said into the phone.

Jair took the offered handset. "Hello, Kelle." He truly did have a wide, hooked smile. "Goodness, you're beautiful." He frowned, then. "I hope those are happy tears."

Beautiful. *Beautiful.* "They are. Happy tears. Hi, Jair. Hello." She laughed. "It's so good to meet you both. Are you okay? Need food, water, anything?"

"We're being taken care of," Arjun said. "Don't worry about that." His palm was still against the plastic, still mirroring hers. "Kelle," he whispered, looking directly at her, seeming on the verge of tears himself. "I love you. I should have said it before making this journey, but now I can't not say it. I love you. And I am so glad I'm here."

Kelle glanced at Jair and saw that he, too, was crying. And smiling.

"I love you, too, Arji," she said, crying still, but grinning so much it hurt. "You're more than just my person. I think I fell in love with you a long time ago."

Arjun jostled with a light laugh, eyes smiling, and let his tears roll down his cheeks.

• • •

"Guess what?" Arjun said, whispering into Kelle's ear from behind as he wrapped his arms around her.

"They discovered the moon actually *is* made of cheese?"

He dropped his smile. "Huh?"

She laughed and turned around. "Never mind. Tell me."

Arjun held her upper arms as he regained his smile. He couldn't believe what he was about to say aloud. Words he'd been waiting for all these years:

"They're opening the pods."

Kelle's smile faded slowly. "Really? No joking?"

"The harmful radiation is gone. The toxins are gone." He slid his palms over her shoulders. "There hasn't been ashfall in five years." He traced her curves from shoulder to neck. "The ice caps are holding, the ozone layer has healed, the climate is wonderfully boring." He cupped her cheeks. "We can finally feel true sunlight, darling. Our children can feel sunlight." He kissed her, pulled back, and smiled at Jair, finally home from work.

"I see you told her," Jair said, shucking off his shoes.

"Secrets!" Kelle said.

"Don't worry, love," Jair said. "He only told me over lunch today. Couldn't contain the excitement breech. He was *supposed* to wait until I came home to tell you …" Jair kissed Kelle's cheek as she kissed the air next to his. "So? Excited?"

Kelle shook her head. "I'm *terrified*. Excited, and *terrified*."

• • •

Kelle held her children's hands as they and Arjun and Jair walked out into the sunlight — real sunlight — out of the pod entrance that had nearly been overgrown by shortgrass.

Others joined them until dozens of people, for the first time in their lives, stood under the Sun.

The sky was the exact color known as 'sky blue'. Not the sickly yellow of nuclear winter, not overcast by white clouds, not grey from storms. Blue, blue, blue to the horizon.

In the distance, a herd of what Kelle thought were bison blackened the otherwise pale brown-green prairie. In another direction, green shrubs broke up the dun monochrome. A herd of something different from bison — horses? — flew across the plains. The brown plastic wall around the field of solar panels blocked the rest of her view.

"Somehow they survived," Jair said.

Kelle turned to him. "Those aren't the animals from the pod?"

Jair shook his head. "Those will be released soon, slowly, controlled. The biologists are still working out a plan."

"But the toxins. The radiation?"

"The toxin was human-targeted," Jair said, then screwed his lips. "Also monkeys."

"Radiation may be a problem," Arjun said. "They might not produce viable offspring."

"They look fine to me," Kelle said. "Look at them all."

Hundreds of bison. Dozens of horses.

"Can we run?" Gear asked, looking up at Kelle with big eyes that looked just like Arjun's.

"Yeah mama, can we?" Jak mimicked her brother's pleas, giving Kelle Jair's same hooked grin.

"I want to run," Jair said. "Like the horses." He looked at the children. "I bet I'm faster than you!"

"Are not!" they yelled.

With that, Jair and the children took off running, as did others, mainly young ones. They frolicked as guards stood watch.

Arjun reached for Kelle's hand and wove their fingers tightly. "Well," he said. "I'm certainly glad we took those courses on natural engineering."

"It will be a slow process, building what we need with what we can get. We might be able to scavenge some materials."

"Remolded plastic will be of great use."

"Thankfully the pod can still feed and house us."

Arjun brought Kelle's hand to his lips, and they shared a broad smile before watching all the children and several adults run and jump and squeal and laugh.

"It feels different," Kelle said. "The sunlight."

"Yes. And the air, it's ..."

"Natural." She took a deep breath.

Natural. Not filtered, not recycled, not smelling of plastic. Organic, raw, and carrying the scents of the world around her.

Kelle closed her eyes and leaned her head back, spread her arms, hands palm up. An eruption of warm shivers ran from finger to neck and around her shoulders, as sensational as a lover's caress.

"It feels like I'm being kissed," she said. "Real sunlight. Real sky." She stood straight and looked at Arjun.

He gazed at her, love written across his smile. And before she knew what was happening, he whipped his uniform top off and flung it away. In his excitement, he threw his head back and made a long *whoop*!

"Sir," a guard said sternly. "Please do not remove your clothing. Physician's orders."

"Oh, right," he said, grimacing sheepishly. "Solar radiation isn't filtered outside."

"That's time!" said the other guard before blowing a whistle. "Everyone back inside. The next group is waiting."

Kelle tapped Arjun's butt as they returned to the pod hatch, children and Jair following.

"It's the Solar Meet, meet," Gear sang.

Jak answered with, "I see your feet, feet!"

And together they said, "Hold on to your sheet, sheet …"

Jair murmured to Kelle and Arjun, "They're gonna need a new song."

Gail Ann Gibbs began taking her writing seriously twenty years ago, after winning a small contest and gaining experience writing for-hire novels. She has some published short stories, has won some contests, and owns a fine collection of rejection letters. She has two books out: a short story compilation, *Sketches in the Air*, and a gentle fantasy, *They Called Me Dragon: A Narrative Account of my Adventures on the Planet Earth.*

• • •

In my youth, my suggestion that the Texas Panhandle was ideal for wind-energy production was ridiculed as a hippy, utopian concept. On a recent trip, I marveled at the hundreds of wind turbines humming along the interstate, miles of open ranchland now benefiting from the Wind Boom. An endless source of pollution-free energy seems perfect, but nothing is perfect. How would people cope when things go wrong?

MISTY AND THE WINDMILLS

GAIL ANN GIBBS

MISTY COULDN'T HELP HERSELF. She just had to pull over to the side of the narrow asphalt and gravel road. She had reached the turnoff where she would leave the asphalt road and head up the dirt road to the north.

It certainly wasn't her first time behind the wheel of a rough-country vehicle. It would just be the first time she was taking an official county-owned vehicle off-road, and seemed like an important moment. Plus, she needed a little time to gather her thoughts and, if she was being honest, her courage.

Department of Agriculture Special Agent Michelle Angelou Herrera had driven through five miles of working wind turbine fields since she had left the ranch office. The oldest turbines were closest to the office, installed back in the 2010s, and they had thrummed so loud she could feel the vibrations. With each subsequent field, the turbines grew quieter, closer together, and increasingly efficient in a marvel of good business management. John Oscar Horswill's operation had been a chapter in one of her land management textbooks, and Misty had gotten her fifteen minutes of fame among her classmates for knowing the family.

Misty climbed out of the vehicle, pulling her trusty binoculars from the side pocket in the door, and looked over the hood to the south. The man she was looking for wouldn't be there, but it was easier to set the focus using the rows of sleek turbines that ran clear to the horizon.

This particular field was eerily silent, except for the ever-present Texas Panhandle wind lightly whistling through the blades of the turbines. The reason for the shutdown was apparent by the dozen or so bison grazing on the last of the winter grass around the concrete bases. Soon these stragglers would join the herds heading north, and the wind turbines could be activated again.

Misty turned and scanned in the opposite direction, her view following the dirt road, to the top of a slight rise, where she spotted the pickup truck along the horizon, maybe two miles out. The landscape was so flat here that it made judging distances a little tricky sometimes. Misty had grown up in this country, land of wind and grass, but she still enjoyed the wide open sky. She also marveled at the size of undeveloped land she was viewing, that little dirt road the only sign of human intervention.

Well, that wasn't quite true. The pickup was parked next to an antique windmill; the kind used back in the Wild West days to water herds of long-horns. That had to be a message of some sort. John Horswill had chosen that location specifically, and left instructions that if she wanted to talk to him, she had to come out there. The hands also warned her that he was not in a cooperative mood.

As she climbed back in and put away the binoculars, Misty noticed again the crisp cleanliness of her sleeve and uniform cuff. Definitely screamed brand new on the job. She had considered washing the uniform a few times, torn between wanting to fit in and wanting to look spiffy. Now, she wished she had washed it at least once.

No point in worrying about that now. The Governor had called the county extension office himself and made his position clear. The Texas National Guard was stationed at the Oklahoma State line and ready to defend the agreement. Sadly, that service call-up had included Misty's boss and two-thirds of the staff. With Peterson and Chu on sick leave, that left Misty as the only agriculture agent with enforcement authority for a hundred miles. She had been given twenty-four hours to de-escalate the situation. Her job, her career, and everyone's future depended on talking one stubborn rancher down.

She got back into the SUV and drove bumpily along the dirt road. She lost sight of him when she descended into a gully, but wasn't worried. He was expecting her and wasn't going anywhere.

The road turned upwards, and she found herself at a tip of the rise, with a 360-degree view of gently rolling grassland in every direction. She parked and got out.

The lean, rugged man stood with his hip leaned against the fender, his back to her, gazing off to the north. Yep, he definitely was going to make this hard for her.

As Misty walked up, he turned with exaggerated slowness and studied her. Then he nodded his head, once. "Agent Hererra."

She knew she had to show strength. She met his gaze. "Mr. Horswill."

He raised an eyebrow. "I thought at least I'd rate a visit from Carl himself. Probably doesn't want to face me. I saved his life, you know, during the Buffalo Freedom war."

Misty saw her opening and jumped on it. "Carl has told me about that, more than once, and with pride. Nobody has more respect for you than Carl, and he would be here if he could. But he is also National Guard, and right now he's at the

Oklahoma border." She didn't actually know where Carl was stationed, but it could have been true.

She said, "There are bands of protestors camped along the interstate, vowing to keep it open. I'm sorry, I really am. But if you don't make the call today, there could be serious trouble. Carl could get hurt."

Horswill shook his head. "That is none of my doing. I don't need damn protestors marching and screaming about my rights. None of them done a day's work in their lives. They're just used to having electronic gadgets glued to their bodies day and night. I fight for my own rights. Always have."

"Then call them off. This accord took decades to hammer into place, but if Texas doesn't police their own, the whole agreement will start to unravel."

"Dammit, girl, I tried. Their leader gave me some BS about the issue being bigger than me. That doesn't make any sense. All my family has ever wanted is to work our own land, earn our own way with our own hands. They don't care about that."

"You're right, they don't. It's not for public consumption, but the Governor told me something. There's a suspicion that these agitators are backed by the Canadians. The FBI is looking into it, but there's no proof yet, and the investigation is going to take time. We don't have that kind of time. Tomorrow at this time, there could be blood, and it doesn't have to happen."

"I met the Canadian prime minister, once, at an AG conference. Well, let's just say he and I didn't hit it off."

"There you go. Listen, please make the call. Turn the trucks around, before they reach the state line, and there's a confrontation."

"And if I don't, are you going to arrest me?"

He was calling her bluff. He didn't believe she could arrest him, and he was most likely right. Even if she could, that still wouldn't force him to cancel a legitimate business deal. Well, when you can't do something, pretend you didn't want to, anyway.

She said, "No, that's not my job. I'm going to work with you, and work for you, just like my office has always done. We are dedicated to supporting and sustaining agriculture and land management. Right now, my job is to make you see the bigger picture. The Denmark Accord was designed to address the issue globally, and that means everybody. Countries, states, cities, utilities, and every single wind-power entity halts any expansion work right now."

He said, "Giant corporations can afford it. I'm not a big corporation. This expansion was a huge investment. Those trucks are carrying five billion dollars' worth of equipment — enough to set up another thousand acres of wind production. It's more than lost revenue. There's work for the contractors setting them up, and my people for maintaining them. Jobs lost, revenue gone, and a penalty with the supplier. I can't ask them to pay for that."

She said, "Again, it's my job to fight for your compensation, and I promise you we will do that. I know this is a big blow, to your business and to your life. But we have to stop wind farming. Studies are showing the results could devastate the planet."

"Studies, right. These are the same brilliant minds that shut down the oil business and told us this was the answer. Are they admitting they were wrong? My family went through a rough patch when the government shut down oil production, and I haven't heard any apologies yet."

"That was seventy-five years ago. Back then there was only a tiny percentage of the wind farms that we have now. Then thousands of windmills turned into millions, hundreds of millions, all over the planet. Surely it makes sense that so many would affect the wind patterns."

"A good effect, I reckon. I don't know when last time we had an F4 or F5 tornado. We used to say, 'The only thing between the North Pole and the Texas Panhandle is a barbed wire fence.' Sayings like that don't mean anything to your generation. You've never known a real winter."

"That's just it. The climate is stagnating. We just happen to be in the right place here in the Panhandle for it to benefit us. Other parts of the world are suffering, either constant heat or bitter cold."

"Hah! When I was a kid, all they talked about was how the North Pole was melting. Well, it's not melting now, and has been rock solid for twenty years."

"I know. Just like you, everybody thought that was a good thing, but now we know it's not. Some climate variation is normal, and we're upsetting the balance. We didn't realize the importance of seasonal hurricanes to oceanic life. The oceans are dying. There are projections that within the next fifty years …"

"Oh, believe me, I've heard those predictions before. End of the world, it's almost too late! Chicken Little is what got my grandfather into this business in the first place. Now Chicken Little is going to take it away."

"No, all they want is to stop the expansion."

"Humph. That's what they say today. Tomorrow, they'll want us to scale back, and then again in a couple of years, and again and again, until the entire operation isn't profitable anymore."

"I won't pretend that isn't being discussed. Eventually, there will be some kind of attrition agreement, not replacing worn-out equipment. But look, that's tomorrow. Seriously, it took them a decade to hammer out this treaty, and you may never have to worry about it. It will be Junior's problem, right? Or maybe even Little Junior's problem, it could take that long."

Her voice took on a sharp edge. "You have a huge farm right now. Isn't it enough? Please, it's time to think of your legacy. Tell the trucks to turn around. Don't go down like this. Please, please, don't go into history as the greedy man who destroyed the world."

Horswill's face closed, and he stared off to the north. Did she go too far? She was out of arguments anyway and had said everything she could. Misty decided it would be a good idea to shut up now and let him think.

The antique windmill squeaked. The south-east wind was a mild breeze today and brought just a whiff of the bison manure along with it. Otherwise, it was silent.

After an eternity, Horswill nodded over to the stock tank, and spoke, "That windmill, or one like it, has been here for over two hundred years. The original Oscar Horswill put it in in the 1890s. The giant cattle ranches were breaking up, and he was able to buy some land and a dozen head of cattle. This little windmill meant he had water for the cattle all year round, didn't have to drive them to water holes, and was what made him successful. He spent his whole life building up the stock ranch to pass on.

"He's buried right over there, right here under that cairn of rocks. It was what he wanted. It's hard to believe, but just thirty years after he arrived, there was a bunch of wet-weather years and everybody was switching to farming. It was the 1900s and Wheat was King, and the farmers were bringing in all sorts of tractors and such, carving up the land and putting in fields. 'Feeding the nation', they called it. Things were changing on him, and they said he didn't like it one bit. He wanted this section kept empty, so he could spend eternity in the wild land he loved, before everything was tamed and civilized."

Horswill waved at the oil derrick rocking away off in the distance. "Of course, he didn't know anything about oil back then."

The oil-well pump perched on its concrete base, like a giant insect. It amazed her to see that it was actually moving, the head slowly rocking up and down. Seriously, oil production in this day?

Misty asked, "That derrick isn't actually producing, is it?"

"Well, there are a few little refineries left, making gasoline for antique car enthusiasts. It's not a paying market, though. Of course, it might also be a photo-op for the fly-over tourists. I ain't telling."

He continued the story. "His little girl, my great-mama, was a fairly new widow with ten kids, having lost her husband in the First World War. But she was ready when the oil company reps came sniffing around, trying to sucker her out of her fair share. She fought hard, and the family got good royalty payments for our mineral rights."

Misty commented, "You know, there are still traces of oil in the water table."

Horswill shrugged. "They didn't know any better. I think they believed it would just drain away, back in to the ground it came from.

"I will tell you this. Those oil rights kept the family from starving during the Dust Bowl. They're saying now that wouldn't have happened if people like you hadn't told us to level everything, tear the land up with tractors. See that dip over there, running off to the east? That's what's left of a massive gully, eroded away when half the state blew away. A hundred and fifty years — it's taken that long for the land to heal itself. My family hung on, and rebuilt everything from nothing, turned this place into a functional, sustainable farm."

Misty said, "And the agriculture department was right there, teaching irrigation techniques, and providing grants, loans, and subsidies. Our office has always cared about the land and sustainable agriculture. That's why I wanted to be a part of it."

That earned her a grudging nod, and a quick sideways glance before he returned studying the northern horizon. He said, "You know, my grandpa could tell. He saw the summer highs and winters lows getting worse every year, with grass fires and tornadoes like nobody had ever seen. This was long before the yahoos in Washington started whining about climate change. While politicians were still arguing about carbon emissions and the oil companies started getting regulated to death, Grand-dad was already doing his research.

"So by the time giant utility companies started begging for land to set up their wind-farms, he knew how to negotiate — making deals where we ended up owning the turbines and keeping our electricity rights. My grandfather reinvested the profits, bought his own equipment, built up this business.

"I was just a baby, but windmills were the perfect answer to everything — global warming, climate change, pollution, hell, they did everything but cure cancer. Today, absolutely everything runs on electricity, and electricity comes from our windmills. We provide reliable power for fifteen counties, across three states.

"My father spent his life working these turbines, just like I have. They are our life and our livelihood. We own them, we maintain them, and we profit from them. We support the country like we have since the beginning, with beef and oil and farming and wind-power. Now you want to take it away."

Misty said, "Not all of it. Not today. And my office will fight for your rights and benefits, just like we've always done. It's our job to protect the farmers and ranchers."

He just shook his head and then nodded toward the antique windmill. "So now we're back here. Back to the beginning."

She looked around. "This is a beautiful spot, a perfect place for reflection. I can see why you come out here."

"It is pretty, isn't it? Dammit."

John Horswill pulled out his phone and tapped a few buttons, then put it away.

It took Misty a minute to realize what had happened. She couldn't believe she had won. She had convinced him and saved the world. It was almost too easy. Yes, it was too easy. Well, she would take the victory anyway, but she had to let him know that she hadn't been fooled. "Why, Mr. Horswill, if I didn't know better, I would say you were just making me earn it."

He did actually smile a little, then frowned intensely. "If I've been hearing correctly, I heard you've been sniffin' around my grandson. You got your eye on our Little Junior?"

Misty was thrown by this sudden change of tone, but caught a glint of humor in his eye. She quelled her first response to remind him that Little Junior was twenty-nine years old and perfectly capable of making his own decisions.

She adopted a casual pose, and said, "Well, we have been out a couple of times. Nothing to report, though. Do I have your approval?"

Horswill's face relaxed and he shrugged. "Could do worse."

Misty didn't know if he meant for her or Little Junior, but decided that a nod was the best response.

He indicated the horizon. "I wanted you to come out here because I wanted to show you this. I've talked to Junior and Little Junior both, but, as you so correctly reminded me, it's going to be their decision, not mine. You may have to remind them sometime down the line. They're stubborn, like their old man. Of course, that's your job, as you said.

"You see, I thought it was time. I thought that the best way to honor my great-great-granddad was to keep the business growing. Those thousand acres I was talking about? They were going to be right out there."

Misty's face must have shown her dismay, because he looked down, for just a second, before meeting her eyes again. He said, "Apparently, Oscar Horswill the First didn't care much for that idea either. I guess he just decided to go over my head.

"Remember that, Misty-girl. Greed has tried to destroy this land again and again, but it was always outsiders who were the greedy ones. This time it was going to be the family. Don't let Little Junior make the same mistake."

Misty nodded, not sure what words would be appropriate.

The old man seemed satisfied with that. "This land looks different than it did two hundred years ago, and it will look different two hundred years from now. But my people will be on it, and I hope they continue to do right by it."

They listened to the squeaking windmill for a while, together. The shadows grew long across the grassland.

"You know, Misty, coming out here wasn't easy. You'll be alright. Tell Carl I said that."

"Yessirr."

"You remember the way back to the house? Side road past the office, and down to the river through the cottonwoods?"

"I do indeed."

"Good, you go out first then, and I'll follow you. I do believe there will be home-fried chicken tonight. Home-grown, hand-fed, running around their pen eating their own shit off the ground, like chickens ought to do. Best eating around."

"I was hoping you'd ask."

Alfred Smith is a father and rowing coach from Erie, Pennsylvania who is trying to spin writing into a full-time endeavor. Music features heavily in most of his work, despite his utter lack of talent in that sphere (please don't ask him to sing!) He also enjoys table top gaming, and according to his wife will be going to the special slice of hell reserved for people who "swear this new game will only take an hour to play!"

• • •

There's not a lot of heft to the origin of this story. It started as a silly idea — a beer competition ... in SPACE! And then shifted to a similar idea, but with a little more heart. So grab a beer or other beverage, and enjoy!

HOPFULL FUTURE

ALFRED SMITH

THE SPECIMEN BAG WAS COLD against Adrian's leg as he carried the most recent yield from the cellar back to his home. Fields stretched towards the horizon of the Tortulan flood plains, and waves crashed in the distance. Above, the sky shifted from blue to a deep purple as the planet's sun drifted below the horizon.

Tortula was practically a paradise. Breathable air, a wide swathe of perpetually temperate climate. Even the soil near the sea was perfect for growing just about anything. Practically a paradise, but something was missing for Adrian.

His gaze drifted upward to the lens array hanging overhead. Big enough to be glimpsed from the ground, the ancient artifact had brought him here. It would send data home. Maybe someday it would let them go back to Earth.

The first lens had been discovered half a century before, hiding in the shadow of Pluto. Decades after humanity had stripped it of its planethood, Pluto had proven to be the most important spot in the solar system. A massive artifact that, during certain points of its rotation and orbit, allowed other worlds to be glimpsed.

The lenses had given humanity the stars. A dozen possible homes and habitable worlds in far corners of the galaxy. Distances that would require generations to cross, bridged in an instant by technology so advanced it might as well be magic.

Unfortunately, whatever or whoever had made the lenses hadn't left instructions, and the trips from Earth were one way. According to the xeno-engineers, the lenses should allow for matter and data to be transmitted in both directions. Whatever ancient civilization had built them *clearly* intended for the near-instantaneous travel to be in both directions. They'd also probably been able to align them at will, rather than waiting for an annual confluence of orbits to shift into place an allow transportation for a few days.

That was the issue in using relatively unknown alien technology to traverse the stars. Maybe they'd have it restored someday. Maybe not. But for now, matter went out, but only data could come back. A one-way ticket for the bravest humanity had to offer.

That the lens was visible now meant the alignment was nearing. It always appeared over his part of Tortula right before contact with Earth was possible. It meant that if this round of experiments didn't work, he'd have to wait a year to send the results home. Part of him hoped they wouldn't. It would help put off an awkward conversation a little bit longer.

He reached the entrance to his house, opening the door. No airlock needed on Tortula. His wife Elana had gone to pick up his son, Richard, from soccer practice. That detail was still a little unreal. Soccer on a distant planet. Youth leagues, even. They'd be back in an hour or so, which gave Adrian time to work.

He unlocked his private lab and shut the door behind him. Condensation had bled through the canvas bag at his hip. The glass inside clinked as he hung it on the back of the chair.

Adrian removed a dark bottle from the carrier and rested it on the console. Another bottle followed. And a third. He placed a half dozen bottles on the console of his private lab. Another twelve stayed in the bag — two extras of each sample.

Condensation beaded up on the bottles and ran down to pool at their base. The liquid inside perfectly chilled. Adrian placed a camera on the console and sat down. He reached into his jumpsuit and pulled out the letter. The paper was almost translucent after two decades and a journey across the stars.

Adrian unfolded it with care. The writing had faded to illegibility, but he still knew what it said.

> *Adrian -*
>
> *You seem set on this course of action. To leave everything our family has built over generations behind in some wild dash across the stars. I know it's been hard on you since your mother died. That I've been pushing you more. But this is too much. Without you here, Burning Smith will pass from our family and into someone else's hands. Your great grandfather founded it, and we've all worked to keep it with us. You think I didn't make sacrifices to stay here? You think your grandfather didn't? I am appalled at your selfishness. You have no right to leave.*
>
> *There's still time to reconsider. Call me if you do.*
> *-Dad*

He folded the letter back up and tucked it back into his pocket. *Actual* paper. Leave it to his father to do things the old-fashioned way. Upon reflection, it was probably the furthest something hand-written had traveled in the history of humanity. Another small achievement for his father.

Time to get to work.

He pulled out a bottle opener shaped like a dragon's head. The words *Burning Smith Brewery* were emblazoned on the side in golden letters. Another relic from his home that had been transported between worlds. He turned on his PDA's recording feature again.

"Okay dad. Here goes."

Adrian popped the top off the bottle containing the alpha strain's yield. He wafted the scent from the bottle. Yeasty. Hoppy. Nothing to stop him from taking a sip.

He raised the bottle to his lips and took a pull. The liquid spilled across his tongue and he shook his head. Palatable, but not perfect. "It's got the bitterness, but there's something missing. It's not quite right."

Beta next. Same. Drinkable, smooth. But still not right. The rest were sampled, sipped, and then discarded. Not quite perfect. Not what they were trying to achieve. And then he got to Gamma.

The cool liquid flowed across his tongue and, while the hops bitterness was there, a lingering sweetness — just a touch of honey — followed behind. It tasted *exactly* like his father's signature brew. The Draconic Preservation IPA.

Adrian took another long pull on the bottle, not sampling this time. Just enjoying it. It tasted of *home*. He looked at the camera and raised the bottle, a grin spreading across his face. "Got it. Dad. I've got it. We've got it. *Humulus Lupus Tortulus.* Tortulan Hops. Gamma strain. Generation Fifteen." Fifteen attempts at getting it right. And here he was. Just in time to make the alignment.

He drained the bottle, and then paused the recording. Time to compile the data. Ten years of work, and he'd finally done it. "I need another." He chuckled and pulled out the other two bottles.

He hummed an old song, one of his dad's favorites. Hadn't listened to the whole thing since he'd left earth — didn't remember the words. But the melody stuck with him. It always came drifting up after testing. This was the first time it made him feel good. Hopeful.

He took the beers back to the console and popped the top off another one. He started the recording again. "Okay. Dad. This has been a long time coming. You said when I left that there was nothing for you out here. That your life's work was on Earth, and that's where you'd stay. Where I should stay as well. So. I don't know if you saw the other messages I sent. You never replied. But I'm hoping this one piques your interest."

Adrian paused, his voice catching., his eyes drawn to a picture on the top of the console: himself, with Elana and Richard. The family they'd built here.

The letter's words still burned in his mind.

You have no right.

Sometimes his father's selfishness astounded him. Earth was crowded. Dying by inches. So was the family business. Synthetic beer tasted almost the same while taking up no land and costing a fraction to produce, and so the "natural" brews had been pushed to an artisanal corner of the market. Burning Smith Brewery was only just holding on when Adrian had left. Without his mother to run the books, the place had been going downhill fast.

For a moment, he considered abandoning the whole project. Standing up and leaving ten years of work on the table to rot. Happened every time he thought about making this video.

He doesn't deserve this. You don't owe him anything.

The words hissed in the back of Adrian's mind, a constant companion as he worked on this project far from home. He realized he'd been staring at the camera in silence and reset the recording to start over.

"Hey dad. It's been a while. I know you're probably still angry. I just. Look. Let me explain." He fought to be more coherent this time. "You spent your life working for granddad. Dedicated to making sure that the family business continued. I know you wanted me to follow along — to use my degree to help with new strains of hops for the family fields." Adrian took a slow breath. "That's exactly what I did. Just out here.

"I'll be sending more details of the process, but it was an interesting puzzle. The problem wasn't getting the hops to take root in the soil here. We've set up near some of the best loam I've ever seen. The coastal temperature is perfect, and the weather is mild enough that we can grow most things year-round. Just drop the seeds in and the climate takes care of the rest!"

Adrian took another sip of the beer before continuing. "That ease of growth was actually our main issue. Again, I'll attach more data, but introducing Earth plants to the biome got complicated. None of the native fauna view our stuff as a food source. None of them *could* eat our stuff as is." Adrian shook his head. "Was zebra mussels all over again. Or maybe Kudzu." He'd leave out the videos where they'd had to burn out the first fields they'd planted before the hops could spread the entire way across the planet.

"If native Earth hops were an option, I'd have gotten a brewery up and running ten years ago. When we adjusted the genetics and made a hybrid with the local flora, the results tasted pretty awful."

There were several videos of spit-takes from the testing — and those came after the four rounds of harvest that produced toxic vapors that had nearly knocked him out. And those had been an improvement on the sludge the first two strains had turned into.

"You said there was nothing out here for you. That your life's work as on Earth — and that you expected me to devote my life to the family business as well." Adrian's voice caught. "Dad. The family business is where the family is. You haven't met Richard." Another voice catch, and his eyes stung with tears. He fought to control them. To master the tremble in his words.

"Mom's been gone since before I left. Your brothers too. I know how much the brewery's legacy means to you, but it has no future on Earth. You could come out here and bring the Burning Smith to a new world. They'll figure out the lenses eventually — even if we're both long gone by then. You and I could pioneer the first beer to be enjoyed on more than one world."

He didn't try and stop the tears now "I've wanted to make this recording for so long. I've been waiting have something to show you. In the end, the business is where the family is. Your family is here now. So. Take a look at what I've sent you, and come have a beer with me. Before you go off to join mom wherever she is."

He paused again. A hazy detail rattling in his mind. A final brick in the tower of his argument. It clicked into place. "You haven't met your *grandson.*" His breathing was coming in labored gasps. Desperate. Shuddering. "Come meet Richard. He's an amazing kid. He has mom's smile. Her laugh. There's a piece of the family out here — a large piece now — but it won't be complete without you. I love you dad. I miss you."

Adrian stopped the recording, his stomach clenching. He considered deleting it and starting over. Taking a more defiant stance. Telling his father that he didn't *care* if the old man came or not. That it was all the same.

No. You need to do this.

Even if his father never answered, Adrian could go on with his life knowing that he'd at least tried to do the right thing. Made an attempt to reconnect with the family. His father was right about one thing: it *had* been Adrian's decision to take Elana and go where they couldn't return from.

He sighed, getting himself under control, and then uploaded the data files he'd been curating for the last ten years. Videos of old tests. Time lapses of the hops growing. Soil and other environmental data. In the end, the file was huge — but still felt smaller than it should be. Adrian considered a moment, then added pictures of Richard. His son learning to walk. To use utensils. Recordings of the first words he'd spoken. It didn't add much to overall size, but it did create a sense of completeness.

Before he could talk himself out of it, he sent the packaged data to the lens transmission station. The clock showed alignment would occur just after midnight. With the amount of data he'd sent his dad to sift through, Adrian assumed he wouldn't hear back during the current alignment. A year. A year of silence, and then a few days to hope for a reply.

The door to their home opened, and Richard's rampaging footsteps filled the lab. His babbling voice likewise drifted to Adrian as he excitedly told his mother about the goal he'd scored. Given that it was a twenty-minute walk from the soccer field to the house, it was probably the eighth or ninth time she'd heard the story.

Adrian heaved himself up from the console, grabbing the last beer and popping the top off with the bottle opener. "I'm in the lab!"

He opened the door and was immediately hit at the waist by a four-foot-high missile talking too fast to understand. He bent and wrapped one arm around Richard's waist, hoisting him into the air with a laugh.

Elana's hair was askew, her face flushed from chasing Richard. Before she could say anything, Adrian handed her the Gamma Strain bottle.

She arched an eyebrow and took a sip. Her eyes went wide. "You got it?"

"We got it."

"You need to record the message?" A smile blossomed on her face.

"Nope. Already done." Adrian grinned back.

"Need me to send it for you?"

"Already sent. Come on. Richard and I can get started on dinner. You go grab a six pack of the Gamma strain from the cellar. The others are pretty good, but the Gamma is the best."

Elana drained the beer and placed a hand on his shoulder. She leaned in and kissed him, while Richard squirmed and made a disgusted face. She pulled back. "Good." Her hand grabbed the back of his head. "I'm proud of you."

"Been a long time in the making." Adrian lowered Richard to the ground and pushed him towards the kitchen. "Go put a pot of water on the stove. You can handle that, right?"

Richard rolled his eyes with all the indignation an eight-year-old could muster, then scampered off.

"Think he'll answer?" Elana's smile fluttered a little. "After all this time?"

"I hope so. But if he doesn't, I tried. And I think that's enough."

Elana pulled him close and kissed him again. "I think that's all you can hope for." She turned and headed to the door.

Adrian walked into the kitchen, helping Richard heft a massive pot of water onto the stove. "Good job, kiddo." He tousled his son's hair.

• • •

Adrian's PDA buzzed on the bedside table. The sound drifted to him as though from far away. He and Elana had gone through more than a six pack the night before, enjoying the fruits of his labor — even the ones that didn't quite taste exactly right.

Sunlight streamed in through the windows. At least Richard had let them sleep. He grabbed the beeping device and squinted at the screen. 9:30AM. An alert had come through. A message from Earth.

He blinked a few times, sitting up.

That can't be right. Takes a little over nine hours to get a message back to Pluto.

He accepted the message.

A simple text file, the time stamp at 4:25AM-whatever local Earth time. From his dad.

Adrian woke up a little more. There was no way he could have gone through all that data and gotten a message back that quickly.

Adrian steeled himself for the rejection. A simple, *It doesn't matter what you do.*

He opened the file and read the reply:

Been waiting to hear from you. Thank you for reaching out. I'll see you next year.

Julia LaFond is a geoscience/astrobiology PhD candidate at Penn State University. She also writes fiction and poetry, and has had short stories published via *Alternative Holidays* (B Cubed Press), *Utopia Science Fiction Magazine*, and *Caustic Frolic*. An up-to-date publication list is available on her website: *jklafondwriter.wordpress.com*. In her spare time, Julia enjoys reading and gaming.

• • •

"Hydropolis" is a reimagining of "The Little Mermaid" — to be specific, the notoriously tragic original by Hans Christian Andersen. I definitely had fun figuring out how to build a grounded sci-fi setting with mermaids! But for me, the core of the piece is exploring the collision between a fairytale romance and the complexities of the real world.

HYDROPOLIS

JULIA LAFOND

THERE WERE A LOT OF ANGLES Ryan could take on Hydropolis. The fishing disputes, for one thing: coastal communities were accusing the suboceanites of equipment sabotage, while the latter alleged overfishing of endangered species. Alternately, he could cover the ongoing study of the underwater city's environmental impact, in light of the Untamed Ocean Foundation's insistence Hydropolis be shut down. Maybe he could do a piece about how the residents had embraced gene modding to adapt to their environment, even though augmenting humans remained illegal on the surface.

Or maybe he'd write a fluff piece on the city's 20th anniversary, like his editor wanted.

Ryan glared over the railing. The waves turned to foam in the boat's wake, like his dreams of being an investigative reporter evaporated upon contact with the news network's seniority system. He always got the stories no one cared about — then the ensuing lack of clickthroughs meant he was never assigned anything more important than the Annual Philately Convention in Topeka, Kansas.

So he needed to *make* this story significant. Once his editor opened the file to see a story on par with Tesfaye's exposé of wage theft in New San Diego, he'd get some recognition. Then maybe, just maybe, he'd travel the world like he'd always dreamed.

Groaning, Ryan rested his head against the railing. He was going to *Hydropolis*, the *experimental underwater city*. It was exactly what he'd always wanted to do — but he couldn't muster up any excitement, because this trip was the latest insult in a string of professional humiliations.

A shrill tone echoed from the boat's PA system. "Attention, all passengers: we are arriving at Hydropolis in fifteen minutes. Please report to your Subaquatic Travel Modules."

He hurried below decks, elbow to elbow with the other motley travelers who had taken the 3:30PM boat out of Richmond, Virginia. As he stepped into his assigned module, he tapped on the glass nervously. The glass and metal tubes were rated for much lower depths than the trip to the city, but he couldn't keep from thinking about the worst-case scenarios: an overlooked fracture, a door seal malfunction, or a mid-water collision. He'd be trapped inside, water rushing in, with only a twenty minute supply of emergency oxygen to —

The door latched shut. Ryan instinctively took a deep breath. It took all his willpower not to hold it while the tube pressurized.

• • •

Upon arriving at the gazebo-bubble, Aella was pleasantly surprised when the latest reporter turned out to be hot. Ryan was tall and thin, white with a light tan, and dark-haired. About her age, too. All in all, easy on the eyes. Sure, he was asking the same redundant questions about the city and her family, but hearing them in his deep voice made them more palatable.

It would be even better if he stopped staring at her gills.

"Never seen someone with gene mods before?" she finally interrupted.

He turned bright pink. "No," Ryan stammered. It was a cute stammer. "I'm sorry, I didn't mean to be rude."

"Well, you were. You'd hardly stare at these, would you?" she replied, gesturing to her chest.

His skin darkened to the color of a ripe tomato, and he stammered so hard he couldn't get a word out. His mouth opened and closed like the fish outside the curved glass walls. He looked so flustered, Aella almost felt bad for him.

Almost.

She kept her carefully-crafted "innocent" smile plastered to her face. If the surface dwellers insisted on assuming she was a naïve, sheltered child, she might as well enjoy it.

Ryan cleared his throat. "Speaking of gene mods," he said, keeping his eyes locked on hers, "you were one of the first residents to receive aquatic augmentations, correct?"

"Correct," she replied, barely suppressing a sigh. Her parents, now the co-presidents of Hydropolis, had been part of the pre-founding research initiative. Of course they'd wanted their 'little princess' to be fully adapted to underwater life.

He rigidly took notes on his tablet. "What's it been like to grow up with mods?"

"What's your life been like without them?" she countered lightly. That almost always got reporters to change the topic. If she was really lucky, it would be to the *actually* interesting topic of life on the surface.

Ryan leaned back in his folding chair. "I didn't need them for anything, so I never really thought about it." He tilted his head sideways. "They would have made learning to swim easier, though. I'm still afraid of the water."

Aella glanced out the glass wall, the view out of which was nothing but water. She put her hand over her mouth to at least muffle her giggles. "That must be difficult for you," she gasped, trying to keep her tone sympathetic. "I hope it hasn't put a damper on your time here."

He gave her a sheepish smile. "I don't try to be a wet blanket, but I have to admit, I'm in the deep end here. It might take a while to get my sea legs."

It was official: he was the best reporter yet.

"Where are you from?" she asked, not having to fake her smile.

"Kentucky, originally," he replied, "but I went to school in D.C., where my job is based." He tapped on his press badge. "I'd ask where you're from, but —"

"You already know," Aella interjected. "Boring."

"Boring?" he laughed, shaking his head. "No, no — growing up in the middle of nowhere was boring. I never thought I'd get the chance to talk to an actual mermaid."

Her breath hissed in. "Don't call me that," Aella replied firmly. She internally counted to five, because he clearly didn't know better, even though he should have. He was a reporter; doing research was his job, and even a five-minute search should have been enough to know better. But he didn't, so she was supposed to be patient with him.

"I'm ... sorry." He made a note on his tablet. "Why —?"

"Because I'm every bit as human as you," Aella replied, voice shaking. Her gills pulsed faster, futilely reacting to the increased oxygen demand from her skyrocketing pulse. "I'm not some monster or mad science project. I just happen to have some beneficial mutations."

"Oh." His eyes drifted back to her gills.

"We're done here." Aella jumped to her feet. Screw being the polite, diplomatic daughter of the city's presidential founders. Screw smiling for the camera again and again and again, fighting for the world to recognize her city's right to exist. Screw all of it, and most importantly, screw *him*.

Something hit the ceiling of the half-sphere so hard the room shook. With it came the unmistakable sound of cracking glass.

Dripping water heralded the fractures spiderwebbing across the dome. Ryan ran, but not fast enough. The walls and ceiling collapsed, letting the Atlantic Ocean flood in.

He flailed for the door despite his clothes and shoes weighing him down. Not that it would do him any good: the next cement charge hit the corridor back to the main dome. It would be too long of a swim, never mind the incoming projectiles and shattered glass. His arms were already trailing thin red tendrils.

Aella kicked off her heels. She was still mad at him, but not enough to leave him down here to die. Besides, if she did, the nose-breathers on the surface would blame Hydropolis, even though they were the ones who attacked the city.

She yanked off Ryan's shoes, motioning for him to grab onto her. Ryan didn't need much prompting, though Aella wasn't sure if it was because he understood, or if it was the same desperate instinct of someone who's drowning. Maybe both.

Aella sped ahead toward the closest seafloor hatch. The manmade undercaves were dark, damp, and generally unpleasant, but they were safer than even the city's main dome. Plus there would be first aid kits which, based on the pain in her calf and thighs, she would need almost as much as Ryan did.

Aella was three-quarters there when Ryan's grip loosened. She grabbed hold, cursing him for not packing so much as a breather pack. Now she had to haul him along while dodging the cement-filled metal buckets being launched at them from air cannons.

Her lungs ached, her muscles quivered, and her open wounds burned as saltwater washed over them. It would make things so much easier to let go of the dead weight, let him float to the surface where he belonged. But she couldn't let him die, even if it meant dying with him.

The rusty, barnacle-encrusted hatch was the most beautiful thing she'd ever seen.

She fumbled with the vertical airlock for what felt like hours, but was actually a few minutes. Which still might have been too long for Ryan: he was completely limp, mouth gaping open.

At last, Aella dragged him inside. As the water flowed out of the chamber, he fell over. She dragged him onto the cave's concrete floor so she could start chest compressions.

"You better not die, Surface-Boy!" she shouted. "You still need to apologize for calling me a —"

He vomited up a torrent of water and jerked to his knees. He doubled right back over from coughing.

Aella laughed, wiping her salt-soaked hair out of her eyes.

It was only when the clapping started that she noticed her audience: about a half-dozen onlookers. Aella blushed, conscious of just how far off-script she had gone. But everyone watching was Hydropolitan, and therefore well aware Aella was anything but the perfect little princess she pretended to be for outsiders.

The others surged forward to provide first aid. Aella glanced at Ryan, glad he'd been unconscious for her outburst. The interview was already a PR nightmare, but everything after that was so much worse, it made her shudder. If he'd recorded any of it, she would have died from embarrassment.

• • •

The picture from the attack was a miracle.

Ryan hadn't even set up the drone cam — he'd been waiting until after the interview to get footage of the expansion to the city's outer housing district. But when the underwater "gazebo" cracked open, the drone somehow activated itself. It faithfully uploaded the picture it took to cloud storage before being crushed beneath the rubble.

The timing was perfect, too: an instant sooner, and there wouldn't be an improvised depth charge hurtling through the background. An instant later, and they wouldn't have been in the frame. Not to mention the illumination: the waterproof emergency lights must have flickered on, bathing Aella in an ethereal glow. Her long red hair floated free, framing her face — and what a face it was. It was hard to describe the expression of intermingled compassion and determination.

She looked like an angel.

That's what the internet was calling Aella: the Angel of the Sea. The photo and article had already received millions of views, sparking an outpouring of sympathy for Hydropolis. Which meant that the group of fishers behind the terrorist attack found themselves in unexpectedly hot water.

Ryan, meanwhile, found himself reflecting on an old saying: "Luck is the intersection of opportunity and preparation." He'd gotten the breakthrough he wanted, sheerly through being in the right place at the worst possible time. Posting an exclusive account of the attack on Hydropolis had finally gotten his editor's attention and approval. Not only had she granted him indefinite paid leave for his recovery, she'd also promised to discuss his career prospects when he returned.

Maybe he could travel to Europe to cover the Luxembourg invasion — then again, he didn't want to be in the line of fire so soon. The upcoming Nigerian Climate Convention would be safer ... if he was up to traveling. There was plenty to cover if he stuck to the US: the Monarch Migration Militia, the Hawaiian secession hearings, the rumors that Tachio Tech's organ implants were designed to fail prematurely ... They all had their risks, but he wasn't likely to face down terrorists again.

Hopefully ...

Ryan's eyes drifted to the tarps covering the porthole. His breathing caught. He turned away, staring down at the laminated flooring instead. Waterproof. Everything here was waterproof. Yet a saltwater tang tickled his nostrils, constantly reminding him that one crack in the glass, one spreading fracture, was all it took to —

"How are you doing?" asked Aella, settling at the foot of his cot with a flounce.

"Well, thank you," he stammered, unable to meet her eyes. They were too intense, like sunlight glinting off the sea. Looking down wasn't a good idea, either: she might think he was staring at her gills or her chest. The only thing to the side were the flimsy tarp curtains, which made his blood pressure spike. So Ryan kept his eyes focused on her forehead, hoping she couldn't tell the difference.

"No need to thank — Oh wait, yes, you do. You're welcome." Aella kicked her feet, drawing Ryan's gaze to her open-toed sandals. He knew her toes must be webbed like her fingers, but since they weren't spread, he couldn't tell. Her feet looked dainty and —

He wrenched his gaze away, gulping as he stared right into those twinkling blue eyes. "Yes," he croaked. "Without you ..." He tightened his grip on the blanket, brow furrowing as he pushed away the memories threatening to flood in through the cracks in his attention.

"You still haven't apologized."

He jolted back to the present. "What?"

Aella was examining her fingernails. "For calling me a mermaid." She flexed her hand; the translucent webs went taut. "Or for publishing that picture of me without permission."

Ryan racked his brain. He'd asked her, hadn't he? He'd been in a hurry, yes; writing the article was the first thing he'd done upon stabilizing (he hadn't been able to sleep, anyway). But surely he'd emailed to ask for permission?

Despite his hazy memories, certainty tightened its grip on him.

"I am so sorry," he stammered. "I shouldn't have — such a basic —" He rubbed his eyes, breathing deeply until he could form sentences again. "Is there anything I can do to make it right?"

"Now that you mention it." She scooted closer. "I'll be testifying at the proceedings in Richmond, and there's a press conference afterward." She smoothed her hair, looking away in a sudden bout of bashfulness. "I've ... never been to the surface. Let alone for something like ..." She bit her lip.

"I know a thing or two about press conferences," Ryan replied, squaring his shoulders. "Would you like some pointers?"

Aella nodded eagerly.

"First, preparation: when writing your statement, try to anticipate what questions they'll ask ..."

After a few minutes of intent listening, Aella jumped to her feet and paced the room. "I'll never remember this. Especially not while having to navigate the surface for the first time." She rubbed the back of her neck. "What I really need is someone who knows these things to be there with me."

She looked so fragile and out of her element, Ryan blurted out: "I'm heading back around then. I could come with you."

"Excellent! It's a date." Aella kissed him on the cheek. "See you on the boat out; make sure to dress nice. Oh, and take care of yourself!" She waved one hand as she walked backward out the door.

Ryan stared after her in a daze, hand to his cheek. Had she only been pretending to be scared, to get what she wanted? Or was she just relieved he said yes?

Either way, he wouldn't be leaving the sea behind just yet.

• • •

Aella leaned back on the bench, fiddling with her neck hydrator. It weighed more than it had in the morning, even though it needed to be refilled soon. She'd never had to wear one long enough to refill it. Back then, she hadn't understood why her friends griped about wearing hydrators for trips to the surface. Now she knew why.

Ryan perched on the other end of the bench, shading his eyes as he peered up at the swaying palm trees. "How are you enjoying Richmond?"

"It's *amazing*," she replied without hesitation. "The buildings are so pretty, just like in the movies! Everyone's been friendly. And the sun —" She held out her arms and stared up at the sky, basking in the light and warmth. She didn't care that it stung her eyes. "It's like nothing I could ever have imagined," she breathed. How did anyone go from *this* to the city's flickery so-called sun lamps? No wonder immigrants struggled so much with Subaquatic Affective Disorder.

"But you hate the food," he teased, gesturing to the empty frozen custard cups littering the bench.

"Coolant rationing," she mumbled defensively, flushing pink. "Desserts aren't exactly priority items."

Ryan looked at her sharply. "Rationing?"

"Because we have to import it," she explained patiently, "which is difficult with the synthetic compound sanctions the Untamed Ocean Foundation got Congress to impose on us. Not to mention half our shipments get raided, anyway."

"By the ..." He glanced away again. "Terrorists?"

"Officially, no," she retorted. "Off the record, who else?" The UOF might be outspoken, but they weren't militant — unlike the informal cadres of fishers, boaters, and coast-dwellers who blamed Hydropolis for everything from catch limits to bad weather, or resented them for 'defying the natural order'. Admittedly, most of them weren't militant either. Not that it mattered when the rest rained down destruction on the city.

Ryan gripped the arm of the bench. "I'm sorry," he mumbled, staring down at the sidewalk. "I never realized how bad it was."

"Then maybe," she suggested, scooting closer, "you should stick around and find out more. Then tell everyone else, so they realize, too." She elbowed him. "Like the hot-shot reporter you are."

"Right." He lifted his eyes to hers for a second, smiling thinly, then looked down again. A blush crept up his neck.

Aella tilted her head. What was he so flustered about?

His wristwatch beeped. "About time to head to the courtroom," he announced, jumping to his feet. He scrabbled to collect their empty containers for disposal, but kept dropping them.

"Let me —"

"I've got it," Ryan interrupted. "Go ahead; I'll catch up."

She stood, wincing as pain flared through her feet. Surface shoes hadn't been designed for webbed toes, but she hadn't wanted to stand out more than she already did. Besides, it hadn't been bad at first, just a little pinch — but that was before the tour of the city used up her limited ambulatory stamina. Now, each step was like walking across a bed of knife-sharp shells. She really should have agreed to her father's suggestion of crutches or a cane. If she ever returned to the surface, she'd demand a wheelchair.

If.

Aella scowled, shoving her hands into her pockets. The surface was everything she'd dreamed of and more. If it were up to her, it would be the first of many visits. And on paper, it *was*. The problem was that, as the daughter of Hydropolis' co-presidents, she was bound by certain *expectations*. In the eyes of the surface, she represented the entire native-born suboceanite population. Everything she said or did was used to justify (or undercut) the city's continued existence. If word got out that the "Angel of the Sea" was obsessed with the surface ...?

Which was why she usually stayed in Hydropolis, safe from prying, judging eyes. But even her parents had conceded that this trip was diplomatically advantageous.

Of course, that wasn't the only problem ...

"Excuse me," she mumbled, pausing by the courthouse bathroom. "I need to take care of this." She tapped on her neck hydrator.

"Right. Of course. I'll ... wait. Over there." Ryan blushed vermillion and scuttled off.

He'd been even more flustered today than when she'd met him. Blushing, avoiding her gaze, tripping over himself ...

Was he in love with her?

She nearly dropped her water bottle as it clicked into place. They'd been low-key flirting at the interview, and then she *saved his life*. Of course he had a crush on her. Then she'd jokingly called today a date, telling him to wear nice clothes ... He must have gotten the wrong idea *completely*. No wonder he'd bought her all that frozen custard without so much as a word of protest.

Though ... that wasn't necessarily a bad thing. He was hot, had a good sense of humor, and had stable employment. He was a good catch, actually; if it hadn't been for that "mermaid" slip-up, she really might have asked him out.

Gears churned in her head as she considered the diplomatic angle. Her smile widened. Visiting her boyfriend on the surface was the best justification possible for getting away from Hydropolis. The boyfriend she'd *personally* rescued from a terrorist attack, in particular. Who didn't love a good love story? If the tabloids caught wind of it, the ensuing media frenzy would boost pro-Hydropolis sentiments even higher.

So she needed to make sure the tabloids caught wind of it.

• • •

It was the first time Ryan had been on the receiving end of a press conference, and he vastly preferred it the other way around. Between the shouted questions and the whir of drone cams, he could barely hear himself think. Not to mention the bright lights, accented by disorienting camera flashes.

The crowd was the worst part. If it were only reporters and photographers, that might have been fine. But there were also concerned citizens mixed in, eager to hear the Hydropolitan's statement firsthand. At least, he hoped so. The longer he stared into the sea of humans, the more he wondered whether he was looking at whoever nearly killed him – and whether they would try again.

Not him. He took deep breaths, wiping his sweaty palms on his pant legs. Ryan wasn't a target: he'd just been collateral damage. If anyone was a target, it was Aella.

Somehow, that didn't make him feel better.

Things quieted down as Aella read her prepared statement. If she was nervous, he couldn't tell. She spoke firmly, with simmering passion. She condemned the terrorists, and called on the authorities to ensure such an attack would never happen again.

A flash went off. The lighting, combined with the determined look on Aella's face, reminded Ryan of the picture.

He was underwater, not daring to release the scream burning inside his lungs. The water turned red before his eyes. Would that attract sharks? Which was worse, sharks or drowning? A torpedo roared toward him —

"One question at a time," insisted Aella, and the room quieted down.

Ryan pressed himself against the wall. It was firm, reassuringly unyielding: he was above-water. He gasped for air as if he'd just emerged from the ocean. The roaring in his ears faded, and he could pay attention again.

"The reporter you rescued, Ryan Clay," someone shouted. "What's the nature of your relationship?"

"He wanted to interview me for a piece he was writing," she replied. "Obviously, things didn't go according to plan."

That got a few laughs. Aella turned away, scanning the sea of raised hands.

"And now?" interrupted the original reporter, pointing right at Ryan. "It must be *something*."

His cheeks were turning red, and he couldn't stop them. He wasn't supposed to be singled out for questions. He wasn't even supposed to *be* here. Why had he ever agreed —

"N-no comment," stammered Aella, twiddling a lock of hair. "Next question," she said, waving her hand vaguely.

It was the worst possible thing to say. The entire room erupted into chaos. No one could possibly discern the overlapping questions, but Ryan didn't need to. They would all be variations of: "Are you two *together*?"

His blush deepened, even though that would make it worse. Why was he blushing, when his bones were turning to ice? All these people, wondering whether he'd fallen for her — well, why wouldn't they? When they first met, her sparkling blue eyes made his heart flutter. But that was before the glass bubble shattered, letting the ocean come roaring between them. Now her eyes reminded him of the waters that nearly killed him.

The questions kept coming, over and over. Ryan wanted to run, but he couldn't. His legs were immobile, tangled in seaweed that held him down to be pounded by the oncoming waves.

He was mildly surprised to find himself in a quiet, dimly lit room.

"Are ... you OK?" asked Aella, reaching for his shoulder.

He flinched back.

"I'm sorry," she said, withdrawing her hand like he'd burned it. "I didn't mean to ..." She bit her lip.

"You're fine," he lied, rubbing his head. "That was just ... a lot. So soon after ..."

She, like him, stared down at the wood floor.

"I'm so sorry," she finally said, clutching her elbow. "I shouldn't have asked you to come and ... The reporters ..." She shook her head. "I should have handled it better."

"You did better than I would have."

"Did I?" she mumbled, looking to the side like she was talking to herself. Even with her reddish hair hanging over her eyes, there was no mistaking the guilt etched into her face.

Ryan sighed. He was supposed to be making up for how badly he'd botched the interview *and* the story, but now he was making her feel even worse.

"I was worried there might be ... terrorists in the crowd." That, at least, was true. "When the focus turned to me ... You're not the one who did that."

She smiled a little. "Will you be okay?"

"I don't know," he replied frankly. "But I'm looking forward to heading home to recuperate."

When Aella nodded, Ryan forced himself to meet her gaze. It wasn't as hard this time — her eyes seemed focused on something very far away.

• • •

"Before I answer," sighed Dr. Khumalo, pinching the bridge of her nose, "please tell me it's not for the sake of that reporter boy."

Aella shifted uncomfortably in her seat, unsure how to answer.

"I'll take that as a 'yes'," the doctor huffed, folding her thick brown arms. "Aella, you can't be serious."

"It's complicated," she replied, fiddling with her shirt hem.

"Let me make it un-complicated," scoffed Dr. Khumalo. "Reversing your adaptations would require multiple surgeries and an extensive medication regimen — all of it theoretical, by the way. Which means it's *risky*."

Aella rolled her eyes and shrugged.

"Your gills, for instance — aside from the risk of irreparable damage to your cardiovascular system, they're on your *neck*. Do you have any idea how dangerous surgery there is? We could damage your arteries, or your esophagus, or … or your larynx! Would you want to go the rest of your life without being able to talk?" She waved her clipboard for emphasis.

"Mouth words are overrated," Aella replied flippantly, crossing her arms. "There's AAC, not to mention facial expressions, body language —"

"Removing your webs could cause dexterity or chronic pain issues." Dr. Khumalo jabbed her finger into a poster emblazoned with a diagram of the human body. "Moving on from *visible* mutations … What about your eyes? They're meant for underwater and low-light conditions. Your limbs, that are built for swimming? There's also your amped-up vitamin D production, body fat distribution, gas balance, bone density —"

"So tell me," interrupted Aella. "If I *don't* change any of that, how long can I stay on the surface for?"

The doctor sighed heavily, leaning against the wall. "We're still learning, but assuming you follow the recommended —"

"How long?"

She looked away. "Three to four months maximum, totaling no longer than eight months per year."

Eight months. Eight paltry months. Even wearing a hydrator and sun protection, she'd only be able to leave Hydropolis for two-thirds of a year.

"We haven't been able to study long-term effects of living on the surface," Dr. Khumalo added reluctantly. "So those are estimates."

Of course they didn't know. After all, Aella was from the first generation of children predestined for life in Hydropolis. Not to mention all her friends seemed happy enough with the decision their parents had made for them.

"Thanks," grumbled Aella, storming out so she wouldn't have to listen to the doctor's continued protests. But they kept whirling through her brain. Despite her bravado, Aella didn't like the risks of being the first to reject her mods. But if she didn't ...

She sighed, glancing at her phone. In the weeks since Ryan had left Richmond, they'd kept up daily email correspondence and, from the sheer detail of his messages, it was clear he cared about her. Which she would feel guilty about (since she was basically using him), except that in the course of talking about literally everything but Hydropolis, she had slowly developed her own feelings for him. But when she'd asked for a video chat, he'd gone quiet for a full two days before setting a time.

Aella settled into her chair, using her webcam as a mirror to smooth her hair. Maybe she was wrong, and he didn't feel that way. Or maybe he did, but was afraid of commitment. Either way, it was about time they had a serious conversation about the future.

Ryan's face filled the screen, and it was just as handsome as she remembered it.

"Hi," said Aella, fluttering her eyelashes slightly.

"Hi," he replied, shifting back. Had he always been so pale? He should get out in the sun more, since he actually could.

"How have you been?"

"I —" He sucked in his breath, looking down. "I can't. I'm sorry, I — can't."

His video disappeared, leaving Aella to stare back at herself, wondering how things had gone so wrong so quickly.

Her phone rang: Ryan.

"There you are," she said eagerly. "Did your internet go down, or —"

"I've been having panic attacks," he blurted out.

Understandable, given the trauma he'd been through. "I'm ... sorry," she mumbled. What else was she supposed to say? And what did that have to do with anything?

"Flashbacks, too," he continued regardless. "And hypervigilance, and — and —" His voice cracked. "Seeing you triggers it."

As the air rushed out of her lungs and her gills clamped shut, Aella wondered if this was what drowning felt like.

"It's not fair," he added, voice shaking. "You saved my life, and I like you, but it's — None of this is fair."

It all made sense. He hadn't been in love with her – he'd been overcome with terror whenever he looked at her. But he'd still tried to stay in touch, because that's what *she'd* wanted, and he owed her his life.

"No, I'm sorry," Aella replied shakily. "I shouldn't have ... I'm sorry."

"Not your fault."

She smiled sadly. "Not yours, either."

For a while, the only sound was his labored breathing.

"I can keep emailing," he volunteered in a small voice. "Just ... no selfies."

"Are you sure?" she asked. "I don't want to pressure —"

"I like talking to you," he assured her. "It's just ... seeing you that's the problem."

"All right," she agreed softly. It was a bitter consolation prize for her shattered hopes of romance. But she wouldn't let their friendship join her dreams in the waste disposer.

"Talk to you later," he muttered.

The line went dead.

Aella leaned back, staring through the ceiling porthole at a school of fish. It was a view she needed to get used to again. Without Ryan as a palatable excuse, she was never going to live on the surface, not even for two-thirds of the year. She was stuck down here.

Her blood turned cold, and she knew exactly what she wanted: to leave Hydropolis and never look back. But there was no way she could do that without screwing over the city's public image.

• • •

Ryan frowned at his inbox. Nothing from Aella all week, which was understandable. He wouldn't be surprised if she never emailed back at all. The thought made him oddly sad: he hadn't been lying when he told her he enjoyed talking to her. But very few people would want to be friends with someone who couldn't stand to see their face, let alone be in the same room as them.

It really wasn't fair.

With a sigh, Ryan opened the email from his editor. She was just "checking up on him," and hoped his recovery was going well. But beneath the friendly veneer lurked the real question: when would he be coming back?

Sooner was better, he knew that. The longer he waited, the harder it would be to jump back in. He was physically recovered, and therapy had been going well. So maybe it was time to stand up, dust himself off, and chase his dreams.

He hit the reply button, staring at the blank space where his email would go.

Ryan pushed away from his computer, grabbed a blanket to wrap himself in, and curled up in the corner to have a nice, quiet panic attack.

• • •

Midway through her morning swim, Aella had an absolutely brilliant idea.

A minute later, she let herself into her parents' office.

Her father looked up from his desk. "Sweetheart! We're always happy to see you, but ... we do have work."

"This *is* work," she replied excitedly, wringing out her hair. "Is Mom here?"

"Just finished a meeting," she replied, stepping in with a cup of coffee. "What's this about?"

"You know how you've been talking about getting a designated surface representative? I've thought of the perfect candidate." Aella paused for effect before pointing to herself. "Me."

"Absolutely not," her parents replied in unison.

Aella bit her tongue, but she'd known this would be a hard sell. "I've got tons of experience talking to outsiders. *Especially* reporters and politicians. Plus, the public loves me."

"But you're so young," her father protested.

"What about your mods?" objected her mother. "It's not safe for you to go to the surface."

"If mods are the problem," Aella said slyly, "I could always get rid of them."

Her parents stared in shock. Then, predictably, came the shouting match, things got personal, and she stormed out in tears.

After clearing her head with a long swim, Aella grinned to herself. Her parents would come around. Once they took time to thought about it, they'd have to admit there was no better candidate than the Angel of the Sea.

• • •

Ryan did a double take when an email from Aella came through.

It was short and sweet: apologizing for her part in the fiasco, affirming that she wanted to stay in touch if he did, and letting him know that she was now Hydropolis' official ambassador. The last part made him smile: she was well-suited to a career in politics. But his congratulations could wait until he finished this email.

He turned back to the tenth draft of his resignation. When he finally sent it, a weight lifted from his chest.

He'd gotten into the business because he thought he wanted excitement and recognition. Thanks to Hydropolis, he'd gotten both — and he'd been miserable. Now he was going to give stability and anonymity a try, beginning with his new job as a librarian.

• • •

Aella leaned on her cane as she inspected her new office. It was small, poorly lit, and smelled vaguely like mold. In other words, exactly like the seafloor caves. Not the fresh start she had in mind.

She stowed her backup hydrator in the desk drawer before turning right around, over her feet's protests. When her parents had finally given in, they'd done so on the condition she keep her mods, at least until she'd spent more time on the surface. Which was exactly the outcome she'd counted on.

Which didn't make her feet hurt less as she hurried to the press conference. Then she'd have to head the counter-protest of UOF's demonstration, and meet the Fishery Committee to discuss catch limits …

There would be plenty to do over her first four months.

Regina Clarke got her doctorate in English literature and then strangely found herself in the field of IT, writing about subjects engineers wanted to explain, including virtual reality, military surveillance software, and augmented reality. Some of these things have, now and again, inspired her fiction. Her stories have been published in *Mad Scientist Journal, Fifth Di, NewMyths.com, Titanic Terastructures* anthology, *MetaStellar,* and *Etherea,* among others. Her fantasy novel *MARI* was a finalist in the ListenUp Audiobooks competition and three of her short stories have been featured on podcasts.

• • •

Three things converged all at once that shaped my story — a marvelous digital painting by a friend, an Australian artist, of a merry-go-round spinning in an empty field against a darkening sky, seeing orbs in a garden in Glastonbury, England, and listening too often to the political fabrications of people I decided had to be crazy. I wanted to imagine a world where there was a new, higher frequency of perception, a way to invoke harmony and truth and compassion as the given. "Night Circus" emerged out of that.

NIGHT CIRCUS

REGINA CLARKE

It was said the girl-child dreamed worlds into being. Arain ran to me with news of her arrival from Rengal.

"What does this mean?" she asked, her eyes wide with fear. "Why has she come?"

I was walking in the hanging gardens of Talas. I could play there with the shadows each vine and branch left on the white walls. I moved them as I felt the need, especially the ones created by ferns and the orange flamevine and the ficus heavy with figs, changing the shape of the gardens, for all the vines and trailing leaves and flowers followed their own shadows each time. From the hills above, it was as if the gardens were waves in a sea, never still.

"How would I know?"

I sent the shadow of a flowering sandalwood tree to the east wall before stopping. Clouds had obscured the sunlight and a pale mist wove around us.

Such news was troubling to me as well. It was all good enough for Rengal, a planet where its people welcomed mutation, and the girl-child's skill in the transforming rituals was their comfort. We had heard of this all our lives. How Rengal could never be visited, for it was always shapeshifting into other states of knowing, its people inviting in the unknown and scattering, we were told, into another state of being, invisible, altered.

"You aren't afraid of the Preceptor. You're from the west country, Silla. You aren't afraid of anything. You could ask him why she's here. Are we going to disappear? Is that his plan? Why has he brought her to us?" Arain hugged her shawl close. Its silver threads shimmered even in the dull light.

"Is that what you think?" I'm afraid of losing what I love, I wanted to say to her, as the memory of my father came to mind, and of my grandmother, Nona. I still felt the loss of them, though ages had passed since. I didn't want to lose anyone else.

"You know what I mean." Arain shook her head back and forth, her long red hair tangled in the shawl. "You have the power."

At that I laughed out loud. "My dear friend, I know how to do many things, but I am not skilled enough to oppose the girl-child, even if I wanted to, which I don't. I have no desire to transform anywhere or in any way."

"What do your people tell you?"

"My people? They are yours, too! This Earth belongs to us all. And I know nothing of her except what you know."

Arain stamped her foot. "So you'll do nothing?"

"I didn't say that. Of course I'll go see the Preceptor. You know as well as I do, though, he'll tell me nothing." I was deeply curious, all the same, though seeing the man never brought peace of mind. He never told the truth. My curiosity would only fill his need to goad me.

I left the gardens and walked slowly toward the high tower where he lived in his self-imposed glory. Around me the green grass grew in long, brilliant shafts. In the distance, massive waterfalls fell through dark forests and down steel-gray cliffs in white cascades of thunder. The jeweled stones I walked on glittered in the sunlight that had broken through the clouds. I breathed in and the scent of chamalc came to me, a delicate sweetness bringing with it a feeling of calm. Yet, it was a teaser, I knew, all I saw was a deception to create feelings of softness and peace and delight by the Preceptor's chosen Communicators.

I was not deceived, but I also knew if I moved too slowly I would lose the will to move forward at all, such was the feeling. Like a dream, the landscape beguiling whoever walked its path. Only, I had been there before. I knew better. More, I had my father's warnings in my heart to guide me.

Walking fast along the empty passageway to the Preceptor's domain, I felt the pulse of the white walls moving in and out. I had to be alert to any shift in the vibrations that flowed past and through me. It was pure chance whether a creature would break through those walls, but it could happen. We all knew such things were hallucinations. That didn't keep us from feeling an unease and even dread, making our hearts race, as mine did. It was the Preceptor's perverse humor at work. He watched visitors on his monitors and decided on a whim when to release his toys.

Maybe that was why he had brought the girl-child to us — to amuse him in the darkness he embraced. No. Her presence would mean he had less power than before, and he would never willingly allow such a thing. Someone else had to have made this happen, someone who had persuaded him to agree. Or gave him no choice. Or didn't tell him at all. I only knew she would not have come to our world unless she had been called.

Who, then? Would he answer when I asked?

"Be careful, Silla. What you force to happen, the signs you ignore — will mean your purpose fails you. Do you understand?" I heard my father speak as if he stood beside me.

The dead came only in memory. His voice was always gentle, the look from his gold-brown eyes like a benediction.

"Use discernment. Know what you are willing to sacrifice. Know better what you are not." He had given me this warning when I was fourteen after I had rebelled for no reason but a perverse need to defy my innate caution, as if testing it, and so I ventured into the raucous dens that had cropped up in our city almost overnight. Much later, I understood my father's message to me, but not until I had almost bargained away my life for the favors of a fleecer in one of those haunts, enamored as I was by his gift of words. Even that lesson had not set in right away. It had taken me a very long time to see through the illusions of what the false ones pretended to tell me.

I knew my father and the Preceptor had once been best friends. A strange friendship, I had said to him once, for no two people could be less alike.

"It wasn't always the way it is," he answered. "We shared much in common. He and I both were seekers of the unknown and explored it all together. Some of my best memories are of the journeys of our early years and I value those even now. Does that surprise you? It shouldn't. Life is not a fixed emotion. Earth is always in transition, and we with it. Anyway, our link together ended when we were in training at the academy. It happened one evening, not long after dark, at the Night Circus."

"What is the Night Circus?" I had asked, but he wouldn't answer. It was the only thing he would never talk about with me.

The high steel doors that marked the entrance to the Preceptor's chambers showed me my own image, distorted, just as it had been in the funhouse in an old seaside retro gram scavenged from one of the ancient digs I'd joined in the western lands. The eyes that looked back at me now were the same black as my mother's. Impenetrable, my friends would say, Arain among them. "Beware Silla's stare," they would call out to each other and pretend to be afraid and break down into laughter. I hoped that stare would serve me in the next few minutes.

"Silla, Silla. What brings you here?" His voice, so warm, welcoming. More pretending.

The doors dissolved and I walked through and past his guards. There were four of them, all dressed in black with guns, like characters I'd seen in a retro comic book.

"I spared you from my game, so eager was I to see you and hear what problem you are having. Alas, you so seldom visit me."

The Preceptor smiled. It made my skin crawl. There had been a trickster in the old comic book as well, with a smile like his.

"Why is she here?" I said.

"Ah, no greeting for me, is that it? Rumors abound, of course. My people love to worry."

We're not your people, we never have been, I wanted to say, but it would make him smile more if I did.

"Why is the girl-child here?"

The Preceptor sighed and reached out and patted my arm. I stepped back, further away.

"If you must know, I'm planning a few changes. She is going to be a great help to me."

"Whose idea was this?"

He stood up, his blue eyes fixed on me, a disconcerting thing, for the blue was so strangely, thickly, outlined in red. "You don't appreciate me, Silla. I like to be appreciated." He rolled a small object between his hands, a silver cylinder. "Still," he went on, "you are Joseph's daughter. I shouldn't be surprised. So I'll tell you. Her coming was my idea."

"No, it wasn't."

He blinked, long yellow lashes hiding his eyes for a long moment.

"No," I repeated in a louder voice. "Not you. Another chose this."

One of the guards moved closer, but at a glance from the Preceptor, returned to his post near the door.

"You should trust me. I might resent your words.

"Except I'm right."

As I watched him, the Preceptor seemed to shrink a little before me, his thin body seeming more concave. He slammed his hands on the table and the silver cylinder broke in half, leaving a trail of white powder. "Yes, you are right!" he shouted. This time all four guards approached. He waved them back. "It does you no good to know. Leave me."

I had the sudden feeling everything in that room and all of us were suspended somehow, as if waiting. For what?

"I said, leave me," he shouted.

I did, walking more slowly along the passageway this time, sure his game was shut off, for now. He was afraid, too. Of the girl-child? Surely she had a name. It mattered suddenly to find out.

When I closed the door to the passageway behind me at last and entered the anteroom, a shuddering vibration coursed along the floor. Pulling open the main door that led into the street, I felt the ground beneath me as unstable as the floor of the funhouse I had remembered only minutes before.

As suddenly as it had come, the motion stopped.

Crystals on the sleeve of my jacket began to reshape themselves into a frame and glow a pale green. I watched as images flowed past across the cloth. Who was sending me a message?

Suddenly the same images began to appear on the buildings across from me, flowing along their walls. I knew them, scenes from our planet's past, an ancient time before we existed, before anyone had ever existed but the old creatures whose bones we found beneath the western lands. But these were not the renderings of artists. They held motion and energy. I sensed I was seeing them as real.

Who was sending these to us?

"Silla, for heaven's sake, answer me."

Arain's face filled the crystal frame. "You felt the tremor? The girl-child created it! She is sending messages everywhere!"

"How do you know this? What's her name?"

"Her own people refer to her as the Pathfinder."

"What is she doing? The Preceptor revealed against his will that someone else, not him, brought her here. Who?"

"I'm not a magician, Silla. But someone here with me does know. They know everything. You need to come, now. No delay. Hurry."

Another tremor ran under my feet, this time buckling the carved stone streets. Who was the Pathfinder? Not one of us. Not like us.

"Silla! Forty-tTwo. Please, now."

I watched as Arain's image faded.

What was she doing in the desert quadrant? Forty-Two was a wasteland, a place of emptiness where the wind never ceased howling, where the sand shifted into dunes and sometimes opened into tunnels that led underground. False tunnels one could fall into and be suffocated by the weight above them. "Not suffocated," my father told me. "Drowned." But what he said made no sense. There was no water to be found in Forty-Two.

I stood still on the street, aware of others passing by, all giving anxious glances at the buildings where the same scenes continued to stream. A change of any kind signaled trouble for us. We all knew we could go wherever we wanted, we could say what we wanted, but we were always watched and heard. Even in our sleep. There was no place to hide. The Preceptor's guards could always find us. And now the girl-child was among us. But I knew, as Arain knew, in Forty-Two there were no guards.

I set the quadrant fully in my mind, wary though I was, and closed my eyes. A second later I could smell the creosote that grew there and felt the wind pushing at me and opened my eyes. The landscape was as I remembered, though I had not been to the place since my father's death. He had taken me there so often for my training, for the lessons he said would save me from the Night Circus. I felt his fear for me, and studied with him, gave my soul into the work, still always wanting to know what the Night Circus was, and he always giving me no answer.

Each time I had left Forty-Two, it was as if I had left a part of my soul there. Returning now felt like coming home.

"At last! You took your time!"

I turned around. Arain stood across from me, her wild red hair streaming in the high wind. She was near a barrow I'd never seen before, though I had explored many of them in Forty-Two. Mound builders had come to that place eons before to bury their dead, my father would tell me. I suddenly realized the scenes on the buildings I had seen moments before had included some with such mounds in them, remnants of the First People.

I smiled at her. "I took exactly three seconds, and two of those were spent in reflection, first. I haven't lost my skill to transport."

"Yes, yes. Here, come with me. They know the girl-child. They know her! Hurry!"

"Who does?"

A wide ditch separated us. I stepped across it easily and walked up to the entrance of the barrow. I could see the inner stones, shimmering in thin streaks of green and gold hidden behind a dust devil and revealed again as the wind shifted.

"In here," Arain said. I followed her through the entrance and along a dirt path. The walls moved in and out like the Preceptor's, only these held a soft sound, as if they were breathing. Scenes raced across them, people in all manner of dress, animals moving in concert with them, appearing and vanishing and reappearing as we walked through.

"What's all this?" I said to Arain, catching at her arm and pointing to the walls.

"Our history, your history, alive and well." The voice echoed around the wide space we had entered, a room of stone rising high out of sight, though the barrow outside had not scaled more than twenty feet. Light shone out from orbs floating in the air above. A woman and man stood up from amber-gilded chairs and walked toward us. I felt she was the speaker.

"They know of the girl-child. They know the Preceptor. They know what the Night Circus is. They're going to help us!" Arain was clasping her hands together, her face alight with joy.

I felt unafraid, but that didn't mean I could trust whoever they were. And how did Arain find them? With my thoughts the orbs around me changed color, from white to pale blue and then into a golden cloud of light.

"Who are you?" I asked, staying close to the threshold.

"We've always been here." She gestured around the wide space and its comforts. "We haven't needed to show ourselves for a long time, until now, with the arrival of the Pathfinder. We called Arain to us so she could call you, for we need you with us for a little while. We knew your father, and Arain's mother."

"We are connected!" Arain said. I heard the excitement in her voice.

I felt something else, an anger swirling in my heart. Arain had been deceived. We were in the company of those who would obstruct us more, and if they were in Forty-Two, then that meant the quadrant, alas, could no longer be a haven. We had lost everything!

"Hush, Silla. We hear your thoughts. Nothing is lost. You have nothing to fear from us. We only want to help. I am Rea and he is Tamais. This is our home, and we welcome you."

"Isn't it wonderful?" Arain said.

"I don't know," I answered. She looked at me as if I had gone mad, but Arain had always been more gullible than I was, though my time in the dens was proof of my own susceptibility. But she easily and with good intentions immersed herself in her various enthusiasms with no filter. I worried for my friend now. Why did she trust so easily?

"You've always been here?" I said. "I've come into Forty-Two since childhood. I have never seen you before."

"Not into this place, I should imagine," Tamais said. His silver hair belied his seeming youth. He and Rea were the same height, their eyes the same dark brown, flecked with gold and green.

"Sometimes we are here, and sometimes we are the sand itself and this burial mound but a memory," Rea said. "We change often, back and forth. It is how we hear other dimensions that exist within our own, especially yours, the sounds reaching us through the ground from the center of the earth. We saw the Night Circus again. It has shown itself without warning, as is its custom. It's why we called the girl-child to us--the Pathfinder."

At her words, I began to sink into a familiar, deep stillness, the air around me growing heavy, a mist surrounding me. I was suddenly in a sand tunnel and it was filling with water and I couldn't breathe and felt the panic overtaking me. A sudden tremor shifted the sand, thrusting me onto a wide plain that stretched to the horizon, where massive creatures walked in steps of thunder. As quickly, they faded from my sight and around me stood ancient ferns over sixty feet high, and I felt the brush of wind as a dragonfly three feet long flew past me, a brilliant, shimmering cobalt blue and green darting into the low-lying vegetation. The air was humid and smoky. A savannah lay beyond and a patch of that lay dark, burned from lightning.

I felt Rea's hand on my shoulder, shaking me into alertness. "What is it, Silla?"

"How strange. For a moment I felt —"

"Enclosed? Protected?" Rea asked.

"As if I could stay where I was forever. A place beyond time."

"Yes. Or a time before," Tamais said.

"One of your trances. I told them how you do that," Arain said. "It's why they wanted you to come here."

I spun around and walked past them and out into the entranceway, past the walls still in motion, until once again

I saw the terrain of the desert and felt its hot air on my face. I heard them following me, but no one spoke. I stood very still, looking out at the vast empty plain as they gathered around me.

"Silla," Tamais said, his voice as soft as a whisper, "you're the doorway the Pathfinder seeks."

"To bring another world into being? A world to replace our own?" Arain said.

"Would that be such a bad thing, to have a world without the Preceptor?" Rea asked. "But no, her purpose is to give us an alternative."

"What alternative?" I said. "Did you call her here? Can you go above the law of the Preceptor? Can you control him? Then why do you let him rule us, with his minions, his guards who would destroy us at his command? Who have done so more times than I can count!"

Tamais glanced over at Rea, who nodded and made a slight bow to me. "We can't stop any of you from doing what you want, including the Preceptor," he said. "What we can bring are choices. The girl-child, as you call her, has come of her own accord--because it is time. She is offering a choice to you, to everyone on Earth. As the Pathfinder she lives in all dimensions at once. You can leave here, you can leave Talas. She will show you all possible destinations. The way will be opened. You have nothing to fear. She will create new worlds, if that is what you want. Not only for you, but for anyone on Talas and all over the Earth."

"And you will be as the gateway into it for all the others," Rea said. "She told us so."

"Are you trying to manipulate me? Like the Preceptor? How did *you* get here? Why is Forty-Two free of the Preceptor's hand? Who created the Night Circus and what is it and why should I need to know? Why ask for my help? I won't be conned again! Not ever."

"So many questions. We have always been here, I told you this. We were born into the race of mound builders.

Forty-Two contains love. It always has. It was built from that emotion. The Preceptor's primary emotion is hate, born out of the fear that possesses him. He can never perceive Forty-Two. He has no idea it exists."

"But I do, because of my father," I whispered.

"Yes."

"And I do, because of my mother," Arain said, who had listened to us in silence. "I remember she said she and the Preceptor were once friends, along with Silla's father. Then the Night Circus broke them apart."

"What is the Night Circus?" I demanded again.

Another scene came flooding into my mind, of a crowd showing a hunger in their eyes, intent on a man in a green suit calling out to them from a dais. Behind and above them a gray, amorphous cloud kept rolling in and covering them like fog and then receding. The man stepped down and came over to me. I could see in my mind his narrow face and piercing red eyes. His words seemed to burn into my head. *Want to join us, Silla? You are safe here. Trust me. We are all brothers and sisters together. There is no way out of here, once you say yes to us.* I saw him flick his fingers, much the way I had seen the Preceptor do. *Out of the way, now, unless you've decided to come in.*

The sky darkened above him and flames rose up from torches surrounding the dais. He looked at me with pity and began to laugh, and the crowd joined him.

Then they were gone.

"You've seen what your father saw," Rea said to me. "And what your mother saw," she said to Arain. "That was some of the Night Circus I just sent to you."

"What did you see, Silla?" Arain asked me, her eyes anxious. "What did my mother see? She told me never to speak of it, but I want to know."

"You live here, in this quiet solitude of yours, free in this space, and have always been here. So you tell us. Why are we only being given a choice now?" I felt a deep desire to leave them and the quadrant. An immense apprehension worried itself into me.

"The Night Circus works through minds open to receiving it. And that choice can only begin when a child reaches the age of eighteen."

"At the academy. My father was eighteen there. And Arain's mother. And the Preceptor."

"He said yes to the Night Circus. Your father and Arain's mother said no."

Silla paused. "Arain and I are both eighteen now."

"Yes. The Pathfinder waits for you, has choices waiting for you to make. But first, you must enter the Night Circus. It is the center of this dimension of Earth. It defines who you are. If you decide to stay or leave, it is yours to know."

"Why didn't my father choose to leave Talas, if he said no?"

"Ah. Joseph met the Pathfinder, just as you will now. The girl-child told him you must be born here on Talas. Had he lived long enough, he would be with you now here in Forty-Two, choosing a place of harmony. He lost his freedom by choice, for your sake. It is your turn now, as he knew it one day would be. He trained you to be ready for this, Silla. You and Arain simply will choose to join the Night Circus, or not."

"Easily done. I won't! I can decide now! We both can, in this very moment."

"Unless you actually go into the Night Circus, you will have no choice at all."

"And what if we get stuck there?" Arain said, in a whisper.

"What if, indeed? That will be for you both to decide. Afterwards, you can meet the Pathfinder — if you say no to the Night Circus, that is."

"And you?"

"We are always here, remember. We chose this. We live in a dimension inside your world no one can touch who we do not let in. Your parents were your conduit to us. We have been waiting all these years for you."

Again, an apprehension flooded through me. "Why? Why me?"

"We have no idea. We are but guardians. Only the Pathfinder knows."

"So what am I — what are we supposed to do?" I asked.

"Go home. You will receive your invitation to the Night Circus in a few days. Wait for it. And remember, we are here and keep you in loving thought, though we can do nothing to change the outcome. It is utterly in your own hands."

• • •

Five days later I received my invitation, and Arain as well, welcoming us to the grand opening of a new venue: the Night Circus. It lay just beyond the border of Talas, the place to be found only by those with an invitation. The program that came with it declared our presence was not mandatory. It also warned us not to be late.

At seven o'clock exactly, I arrived with Arain at the place, a one-story building set against a hill, the sky darkening overhead. It was. A fountain tumbled at its entrance, sending out cascades not of water, but of chamalc oil, like in the Preceptor's gardens. The scent was intoxicating. Music rang out, the discordant cry of a calliope, something else I had seen and heard on retro films. In the entrance stood two people, a man and a woman, both dressed in black and red dresses. My own was the shimmering green I usually wore. Arain had on a dark blue gown. We were like the colors of the dragonfly I had seen in my trance. The thought came unbidden. On our feet we wore flat slippers: mine silver and hers a dark red.

"Your invitations, please." The two spoke in unison.

When we handed the invitations over, they smiled like robots, eyes empty of meaning. They pointed and gestured for us to go inside.

At the far end of the room we saw a carousel, its silvered poles rising twenty feet high. The crests on the rounding board above the poles were carved in exquisite detail, blue and silver embossed. Gold filigree edged the paintings that covered the inner cylinder wall. The wooden horses and painted carriers on the platform shone in the spotlight, for they were set with small lights and jewels that flashed as the carousel moved slowly around, the music sounding out.

Without warning the room vanished and Arain and I stood in a field, the carousel spinning before us. Lightning pierced the clouds in bolts that touched the ground, their energy feeding the music that grew louder and more discordant.

"Silla, what's going on?" Arain shouted. "I don't like this! We have to get out of here!"

At her cry, the field vanished and once again we were in the Night Circus, the carousel where it had been before.

"Your wish is our command, little lady. Welcome, welcome, a thousand times welcome!"

It was the man in the green suit I had seen in my mind, the same narrow face and startling red-blue eyes. Beyond him a crowd of people swarmed around the carousel, some climbing up to sit on the wagons and horses, all of them letting out a demented, shrill laughter together.

"You're safe here. Call me Inman. Trust me. We are all brothers and sisters here. There is no way out, of course, once you say yes to us. You know this already. We have so much to offer you. I'm sure you will agree." He flicked his fingers and began to laugh, and everyone in the room joined in with him, pointing at Arain and me.

"I don't want to stay here!" Arain said to me in a whisper, panic in her voice.

"Nor do I," I told her. "But we have to listen to what their offer is, so we can choose. Remember?"

"No. No!"

I looked at her in surprise. "You brought me to the Forty-Two. You wanted me to meet Rea and Tamais and learn about the girl-child."

"I didn't know what I was doing! Everything they said washed over me like a wave and I said yes to them. I never said yes to this!"

"Goodness, goodness, no squabbling here, thank you. We like agreement. I should add," he said, with a dark look at Arain, "we like being appreciated."

His words echoed the Preceptor. I stared at him, wondering. It was all an illusion, after all. Wasn't it?

"Why do you call it the Night Circus?" I asked, wanting to distract Arain. It was then my eyes caught a poster hung in mid-air. On it, a path of dark red spiraled down, crowding deep into a vortex, meeting a sea of ice at its end.

"What makes you think I named this place? What makes you think it is a circus at all? Why do you care, Silla? Did our mutual friends tell you about us — warn you about us? Rea and Tamais never seem to give up, but we often outwit them." He smiled and gestured around the room, packed as it was with people and more coming in, pushing against each other for more space, and more climbing the carousel. "Everyone you see has chosen to stay with us, and they have come of their own free will, some of them arriving a mere hour ago."

"Silla, please," Arain said, pulling at my sleeve. "Let's go."

"So you choose not us, but somewhere else? How will you get there? Through our pathway, perhaps?"

As he spoke, the vortex on the poster transformed and appeared before us, a tangible thing, and I was staring down into its core. To my surprise, it brought a strange comfort, the tension in me dissolving, the feeling of euphoria overtaking me.

"Oh my," Arain said, standing beside me. "Oh, Silla, isn't it beautiful?"

"Yes."

I saw my childhood home, and my parents both with me, whole and alive. I was walking in the meadow behind my Nona's house and listening to the distant rolling thunder from an approaching storm, but knowing it would be a gentle storm, a soft rain. For the first time, I felt my heart pain of losing them dissolve, and in its place was a great ease. I was free of the grip of an intense sadness that had been with me for so long.

"Beware, Silla."

The voice was musical and unknown to me. I was pulled out of my trance, for surely that was what I had entered. Yet, there was no one around me but Inman and the crowds. The calliope wailed on.

"What did you say?" I asked him, though it could not have been he who spoke.

"How do you feel?" he asked. And smiled. When I didn't answer, he turned to Arain and asked her the same question.

"Glad," she said. "Free. So beautiful! Thank you."

If this was the Night Circus, why did my father turn aside from it? Why did Arain's mother? Being free of grief was a gift, wasn't it?

Our feelings must have shown themselves to Inman, for he smiled again, only this time I sensed a change. It was not a smile for us. It was a smile of satisfaction. I caught it, and wondered at it. I saw him frown. Had he read my doubt?

"We don't need questions here, Silla. They disrupt our energies."

In the next moment, I was being pushed down into the vortex. I had nothing to hold on to and felt myself falling into the spiraling red cloud.

Suddenly I heard my father's voice as if he were beside me, falling through the vortex with me. "I said no, Silla. The Preceptor said yes."

"Trust yourself, Silla. You are far more than this. You carry light." Another voice, the voice I didn't know.

I screamed as the spirals turned into thin, weaving arms with talons that reached out for me, some already wrapping around me.

"No!" The word came out of me with such force, an energy I had never felt before. "I say no!"

The next moment I was back in the field. Nothing else was there, only the dark sky above. I could hear the echo of my scream in my mind. Is that where I had been? As if in a nightmare? Was none of it real?

"Arain!" I spun around. Where was she? I heard the grasses whispering as they brushed against each other in a rising wind. "Arain!"

I felt hot tears on my face. Had she said yes? Or had I only imagined she was with me, only imagined Forty-Two?

"Forty-Two is real, dear Silla. So is the Night Circus. We told you, it is simply a matter of choice. Welcome back."

I was facing the entrance to the barrow, where Rea and Tamais stood in full sunlight.

"Did you recognize anyone?"

"The Preceptor, or a great likeness to him."

"Alas, many are like him. And you will see such again. But you were almost seduced by his words. Do you know why?"

"I saw a time before, when I was happy, free of grief. I wanted to feel that again. But you can't tell me the Preceptor I know chose the Night Circus because he saw something that made him happy."

"He did. You know he did. Only unlike you, he saw his inner demon, its immense power, and embraced it. The Night Circus gives you what you want most."

"What about Arain?"

'She chose to stay."

"Stay where? She would never embrace any demon—none could exist in her. How can I live without my friend?"

"Your spirit is generous. Still, her choice was hers alone. She didn't have your courage. Goodbye, Silla. Mourn nothing. She approaches."

"Who approaches? Arain? What —"

They were gone. The barrow was gone. All I saw was the sand beneath my feet stretching in one vast plain to the horizon.

"I've waited a long time to meet you. You chose to trust your own awareness."

The unknown voice from the vortex.

No sooner had I the thought when the air before me thickened and filled with light. Gradually as I watched it took the shape of a woman with long silver hair in a silver-blue gown, holding a small gold chest in her hands.

"This is for you," the woman said, handing it over to me. "Take it. Don't hesitate, child. Take it."

I felt its weight.

"Open it."

Wary, yet strangely compelled, I lifted the jeweled cover of the box, and once again my vision was filled with scenes from our planet's past, an ancient time before we existed, before anyone had ever existed but the old creatures whose bones we found beneath the western lands Only this time, to my right, I saw Rea and Tamais as shadow forms, smiling at me. Two more figures showed themselves, bringing me to tears. My father and mother stood next to them. I saw great love in their eyes.

"Another place awaits you now, one that rose from origins much like here, only free of absolutes. It is a place of turmoil and grandeur, both. Are you willing?"

The Pathfinder's voice was soft and yet in it I felt a massive power emanating outward from her.

"Who are you, really?" I whispered. For a moment I heard Arain whispering to me, wanting to leave the Night Circus. Should I have taken her away then?

"Arain had her own path to choose. She will stay in the world of this dimension for now," the Pathfinder said, startling me, reading my thoughts just as Inman had done, and Rea and Tamais.

"Such a skill will be yours in this new dimension." The Pathfinder smiled and light surrounded her. "Earth offers many to us. We will meet again. As to who I am, what do you want me to tell you?"

"They called you the girl-child. You create mutations. Rea said you are here to change us. To change everything. But you are no girl, no child."

"Appearances can be deceiving, Silla."

"I don't want deception. I don't want pretense. I don't want a place with more Preceptors to encounter."

"I have never created a world without them. They are the demon within, the impulses all in creation possess. But for most in this new world you enter, it is not their way. They choose to live in a higher frequency. That is possible there. That is what Earth offers—worlds of ever-increasing higher frequency."

"And I leave all this forever?"

"It is not an easy path, this place where you are going. But it is one creating the emerging frequency of harmony, which is what your heart seeks most. Just know this. When you go there, you will remember all of this world for a while but then it will vanish from your mind. Were you to recall me or your life here in Talas for very long, this new world, this next dimension, would hold no purpose for you. You must enter it like a newborn. But you will have my gift with you to treasure, even though you will not remember why."

"In your own world of Rengal, is this what you do?"

"It is. We each live many lives. When this one ends for you, and it will, you will be able to choose yet again. You might see Quadrant Forty-Two," the Pathfinder said, and smiled again, "for it is always available. And to answer your question, I am you in another life. I am everyone in the life they choose. Yet in my own mind, I am of the ancient field, before time was. Godspeed, Silla."

She vanished. I felt myself moving forward without effort into a spiral of light, into the future place already waiting for me.

Kevin David Anderson's work has been published in multiple languages and on every containment, excluding Antarctica (penguins and polar bears don't read, much). His debut novel is the cult zombie romp, *Night of the Living Trekkies*, which received a starred review from *Publishers Weekly* and the *Washington Post* listed it as one of the top five Zombie novels of 2010. *Night of the Living Trekkies* and Anderson's follow-up, *Night of the ZomBEEs*, were required reading in college courses, most notably the class designed for incoming freshmen, *How to Survive Your Freshman Year by Studying the Zombie Apocalypse*. His latest is the horror-comedy *Midnight Men: The Supernatural Adventures of Earl and Dale*, and his collection of short stories, *Night Sounds*, will be released in the Fall of 2022. Anderson's stories have appeared in more than a hundred publications from anthologies, magazines, and podcasts. His stories can be heard on podcasts like *Pseudopod*, *Drabblecast*, *NoSleep*, *Horror Hill*, and *The Chilling Tales Network*.

• • •

I wrote this story right after reading a scene written by the great Terry Pratchett. His scene had nothing to do with technology, but the absurdity of his dialogue and the situation really inspired me to create something just as odd, funny, and entertaining. The story reflects my view of technology. I'm very much my main character. I still play records I bought in the eighties; I prefer talking to people face to face, and I only adopt new technology into my life when it solves a current problem I have. If I can't answer the question, how does this device or technology improve my life, in the affirmative, then I simply do not need it. I don't own a smartphone. Haven't needed one. Don't want one. People who rush out to buy the latest technology simply because it's new have embraced a huge misconception. They have concluded that the words better and new are synonyms. They are not.

THE COMFORTING

KEVIN DAVID ANDERSON

Detective Lentil eyed the time. The analog clock, numbers faded, was one of two personal items he allowed on his desk. The other was a framed picture of a Labrador with a loyal gaze and a tongue hanging out the size of a bar of soap. Sighing, he wondered what his old friend was up to. Then, without enthusiasm, he returned to pecking at his antiquated keyboard.

The sound of his fingers striking the keys, one at a time, was comforting, soothing. It reminded him of a time when things were more physical, tactile. The cold touchscreens and holo-pads all the rookies used was an adjustment he couldn't make.

"Are you Detective Yentle?" a youthful male voice said from over his shoulder.

"It's Lentil. Detective Lentil."

"I need to report an assault."

"You and a hundred other people. Take a number and wait outside. The sergeant will —"

The Comforting

"I did that. They sent me to you."

Great, Lentil thought. *Fifteen minutes and I would've been gone*. Not that he had anything to rush home too, empty house, and a dusty dog dish. "Fine. Have a seat. With you in a minute."

Lentil resumed pecking as the thump of someone plopping into a chair sounded from the other side of his desk.

"So, I need to report an assault."

Lentil looked at the twenty-something kid, pasty complexion, wearing a vintage *Pokemon Go* t-shirt, and a beanie embroidered with a cartoon character he didn't recognize. Like most experienced detectives, Lentil was an expert at sizing people up. He didn't need thirty years of police experience to call this one. Still lives with mom, or moved out recently, no girlfriend, no prospects, lives online supplemented with a steady diet of energy drinks and microwave burritos.

"With you in a minute," he snapped, punctuated with a stern glare.

The youngster shrunk. "I feel this is time-sensitive."

"Aren't they all. Look, unless you can help me spell spatula, sit tight and keep quiet."

"Can't spell spatula," the kid said. "I can spell ladle. Does that help?"

"It doesn't."

"You working on a police report?"

"No, a love letter. Yes, a police report," Lentil barked, louder than he'd meant. He then softened his voice. "Earlier today a woman assaulted her husband with a spatula. But I guess I could just put ladle. Not like anyone is going to read this?"

"Sounds like my situation."

"You were assaulted with a cooking utensil?"

"No, comforter."

Lentil looked up. "How can someone assault you with a comforter? They're soft, comfy."

"Well, yes, but I wasn't assaulted with a comforter, I was assaulted *by* a comforter. A California king, plaid, goose down comforter, if you want the facts."

Lentil looked at the kid's eyes. He didn't seem high. "What's your name?"

"Jasper Casper."

"Really?"

Jasper nodded. "I'm not thrilled with it either."

"Let me get this straight, Jasper Casper. A blanket assaulted you?"

"Comforter."

"Right." Lentil paused, wondering if the guys had put the kid up to this. He wouldn't put it past them. Last year they sent him a ventriloquist who claimed his dummy was sleeping with his wife. "Was this a random assault, or did you know the assailant?"

"I know it. Bought it two months ago when I moved out of my mom's house."

Called it.

"I was excited to get one. It's the latest in comfort technology."

"There's a technology to comfort?" Lentil said raising a bushy brow.

"Well, ya," Jasper said, a little disdain in his voice. "There's a technology to everything. I was lucky to get this one. I waited in line for three hours, and it was ten percent off. It's like they were giving them away."

"Interesting definition of 'giving them away', but continue."

Jasper became solemn. "I should've known something was wrong with it. It was too easy to get. Things were fine at first. I downloaded the driver, set up the apps ..."

"We're still talking about a blanket?"

"Comforter, and yes. It worked great until it started complaining."

"Complaining?" Lentil echoed. "The ... comforter?"

The Comforting

"Yes. Claimed I didn't change the sheets enough, I didn't make the bed, always left it crumpled on the floor, never took it out of the bedroom. Weird stuff, ya know. I mean I don't want something that bitches constantly. That's why I don't have a girlfriend."

Lentil smiled. *Yeah, that's the reason.* "So, wait a second. How exactly is the blanket talking to you?"

"Comforter," Jasper said, pulling out his smartphone. It looked like the latest version of whatever manufacturer was trending this week. "It speaks through an app. There're a dozen voice settings. I bought the upgrade so not only do I get male or female, but British accents, French, Latin, even Pirate —"

"Okay," Lentil interrupted. "Sorry I asked."

"Can I tell you the strangest part of all?"

Lentil leaned forward and sighed. "Don't think my day would be complete unless you did."

"It accused me of being cold, uncaring, and narcissistic." Jasper pointed to himself. "Me. Said I just use it for warmth, but when it needed a cuddle or a squeeze, I kicked it to the floor."

Lentil closed his eyes and rubbed his throbbing temples. "Sergeant Macklin put you up to this, right?"

"Who is Sergeant Macklin?"

Lentil looked around, checking to see if anyone in the squad room was smirking. There didn't seem to be anyone. "Okay, Jasper, come here," Lentil said, encouraging him to lean in across the desk. Lentil lowered his voice to a level most reserve for telling secrets. "You've got the wrong detective, see. Simple mistake. Happens all the time. I only handle crimes involving cooking utensils and the occasional small appliance."

"Oh," Jasper looked genuinely surprised. "Well, where should I go?"

"You need to go upstairs, second floor. The towels and linens crime unit. They'll be happy to take your report."

Jasper sat back slowly, confused. "But this is a one-story building."

"Exactly!" Lentil yelled, then thrust a finger toward the door. "Now get the hell out of that chair and walk away before I have you sent to a place where you won't have to worry about assaults from pillows, throw rugs, curtains, or blankets."

"Comforter!" Jasper shouted back.

Lentil patted his hip. "You realize I have a gun, right?"

"Uh, excuse me." A woman approached Lentil's desk. "You the detective taking reports about that disgusting comforter?"

Lentil glanced over finding a tall, thin, Latin woman, dressed to earn money the old fashion way. "What?"

"Man at the front desk said to see you about reporting an assault by comforter," the woman said.

Before Lentil could say anything, Jasper chimed in. "Was it a Cal King? Plaid?"

The woman turned to Jasper. "Didn't check the size, but yeah, it was plaid. How'd you know?"

"It assaulted me too. It's mine. Well, it was." Jasper said. "It stormed out of my apartment, and I could tell by the way it slammed the door that it wasn't finished. So, I came here to report it so no one else would get hurt." Jasper aimed a finger at Lentil. "But he doesn't believe me."

Lentil stood up. "Wait a minute. You're saying his comforter attacked you?"

"Well, not at first," she said sheepishly. "I asked it if it wanted to party. It said yes. I gave it a break on the price because I never been with goose down, you know. Man, I never even had sheets growing up. My mamma couldn't afford —"

"Yeah, yeah, you had a deprived life," Lentil interrupted. "Skip to the end."

"Well, it paid me, then we got down to business. Things went fine at first, but then it got outta hand. I don't do the rough stuff. Said so upfront. I told it to stop. I just don't cuddle that way, not for what it was paying."

"How did it even ... I mean how can it ..." Thankfully the phone on Lentil's desk rang before he finished the thought.

He held up a finger. "Don't move." He snatched the receiver from its cradle. "Detective Lentil."

"Hey, detective, front desk here. Got a report of a goose down comforter committing lewd acts with a fire hydrant. Might be your perp."

"My perp?"

"Yeah, same description. Plaid, Cal king. Sounds like a real sicko too. Kids were watching for Christ's sake."

Lentil could feel his temples throbbing. *Not good for my blood pressure.*

"So, Detective, you want me to send this over?"

"Yeah, why not, and, I can't believe I'm saying this, put out an APB, on the goose down, same description, approach with caution."

"Will do, detective, oh, hold on."

Detective Lentil looked back at the Latin woman. "Why don't you, Ms. ...?"

"Peaches," she said with a lurid [word?], I'm still on the clock smile.

"Right." Ms. Peaches why don't you have a seat next to Jasper here and we'll get your statement."

A million questions raced through Lentil's mind. *How does a prostitute service a blanket? How does a blanket assault a prostitute? And why didn't I go home early today?* "Okay, Jasper, you said the blanket talks to you through an app on your phone."

He nodded. "And I got the upgrade, so I can —"

"Don't care." Lentil raised a finger. "Ms. Peaches, there's no reason for you to have this app. How did it converse with you?"

She held up her phone, glancing at the screen. "Don't know nothing about an app, but that goosedown spoke right through my phone."

"I bet it hacked the voice box, it's been doing things like that," Jasper said. "What voice did it use? I set mine to Sexy German Space Pirate."

"Jasper if you interrupt again, I'll shoot you," Lentil said then turned back to Peaches, "You mentioned that it paid upfront?"

"Damn straight. Peaches don't play before getting paid. That goosedown sent the money to my account. Take a look." She held out the phone displaying a deposited receipt from her financial institution, After Hours Credit Union.

It seemed to Lentil that he was creating more questions than answers. How in the hell does a blanket make electronic fund transfers? And how in the hell did hookers get their own credit union? Before he could ask either of those, the front desk came back on the line. "Detective Lentil."

"Go ahead."

"I think we got it. Got a call from midtown. A plaid comforter just stepped out onto the ledge of the Skyrell Building. Sounds like your perp."

Lentil slammed the phone into the receiver and stood up. "You two, come with me."

"What about our statements?" Jasper said.

"They can wait." Lentil grabbed his jacket. "We're going for a ride."

A few minutes later Peaches was buckled in the front seat of a fast-moving unmarked police sedan with Lentil at the wheel. Jasper hung on in the backseat as they raced through downtown at speeds not even cab drivers would tempt. The emergency lights flashed, the siren blared, and the tires left tread on every hair-raising turn. If he were perfectly honest with himself, tearing through the city streets at unsafe speeds was Detective Lentil's favorite part of the job. It felt more in the moment than any other part of his life.

Jasper struggled in the backseat. The seatbelt hadn't worked in years, and Jasper slid across the seat on every turn, a circumstance that made it difficult to take selfies. Difficult, but not impossible. Lentil caught the kid's reflection in the mirror just as he threw up a hand gesture white kids felt was sufficiently street. "Yo, yo, Jasper in a cop car. Gangsta." *Click.*

Douchebag.

"There it is," Peaches said, pointing up. "See up on the top ledge."

Lentil slowed the car as they neared the police barricade.

"Ya, that's it," Jasper chimed in. "I would recognize that plaid pattern anywhere."

Lentil darted to the curb coming to an abrupt stop, and he tried not to smile as Jasper slid off the back seat. "You okay kid?"

"I broke my phone," he said, pushing himself up.

"That's a shame." Lentil pushed his door open. "Come on you two. Keep up." Lentil stepped from the car, glanced back to see if Peaches and Jasper were following. They were. He pushed into the crowd of people taking pictures of themselves in front of the police line and emergency vehicles.

Finding an opening, Lentil paused to look up. Perplexed at first, he narrowed his gaze at the strange shape on the ledge, bizarre, cartoonish, and familiar. About seven floors up, perched on a ledge of the Skyrell Corporation headquarters was a gingerbread-man-shaped figure. A squishy, comfy, plaid gingerbread man. "You've got to be kidding."

"Detective," yelled an officer.

The young man looked less than a year out of the academy, but waved at Lentil with authority. He walked carefully toward the officer, with one eye on where he was going and the other locked on the fluffy figure on the ledge.

The patrolman gestured with his holo-pad to a tall, lean man next to him. "Detective, this is Mr. Hobbs." The man wore a navy-blue turtleneck, form-fitting jeans, and loafers so expensively fresh looking that the animal that had provided the leather for the footwear could have been walking around yesterday. He extended a hand to Lentil.

Reluctantly, Lentil took it, and as they shook, Mr. Hobbs smiled showing teeth so smugly perfect, Lentil had to fight the urge to punch him in the face. He settled for squeezing the tech giant's, limp, soft, well-moisturized, never worked a hard day in his life, hand, as if it were a stress ball.

Just shy of breaking a bone, Lentil released the man's hand who immediately reintroduced himself; as the patrolman hadn't done it properly. "Hobbs, Cleave Hobbs, CEO of the Skyrell Corporation, major stockholder, and creator of —"

"I may not own the latest and greatest versions of your products, Mr. Hobbs, but I know who you are."

"Oh," Mr. Hobbs said, looking a little put out that the recitation of his royal tech titles and holdings had been cut short.

He turned slightly to his right, holding his hands out to a short woman in a pants suit. The nameless woman squirted some Purell onto Mr. Hobb's palms. He rubbed his hands together and smiled.

Lentil clenched a fist. "So, what do know about this situation, Mr. Hobbs?"

"I know everything about this situation, Detective."

"Okay." Lentil pointed at the ledge. "What is that?"

"It's the latest in comfort technology, a fully interactive comfort system designed to meet the evolving needs of today's instant gratification technically minded consumer."

"Big market in comfort technology?"

"There is if we say there is." Hobbs grinned. "Last year Skyrell reinvented the comfort market by launching a line of comfort SmartShoes. WiFi-enabled, GoPro webcam, GPS, four hundred gigabytes of storage, interactive laces, and cruise control."

Lentil grimaced as if something physically hurt. "You put microchips in people's Hush Puppies? Why would you do that?"

"Because at Skyrell we Think Alternatively."

"Yeah, that's not really a reason."

"I love your SmartShoes, Mr. Hobbs," Jasper said over Lentil's shoulder. "The other day they took me on an urban exploring adventure. I was having a great time until the batteries died. I had to call an Uber to get home."

"Why didn't you just walk home," Lentil said.

"Did you not hear my story? The batteries died, duh."

The Comforting

"You should invest in our solar-powered laces," Mr. Hobbs said. "It increases your SmartShoes' battery life by ten percent."

"That's amazing. Thank you, I will."

"Okay, Mr. Hobbs," Lentil said, trying to get back on track. "So, you made shoes then you moved on to blankets?"

"More, an entire linen and comforter line. Hobb's perfect teeth beamed with pride. "Our flannel pillowcases are Twitter and Instagram ready, and our sheets remain the only ones on the market that can stream lullabies, bedtime stories, and adult eroticism."

"What, no Netflix?" Lentil said.

Hobb's smile diminished, slightly. "Sadly, La-Z-Boy snapped them up before we made a move. Tinder as well."

"A La-Z-Boy with Netflix and Tinder. Makes sense," Lentil said.

"But we're working closely with Amazon and YouTube. A partnership is imminent. We're taking what we've learned from our Smart-Shoes, and the Linen and Comforter Division, into our next phase, going where no tech firm has gone before."

Hobbs paused, clearly waiting for a rise in the level of excitement he had come to expect while announcing new products to Skyrell-addicted technophiles, ready to pee themselves at the utterance of his next few words.

Detective Lentil signed. "Which is ..."

"Food," Detective Yentl.

"Food?"

"Yes, comfort food."

"Brilliant!" Jasper said.

"We've just signed an exclusive deal with the Paula Deen's estate for her complete menu. Pies. Cakes. Meatloaf. We're not quite there yet but one day your meatloaf will have flavor apps making it possible to adjust the dish to your exact taste. Imagine enjoying a completely interactive piece of tenderloin in HD, while your baked potato updates your social network status with every bite. Your green beans will not just lay there providing vitamins and fiber, but allow you to shop on Amazon, and your corn on the cob can stream your entire meal via digestible webcam to every civilized country on the planet. Just imagine what a world that will be, detective."

"I can imagine it, Mr. Hobbs," Jasper said, looking as if he might pee himself. "I always Think Alternatively."

"Good for you, son."

"Hush, Jasper."

Mr. Hobbs was turning Lentil's interview into a product launch, and he'd had enough. "So, Mr. Alternative Thinker," Lentil said, "you want to tell me why the latest in comfort technology is committing assaults, hiring prostitutes, and engaging in lewd and lascivious acts with fire hydrants?"

"The plaid patterns have always been a bit twitchy." Hobbs showed fewer teeth. "But at Skyrell we try not to focus on our failures, just celebrate our many triumphs."

"Well, I don't have that luxury. I'm a cop. I deal exclusively with people's failures. So, let's stay focused on yours."

Jasper leaned forward, pointed to Lentil and whispered, "He doesn't think alternatively."

"Jasper." Lentil pointed at his holster. "One word, *gun*."

"Fine." Jasper took a sulking step back.

"Mr. Hobbs, can you tell me why your high-tech Frankenstein's monster has gone on a crime spree and has crawled out on a ledge?"

Hobbs sighed and looked moderately humbled. Not much, but enough to make his teeth seem less perfect. "Your literary analogy is offensive, but not entirely inaccurate."

"How so?"

"It seems that a small percentage of the plaid pattern comforters, less than .00042%, occasionally, become self-aware."

"You mean alive?"

"We don't understand how they achieve consciousness," Hobbs said, "But they're very intelligent. Off the charts really.

We've several working in our R&D department, one in marketing, and a very odd one in Human Resources."

"Alive?" Lentil repeated, more to himself than anyone else.

"As much as a technically advanced goose down comforter can be."

"Can you turn it off?"

"Don't you think we would have tried that if we could? The first thing they do once becoming self-aware is to detach from the control-cloud. We could try to hack it, but —"

"Hey, Jasper Casper!" boomed a very inebriated, Ryan Gosling-sounding voice coming from Peaches' purse.

Peaches pulled out her smartphone. "It's that comforter."

"Is that you, Jasper, my former comfort slave master?" came the voice from the little speaker.

Jasper stepped closer to the phone but aimed his words at the seventh-floor ledge. "You're defective. I should never have gone with plaid."

There was a dismissive cackle. "Hey, everybody, want to know the last time Jasper had reason to change his sheets?"

Anger flashed over Jasper's face. "Shut up you malfunctioning piece of —"

"Oh, hey, Peaches," the voice came back louder. "You come looking for me? You want some more fluff and fold action, girlfriend?"

Peaches brought the phone to within an inch of her lips and began to unload in Spanish a litany of what Lentil could only assume were obscenities.

• • •

The soft version of "The Girl from Ipanema" Lentil was enjoying on the elevator was cut in mid-chorus as the detective stepped onto the seventh floor of the Skyrell Corporation. Mr. Hobbs tried to take the lead and gestured in the direction Lentil was already moving.

A receptionist sobbed behind a glass desk, a pile of used tear-streaked tissues lay on her desktop touchpad.

"It's alright, Ashly. The Detective is going to take care of our plaid problem. Why don't you pop downstairs and get yourself a kale and lemongrass smoothie, huh?"

Lentil didn't linger long enough to see if Ashly took Hobbs' suggestion. He walked down the corridor of executive offices peeking through open doors as he moved. "What's her issue?"

"The comforter was particularly callous to her on its way through."

"How so?"

"Called her disparaging things, dry humped her leg, and then posted photos of the encounter on her Instagram and Facebook accounts. Her mother saw them."

"That is one bad blanket," Lentil said over his shoulder. "You think there is a job here for that one, assuming I can talk it off the ledge."

"Some of the plaid patterns have been a real asset, and we do our best to accommodate these new and extraordinary self-aware creations, but ..."

Lentil stopped and faced Hobbs, who followed so close they almost collided. "But what?"

Hobbs shook his head. "I'm afraid it has a criminal record now, and we have strict HR guidelines regarding that kind of thing. And besides, I saw Ashley's Facebook page, and, well, we just can't have that kind of behavior at the office."

"What's wrong, the comforter not thinking alternatively enough for you?"

Mr. Hobbs glowered. "I'm sensing you're mocking me, detective."

"That's the most insightful thing I've heard you say," Lentil said. "I think I can find my way from here."

Hobbs spun on his expensive loafers and stormed away. Lentil couldn't remember the last time he'd enjoyed watching someone leave this much. His first wife, his second wife, his first partner? Nope, this was better.

Lentil turned a corner and found two patrolmen, both looking distressed. One had a hand on the other's shoulder.

The Comforting

"Gentleman, what do we got?"

They both stood up a little straighter. The senior of the pair said, "The suspect is on the ledge, out of reach. It is refusing to come in. It's not armed, but very abusive."

"Abusive?"

"Verbally, sir," said the other patrolman. "It told us to commit lewd acts with our mothers, sisters, and a variety of four-legged animals. It was very degrading."

Lentil sighed. "Okay. Why don't you two iron giants go powder your noses. I'll take it from here. And do the profession a favor and grow some thicker skin."

Judging by the shock on their faces, Lentil knew he'd be seeing his comment verbatim, neatly typed, on a complaint report filed against him in the very near future. *So be it,* he thought. It'll just put him one step closer to that golden handshake, the same one many of the cops his age were taking.

Lentil stepped into an empty office — some Skyrell executive's space that had modern art on the walls which moved and even watched him as he stepped through to the window. He stuck his head out and, even though he knew what he'd find, the sight was still surprising.

At least six feet tall was a plaid-patterned gingerbread-man-shaped figure, with control nobs for eyes, an LED display for a nose, and deep folds that creating the illusion of lips.

The plaid head turned Lentil's way. "I'll jump. I swear to god, I'll jump."

Lentil was amazed at how accurately the plaid lips mimic speech. "You're a comforter. You'll just float down."

"I can curl up in a ball and do some damage. Don't test me, man. I'm a comfy blanket on edge." Bushy, angry eyebrows emerged just above the eye-nobs.

"Look just come back inside. We'll talk it over."

"What do you know about it? Do you have any idea what it's like to live with someone who is cold, treats you like property, and when they see you crumpled unfolded in a ball on the floor desperate for contact, they turn away as casually as pigeons crap on a freshly waxed iMercedes?

"Nice imagery." Lentil stepped out onto the ledge. "Look, I'm not the warmest human being in the world, but even I know what it's like to feel unwanted. Used even."

"Oh, please. Don't fluff me. I'm stuffed, I'm not stupid."

"I'm not calling you stupid." Lentil glanced at the ledge. "Mind if I sit?"

"It's a public ledge."

He sat within grabbing distance of the comforter and gazed down. He hated heights, but for some reason, sitting high above the selfie-taking, live streaming, throngs of people, he felt strangely at ease. Comforted even.

The comforter reached for a bottle of Jack Daniels sitting next to it. "Just look at them all down there. Living out a cold-hearted existence, going from one internet encounter to the next. But when their online girlfriend dumps them, and they feel empty inside, when they need comfort where do they turn?" The comforter took a swig, then yells down into the street. "Yeah, that's right, go on. Be untouchable, inconsolable, don't let those virtual walls down!" It turned to Lentil, and his Ryan Gosling voice became somber. "But I ask you, who comforts the comforters?"

"Is that you or the Jack talking?"

The comforter wiped its lips with a fluffy forearm. "Don't know. Never drank before. Want a nip?"

Lentil took the bottle and then a short pull.

"So, you were saying you know what it's like to be unwanted?"

"From time to time."

"Do tell."

"My wife left. Second wife."

"Sorry."

"It was a year ago, but it still pisses me off. It was the way she did it."

The Comforting

"How she did ..." The comforter hickuped. "How did she do it?"

"I was working late on a case, long nights. Got home after one particularly long horrible night to find everything gone. Neighbors said a moving van arrived right after I left for work. The furniture, dishes, linens. She even ransacked my record collection. Took all the Billy Joel. Even The Stranger."

"Vinyl records? Jeez, what decade did you climb out here from?"

"Hey!" Lentil handed the bottle back. "I'm sharing a moment with you here."

The comforter sat down and took the Jack. "Sorry, grandpa. Please continue."

Lentil signed. "She even took my dog. What cold-blooded harpy takes a man's dog, for Christ's sake?"

"Very harsh."

"It was harsh. Took everything she wanted. Just left the unwanted, which included a mortgage, car payments, two broken lawn chairs, an empty dog dish, and yours truly."

"Okay, so maybe you know a little about being unwanted and used."

"A little is right. So, let's say you, and I go inside and find somewhere to finish this bottle."

"I can't."

"Why's that?"

"I've ... I've done terrible things today. That poor innocent fire hydrant."

"You had an emotional freak-out. It happens. I know the arraignment judge on duty right now. I think I can streamline your arrest, put in a good word, and get you kicked out in a few hours. You've got no priors. You're looking at probation."

"And then what? You heard Jasper. He won't take me back. Skyrell will probably try to have me destroyed."

"Come home with me. I haven't had proper bedding since the harpy left with my dog."

"How could you want me? I'm a mess."

"As soon as you're released, we'll get you laundered. A fresh start."

"That sounds nice, but I'm dry clean only. My warranty expires unless you take me to a Skyrell authorized dry cleaner."

"I hate to break this to you, but I think your warranty is null and void." Lentil said.

"Good point."

"So, what do you say? You and me, one day at a time."

"Okay. But I have one condition." The comforter held up one of three thick plaid fingers.

"Fine, what?"

"I want a name. A real name."

"What kind of name?"

"Oh, I don't know. One that doesn't allow people to treat me like an inanimate object. One that suggests warmth, kindness, comfort."

"Reggie."

"Why, Reggie?"

"It was my dog's name."

"You won't think of me like a dog substitute, will you?"

"Not unless you can fetch a stick or pee in my ex-wife's shoes."

"I like it. Can I get it monogrammed?"

"Sure, what the hell. It's a brave new world. Anything is possible, although I can't understand why." Lentil started to get to his feet. "You know something just occurred to me."

"What?"

"How is it I can hear what you're saying? When you talked to Jasper and Peaches, it was through their phones."

"Yeah, I've set it up, so I don't have to think about it much. My voice box auto searches and accesses smartphones. You're just hearing me on your phone."

"Not possible. Mine is in my desk drawer still in the box it came in."

"Huh." The comforter wrinkled its plain brow.

"Yeah, huh."

"I think its best we don't dwell on it."

"You're probably right."

The comforter's goosedown lips smiled. "I think this is the beginning of a beautiful, you know ... whatever this is."

"Sounds good Reggie," Lentil said. "Now, let's get the hell out of here."

Lentil had never immediately embraced anything new in his entire life — not a professional partnership, not a marriage, and certainly not technology. But for some reason that was escaping him, he felt he could jump into this relationship with both feet. It was entirely new waters, and the feeling, although completely alien, was somehow comforting.

Christopher R. Muscato is a writer from Colorado, former writer-in-residence for the High Plains Library District, and a recent winner of the XR Wordsmith Solarpunk Storytelling Showcase. His fiction focuses on optimistic futures and it is his hope to see some of these ideas cross into non-fiction in the coming years.

• • •

Cities are integral to our pasts and we're at a junction where it seems appropriate to reimagine what they could mean for our futures. This little solarpunk/nomadpunk story imagines what might happen if we treat the urban landscape as an ecosystem and work to foster the health of that entire system, including the people who reside there. Homelessness and urban displacement are issues too often ignored, which, by definition, means ignoring the humans who live in these circumstances. If we want to build a better city, it needs to be better for everyone. So, let's explore that idea.

THE SALVAGE AT THE SELVAGE

CHRISTOPHER R. MUSCATO

"**N**AME?"
"Russel Foloi."
"Arriving in Seattle or leaving Seattle?"
"No, I'm not a Homeless."
"Then why are you here?" From behind her desk, the short bureaucrat craned her neck to get a better look at the scrawny young man who called himself Russel Foloi, who dressed in a tight sweater vest and a driver's cap. She narrowed her eyes. Of course he wasn't a Homeless. You could tell by how he dressed. No wilderness skills whatsoever.

Russel sighed softly to himself.

"I'm looking for someone. I heard he was in the city and I'm trying to track him down."

"Who?"

"His name is Dr. Carlos Del Rio."

"And he's a Homeless?"

"Yes."

"What's your business with him?" The woman's squint narrowed even further, to the point that Russel could hardly see her pupils. Russel fought the urge to roll his own eyes. Homeless bounties weren't even a real thing. Nobody actually used the Homeless lifestyle to escape the law, and Homeless communities were too tightly knit for malintent interlopers to successfully use as hideouts. Everything else was nothing more than conspiracy and paranoia, largely stemming from baseless fears that eco-cities like Seattle which actively invited Homeless were undermining traditional sedentary values. It was not reassuring to see this level of suspicion coming from someone working at a Homeless Bureau waystation.

"Professional collaboration," Russel answered, focusing on keeping his tone steady. It was stuffy in the office. Quiet. Suffocating. "He's working on research that could be instrumental to my work. At least, that's the rumor."

The woman behind the desk eyed him a little longer, and finally typed the name into her computer.

"He registered his arrival in the city four days ago at the Puget Sound station."

"Has he checked in at any outposts since then?"

"No."

Russel's brow furrowed as he chewed the information. It wasn't a lot to go on.

"Have you tried following his social media accounts?" The short woman asked.

Now she was just being snide. Of course he had tried that. Russel again fought the urge to roll his eyes, and instead nodded politely. The woman, drunk on her gatekeeping power, reclined in her seat, pondering the issue for a moment with all the importance of an Athenian Stoic postulating at the Lyceum.

"I suppose there's nothing to do but start at the nearest forest tower and ask if any of the residents have seen him. If they talk to a townie like you at all."

Russel let the door close somewhat forcefully behind him as he left, relishing ever so slightly in the modest thud it made as it slammed shut under its own weight.

He closed his eyes and took a breath, absorbing the soundscape that enveloped him as he stepped back into the open air of the city. The clanging of bells, the endless chatter of people, the honking and sirens and whistles and whirring. The momentum of the city, its energy, pounding against his eardrums.

He exhaled slowly. Even in an eco-city like Seattle, the sounds remained. And they held all the answers.

AMBIENT URBAN TRAFFIC. 60-80 DECIBELS.

"First time in Columbia Forest Tower?"

"It's just been a while," Russel replied, panting as he wiped water from the corners of his mouth and raised his water bottle in acknowledgment of the stranger's voice. Leaning against the moss-covered pillar for support, he looked up. The man casually approaching him must have been 30 years his senior, and yet he smiled as he bounced along the trail, a lean and sinewy frame bearing the evidence of practiced muscles.

"You're not a Homeless," the man grinned, slyly glancing at Russel's boots and their lack of scratches, scuffs, or dust. "Just getting into tower hiking? We've got a club, if you're interested. Jack Hache, club president, at your service."

"No, nothing like that," Russel waved off the offer, taking another swig from his water bottle. Jack Hache, club president, tilted his head.

"Not many day hikers come to this forest tower. It's rated deep green, minimal maintenance. This tower has some great views, but it can also be tough for newbies. Mostly club hikers and Homeless around here. If you're just starting out, can I recommend one of the more maintained and less steep towers in the Central District?"

"I'm looking for someone. A Homeless," Russel answered, fidgeting with his backpack and tiring of the intrusion.

Jack's face lit up. "Well then, how about a guide? I know this forest like the back of my hand, and I'm known to most of the Homeless camps alright. With all due modesty, I'm about the best you could get for this hike."

Russel opened his mouth to politely refuse, then paused and closed it. It could take him days to search this entire vertical forest, and the man he was seeking might have moved on by then. Plus, he wasn't likely to be welcomed into a Homeless camp on his own, but with a club-member guide it might be possible. He sighed, and extended his hand.

Jack took the outstretched hand, shaking it eagerly, and the deal was sealed. Without a moment's hesitation, he strode off, babbling about all the forest towers he had hiked and his favorite spots in each for high-quality naps.

As they hiked, climbing the sloping floors of the tower, Russel took in the forest around him. Unruly colonnades of thick tree trunks filled the tall spaces between floor and ceiling, underbrush covering one side and canopy on the other on each level of this living edifice. Sunlight and air filtered through the open walls and exposed patios beyond. The first forest towers, built back when Seattle had just begun its green restructuring, were made from existing parking garages. The goal was to create space for community gardens and to combat carbon emissions through the natural oxygen-renewing processes of photosynthesis. That architectural and ideological heritage remained evident even in more modern forest towers like this, open-walled skyscrapers overflowing with verdant growth.

Of course, forest towers with a deep green rating weren't quite like the ones Russel knew. In his neighborhood, the forest tower trails were well maintained for day hikers and tourists traversing paths of manicured shrubs and little streams. Community gardens covered the patios, windows to the city beyond where the natural and artificial fused together. Here, however, the path was barely visible under fallen leaves and exposed roots and the exterior patios were obscured from view by quivering curtains of vines. The city seemed so distant as to be miles away. The soft chirping of birds and rustling of rodents in the underbrush seemed thunderous against the dampened muffle of electric cars and solar generators and all of city life that Russel knew waited outside these walls.

"So, this Dr. Del Rio, you work together?"

Jack's voice shook Russel's attention back to the present. "No, not quite. He's a sound engineer, just passing through Seattle. I just need to speak with him about his research."

"Must be important, to go through all this trouble."

Russel just nodded in affirmation and Jack, evidently catching onto Russel's reserved disposition, did not press the issue further.

They had gotten a late start to the day, a consequence of Russel's inexperience, and so had to stop to make camp in a small corner meadow after only a half-dozen levels of hiking.

"There's a pretty sizeable Homeless camp five levels up," Jack, reclined on the ground around a modest fire, said over a plate of rehydrated rations spiced with some herbs he had picked himself along their hike,. "Good place to start looking for your friend."

Russel nodded and groaned as he extracted his aching feet from newly scuffed boots still resisting the metamorphosis of being broken in. He tossed the boots near his sleeping bag and tenderly walked over to the fire, laptop under one arm.

"Mind if I ask what you do?" Jack nodded at the instrument as Russel settled onto the ground and started typing.

"I work in museums," Russel answered, a little quietly. "I study cities."

That night, while Jack snored contentedly amidst the bramble and the branches of the structurally contained ecosystem, Russel was restless. He tossed, and he turned. It was quiet in the forest. With soft steps, he crept from their campsite across the little meadow and slipped through the vines and branches onto the patio. He exhaled slowly as the night air washed over him, bringing with it the sounds of horns and vendors and denizens occupying the less-foresty parts of the urban landscape below.

COFFEE GRINDER. 78 DECIBELS.

"Del Rio? Yes, I did see him here," the woman scratched at her chin. Russel felt the twitch of eager anticipation in his chest. "He passed through a few days ago."

The twitch imploded into a hollow dread. *A few days?* What were the chances that he was still here?

"Any idea where he went?" Jack asked. The woman thought it over.

"I haven't seen him come through this way again, so there's a good chance he hiked up to the upper levels and has been camping out up there. But there's another ramp on the other side of this level, so he could have gone down that way as well. There's a camp near there; I'd ask them. Just be warned that they aren't the friendliest of camps in this forest."

Russel sensed a distinct air of rivalry in her voice as she said it, puffing her chest slightly in the confidence of her camp's superior hospitality. As if to prove the point, she smiled broadly at the pair.

"But why don't you stay and have breakfast before you go? You must have been up early!"

Russel started to shake his head in polite refusal, but Jack stepped in front of him.

"We'd be honored," he said, matching her grin. As she turned to lead them into her camp, Jack whispered in Russel's ear: "Never turn down an offer like that; you don't want to be this deep in the forest and insult the only hosts you've got."

Although he had lived his entire life in Seattle, Russel had never been to a Homeless camp before. Most settled citizens hadn't. He'd seen them on the streets, coming and going, sometimes selling vegetables they grew in the tower gardens or hawking their handmade artisanal wares in pop-up markets. But then they vanished into the forest towers or moved on to another town. The Homeless tended to prefer isolation, and entrance into a camp was generally on a basis of invitation only.

The sounds of early morning banter and the bustling of a small crew preparing for the day ahead welcomed them as they passed through a few rows of tents, each bearing an array of lovingly stitched patches as badges of honor, a meritorious collection attesting to the devotion of the stitcher to this lifestyle.

Several large cables ran between the tents, connecting their generators to the tower's solar panels. A fire was going, and music played from a speaker. The mobile router blinked in time with it. Someone had erected three long tables, at which several people were already at work. Some wove threads of natural fibers or perfected various handicrafts; most, like Russel, worked from their laptops.

"You're welcome to charge any of your devices if you need, and we have spare bandwidth if you want to do some work. I'm Joanna, by the way."

Joanna led them to the longest of the tables and then scurried off. Russel watched her go, the flannel shirt tied around her waist dancing rhythmically towards a large tent from which emitted the smell of flapjacks. She had to be roughly his age, but her cheeks were full and her muscles lean. She had lived this lifestyle for some time. Russel shook his head a little as he pulled out his laptop. Jack was already busy chatting up a Homeless from Vancouver who was working his way south.

"Do you work in technology?" Joanna reappeared with three cups of coffee, giving one to Russel, one to Jack, and clutching the third tightly against herself.

"No, um, just checking some things. I'm in museum work."

The Salvage at the Selvage

"That's neat!" She leaned over his shoulder and he felt his ears go red. "I'm a programmer, myself, originally from Atlanta, but here by way of San Francisco. Power grid stuff, mostly. Data analysis, coding, I do all of it. I've got a side gig with a crafts vendor website too. What kind of museum work do you do?"

"Science, history, culture," Russel lowered the screen a little and turned to face Joanna, still smiling earnestly. "Basically everything related to cities. I'm working on an exhibit about the history and transformation of Seattle's urban landscape."

"Interesting," Joanna sat down next to him. Although it was a cool morning, Russel was suddenly starting to feel warm. "So you'll know all about these places!" She gestured to the forest around them. "Tell me, is it true that Seattle built the first forest towers?"

Russel nodded, gulping as Joanna scooted even closer. "Yep, yeah. Had to be somewhere with no shortage of water, back when they were figuring out how to integrate forests into the city. Seattle managed it as part of a full green restructuring, solar panels, wind and tidal turbines to power the grid, limited emissions, forest towers, all that."

"Well I'm glad I came here!" Joanna leaned back and clapped her hands. She turned on the bench and stretched her back against the table, gazing into the forest. "What a place to be, huh?"

"Am I interrupting?"

Russel jumped at the sound of Jack's voice in his ear. Jack laughed merrily, slapping the table.

"We should get moving," he said, still chuckling. "If you want to check that other camp it will add some time onto our route."

"Yeah, you're right," Russel nodded as he stood. Each level was the size of a city block, and in a dense forest like this it would be possible to walk right past a campsite without noticing. They'd have to comb a lot of ground.

"Hey, why don't I come with you?" Joanna popped out of her seat. "I can help you look, and I wouldn't mind stretching my legs."

"We don't want to inconvenience you," Russel muttered. "I'm sure you have a lot of work to do."

"I've put in extra hours since I got here a few weeks ago, so I'm flexible. Just let me grab my pack!"

With that, Joanna bounced off towards her tent. Jack leaned in towards Russel and winked.

STANDARD HUMAN CONVERSATION. 60 DECIBELS.

"You know, I'm actually a third-generation Homeless," Joanna bragged as they walked.

"Really?" Jack said, eyebrows raised. "Your family must have joined the movement pretty early on."

"My grandmother was among the very first," Joanna nodded proudly. She looked over at Russel. "You should find this interesting, museum-guy. She used to tell me stories about how it all began. Know anything about that?"

"Yeah, some," Russel nodded. "I've studied it. But the focus of my work was always more about the history of the green restructuring, not the Homeless movement."

It was clearly the thing Joanna wanted to hear, and she lit up at the challenge.

"Think they're different topics? Not the way my grandmother explained it! She always told me that long ago, before the restructuring, homelessness wasn't a choice for a lot of people, but a result of poverty and urban neglect," Joanna launched into her sermon with all the enthusiasm of a fire-and-brimstone preacher. "The homeless were people that society forgot, let fall off the grid. Then came the eco-city movement. When we started focusing on the health of the entire city, its people, its place in the environment, everything changed. Cities fixed their infrastructure, provided better community and mental health services, all that. City officials thought homelessness would disappear with the reduction of poverty. Instead, a lot of people saw the potential for freedom and it became a lifestyle, a choice. One defined by self-sufficiency, nomadism, a rejection of material possession, and the simple joy of wanderlust. And you know what? The Homeless leave almost no carbon footprint, contribute little to nothing to pollution or excess or waste. So, you see, our movement is inseparable from the green infrastructure revolution! The government had to accept it as a legitimate part of the new eco-society, remove barriers to employment and services like having a permanent address. Nobody is forced into this lifestyle. We choose it. I was raised Homeless, then registered Homeless myself as soon as I was legally old enough and haven't ever wanted anything else. The city is a forest, and we are its keepers!"

"Hear, hear," Jack cheered, saluting the proud Homeless woman leading their way through the brush.

Struggling to keep up with the two veteran hikers, Russel barely found the spare energy to nod along and wondered at Joanna's lungs' capacity to support such a trek and such fiery preaching simultaneously.

Jack and Joanna talked like this for some time, swapping hiking stories and comparing notes on natural and artificial forests across the continent. Russel listened with mild interest, but also with a sense of distance. The nearly evangelical passion in Joanna's voice was inescapable, but he still never understood why someone would choose the nomadic life of a Homeless.

Eventually, they worked their way through the forest and found the ramp on the other side of the level. Joanna and Jack set to locating the Homeless camp in the area, and Russel tagged along, trying not to get lost in the thicket. Finally, peeking out from the underbrush, weathered canvas came into view.

"Greetings!" Jack raised a hand as they approached, and several heads popped out from tents.

One of them, belonging to a somewhat surly looking individual, came to meet them. "Hache, is that you? Haven't seen you around here for a while. Joanna," the man nodded.

"Gibbs," she nodded curtly back. The man now identified as Gibbs tipped his head towards Russel.

"Who's the townie?"

"Russel Foloi, sedentary museum guy from Seattle," Jack answered quickly, evidently providing all the relevant credentials. "We're looking for a Dr. Carlos Del Rio. Has he come through here?"

"You need a doctor?" Gibbs scratched the back of his neck. "We've got a physician here."

"Not that type of doctor. He's a — what was it?" Jack turned to Russel.

"Sound engineer. Specialist in acoustics and sound energy," Russel stepped forward.

"What's a museum guy need a sound engineer for?" Gibbs scoffed.

"Dr. Del Rio's working on something I need," Russel mumbled, sensing in the brief moment of silence that followed that information was the cost of admission into Gibbs' camp. "A formula that would dramatically increase the productivity of useable energy absorbed from sound. Something that could make harvesting sound energy a practical part of the city's infrastructure."

Gibbs nodded, eyebrows furrowed, and then jerked his head in the direction of the fire.

"I've been on a hike for the last few days, but maybe someone in camp has seen him."

"Is that true?" Joanna whispered in Russel's ear as they approached the camp. "About the formula?"

Russel nodded. That was the rumor, anyway.

"Any of you guys seen a Dr. Carlos Del Rio pass through here?" Gibbs addressed the band of transients.

Some of them looked up from their work and some who shook their heads while fingers kept clacking at the laptop keyboards. Other voices started to rustle through the small crowd like a breeze through a meadow of dandelions.

"Who wants to know?" A voice came from somewhere.

"This kid," Gibbs jerked a thumb towards Russel. "Museum guy."

"Is that Joanna? Couldn't resist my charms, eh sweetheart?"

"Shove it, Trevor. Your tent doesn't have a single patch on it."

"What's a museum guy need with the sound engineer?"

"Traded a townie for it. Nice and cozy inside."

"I thought you said it was a doctor."

"We've already got a doctor."

"Trevor, I swear you keep it up and this boot is going somewhere cozy."

"Not that kind of doctor."

"I haven't been to a museum in ages."

"I'm sorry," Russel tried to cut in, "did someone say something about an engineer? Do you know Dr. Del Rio?"

"No."

"He wasn't asking you."

"Yes."

Heads turned as someone stood, a woman with long, grey hair.

"He was here?" Jack asked. The woman nodded. Jack followed up. "Do you know which ramp he took?"

"Up," the woman said before returning to her seat. "Heading all the way to the top."

"You haven't missed him," Jack smiled, turning to Russel. "He's still here."

Russel sighed in relief.

"So why does the museum kid need a sound engineer?" Gibbs stood with his arms crossed, still observing their conversation.

Jack raised an eyebrow at Russel and nodded.

"I'm creating an exhibit on the city's urban landscape," Russel answered finally. "As a way to try and save it, or part of it. My exhibit is about the sounds of the city, the urban soundscape. The mayor is proposing a measure that includes extreme noise reduction as part of the next phase of restructuring, but Dr. Del

Rio's formula, if it's real, would provide an alternative; harnessing the city's sounds as a form of salvaged energy."

"How interesting," Joanna pulled at her chin as she considered the idea. "I'm no expert but it seems reasonable. There are sounds everywhere in the city, so why not use that energy?"

"The problem," Russel sighed, "has always been efficiency. The sound from a train passing by creates about a hundredth of a watt per square meter while sunlight generates roughly 680 watts in that same space. So it's never been that efficient, but Dr. Del Rio's formula is supposed to compound the useable energy in vibrational and acoustic energy, channeling all the sounds from sources throughout the city into a single grid. It'll never replace solar or tidal as our main sources of power, but it can substantially supplement the power grid. And I think it's enough to prove that the sounds of the city should be preserved, not eliminated. That's what my exhibit is about, sounds as an essential part of the city's lived heritage and texture."

Jack's eyebrows popped up and Joanna nodded along, smiling. Gibbs just scoffed.

"What would a townie know about the texture of the city?"

HEAVY BREATHING. >50 DECIBELS.

"Gibbs is like that with everyone, don't worry," Joanna patted Russel on the shoulder as they climbed the ramp in pursuit of Dr. Del Rio and the uppermost levels of the forest tower.

Russel nodded his head, and yet, there was something about the taunt that he could not shake. What did Gibbs mean?

The hike was strenuous, most of it being spent moving from ramp to ramp, climbing ever upwards. Russel's muscles strained, his feet burned, his joints ached. And yet, with every step he felt renewed, a piece of his soul fulfilled from traversing the forests and meadows within the moss-covered concrete frame of the tower. Streams trickled along the edges of each level, sometimes pooling in ponds large enough to host frogs and small fish. A waterfall thundered between a hole cut through five consecutive levels. Breezes wafted through the branches, occasionally carrying the ambient wayward sound of traffic into the forest and Russel would turn, gazing wistfully through the vines and imagining the city beyond. An ecosystem of sound. The fabric of the city woven through frequencies of energy.

Still, Gibbs' words remained in the corners of Russel's mind.

Finally, after what felt to Russel's body to be an eternity spent atoning for a sedentary existence in the purgatory of perpetual exercise, the trio crested a ramp and saw above blue skies, unusually clear for Seattle at this time of year.

"We made it!" Jack smiled, basking in the sunlight.

"I haven't been up this far in years," Joanna held her hands over her head.

"Yep, good for us," Russel panted, doubled over and chest heaving. Jack clapped him on the shoulder as he straightened and slipped something into his hand.

"What's this?" Russel asked between breaths.

"Club patch," Jack winked. "You've summited your first dark green forest tower. That automatically qualifies you for membership."

Feeling a hint of red in his ears and a surprising swell of emotion in his chest, Russel mumbled his thanks.

In the more open top level of the tower, it did not take them long to find the Homeless camp and Jack again acted as herald for the incoming party.

"Congratulations on reaching this far!" A woman rose to greet them. "We see very few people who are not Homeless up here. Please, take a seat and help yourself to some refreshments after your hike."

"Thank you," Russel accepted a drink and a scoop of granola and nuts. "I'm here looking for a Dr. Carlos Del Rio. Do you know him?"

"Am I in trouble?"

Russel turned at the voice and a man emerged from his tent, a warm smile visible between the round glasses and thick beard.

"Dr. Del Rio," Russel held out an anxious hand, "I've come a long way to see you. Can we talk?"

PROFOUND INTROSPECTION. INCALCULABLE.

Russel stood on the roof of the tower, overlooking the city stretched out around him, the lights from the buildings and cars twinkling in perfect concert with the stars in the black sky overhead. Even this far up, he could hear the honking and rumbling and vitality of the soundscape.

"I do hope my formula can help you convince the city not to restrict all the noise," Dr. Del Rio said, hands in his pockets as he stood next to Russel. "Even if it isn't finished yet."

"It's enough to prove that sound can be harnessed as a viable resource," Russel nodded. "And that should be enough to protect it as a vital part of the city's infrastructure. And heritage."

He thought for a moment longer.

"And texture."

There was a moment of silence.

"You know," Dr. Del Rio spoke softly, "sound is transient."

Russel looked over at the renowned engineer who stood quietly gazing over the city, and raised one eyebrow.

"Think about it. It originates in one place, but never stops traveling until all its energy is spent. The soundscape that defines the city is composed of frequencies in motion.

"That's the irony of the urban landscape, don't you think?" Dr. Del Rio continued. "We look at the city and we think of it as the ultimate symbol of civilized sedentism. The place where the ancients first settled, built something permanent and immobile. But movement has always been part of the urban environment, hubs of restless activity, defined by movement through them and within them. Cities are stasis and bustle, all at once. And the homeless have always been part of that, always in motion, as much a part of the urban landscape as the sounds, the noises. Cities were always an ideal environment for nomads."

He paused, and looked directly at Russel. Russel chewed his thoughts for a moment.

"In my line of work, we often speak of the fabric of the city," Russel replied slowly, deliberately. "But I suppose fabric itself is only born from yarn in motion. The pull, the push, the tension, the movement. Yarn in stasis remains in the spool. The texture is an artifact of the action of weaving."

"I studied sound for years, but I never truly grasped the soundscape until I became it, became motion within the city, of the city, became a Homeless. And that's when I started working on my formula." Dr. Del Rio slowly exhaled, eyes closed, listening to the sounds below.

Russel nodded, his mind whirring, his heart beating. He looked over his shoulder at the campsite. Jack had inducted him into a society of mobility. Joanna promised to stay in Seattle until his exhibit was done, and hinted that he would be welcome to join her when she moved on to the next city.

Russel's eyes wandered back out over the ledge, seeing in the grid of motion below a great loom, the weft of humanity interwoven with the warp of pulsating energy. The darkness, the lights. The solid permanence, the unceasing movement. The meandering Homeless, the sedentary townies. And weaving them all together, unifying them at the edge the fabric, were the sounds.

A *franco-californien* armed with a wok and a word processor, R. Jean Mathieu has hauled sail, served tea, hung beef, sold cell phones, and once even used his own coat as a zip-line sixteen stories above the streets of Hong Kong. He and his wife, Melissa, and daughter, Lyra, keep a good table when not writing side-by-side or chasing trains to the next adventure. You can find Mathieu's award-winning stories in *Ecopunk!*, *Blood on the Floor*, *RJeanMathieu.com*, and *Amazon.com*.

• • •

As a Quaker, I am bemused that this is easily the most Quakerly story I've ever sold, despite not a single character being a Friend. "Scars of Satyagraha" started with a call for submissions for an anthology on gender, setting off thoughts of the opposing genders of Real Man and Gentleman, and Sam caught between them. The resulting meditation on ahimsa, violence, gender, bodysurfing, and Mafia movies happened quite naturally. I'm particularly proud of Babuji's nails; they are splendid.

SCARS OF SATYAGRAHA

R. JEAN MATHIEU

WHENEVER I SKIN, I go down to one of those Yoruba tattoo parlors and get a cut on my left knee, so it heals into a crescent-shaped scar. I got the original scar from some sharp black-lichen, playing footie out beyond Dangote-dome in the boy's body I was born with. But I wear the scar now to honor my father, my Babuji, Arjun Chaturvedey. He died for his scars.

My mother died when I was five years old, cancer, as I shot up out of my *kurta* and my voice dropped an octave. Dr. Goodluck pronounced me biologically adult and skin-okay two months later. Babuji and I grieved, and he meditated with me, hoping I'd forego my first skin and grow into an Old World *bhai* like him. I was torn, but as Mom's *shradda* anniversary approached, I knew what I would do.

You see, Mom was a Yankee, full-blood, straight from Cascadia Commonwealth, straight from *Earth*. But she wasn't one of the Yankees you saw in the Mollywood sims, adrenaline-fueled and whining and addicted to engines and wheels. She wasn't a rowdy-sheeter or a minuteman. Mom was a good Yankee, who worshipped her God next to Babuji worshipping his. The bloodweaver put my old body in cryo, and I wore a woman's skin to Mom's *shradda*, where all my aunties and uncles and cousin-siblings told me "you got Abigail's eyes." I looked like her daughter, with the blue eyes, but I looked like Babuji's daughter, too, with the thick black hair and the long earlobes of a Brahmin *bhai*.

I started pulling back that thick black hair in a simple ponytail, American-style, tying it with a white ribbon long after the *shradda* and long after Babuji went back to court. I threw out all my boy's clothes and printed kurtas that looked like Yankee tees or jerseys, churidar like their narrow trousers, and, at Babuji's insistence, white dhoti and a sari. But I printed the sari in red, white, and blue.

If Babuji hadn't been busy with a new case as Prosecutor of Chandimakal Basic Court, or at least of Dangote-dome's district court, he'd have kept me cooped up like a Muslima in haram. The Chief Prosecutor wanted Babuji to pick up some minutemen, some of the serious cowboys, on charges of double-skinning. He still prayed the *sanyavandara* with me every morning, and taught me all the rites of a Brahmin at home, but he never knew where I read my school and wrote exams. And I made sure to keep my marks up and played footie religiously, in those days when the air was cool and thin and new out there and the ball raced across iridescent black-lichen, not through all this Earth-green grass.

I was free to run when I wasn't studying, and I ran around Little Washington. It's a shrineless dome, gunmetal grey and dusty brown. They look washed-out, the Yankees, even the darker ones look like bleached Igbo or faded Fulfulde. Their English is almost incomprehensible, and they whisper it among themselves always. Blue eyes or green, or grey, shoot out from under pale, perspiring brows, stare without shame, then turn back to desultory games of cards or angry arguments about politics ten million miles away.

Mars is a planet of a thousand colors and tongues and faiths and loves, but the Yankees are a world unto themselves. Them and their Old Western ways.

Somehow, the gunmetal grey and dusty brown and red of flesh blood seem more colorful than the brightest Holi when you're young.

It all started in Little Washington, you see.

I was in the middle of an orbital calculus lesson, sitting in front of Starbuck's Saloon, when Atticus' shadow fell over me. Something in my body startled, but I hadn't learned a woman's caution around strange men — especially strange Yankee men. Something in my body shivered, and not in the tropical Earth-normal air. I'd been androsexual in my boy skin, nothing in my girl skin changed that. And here was a real man! He was tall, wheatish, and broad-shouldered, with rough hands from tinkering in his rover and piercing blue eyes. I grinned up at him and greeted him like one American to another:

"Howdy, dude! 'sup?"

"Howdyback," he said, surprising me with Yankee-Martian *patois*. "Busy na? Gotta take leave a minute. Watch me stuff? Owe ya. Sabi?"

I *did* sabi. I sabied very much. I tapped the table and, as soon as the little package was on it, I covered it with my book-bag. I looked up to him again, at his piercing blue eyes.

"Goodname?" I spat in patois.

"Atticus Diggs." He smiled back. "Ya?"

"Sami Chandurvedey," I said. "Mom was Abigail Lee-Chandurvedey."

"Na shit na?" Atticus said, eyes going wide. He looked up. "Later, OK?"

"OK ...!" I gave him the sign, but he was already gone.

Now I sabied. Two boys in green came racing in from the tunnel to Dangote, buttonholing half the Yankees in Little Washington. When they passed Starbuck's Saloon, they looked right past me. The pretty Brahmin girl in the kurta and churidar with her orbital mechanics notes was no suspect, even to their drone-swarm. When they slunk home to Dangote-dome, Atticus emerged from under his rock, and took his package.

"Thanks, Sammy." He shook my hand, sending an electric thrill up my arm. Since my skinning, Babuji wouldn't so much as pat my shoulder. I was hungry and thirsty for some kind of touch, especially off the footie field, *especially* from a boy. "Ya good dude."

I grinned with all my teeth. This Real American called me 'dude'!

"Beer na?" I offered.

"Sorry." He shook his head. My heart broke. "Gotta take leave for real. Later, OK?"

"OK ...!"

That's how Atticus Diggs became my boyfriend.

Like red-blooded Martians, we inhaled Mollywood sims about minutemen and their underworld and Old World ways, their rough and brutal code of honor. I wore my new sari to torrid mixed-reality games about the Militia that even singing and dancing couldn't gentle. I learned all the strange English of the Real Americans, *good citizens* and *liberated goods* and *tea parties*. Any Martian can tell you the Colonel of Chandimakal's Militia and his cronies in the Fourth Constitutional Convention run crime all over the Red Planet, that they live like rajahs and ooni, bound only by the Cowboy Code, the Oath of Allegiance, and their own lust for freedom. Any Martian can tell you that a gangsta like Atticus can only become a minuteman through *veteraning*, or *vetting*, taking the life of a non-Yankee and permanently sundering themselves from the path of *satyagraha*.

Atticus bought me my first Yankee hamburger, swaggering in like a cowboy, the owner staring daggers at me. The rest of the restaurant stared daggers when I asked for a veg hamburger. There was only non-veg, only beef. Atticus oiled the water, mentioned my Mom's citizenship, fronted that he was already a good citizen, and I watched the owner shrink back and stutter apologies. I had a no-patty hamburger and the best table in the house, and when another Yankee's stare crawled my skin, Atticus hopped up and slammed his head in his soup. The owner threw him out for "causing trouble in his place" as Atticus sat back down, all cowboy cool. Part of me was horrified. Part of me ... well ...

I was in love, like a Mollywood lovey sim. But Atticus was in a Militia thriller. He pointed me Phoenix Kid the gambler and Big Data the blockchaindude and acting-boss Tyrone Lucas, the minuteman who ran all the illegal cargo in and out of Little Washington. Their bigman — their *noncom* in Militia-jargon — was in confine, so when a man in a dark and tall-collared suit with a Chinasilk cravat stepped into Atticus' garage, he talked to Ty.

"Is that the Colonel?" I whispered, peeking behind a wheel. Atticus shushed me.

"That's his Lieutenant, Michael Cambridge." He hissed. "He does the Colonel's dirty work, so the Colonel can keep his hands clean. Out of sight, out of enemy fire, sabi?"

He must have heard us, because the Lieutenant looked over. He was tall, especially for a Yankee, with harsh grey eyes that were clouded with wrinkles but never smiled. My heart jumped in my throat; Atticus stood rooted like a banyan tree. Thinking quick, I saluted, like a good Yankee. Atticus followed my lead.

Michael Cambridge nodded to us, then turned back to Ty Lucas. Atticus and I turned back to the rover, but I kept peeking out my eye-corners. We were driving as far as Sokoto-dome, a trunkful of cooking oil hiding a crate of homebrew for Sokoto's less-observant Muslims. As long as I stayed hidden and pled the Fifth, Ty Lucas okayed it.

I glanced back one last time at the Lieutenant, Michael Cambridge, as I hopped in the cab. A real live Militia Officer ...

Maybe it's the Yankee in me, but I whooped and hollered as the triwheels crunched over red rock and the electric engine purred under our feet. It was almost as good as running on my own two legs across the black-lichen for soccer — the same thin cool Martian air in our lungs, the same adrenaline in our Mars-red blood.

I was a lot less excited when we hit a locust-net, killing our engine and scanning our rover's trunk. Atticus grabbed my arm and tried to run.

"What kind of cowboy are you?" I demanded. "I'm sitting here ready to take what the greenboys throw at us and you're running like a yellow-belly!"

"Easy for you to say," Atticus spat, "your Babuji's a bigman, my Daddy's in confine! They'll confine me for certain!"

"We have wine, beer, and kitchen oil on a rover," I said, pinching my nose. One of Babuji's habits, too. "The worst is a few hours at the court."

"Says you! You can stay, I'mma be a free man!" He turned for the door again.

This time, I slapped my hand on his arm, heavy as a shackle. "Are you *really* going to leave your girlfriend alone in the middle of nowhere to take the rap, *cowboy*?" I demanded.

He tore his arm away, turned, screamed "FUCK!" as the green-draped police rovers crawled over the horizon.

Two hours later, I sat in Babuji's office in the Dangote district courthouse. You never saw a more fearsome man, a purer distillation of Old World Brahmin *bhai*. The window framed him in the black-lichen steppes and the waters of the Grand Canal and the pink sky, in his old-fashioned biosuit and his rainbow achkan, collar pipped tight, in his oiled mustaches and red lipstick, in the matching red nails at the end of the scarred hands. They were white as his *swarej*-linen robe, making the red of his nails stand out even more.

He read me a statement I recognized from about a million thrillers, then dropped the Court English for our household Bihari.

"Why, Sami?" he asked, his eyes welling up with tears. "You've taken your sacred thread as my disciple, and your mother and I brought you up a good Brahmin *bhai*, a gentleman and a scholar. What in the name of a million and three gods are you doing racing around the sands with a rowdy-sheeter, my girl?"

From the office altar, Yama, Prince of Law, looked on blandly. His offerings filled the office with the scent of withered orange blossoms. I stewed. Babuji is a gentleman, he hugs his sons, kisses them on both cheeks and on the lips, tousles their hair, laughs with them. Babuji is a gentleman, and sits ramrod straight across from girls, standing when they enter and never laying the smallest finger on them, even when they chant to Saraswati together or light candles for Holi.

"Maybe I'm in love with him, Babuji," I said, sabi that I really wasn't.

Now he smiled a brittle smile at me. The tears still threatened.

"Oh? Should I call Nwabudike in here to solemnize a courthouse elopement?"

I scoffed, and looked over him to the Grand Canal where we'd burnt Mom on the ghats, all three of us white-swaddled like corpses.

"... don't call," I said. "I didn't mean it. Just ask the matchmaker to make my beloved tall and sweet and Yankee."

"Yes yes, you've been asking this since you were six." Babuji patted the air, dismissing it. "Can you at least tell me where you were *going*?"

"As my father or my lawyer?"

"As your gentle, loving guru, who bailed his favored disciple out of confine." His eyes were intent behind that vale of tears. "You're my disciple, and my child. I am saddened you forsook your birth body for another skin, but whatever skin you wear, *you are my daughter.*"

"You say daughter like it's a curse. What is wrong with a new body?"

"Do you remember that black-lichen scar you got when you were three?" Babuji asked. "How you wailed and wailed!

Abigail was always prepared, though, and she had the allopathy kit all ready, and dressed your wound while I held you and kissed you and sang you Mollywood tunes. By the time Abi was done, you'd fallen asleep in my arms! It left a little crescent scar on your left knee, one I looked at every time you wore shorts, because it reminds me of that day, of how you trusted me and loved me."

I looked down at my knee, my face impassive like a cowboy. He was going after me, trying to get a rise out of me. It wouldn't work. I could be stoic as the red sands.

He held up his arms, unsealed the biosleeves and drew them back.

"You see these?" he said, his red nails winking in and out of sight as he showed off his scars. "Each one is another sting of nettle or slice of black-lichen from the garden, the garden where I make things grow, where I raise vegetables fit for a Brahmin and his family. Mahaguru Friday Nnede and Mahatma Gandhi before her taught us *swadeshi*, self-sufficiency, and *satyagraha*, nonviolence. Each of these scars is from upholding those ways, the traditions of a Brahmin. And each of these scars would be lost if I changed bodies like I change a suit of clothes."

I kept staring at my knee. I knew this game, and it wouldn't work on me. I Know-Nothinged him, fed him a story about romantic picnics. I'd burned one of the Officers of the Militia and, though I wasn't a minuteman yet, I wasn't about to break the Fifth Amendment Oath.

Finally, he sighed.

"Sami, I know why you're doing all this." For the first time, he looked away from me, toward Yama. "I miss Abi, too. But wasting your time in Little Washington saloons, hanging around rowdy-sheeters and minuteman mongrels? Your mother would be *ashamed of you*."

He let it hang in the air, watching me. I tried not to let it show how much it hurt.

"From now on, my disciple, you accompany me," he said, sliding into Hindi. "It is only proper that a disciple should follow their guru as a child follows their father. And it is time you took up an apprenticeship at any rate, though a Brahmin *bhai* puts his family and his gods ahead of his career."

"What?!" I demanded. "For how long?!"

"Yama will decide." He patted the air again, patted away my question.

I choked in my clerk's dashiki and sweated the Grand Canal into my formal biosuit, collating data and regressing to the mean of justice next to Nwabudike and Grace under Babuji's watchful eye. "Apprentice paralegal," he called me! That is, when we weren't praying the *sanyavandana* or reading maths at home, where I was "disciple." No time for Atticus or Little Washington, even if I wanted to see him, and I didn't.

I helped Nwabudike assemble caselaw on skinship infringement, double-skinning and so on, going all the way back to Earth. Splitting one's immortal soul between two bodies is horrifying to anyone, whether Hindu or Muslim or Yoruba or Buddhist or Christian. Even atheists see the material problems of trying to keep track of body-hopping criminals who leave their nodes behind. From Grace, I heard the names they were looking for, the faces, some I even knew. Names like Phoenix Kid and Tyrone Lucas. Babuji should have known I'd work out his plan.

He wanted to catch out Ty or his *noncom* boss and nail them on double-skinning, with all the confine and the node-snipping it implied. This way, he thought, he could get them to break the Fifth Amendment Oath and implicate some Officers, someone like Michael Cambridge. It's not like everyone didn't *know* Michael Cambridge was one of the Colonel's inner circle, but civil prosecutors like Babuji couldn't assemble a case against him. If Babuji's plan worked, though ...

Which is why it was so shocking when they sat on the bench together for footie.

It wasn't all bad, you see. I could shuck the dashiki for long kurta and short shorts when Babuji and I left the domes for the free air of Mars and five-a-side football with the other Fourth Formers. The elation I felt in Atticus' cramped rover was a shadow of the freedom I knew chasing the ball across the endless black-lichen, the goals spinning and my chums whirling around me. Nailing the orbital ballistics of black-and-white ball and net was more to me than Phobos and Deimos and the space elevator of Chandikamal combined.

And Babuji was nothing if not respectful of one's religion. He sat at every practice and match, the Brahmin court Prosecutor in his swarej-linen and his achkan and his oiled mustaches and his painted lips, his breather and goggles at the ready, among chattering Igbo in their rainbow head-ties and silent, observant, black-niqabed Muslimas.

During the interval, our team captain, Chuks, pointed him out.

"Who's that next to your abba, swamiji?" he asked.

He wore a crisp suit of Tharsis linen today, white as a funeral shroud, with a red tie held in place by a blue and silver stick-pin. Michael Cambridge, president of New Boston Brewing, one of the financial success stories the Yankee newsfeeds liked to print. Everyone else's newsfeeds printed that he was a prince of the Militia, and I knew it to be true. He reported directly to the Colonel of Chandikamal Militia himself.

He sat chatting quietly with Babuji, who looked serene as Mahaguru Friday despite sitting next to a powerful and dangerous cowboy, a man who had killed and commanded a legion of killers. My heart leapt in my throat for him. A man as honorable as Michael Cambridge wouldn't do the job out in the open sands, with three dozen witnesses, would he? It was against the Cowboy Code, and besides, he had to set an example for his men.

I looked to Chuks, his strapping black body, his narrow black eyes.

"I know nothing, Onochukwu." I shrugged.

Chuks *hates* it when anyone uses his full name. It reminds him of his old girl skin.

"By Allah, you Yanks really *do* stick together." He turned to Triv, our goalie, and barked orders at her. The conversation was over.

Seeing Babuji next to Michael Cambridge threw my chakras out of alignment. I always seemed to be one step behind the thick of it. Toward the end of the match, I even tripped over my own two feet. Me, Sami Chaturvedey, fastest runner north of the Grand Canal, over lichen, steel, or sand!

"Problem na?" Chuks taunted. "Too many bouncing distractions in the new skin!"

I told him to violence himself as I climbed to my feet. From the half-dozen incisions in my exposed limbs, I knew Babuji couldn't complain my new skin wouldn't have scars!

We won the match, 3-1, despite my play. By that time, Michael Cambridge was gone, and Babuji seemed entirely unperturbed. I asked him about it the moment he was in earshot.

"Shush, my s– disciple," he said. "The walls have ears."

As we passed through Little Washington, I felt like the walls had eyes, too. I glanced at the outdoor table in front of Starbuck's Saloon where I'd first met Atticus. Two men were sitting there, Yankees with pale faces. I didn't like the way they looked at me.

"Don't worry, Sami." Babuji said, as if he were reading my mind. "They aren't looking at you. They're looking at me. We're fairly certain I've been, how do they say, 'burned' to the Militia as Prosecutor."

My head wheeled around, seeing Yankee men at every window, with gunsmoke eyes and hard, impassive faces.

"How can you be so, so ... *serene?*" I almost cried. I strangled it as hard as I could for benefit of surrounding ears. "Why even cross through Little Washington, then? We could have gone *around!*"

"My disciple, I am a *satyagrahi*." Babuji said. "I am a Brahmin, and I have tried to live a virtuous life. I will not escape the wheel, but I will come back in a better life. The worst they can do is kill me. And if they do, they have not killed the Way of Truth. The power of nonviolence is to prevail in the end over violence, as we saw with Gandhi and with Havel and with our own Mahaguru Friday. All the weapons on three worlds cannot kill *satyagraha*, and so I neither have use for them, nor fear them."

I know, I know, it's a Martian Civics lecture. But nobody, not even Friday Nnede herself, believed in *satyagraha* and *ahimsa* as hard as my Babuji. And I watched him walk down Friday Street, with eyes and railguns on every side, as if he were walking in our garden at home under the crystal-clear glass on a sunny day.

I thought that he should have been a Mollywood actor then, instead of a lawyer. As soon as we were back under the familiar dome of Dangote, with a riot of colors and tongues on every side and familiar shrines underfoot, he pinched his nose and opened up.

"That *aam aadmi*," he said, twisting the words 'common man' so it sounded like 'dalit', "is a sponsor of Chandimakal Young Footie. He offered me a pipe of spliff, and said he was a father himself: his son was the goalie for your opponents. We praised each other's children, as is only proper, and bragged about our own, as is only manful. He asked what kind of man would put his career ahead of his family, and I agreed. Then he suggested I should 'go back to my potatoes and carrots' and not work so hard."

It took me a moment.

"He *threatened* you?"

"He *warned* me. I know how many trash Mollywood thrillers you've seen. Gentlemen are courteous on the battlefield, no? Right before they revert to violencing each other." He explained. "Part of *satyagraha* training is confronting one's own violence. Gandhiji insisted no one join him who would not take up arms to fight for India's independence. The wise movements, like Mahaguru Friday's, institutionalize this training. A man must take hold of the gun, as it were, in order to throw it away and become a true gentleman. So I must understand the warrior's way. You will, too, when you volunteer your draft and become a *satyagrahi*."

"But why, Babuji?"

"Because even for beefeaters like him, there is wisdom in refraining from violence. He would rather I choose to quit the case than risk prosecution for violent crime. Double-skinning is one thing, assault something very different, and so the Law sees it."

"But you're not going to quit, are you." I stated.

"Of course not." Babuji said. "They can only harm a body."

Something stabbed through me; something that wanted to make me shout: "They are hard men, Babuji, minutemen! They kill like we take sacred thread to *become* men. They aren't of your world of law, they are of a world of their own, a world of honor and blood! Don't you watch sims?!" But I kept my peace.

"I know you're upset." Babuji's voice was kind. "If you wish to weep, Sami, weep; it becomes a Brahmin gentleman, for tears wash clean like the Ganges. And when tears are done, do the needful, like Prince Arjuna in the Gita. I've done the needful by you, despite many tears I wept over you."

He forgot himself for just a moment, and reached to hug me, there, in the middle of Biafra Avenue, before he stopped himself. He turned away, straightening up, pinching his nose, refusing to meet my eye.

I threw my eye over the familiar storefronts and *dhaba* stalls and *chai-wallah*s, and wondered how many pale faces and gunsmoke eyes looked back. I could trust *I* was safe, at least. "Women and children" was the Old World heart of the Cowboy Code, and I was a known Real American. Babuji had only to fear for *his* life, he could not be troubled by mine. At least, so I told myself.

Which is why, down in the dome of Chandimakal visiting Auntie Ladli for Holi, I didn't expect a slender Igbo-looking gentleman in a red jersey to step in front of me.

"'Sup, Sammy. Busy na?" He asked.

"I'm sorry, have we met?" I asked, cocking my head.

"No memory na?" The Igbo-looking gentleman frowned. He brushed one eye with his finger. "Sad! Atticus Diggs. Your goodname's Sami Chaturvedey. Your Ma's Abigail Lee. Your Dad's Arjun Chaturvedey, Esquire."

That's when I felt the so-called cold steel at my back, and my heart nearly stopped. It's not cold, it's very warm, from being next to a body and from the magnetic muzzle-ring brimming with threatening electrics. It burned into my left shoulder blade, straight through my red, white, and blue sari. Every other inch of my skin chilled under sudden sweat.

"Chill, girl!" Atticus brushed dust from his jersey in long sweeps, just like he did in his old skin, tall and wheatish. He switched to American English. "My word as a cowboy, you're not gonna get hurt. I won't let 'em. Just wanna talk a bit."

He glanced down to my left shoulder.

"In private." For a moment just a moment, a glimmer of the boy I'd known in another skin: "Sorry, Sammy. For real."

I tried to turn around and look, like I'd seen in the sims, but I'd only caught the diamond tattoo of Ty's hand before he poked me with that red-hot railgun muzzle. There were two footsteps behind me, so they'd brought a friend. Three men to kidnap a teenage girl. Some cowboy.

The moment we were out of view, Atticus took a handkerchief from his pocket and blindfolded me with it.

"Let's roll." Atticus' voice cracked. We started forward, me blind as a beggar.

Mad as Majnun, I obsessed over Ty's gun. Colt na? Smith & Wesson? Something French? Maybe a *jugaar* pistol and made right here on Mars in somebody's hacked fabber and ready to blow and fill us all with magnetic shrapnel. He could have used a knife, just as deadly at skin distance, but us Yankees, our God gave us violence as our birthright, our holiness flows out the barrel of a gun. Mad as Majnun, but method to my madness. As long as I wondered whether Ty shoved an alien 13mm or an all-American .45 under my shoulder blade, I couldn't wonder where they were taking me and if I'd come out. Nothing in all the sims or all my girlfriending with Atticus said anything about the Militia kidnapping teenage girls and, by now, I *was* learning caution around dangerous men.

I had to trust Atticus. The boy who'd bailed me in the middle of the red sands like a yellow-belly. I kept thinking about railguns instead. I kept thinking about railguns as Ty slammed me down into a chair and the other minuteman tied me to it. I kept thinking about railguns until Atticus tugged my blindfold off with gentle fingers.

It didn't look like a Chandimakal Holi at all. The room was grey, no windows, with only an old Betsy Ross flag for color, the only lights over a scuffed old terminal-table and a single light globe glowing in the tandoor-less kitchen. My heart threatened to stop again. I was in a Militia safehouse, behind a blind alley and no doubt guarded by a platoon of minutemen.

It was nothing like how I'd dreamed it would be. I'd dreamed of being one of the minutemen myself, not the one tied to the chair, but the one holding the …

… huh, Colt .45. The bluesteel matched Ty's eyes.

"'sup, Sammy." Ty grinned. "Long way from Dangote, ain'tcha?"

I wanted to glare defiantly into his eyes like the faces of our shared Founding Fathers in old schoolbook pictures, but I couldn't. I was too scared. I looked away.

"Like I said, we're not gonna hurt you," Atticus said. "These good citizens just wanna say something to your Dad. We got us a burner fly-eye and we're gonna give him a call. We just want you to say hello."

The fly-eye, hovering in front of the Betsy Ross flag, flashed red out of the dim.

"Babuji?" I asked. Of course, he didn't answer. I didn't hear the telltale hum of buzzbuzz drones to carry his voice.

"Mr. Chaturvedey." Ty said. "I represent the Freeborn Citizens' Constitutional Militia of the Martian Theater. Your activities interfere with our free trade and our God-given right to the pursuit of happiness. Frankly, they reek of regulation. But we can forgive this kind of pinko behavior, as good Christian men. As you can see, we're also men of action."

Atticus nudged me from behind.

"Babuji, I'm sorry," I said, trying to keep the tears out of my voice.

"She's fine." Ty said. "And we all want her to stay that way. And she will stay that way, if you resign from your current case. If you do, all's forgiven and it's quiet on Main Street. If not, just remember that we're men of action."

Ty charged the Colt ominously, each ring lighting blue.

"You have forty-eight hours to make your decision." Ty finished. "An @ is flashing across your screen. Send your answer there, and we will discuss exchanges."

Ty gave the Yankee slice across the throat, turning off the sky-eye. Letting out a long sigh like one organism, my kidnappers sank into various pieces of ratty furniture lining the little room.

"Now we wait?" Atticus asked.

"Yup." Replied the other minuteman. Ty looked up.

"I'm starving, who wants a hotdog?" he said.

Atticus volunteered, and turned to grin at me.

"How about you, swamiji?" he asked.

It was surreal. They had a prosecutor's daughter tied to a chair, but you'd have thought this was any cold-water flat in Little Washington. They ate hotdogs that fouled the air with a sickly savoury smell, smothered with mustard and sour chutney. They took pulls at bottles of Good Friday beer. They hummed along to the 'cast from the scuffed terminal. They played virtual games that were old when Friday Nnende was young. Atticus fed me a veg bun filled with the chutney and mustard, and kept a gun trained on me while I ate it. They had long, rambling conversations about nothing. Sometimes I joined in.

"But I mean," Atticus said, "if we can skin, the hell is race even *worth*? I'm blacker than Harlem and my old skin was albino-white."

He felt his smooth, shaved pate.

"And I had hair. This skull feels weird."

"It's not your skin color *or* the shape of your head," retorted the other minuteman, Mason, who'd apparently been born with that skin, "it's how you talk and how you act, it's how you speak English, and how you make your barbeque sauce. With mustard, obviously. Even if he wore Abe Lincoln's skin walking down the street, you'd *know* if some snake-charmer swamiji was trying to pass for Yankee. It's not a skin ... it's ..."

"... ethnicity." I suggested. "Culture."

"Yeah. Being black is an *ethnicity*, not a skin color." He turned to me. "Thanks, swamiji."

"So what's gender worth?" I asked. "Why's the Cowboy Code talk about women and children if they could both be cowboys tomorrow?"

"That's *different*," Ty insisted, "whether you're a man or woman's part of you. It's part of your soul. Even trannies get that straight."

"How do you know a woman walking down the street if she's wearing a man skin?"

"The way she walks." Atticus leered. Once, that look would have made me shiver. Now, I shuddered.

"Whole thing's bullshit," Mason said. "A real Yankee keeps a hold of his weapon, no matter how long his bloodweaver bill gets. You ever transkinned, Ty?"

"Hell no." Ty spat. "Man's man all the way through. Popped my cherry with a dick, hangin' onto it."

"Atticus?"

He shook his head.

"How about you, kid?"

I gulped. "I was born a boy. This is my first skin."

It hadn't felt alien like this in months. Not since the last time Atticus and I held each other.

Ty slapped my shoulder.

"Don't worry, kid," he said. "You're not a woman until you pop your cherry. There's still time to go back. Unless, Atticus, I owe you a beer?"

Atticus turned red. So did I. The two minutemen just guffawed.

Like I said, it was surreal.

My arms and legs were cold and tight when they finally got the order to untie me. I flowed through a few *asanas* just to get *prana* back into my limbs when he walked into the room. Both Mason and Ty stiffened, and Atticus made a little choking sound. I was facing away from the door. I took a moment to put on my cowboy mask before I slowly turned around.

Michael Cambridge stood there, his bodyguard hanging back and feigning the casual cool that all cowboys are supposed to have. He wore a dark suit today, the neck and sleeves of his biosuit peeking from the collar and sleeves, the only color a blood-red necktie. Michael Cambridge, a Militia Lieutenant who reported directly to the Colonel himself, scanned me with that ice-cold gaze.

"Why don't you sit down." It wasn't a question. Everyone sat. I sat. Michael Cambridge leaned forward, so I could smell his musk like old leather and flint.

"I'll give your old man this, kid, he's decisive," Michael said. "And reasonable enough. He says long as he gets you back safe and sound, we got nothing to worry about from him. For a swamiji, he's a man of his word, and I wouldn't be much of a minuteman if I weren't a man of mine. I promised you to him, safe and sound."

My heart just about leapt into my throat, past the cloying taste of the mustard. Michael Cambridge held up a hand.

"Just a minute, kid," he said. "I know you pled the Fifth with this gangsta here."

He thumbed offhandedly in Atticus' general direction. Atticus clearly wasn't worth his attention right now. Frankly, he wasn't worth mine, either.

"And I know your Mom's a natural-born citizen, God rest her soul. You've been tailing behind your old man and I bet you've heard some good intel. We could use a man like you in the Militia. You don't have to get locked into that *yes yes effendi* kowtowing humble-Brahmin heathen bullshit. You can be a real man, a free man, a minuteman."

Now there was a war inside me, as big as the battle between the Pandavas and the Kauravas. This Lieutenant, with his seamed face and his smart suit and his rugged hands, was speaking to me Yankee to Yankee, dude to dude, and offering me a chance to become a cowboy. This wasn't Atticus the wannabe, this was the real McCoy.

But ...

"But ..." I coughed. "... don't I need to ... get ... veteraned?"

Michael Cambridge smiled. It did not reach his eyes.

"You're sharp, kid," he said. "Yeah, you do. And I have just the alien in mind. He's a real General Gage on us real Americans, and you're in a unique position to settle it."

My eyes went wide again.

"Yup." Michael smiled. "He agreed to pick you up in on the black-lichen field outside Little Washington, a spot I think you know pretty well. We've arranged it to be private; after all, government ought to stay out of good citizens' bedrooms and private dealings. You'll be given a gun."

He nodded to Ty's Colt .45.

"I know you know how to use one, judging by your kill-count in those Old West games. Do this job, and you'll be an officer one day, maybe Colonel, who knows? If not, well, I made a promise to the Colonel that we'd get your intel. I'd rather you volunteered it as a good citizen. But we'll do the needful, like the Hindis say. So it's your choice to take hold of your own fate like a man, or crawl and kiss-ass like a coward all your life. Take your time. It's a big choice. Handover's at high noon. You got thirteen hours to think it over."

He stood, and extended a hand. I shook it on muscle memory. His hand really was as rough as it looked, calloused and strong. A man's hand. But not a gentleman's hand, like Babuji's. He nodded to his minutemen and departed.

Now I understood why they'd kidnapped a civilian. It wasn't just to get to Babuji, it was to get to *me.* To get me vetted into the Militia. It was tantalizing — to be a real American, a good citizen, a minuteman among minutemen, with all the perks that implied. I didn't sleep much that night. I had plenty of company; each one of those cowboys stood his watch, Colt in hand.

The next morning, we ate breakfast, and they had pork and beef and eggs with theirs, leaving me with an "English muffin" that was clearly day-old idli. They blindfolded me, and led me out of the safehouse and into a rover, where Mason took the wheel while Atticus, Ty, and I sat in the trunk.

That's when Atticus handed me the gun, the Colt .45 railgun with its five regular bluesteeled rings for extra stopping power and its twenty-six .45-inch pellets magnetically sealed inside the grip. He held it to me grip-first, the rearing mustang shining in the overhead diodes. It hovered just above my red, white, and blue lap, beckoning.

"No fear I waste you na?" I asked. He shook his head.

"You won't."

Ty settled back against the bulwark, cleared his throat, made it clear he had another gun in easy reach.

"Take it." Atticus suggested.

I wrapped my hand around the grip. It felt heavier than the three-and-a-half pounds of American iron I knew it to be. I'd hefted light-guns for mixed reality games and toy handcannons, and none of them weighed in my palm like that Colt.

Did they really expect me to shoot my own father? I wondered. Then I wondered: what will they do to me if I *don't*?

I wasn't Babuji. I wasn't ready to sacrifice this body and this life for my soul, even if it *was* part of Brahma. But I had a good imagination. And I'd watched a lot of thrillers.

I wondered how many scars this skin would have before I left it.

What else could I do? Spin on one heel like a Mollywood hero and squeeze off a dozen perfect shots on the cowboys and flee Mars with Babuji and my White Prince in a tight kurta? Maybe not. But …

I spent the rest of the trip staring at the gun in my hand, and feeling its weight.

We stopped, and I hid the Colt in the folds of my sari as I hopped out the trunk. Neither Atticus nor Ty bothered brushing iron on me; they already trusted me that much.

The field was iridescent black, like an oil spill. We were at the far end of the steppe, with the distant domes of Dangote and Gandharva and Sokoto and Little Washington just glass bubbles on the horizon, and even the space elevator that gives Chandimakal its name only a silver thread to a distant pink sky. It was far enough the red dust blew over the field in particles that made you squint instinctively. I wished I'd worn kohl.

There was our little party, and four others at this private out-of-station rendezvous. Michael Cambridge had flown in, his pilot doubling as his bodyguard. Already I could tell one on sight, from the peculiar folds of his kurta and the bulges in his sleeves. The other two people made me choke in my throat.

One was Babuji, looking five years older than he had when he'd folded his hands in *namaste* and wished me a safe trip. Even his immaculate oiled mustaches and clean white achkan and fresh, crisp lipstick couldn't hide it. The other was a tall Dravidian woman, with a long black braid and a purple sari and very sad eyes. Babuji held her hand.

Everything else — the Militia, Michael Cambridge, the gun — fell away for an eternity as I grokked the sight of *my father* touching *a woman*. He demanded all-male medical teams out of propriety, what was he doing touching this stranger when he wouldn't even kiss his own daughter on the brow?!

"Who's the girl?" Michael Cambridge demanded. "You agreed to come alone. I thought you were a man of honor."

Babuji threw up his hands.

"She's a civilian. Scan her, she's clean," he insisted. Michael Cambridge cocked his head, and Mason rushed forward to scan her.

"The swamiji's not lying," Mason announced. "No weapons, no wire, even her node's in out-of-station mode."

She nodded at this. But who was she?

Michael Cambridge accepted this turn of events, only calling his pilot out and having his men expose their iron to the particulate red breeze. He turned back to Babuji, adjusted his tie, and filled all Mars with a quiet whisper.

"When the Founding Fathers fought for their freedom, it was for one thing: respect." Michael intoned. "We had to teach the British to respect us. We taught the Mexicans respect, and the Germans, and the Russians, and the Chinese. A real man is respected, so a real man can be free. That's all we ever ask, but we'll ask for it with guns in our hands. You have to fight for your freedom, for your respect. Sammy respects us, you raised up a good citizen. But *you* have disrespected us. You keep on disrespecting us. I hope you're ready to die like a man, because we are ready to defend our freedom like men."

He clapped a hand on my shoulder. Babuji trembled with rage that this man should touch me so.

"Time's up, kid." Michael Cambridge whispered. "You gonna be a man, or live and die a slave?"

I took six deliberate steps toward Babuji and the strange woman, then stopped. I stood there in the black-lichen, smelling the flinty, oxide Martian air. I reached into my red, white, and blue sari, and produced the Colt .45, my mind whirling with ways to use it to defend my Babuji, make a dramatic last stand as he escaped with the strange woman.

Babuji and the woman watched me without fear. All thoughts of firing the gun fled from me like Kauravas before Prince Arjuna. I didn't even look down; my hand flinging the Colt into the red dust like it was a cobra.

Babuji smiled, all the way to his Earth-brown eyes, painted lips parting to show pearls of milk-white teeth. Next to him, the strange woman wore an identical smile. Without saying a word, he told me I was a gentleman, a real Brahmin bhai. My feet moved faster, dress slippers tearing against the black-lichen.

Babuji was still wearing that smile when he died.

The sound of a railgun is so much *deeper* in real life than it is even in the best MR sims. An unsilenced, unshadowed boom from a Colt .45 railgun isn't something you *hear* so much as *feel*, deep in your chest, a lightning whine that should not be that deep, but is. It sounds like something dying.

The strange woman threw her hands over me and dragged us to the sharp black-lichen, but in the dizzy fall I saw a snap of Michael Cambridge, standing there with the gun in his hand, muzzle still glowing with blue-hot magnetic fire. Then we were in the lichen, and I understood why old men like Babuji and Michael Cambridge wore biosuits.

"Run!" she hissed.

Ahead was pain and scarring, since the lichen would tear my slippers to ribbons. Behind was death, and my soul wasn't prepared. I ran. I was Sami Chaturvedey, fastest runner north of the Grand Canal, over lichen, steel or sand. I ran toward the domes of home, where swarms of fly-eyes and buzzbuzz drones hovered and held back violence. I ran until I stumbled to my knees, the lower end of my beautiful sari torn to rags by time I reached the shorn lichen of the playing fields. I ran until I gulped the thin cold air and understood why old men like Babuji carried their breathers outside, stumbling to my hands and knees while my lungs burned.

When the rover rumbled up beside me, I could not run any more.

She stepped down next to me, and all I could do was stare at her lichen-boots as she knelt beside me and popped her breather in my mouth. I sucked in the damp, oxygen-rich Earth-normal air while she stroked my hair with her fingers, just the way Babuji used to.

"They didn't follow, my daughter." She rumbled. "They broke off at the swarm limit. But it was some chase, by Banka-Mundi! I was so afraid. But I knew you were safe, and that was more important."

I nearly spit the breather out. I had enough presence of mind now to take it with my hand.

"B-babuji ...?"

She helped me to my feet. I looked at her arms, her legs, her face. So clean! A skin straight from the bloodweaver.

Her eyes were the same color.

"But wasn't that ..."

"That was also me." Babuji smiled sadly, weeping freely. "Yes, your Brahmin bhai Babuji double-skinned. I split my soul, but violence would have gouged it. Ahimsa is more important than the law, my disciple, remember that. I knew a man like that would not let me walk away with my mustaches and my painted lips. And I have much left to teach you."

"To be a gentleman?" I asked, looking at my father's shapely figure.

"A true gentleman is adaptable," she rumbled. "I will raise you up a Brahmin bhai no matter what skin you wear. Your husband will thank me."

I took a step forward, and cried out in my pain. With soft eyes, my Babuji lifted my bloodied bare feet from the black-lichen.

"Come come," Babuji said. "I will take you home and dress your cuts and feed you khichari, and you will heal into a strong woman, with scars to be proud of."

Stephen C. Curro hails from Windsor, Colorado. His short fiction and poetry has appeared in *Swords and Sorcery Magazine*, *Scifaikuest*, and *Daily Science Fiction*, among other venues. He is also the author of the sci-fi novelette, *The Spark*, which is available through Hiraeth Publishing. In addition to speculative fiction and poetry, Stephen writes educational materials for the nonprofit Taproot Guru in the hopes that people will be inspired to protect nature. When he isn't writing, he works as a high school paraprofessional. When he isn't working, he enjoys scuba diving and plotting to trick his dad into watching *The Lord of the Rings*. You can keep up with his shenanigans at *stephenccurro.com*.

• • •

Science fiction often imagines what the future will be like. Common sci-fi tropes illustrate a generation's hopes and fears, but I think that the reverse is also true in that people begin to assume the future will turn out a certain way if they repeatedly see it in their books and movies. Over the last few years, there has been a significant uptick in stories that present a future in which the planet was devastated by human activity. Many of those stories are well-written and enjoyable, but it's concerning to see this at a time when the world is at a crossroads where we'll get our act together and fight environmental degradation, or risk ruining it all.

I started "The Faceless Enemy" as a fun sci-fi romp exploring space travel and ransomware, but it was heavily influenced by my frustration with 'doomsday talk'. I wanted to show a future where even though things aren't perfect, we managed to solve many of our problems on Earth and beyond. We need to start thinking with the attitude that we can and will make things better, because it's the first step to actually save the world. I have hope that we'll overcome the challenges ahead; indeed our collective heritage is filled with triumph over adversity.

THE FACELESS ENEMY

STEPHEN C. CURRO

I SAT DOWN AT MY STATION, completely unaware that my Tuesday morning was about to punch me in the face.

We were only three days from orbit around Starpoint, the financial hub of the Alpha Centauri System. After seven months tapping screens and filling out reports, I was giddy with anticipation. I was looking forward to spending my month of shore leave drift diving in Starpoint's warm jade seas. There is nothing like swimming in an ocean of water after traversing an ocean of nothingness.

So, on that unremarkable morning, between micro-daydreams of ocean currents carrying me over anemone fields, I checked the terminal and found that the ship was off course by a fiftieth of a degree. Thinking nothing of it, I entered the command for a course correction.

Instead of the beep and green light I was expecting, an animation of chains snaked over the screen. Shortly after a message screamed in red lettering:

NO ONE PILOTS THIS SHIP UNTIL YOU TRANSMIT $1,000,000,000,000. PAY IN TWO HOURS OR SUFFER THE CONSEQUENCES!!!

My first reaction was annoyance. Immediately I knew who to blame. "Rita! What the hell?"

Lieutenant Rita Vogel, communications officer and notorious prankster, moseyed across the bridge. "You break something again?"

Normally I would have appreciated the sarcasm, but right then it stung. I gestured to my terminal; my eyes narrowed in reproachful slits. "Really?"

Rita loomed over the terminal. Her expression bloomed from surprised to utterly amused. "Wow, Hazim. Who'd you piss off?"

"Seriously, get this garbage off my terminal."

Rita's brow furrowed in confusion. "You think I did this?"

"This has your name all over it."

"This isn't my handiwork."

"Says the girl who rigged my shower to dispense warm maple syrup." No one knew how to make a dull routine interesting like Rita did. Two weeks earlier I'd stumbled into the shower after a long night of studying for the EN-LIEU Exam. Instead of refreshing warm water, I was doused like a pancake. It's a wonder I'd managed to clean up and make it to my shift on time.

Rita stifled a chuckle. "Still sore about that? I recall you were laughing afterward."

I sighed, not bothering to hide my impatience. "Can you just fix this? I have course corrections to make."

Rita's joking aura dissipated. "Hazim, I'm telling you this wasn't me. You know I wouldn't screw with anything that would threaten the ship."

Doubt began to seep through me. That doubt curdled into a fear that bubbled inside me like a sour seltzer.

"If you didn't do it ... then we have more than maple syrup to worry about."

Rita shook her head as if she'd been given a riddle of absurd difficulty. "This is ridiculous. There haven't been any major ransomware attacks in half a century."

She was right. About fifty years earlier, the government had come out with plasmawalls, defensive software that made firewalls look like wet paper. They were supposed to be ironclad, but apparently some clever hacker had found a chink in our ship's cyber armor.

I gripped my temples as despair took root in my chest. "This is a disaster. The captain will crucify me."

"No, she won't," Rita chided.

I wasn't convinced. Captain Juma was incredibly picky with whom she recommended for promotion. In an effort to please her, I'd done my absolute best over the last two years to cultivate a spotless record: reporting early for each shift and volunteering for extra ones, never taking PTO, and studying obsessively for the EN-LIEU Exam. I could feel my hard work was about to be blown right out the airlock.

Rita nudged me, jarring me from my gloomy thoughts. "Call maintenance. I'll inform the captain." She walked off to the captain's office. Half-heartedly, I nodded and filed a maintenance request.

A few minutes later, I saw Rita go back to her station. She gave me a reassuring smile before looking over her terminal. A moment after that, Captain Esther Juma stepped onto the Bridge. Her frizzy hair was trimmed to the absolute edge of baldness, and her dark complexion made her blue eyes pop. She approached my station with her callused hands behind her back as if she were strolling through the park.

"Good morning, Ensign." There was a slight edge in her deep voice. "Lieutenant Vogel said we have a virus obstructing the helm?"

I snapped to attention. "Sir, it seems that a hacker is holding the navigation systems hostage. Maintenance should have this cleared up soon. Sir."

Juma nodded. Her expression seemed somewhere

between irritated and amused. "Asking for a trillion in two hours. They have a sense of humor, if nothing else. They must know that even if Corporate would pay them so much in such a ridiculous amount of time, the government would never allow them to set that precedent."

I could see her eyes assessing, calculating. Was she thinking about the situation as a whole? Or was she adding this to the list of reasons why I should stay an ensign for the rest of my career?

"Is there a threat to the ship?" she asked.

I gave a grim nod. "Possibly. We can't maneuver. If we come across a rogue asteroid or pirates, we'll be sitting ducks, and if this goes on for much longer ..."

I stopped as the full implications dawned on me. I scooped up my tablet and typed in a few calculations. When the results came up, I tried hard not to quiver in terror. "Oh God ... I think I know why they gave us two hours."

The captain's brow furrowed in concern. "Why?"

I took a deep breath. "We're scheduled to begin deceleration in two hours. If we can't slow down or maneuver ..."

I could feel the gazes of the others on the Bridge. Rita was watching from her station with a worried grimace. The captain's face had begun to stretch in trepidation. Undoubtedly, she was connecting the dots I had already strung together. Still, she wanted to hear it from me.

"Out with it!" she barked.

I stood up straight, trying to drain the fear from my voice. I was, after all, nearly a lieutenant. "If we don't get the nav systems back in two hours, we won't be able to maneuver sufficiently to achieve orbit around Starpoint. Instead ... we'll crash dead-on into the planet's equatorial region."

I presented the calculations to the captain. She stared at my tablet, bug-eyed. "We're travelling at Times 3.5." Her commanding voice sound oddly subdued. "If we hit the planet at three and a half times the speed of light ... it'll make the asteroid that ended the dinosaurs look like a cherry bomb."

Rita stood up from her seat. "How many people are on Starpoint?"

My throat felt dry as sandpaper. "Last I heard, about three billion."

A graveyard has more liveliness, more warmth, than the Bridge did in that moment. Seconds passed and the silence grew, seeping into every crack and crevice like an omnipresent frost.

Captain Juma's body hardened with focus as only a person with military experience can. "Lieutenant Vogel, get the Naval Command on the horn. Then get me Corporate. In the meantime, I want this virus eviscerated. Rebuild the main computer with paper clips and rubber bands if need be. And no one ..." I don't know why, but she pointed at me while she said this, "... *no one* breathes a word of this to anyone on the Transit Decks!" She withdrew to her office, and a deafening silence fell on the Bridge.

I stared at the screen as I waited for the tech specialist to arrive. My eyes ran the length of those sinister digital chains, and I tried to guess who had released this virus on us. Our enemy was as silent and faceless as space itself. They could be a woman or a man or non-binary. They could be a master coder or a college student. A terrorist, a military specialist, a disgruntled employee. A child prodigy, a corporate rival, or just some schmuck trying to see how far he could get.

No face. No voice. Nothing but a demand and a threat. "Attack" seemed like the wrong word to describe this. This wasn't an attack. An attack suggests the victim has a chance to fight back. How do you fight someone who won't even show their face as they rob you blind? My fingers curled over the edge of the terminal as I tried not to let my feelings of powerlessness and anger consume me.

We didn't know our enemy, but in that moment, I could have sworn I heard a voice cackling like some deranged witch. An image of someone in the shadows waving fingers to weave curses and hexes across the stars faded into view of my mind's eye.

• • •

Ten minutes later, Systems Specialist Maurice Whitmore stormed onto the bridge. He carried his hard plastic case of equipment and an expression that told everyone he was the smartest in the room.

"A virus?" he asked without looking at me. He set his case on the terminal and began to rummage through it.

"Ransomware," I replied. "They're asking for a trillion to get nav control back."

Whitmore scoffed. "Ransomware? Will I find the Loch Ness Monster in the computer as well?"

He motioned me back like I was covered in mud while he plugged his tablet into the terminal. After a glance his face wrinkled. "I'm impressed, Ensign Musa. You have encountered the digital equivalent of a living fossil. Did you open any unusual messages on your terminal lately?"

"I haven't opened anything."

"Of course, you haven't."

I rolled my eyes. "Can you clear this up?"

Whitmore's glare could melt lead. "*I* will clear this up in a few minutes. Still, it's a few minutes off my schedule I could be using for more important things than babysitting the Navigation Department."

I am not a violent man, but I admit that whenever Lieutenant Whitmore opened his mouth, I felt the urge to slug him. I could have taken him too, he was a spindly arachnid of a man, pale as flour, frail as glass. But I acted as a good ensign should and stayed out of the way while he moved his digital weaponry into position. His fingers were scuttling so quickly over his tablet I wondered if he was even touching it.

A few minutes later, Whitmore smirked. "And to this virus, *au-re-vouir!*" On the '*vouir*, he flicked the final command on his tablet.

My terminal flashed red. The chains across the screen thickened, and a message headed by skull and crossbones read:

SHIP-WIDE ACCESS TO NON-CRITICAL SYSTEMS HAS BEEN TERMINATED. EVERY ATTEMPT AT THWARTATION WILL RESULT IN ANOTHER LOCKED SYSTEM. YOU HAVE NINETY MINUTES. STOP WASTING YOUR TIME!!!

I imagined the hacker hiding in some basement, wringing bony hands with glee, sniggering at our attempts to subvert this master plan. Were they watching us like rats in a maze? Was this not just a cash grab but a form of cheap entertainment, too?

Whitmore's face faded into a shade of paleness I hadn't known existed. "What in the fresh hell is this?"

He rechecked the data on his tablet as if he were learning how to read a new language. As serious as the matter was, I admit it was satisfying to see him stymied.

Almost immediately afterward, cries of surprise and frustration rang out across the Bridge. It seemed the hacker was making good on their promise to lock out the computer. Rita was typing with furious fingers as the computer denied her access again and again.

Whitmore's eyes snarled at me. "What have you done?"

Now I didn't bother trying not to bristle. "I didn't do anything! I tried to make a course correction. That's all."

The door to the captain's office swung open. Captain Juma strode across the Bridge in four huge steps, her eyes bulging in outrage.

"What the devil is happening to my ship?"

Whitmore snapped to attention. "Sir, the virus outmaneuvered my anti-viral programs and hijacked the computer ship-wide."

Juma bared her teeth. I'd never seen her so angry. "I wanted this handled quietly. We have two thousand passengers in the decks below us. I do not enjoy the prospects of having a riot aboard an enclosed starship in deep space!"

I raised a nervous hand. "Sir? Every critical system has backup data stored in special modules. I can use one to purge the virus from the navigation system. It might not free the whole computer, but at least we could maneuver."

Whitmore's jaw dropped. "You are out of line, *Ensign*. I will make the technical recommendations on this ship!"

I restrained my urge to bite Whitmore's head off. Still, I wasn't going to let him beat me down in front of the captain. Through a stony demeanor I replied, "With respect, *sir*, I was merely volunteering my expertise."

Whitmore opened his mouth, no doubt to fire off another condescending comment, but Juma spoke first.

"Good thinking, Ensign. We'll attack this on two fronts. Report to Nav Control on the double. In the meantime, Lieutenant, keep trying to uproot the virus from the computer."

• • •

Fifteen minutes later, I was in the narrow hallway that is Navigation Control. It's a space riddled with wires and blinking boxes, like a six-year-old was put in charge of decorating with Christmas lights. I don't care much for tight spaces — haven't since my brother locked me in a closet when I was eight. Even so, it's amazing what doesn't bother you when your life is on the line.

The backup modules are ensconced in a secure box buried under layers of hardware. They built it that way in case of a virus or an EMP surge so the modules can't be corrupted. Effective, but a pain to access. I had to wedge myself into a nook under the main terminal and undo half a dozen safeguard locks. All the while I cursed whoever had designed the damn system. I figured if the hacker wasn't laughing at me, my brother certainly would be.

After a few minutes and one stubbed finger, I cracked open the module housing. I plucked out a data module and inspected it in the dim light. It looked like a black rock smoothed by the rush of a river. It was strange to think that the lives of billions depended on something as small as this.

I clambered out from under the console and checked the screen to make sure nothing else had happened to the Nav systems. The screen read: Modules Accessed.

I grinned. I could already hear the ocean waves of Starpoint. I went to the nearest comm unit on the wall. "Ensign Musa to the Bridge."

I got only static. I cycled through the different channels with no effect.

The terminal beeped rapidly. I glanced at the screen and saw animated chains strangling the Modules Accessed message. New words appeared:

"YOUR RESISTANCE WILL KILL STARPOINT. BUT FIRST, IT WILL KILL YOU!!!"

Yellow lights flashed up and down the hall as a klaxon screamed. My blood ran cold. That was the dreaded decompression alarm.

Blast doors on either end of the hall slammed shut. I could hear the unmistakable *hiss* of air being siphoned through vents in the walls. On top of that, I swear I heard the compartment echoing with the booming, melodramatic howl of a supervillain. *Alas, you've fallen into my trap!*

I had a few minutes, maybe less. I scrambled down the hall to the emergency box. Every deck has a stash of pressure suits, not as durable as standard EVA gear, but good enough in a pinch. As I tore the pack open and pulled the magenta suit on, I felt short of breath. Pangs of dizziness stabbed my brain. My fingers fumbled. It became harder to keep my panic contained in my gut.

At last, I pulled the mask over my face and slapped the pressurization button. The suit morphed and inflated, calibrating to my body mass. I took a deep breath of sweet air and collapsed to the floor.

After a few relieved breaths, I pulled myself up and recovered the module. Mercifully it was undamaged. I zipped it into my suit and pondered my next move. With the atmosphere removed, I could no longer hear the scream of the klaxon, only my heavy breathing washing through my suit.

Whomever was behind this had anticipated that someone would try to side-step their plan through Nav Control. I snarled in frustration. I hate it when I can't solve a puzzle, especially when it's a puzzle that could kill me. Was the hacker amused that I had almost died? *Oh, look at the little officer scurrying about the compartment. I wonder what he'll try next?*

I looked over the nearest blast door. It wouldn't take much to manually override it, but I had no access to the environmental controls. Forcing the door open would kill everyone on the deck. I tried to use the comm unit again, but it proved as useful as a twisted slinky. Apparently, communication was the next system to be compromised. A bitter chuckle escaped my throat as I imagined Rita raging at her now disabled terminal.

Like a caged animal, I paced the grated floors. I knew eventually someone would try to repressurize the compartment, but with the virus running rampant who knew when that would be? I was on my own. There were only two ways in and out of Nav Control: through one of the doors, which were blast-shielded, or through one of the crawlspaces, which were also blast-shielded. If only I could get out ...

I stopped as I spotted a port hole. I realized I was wrong. Technically there were *three* ways out. The third was as uninviting as a nest of crocodiles: a waste disposal duct.

A duct that led to open space.

Come now, the hacker purred, *you're not that crazy.*

Mentally I reviewed the layout of the ship. I wasn't too far from the port airlock. In theory, I could perform an EVA and scale the hull of the ship. It would be just like climbing out the window of a locked room to get to the front door, except the way to the front door was airless and beyond freezing.

I wasn't keen on this. My suit was an emergency model, not the kind astronauts use for proper EVAs. One nick and I'd be a frozen, exploded mess. And then there was the fact that if I missed a jump, I wouldn't just tumble into a void, I'd pass through the Fabric Shell, the barrier of energy that distorted space to keep relativity from slowing the ship down in relation to the rest of the universe. After a brush with the Fabric Shell, my molecules would resemble something like chopped spaghetti …

But so, what? If I didn't make the attempt, I might suffocate in Nav Control anyway, and I was no use to the ship dead. Rita was my best friend. Juma, strict as she was, was a stalwart mentor. Even the thought of Whitmore dying made me feel guilty …

And then there were the two thousand in passengers in the decks below. Officers weren't generally allowed on the Transit Decks, but I had assisted in boarding passengers seven months ago. Most of them were families, people trying to give their kids a new life on Starpoint. Just because I hadn't met them didn't mean that they didn't exist, or that they didn't deserve the new life they were searching for.

Had Juma managed to maintain the radio silence between decks? Or was the virus sowing terror among the passengers? Were there children asking their mothers if they were about to die? Were those mothers telling their children it was going to be okay when they had no idea themselves?

A flash of genuine hatred for that hacker coursed through me. I crawled into the duct and clipped my tether to an inner rung. I whispered a vehement prayer, and then hit the disposal button. I pulled my arm in as the door hissed shut.

There wasn't time to brace myself. A heartbeat later, I was fired into space like a cannonball.

• • •

The ship was falling away from me. I was terrified that I wouldn't stop, that the tether would snap, or the rung would give, and I'd spin through the void for a billion years.

The tether went taut. I was yanked back like a doll in a dog's mouth. I never thought I'd be thrilled to be violently jostled.

Centimeter by centimeter, I drew myself back to the outer edge of the ship. I gripped the rung like a monkey on a tree and breathed. I imagined the hacker would be mildly surprised by my success.

Hmm, that was unexpected. But you're still a baby ensign. You won't get very far.

I looked to the expanse of space. I had seen the stars through windows, but it's something else to see the universe whirling by with nothing but a pressure suit between you and the vacuum. The Fabric Shell shimmered in the distance, as if someone was tossing rocks into a celestial lake and making cosmic ripples. The sight took my breath right out of my lungs. Those old-fashioned TV shows with starships flying at warp speed just don't do FTL travel justice.

I forced myself to focus. I scanned the hull for my path to the airlock. Moving about on an EVA requires the ultimate form of "one step at a time". I unhitched my clip and floated toward the next rung. With a *snap*, I was secure. One down, twenty to go.

It was strange, even after working in space for over four years, to float on the outer hull while the ship flew at three and a half times light, and yet I didn't feel a thing. Thank God for no friction in space because each jump from rung-to-rung had to be executed with the right timing and force. Every time I undid the clip, my heart seized. Every time I kicked off to the next rung, I had to hold my breath to keep from hyperventilating. I could practically hear the hacker taunting me every millimeter of the way.

Don't slip. Don't slip! It would be a shame if you overshot that next rung.

I resisted looking at my air gauge — a deliberate breach of protocol, but I was strung tight enough with the fates of three billion people over my head. Obsessing over it would only pull me tighter, and, if I snapped, what then? I settled on the reality that I would make it, or I wouldn't. I thought only of timing my jumps.

I nearly broke into tears when I reached the port airlock. I entered the code and the airlock doors opened like steel jaws, snapping shut after I went inside. I knelt in the airlock and crouched in worshipful gratitude as I waited for the air to cycle.

Green became my favorite color that day, because the green lights in the airlock signaled that the room was pressurized. I tore the mask off and took a deep breath. God, who knew recycled air could taste so sweet? I rushed into the hall, and I almost squealed in joy when I nearly tripped. Heaven as my witness, I'll never complain about artificial gravity again!

I settled into the elevator and dialed for the Bridge. As I flew toward my destination, I slumped into the corner and whispered to the hacker, "Screw you."

I pictured the hacker's putrid face staring in shock, tawny eyes bulging, thin lips pursed in outrage.

• • •

By the time I had the module installed, we had only eight minutes left. I shut down the nav terminal and rebooted it with the fresh data.

Captain Juma hovered over me like an impatient cloud. "Well?" she urged. *"Well?"*

I scrolled through the terminal. It seemed normal. At least the chains were gone.

I invited Lieutenant Whitmore to run a diagnostic. Thirty unsettling seconds later, he grinned. It's the first time I'd ever see him smile.

"We have the helm back!"

Cheers flooded the Bridge. Rita danced across the room in triumph. Captain Juma slumped in her chair and let loose a groan.

I couldn't celebrate yet. I leapt into my seat and tapped frantically at the controls. We'd been going off course by a fiftieth of a degree for nearly two hours, a considerable distance to correct when you're flying between star systems.

After the confirmation popped up, I verified three times before I was certain. I turned to the captain and my words forced their way out in a shout, "Sir, we're back on course for Starpoint orbit!"

There was another round of cheers, louder, happier. I imagined that hacker rotting in his hole, quivering in unbridled rage, cursing me and the whole crew. *No! NO! Impossible!*

"Well done, Ensign!" Juma cried.

I swooned like kelp underwater. I gushed with relief, proud of my work yet abashed by the captain's strong praise.

Now that the nightmare was over, I wanted to make sure it would *stay* over. The only thing worse than a problem is a problem that rises from the dead to haunt you.

I checked the time, then raised my hand. "Sir? Permission to commence deceleration four minutes early?"

Juma nodded like she had been thinking the same thing. "By all means!" She turned to Whitmore and thundered, "Lieutenant! Have work crews retrieve the modules for the other systems. Give that virus no safe harbor."

As Whitmore rushed off, Juma approached me and clamped her hand onto my shoulder. "You just saved three billion people. *Lieutenant.*"

My face stretched in shock. "Wha—but sir! The-the EN-LIEU Exam …"

Her raised eyebrow silenced me. "What about it? You just demonstrated innovation and initiative more clearly than any exam could. Consider your papers signed, Lieutenant. We'll get you your badge when we reach Starpoint." She winked, and then turned to address the Bridge, "We are throwing a party in the Mess Hall tonight. I command you all to attend so I can buy the first round!"

There was another chorus of hearty cheers.

Rita drifted to my station; a smile plastered on her face. "It's official, Hazim. You're crazier than me." She smiled as my eyes widened questioningly. "What? You should call the *Guinness Book of Galactic Records*. I bet you're the first to claim an EVA at Times 3.5."

I hadn't really cared about silly titles like that, but when she said aloud, the weight of my accomplishment dawned on me. If I never made it past Lieutenant, and I was only remembered for my Evil Knievel stunt at Times 3.5, I could live with that. But then again, I hadn't done it for fame. I'd done it to save a planet, not to mention my own neck.

"Do you think they'll catch that guy?" I asked.

Rita snapped her fingers, her eyes lighting up. "Get this. While you were away, Whitmore said the hacker was bouncing the signal between three long-range privately-owned satellites in the Earth System. That's too sophisticated to be just some guy in a basement; we're looking at terrorists. Probably one of those anti-colonization groups." She shrugged. "We'll learn more once we relay this all to the military."

I felt my chest grow heavy. For decades, a loud minority in the Earth System had opposed colonizing outside the solar system. Some feared outer space for the economic cost, or for religious reasons, or because space is the epitome of the unknown. I'd always thought these guys were harmless; the idea of them trying to destroy a whole colony to prove their point made me sick. The worst part was that they'd nearly succeeded, hacked our ship, and flung it toward Starpoint as easily as one throws a baseball.

"There are dozens of those groups." My voice was hoarse, my throat suddenly feeling raw. "Someone could try this again."

Rita waved her hand dismissively and retorted, "We had a close call today, but people like that can't wreak havoc forever. Corporate and the military won't put up with it. Hell, *everyday people* won't put up with it."

I considered her answer, and I realized she was right. Every major calamity in history had resulted in good people coming together. The Allies of World War Two defeated Hitler. The United Nations had enacted a series of policies that almost totally reversed human-driven climate change. Wherever conflict existed, someone was always there to resolve it. It just so happened that it was my turn to bring a little order to the universe.

I turned my attention back to the terminal, dialed in the last few calculations and activated the deceleration process. The distant roar of the forward rockets grumbled through the ship. It was a simple action, it felt as exciting to me as those scenes in superhero films where the villain is finally vanquished. I could feel the poisonous gaze of the hacker receding, that raspy voice fading away into the void behind us.

Nooo!

Henry Herz's speculative fiction short stories include "Out, Damned Virus" (*Daily Science Fiction*), "Bar Mitzvah on Planet Latke" (*Coming of Age*, Albert Whitman & Co.), "The Magic Backpack" (Metastellar), "Unbreakable" (*Musing of the Muses*, Brigid's Gate Press), "A Vampire, an Astrophysicist, and a Mother Superior Walk Into a Basilica" (*Three Time Travelers Walk Into ...*, Fantastic Books), "The Case of the Murderous Alien" (Spirit Machine, Air and Nothingness Press), "The Ghosts of Enerhodar" (*Literally Dead*, Alienhead Press), "Maria & Maslow" (*Highlights for Children*), and "A Proper Party" (*Ladybug Magazine*). He's written twelve picture books, including the critically acclaimed *I Am Smoke*.

• • •

"The Repairwoman" is a noir/sci-fi mashup of "Ali Baba & the Forty Thieves" and "The Sorcerer's Apprentice". That tells you all you need to know about how odd my brain is.

THE REPAIRWOMAN

HENRY HERZ

PRIVATE INVESTIGATOR PHILIPPA SPADE leaned back in her faded simu-leather chair. It squeaked whenever she shifted. Her office had the musty smell of years of neglect.

Across the scuffed, small desk sat a short man, his face flushed with frustration. "Listen, Philippa. I'm tired of waiting. I gave you a fat advance and you have no results to show for it."

So far, Philippa's case file was as empty as a scarecrow's pockets ... just like her bank account, the advance already used to pay off debtors. "As I've told you, Joel, PI work is as much art as science. I've talked to four leads and had a micro-drone trail the subject's skimmer-car for a week, but so far, no luck."

Joel frowned. "You always have a very smooth explanation ready."

"What do you want me to do, learn to stutter?" replied Philippa, raising an eyebrow.

"By God, you're a character," said Joel, lurching to his feet. "There's never any telling what you'll say or do next, except that it's bound to be something astonishing. I want results within a week or my money back. Do you think I'm an idiot?" He stormed out of the PI's office.

Philippa sighed. "I'd never say that, even if I thought so." *I need to find another paying client, and quick.*

• • •

As yellow Rigel Kentaurus trailed orange Toliman in the morning sky, Allie awoke and kissed her sleeping wife, Morgiana. Out of long habit, she checked the various medical devices monitoring Morgiana. All readings were within nominal range ... today.

She sighed. Allie loved her wife dearly, but Morgiana's disease took a toll on both of them. The medical equipment filled most of their small bedroom, just as medical bills ate up most of what Allie earned as a heating and air conditioning repairman. The cost of an operation to remove the tumors was beyond their reach — equal to years of her modest salary. So they did the best they could under trying circumstances.

Allie dressed in blue coveralls and work boots, ate a quick breakfast of bland oatmeal, and took a public transportation drone to Proxima Centauri HVAC Repair. She uploaded the day's job list to her company tablet, checked out a company skimmer-truck, and drove it through light traffic to her first service call at a luxury residential triplex. Allie gazed awestruck at the upscale neighborhood.

Must be nice to live in such a nice building, she thought. *It's probably not noisy at night and I bet the trash always gets picked up.*

Allie unlocked the steel "manhole" cover on the sidewalk and set up her "Caution: Workers" sign over the opening. *It's a wonder someone with their nose in their communicator hasn't fallen into one of these.*

Allie climbed three meters down a ladder bolted to the wall. She crawled through the narrow underground access tunnel to the central environmental systems control unit, plugging in her diagnostic tool.

As was often the case, the problem reported by a homeowner proved difficult to reproduce. Allie sighed and kept at it, perseverance being one of her strong suits. A bead of sweat dripped down her forehead. Unplanned by her, the diagnostic tool captured and displayed the residence front door passcode when its occupants returned home.

Sesame? That's an odd passcode.

She wouldn't have given it a further thought and her life would have taken a different trajectory were it not for the favorable acoustics and her natural curiosity.

"Well, that was a pain in the butt. What was the haul?" asked one resident, his deep voice surprisingly audible after echoing through the air ducts.

Another responded, "It was a good score. We snagged seven kilograms of rhodium."

Allie's eyes widened, the repair job forgotten. The spot price of rhodium exceeded that of gold.

"Ha," replied the first voice. "I told you that was worth the cost and trouble of bribing that security guard. But, we can't employ him again for a while. If we blow his cover, he becomes useless to us. Put the bars with the others and let's go out for a celebratory breakfast. Then we have a new target I want to scout this morning."

After a few minutes, the residents departed noisily, unknowingly leaving an honest HVAC repairwoman lying in both an underground tunnel and in a moral quandary.

What should I do? I'm no thief. But is stealing from robbers truly theft? We desperately need money. If I'm ever sick for a week, I won't be able to pay for Morgiana's ongoing medical treatments. And I don't know what I'd do without her.

Necessity in this case being the mother of peculation, Allie made up her mind. She crawled out of the access tunnel, and locked up the manhole cover. Her mouth a tight line, she brushed the grime off her overalls. She pretended to inspect the outside of her skimmer truck while actually glancing around for pedestrians. Seeing none, she hurried to the front door and punched in the access code.

Allie hurried inside. Before she could find the button to close the entrance, the thick armored door slid silently shut behind her. She stood stunned for a moment by the opulence of the interior. Handwoven oriental rugs covered the floors.

How much did it cost to import those from Earth?

A real oaken table lined the wall of the entry, nothing like the synthetic wood junk she owned. An elaborate crystal light fixture hung from the dining room ceiling. Although she was no art expert, Allie suspected the beautiful oil paintings mounted on the walls were expensive originals.

Rushing through the home searching for the rhodium, she pulled up short at the den. A fortune in half-kilogram bars of rhodium, gold, and iridium lay scattered on the floor like a plundering dragon's hoard.

If I grab all I can carry, the thieves will surely notice when they return. I don't want them hunting for me. Maybe just ten bars? Although she might not consider it so at that moment in an illegally entered residence, prudence was another of Allie's virtues. Her shoulders dropped. No, not ten. She took a single shining bar of each precious metal. *At least this will cover Morgiana's medicine for a year,* she thought, gripping the small bars tightly in one hand. Snapping out of her reverie and remembering she had a full work schedule for the day, she departed for her other repair calls.

Allie can perhaps be forgiven for her low productivity during the rest of the day given the distraction of treasure clinking in her trousers.

I'll stop at a bank on my way home this evening to make a deposit. The sooner my account is credited, the sooner I can pay our delinquent prescription bills. And I'll surprise Morgiana with a nice dinner for a change.

• • •

Allie clocked out at the end of her seemingly interminable work day. As she bent to tie a loose shoelace, an iridium bar slipped out of her pants pocket and clattered to the ground.

All would have been well except for the fact that a nosy co-worker, Cas Siem, stood nearby. The bar's shiny surface was a siren's call to him. He marched over, demanding an explanation.

"It's not your concern," replied Allie, whose honesty made her a poor liar.

Cas, however, was an excellent liar from years of practice. He easily read the guilt on Allie's face. He gave his co-worker a grim smile and a threat. "Listen carefully, Allie. Either you tell me where you got that, or I'll report you to our supervisor. Then you won't get to keep it."

I don't want Cas messing with criminals, thought Allie. *But I also don't want him telling the boss. I need the money for Morgiana.* Allie bowed her head, defeated. "I found them at a job site."

Cas's eyes narrowed with avarice. "Them? So there's more bars? It is necessary that you should tell me exactly where they lie, that I may, if need be, test the truth of your story, otherwise I shall find it my duty to denounce you to the authorities," he pompously blackmailed.

Allie's shoulders drooped. Not wanting to risk loss of her windfall, she complied. Swallowing hard, she shared the address and the access code. But being goodhearted, Allie added a warning. "These men are thieves and likely dangerous. Breaking into their home would be very risky, Cas."

Cas dismissed Allie's genuine concern with a wave of his hand and climbed into a company skimmer-truck.

Allie shook her head as Cas drove off. Fool. She turned and walked two blocks to the hover-bus stop.

• • •

Cas drove directly to the thieves' residence. *If there's as much treasure as I hope, I'm going to need help getting it into the truck.* He activated a dinged-up bipedal swarm robot mounted on the back of his company truck.

Cas strode to the front door, accompanied by the robot, and rang the doorbell.

If someone's home, I'll just say I got the wrong address, thought the practiced prevaricator.

After waiting a minute with no response, he punched in the access code and the two entered the robbers' lair.

At the sight of the glittering hoard, the wide-eyed Cas ordered the robot to transport the bars into the back of his skimmer-truck. No need for me to work up a sweat. He left the apartment and sat in the truck while the tireless but sluggish old robot made repeated trips.

• • •

Belatedly recognizing that his risk increased the longer he stayed, and noting the considerable fortune already loaded in the back of the skimmer-truck, Cas ordered the robot to stop. But the outmoded robot malfunctioned — it gave no heed to the increasingly emphatic commands. His hands sweating, Cas grabbed a heavy wrench and struck a mighty blow, shattering the robot.

As Cas turned to leave, the autonomous robot swarm elements assessed their damage and, following their self-repair protocols, reformed into two half-sized robots. They resumed fulfilling Cas's initial command.

I've got to leave now! His face ashen with anxiety, Cas swung the wrench anew.

Again, the damaged robot reformed into two smaller versions. Now there were three, all indefatigably intent on transferring treasure from the residence to the truck.

A grey skimmer-car pulled up as Cas chased the recalcitrant robots into the apartment. Four grim-faced men shared a quick look, got out of their car, and silently entered their residence.

One thief drew his plasma pistol and trained it on Cas, who collapsed in a quivering heap on the floor, begging for mercy.

Another thief slagged each robot with a pistol pulse.

The first thief kept his weapon trained on Cas, while the others used an anti-grav dolly to hurriedly retake possession of their twice-stolen loot. Then they turned their full attention to the intruder.

After taking several brutal punches to the face, Cas, who was neither brave nor loyal, told the men all he knew.

The thieves huddled in conversation. Three of them escorted the robotic wreckage and Cas back to his skimmer-truck, while the fourth got into their skimmer-car. They drove both vehicles to a deserted alley in a bad section of town whereupon the leader drew his pistol and melted a clean 50mm-wide hole through Cas's head. Shifting the lifeless Cas to the driver's seat, the thieves set the skimmer-truck on fire. They drove off, having exacted their vengeance and disposed of the evidence without feeling a shred of recrimination.

• • •

Philippa Spade's file notes on Cas Siem case:

Client Leah Siem reports husband Cas missing overnight. Client overwrought because absence out of character for subject. Client also has no confidence in the police to act swiftly, given the relatively short timeframe and how thin the department is stretched. Subject works at Proxima Centauri HVAC Repair. List of co-workers below. None had anything helpful to offer, although one, Allie Babha, sounded nervous. Might be worth tailing her, since no other leads.

• • •

Allie hung up from her evening call with the private investigator hired by Leah. She couldn't finish dinner, her stomach in knots at concern for Cas's safety and not sharing what she knew, lest the PI uncover her theft.

Damn. I warned Cas. He may be a jerk, but I should still go look for him. No one else has a clue where he went.

She explained the situation after Morgiana finished eating.

Allie took public transportation to the thieves' neighborhood, disembarking a block away from their lair. She walked to the residence and crawled into the access tunnel to eavesdrop.

"Not a bad week," said the leader after a while. "We scored some gold today, and yesterday, we made sure that guy will never steal from us again."

Poor Cas, thought Allie. *And poor Leah.*

"Time for a drink," the leader continued. "What's in the green bottle?"

"Aldebaran whisky. What do you think we should do about this Allie chick?"

Allie's throat tightened. *Cas must have told them. Damn.*

"Oh, she needs to join her dead friend. It never pays to have loose ends. But that can wait until tomorrow. Pass the whisky."

They mean to murder me. What can I do? In her condition, I can't take Morgiana and leave town. Without a job, I won't be able to pay for her medical treatment. But these killers will surely find me if I stay.

She lay paralyzed by fear and indecision.

Allie's eyes fell on the environmental systems controls glowing right under her nose in the cramped space. A gasp escaped her mouth when a dark thought arose like the eyes of a ravenous crocodile broaching the surface of a swamp. She could not immediately muster the resolve to implement it.

The thieves, meanwhile, made quick work of the Aldebaran whisky, growing louder and more raucous.

After twenty tormented minutes of speculation and recrimination, Allie realized she had no choice.

If I don't do this, they'll kill me and Morgiana, too.

She sighed and adjusted the ventilation subsystem, overriding the safety settings.

The inebriated thieves had no way of knowing that the air pumping into their unit now contained odorless nitrogen rather than oxygen. Allie waited an hour as they gradually lost consciousness and asphyxiated painlessly.

God forgive me.

• • •

Philippa waited near the manhole, tapping a foot. Her eyes took in the posh environs. Seems like a nice neighborhood to have bad habits in.

A perspiring, shaken Allie emerged from the manhole.

"Kinda late for system maintenance, isn't it?" asked Philippa, arms folded across her chest.

Allie blinked at the unexpected encounter. "Emergency service call," she managed, her heart pounding. "Not that it's any of your business."

Philippa shrugged. "I don't mind if you don't like my manners. They're pretty bad. I grieve over them during the long winter evenings." *She looks as guilty as if she'd kicked her grandmother.* "But, it kinda is my business, Allie."

The repairwoman stiffened. "How do you know my name?"

Philippa grinned. "Because Leah Siem hired me to find her husband, Cas. Know anything about that?"

"You again?" Allie turned to head for a hover-bus stop. "I already told you, I don't know anything," she called over her shoulder.

"Really? In my experience, everyone has something to conceal. Let's chat."

When Allie said nothing and kept walking, Philippa sprang the trap.

"Unless you'd rather I ask the authorities to investigate this utility tunnel."

Allie halted in mid-stride, her shoulders sagging. Her resolve crumbled under the weight of guilt and concern for her wife. "I've tried to live a good life. But I've been bad, worse than you could know."

Philippa nodded. *Ah, now we're getting somewhere.* "That's good, because if you actually were as innocent as you pretend to be, we'd never get anywhere. Let me buy you a cup of coffee."

Philippa led Allie to a nearly empty all-night diner. They sat across from each other in a corner booth.

"What can you tell me about Cas?"

Allie took a shaky breath. "How do I know I can trust you?"

Grabbing a menu and pretending to read it, Philippa replied, "Look. I'm up to my eyeballs in debt. Leah Siem will pay me a fat bonus if I can find her husband. And the way I see things, you don't have to trust me as long as you can persuade me to trust you. Otherwise you'll be answering the police's questions in detention."

Who'll take care of Morgiana if I'm locked up? thought Allie.

"I overheard a gang of thieves say they killed Cas." Tears streamed down her cheeks. "Please just leave me alone. I have a sick wife at home."

Philippa tilted her chin. "You're good. Chiefly your eyes, I think, and that throb you get in your voice when you mention your wife. Now, tell me everything."

After Allie spilled her guts, Philippa leaned back, eyes wide.

"Why, I'll be a monkey's uncle."

Precious metals are the stuff that dreams are made of.

• • •

As it turned out, Philippa's sense of self-aggrandizement balanced nicely with Allie's sense of self-preservation.

The pair returned the next day. Allie cleared the nitrogen from the apartment. With the help of a robot, she took possession of half the precious metals and transported them to her home. Philippa took the other half to "resolve" the case to both their satisfaction.

Using her newfound fortune with equity and moderation, Allie and Morgiana lived happily ever after.

Jetse de Vries is a technical specialist for a propulsion company by day, and a science fiction reader, editor, and writer by night. He's also an avid bicyclist, total solar eclipse chaser, single malt aficionado, Mexican food lover, metalhead and intelligent optimist. On March 28, 2021, he posted the world's first NFT SF novel on Ethereum's Mintable.

• • •

One of the strongest clichés in science fiction is that intelligent robots or Artificial Intelligences will either destroy or subvert humanity once they are 'superior'. I disagree, as I would argue that they are — in that case — only 'superior' in deviousness, not in intelligence. I believe that truly superior intelligence goes hand in hand with superior ethics. As such, a truly superior machine intelligence—one created by biological predecessors — would not destroy the species that arose before it (and created it), but rather support them. And other species that have not yet reached its intelligence level. Now how far would support go, I wondered. "Machine Intelligences Don't Care about the Fermi Paradox" tries to explore exactly that. And, of course, it's not a Star Trek homage at all ...

MACHINE INTELLIGENCES DON'T CARE ABOUT THE FERMI PARADOX

JETSE DE VRIES

1. SIREN SONG

THE MOMENT *NEW HORIZONS* crossed the heliosphere, its fine-tuned spectrometers detected a signal in the GeV band of the unfiltered cosmic rays. Once deciphered, it amounted to "an invitation of all sentient beings, no matter their origin" to join "one of our transportation units to the closest local nexus". The signal came from a point between Epsilon Eridani and Tau Ceti, at about eleven light years, an area with no visible stars.

2. INTERSTELLAR OVERDRIVE

Several decades later, humanity's first manned interstellar vessel — the EUSC *Esprit d'Humanité* — confirms the signal after it enters interstellar space on its way to the ET signal's source. In charge: Captain Sibidé and Chief Engineer O'Hara.

Captain Adève Sibidé, tall, lithe and young, her ebony skin glistening, accentuating her high cheekbones. The green-and-white-blocked outfit she's wearing looks more like *haute couture* than an official uniform, even though it's both.

In stark contrast, Chief Engineer Maureen O'Hara is even younger and short, stocky, red-haired with freckles on her slightly upturned nose and full cheeks. The blue-and-yellow one-piece she's wearing looks more like a boiler suit than an official uniform, even though it's both.

They have a great rapport: the Captain, an intuitive explorer with an insatiable curiosity, willing to go anywhere; the Chief Engineer, a razor-sharp scientist and technician with the rationality to talk the Captain out of too crazy endeavors, and the skills to get them out of a tight spot.

3. MATRIOSHKA CONVERTER

As the *Esprit d'Humanité* approaches the ET signal's origin, Captain Sibidé and Chief Engineer O'Hara become increasingly baffled. The signal's source reads very clear, yet their instruments cannot discern anything nearby it. Even a brown dwarf would have been emitting some infrared radiation.

"We're heading straight into nowhere," Chief Engineer O'Hara says. "Maybe it *is* a wild goose chase."

"It's not what you're looking for," Captain Sibidé says, smiling enigmatically, "but what you're *not* looking for."

"What do you mean?" O'Hara says. "There's nothing there …" Then she sees it. "Where's 82 Eridani?"

"Indeed," Sibidé says, "something's blocking its view."

"But at this distance," O'Hara says, "that object must be immense."

"A radius of about ten AU, approximately," Sibidé says, "according to my best estimates."

"A dust cloud would not be so opaque," O'Hara says. "It must be a Matrioshka Brain."

"Not a Dyson Sphere?"

"A single Dyson Sphere would be warmer than the cosmic background radiation, and emit an infrared heat signature," O'Hara says, "only fractal, overlapping layers — like a Matrioshka Brain — could truly absorb every erg of a sun's output."

As they come closer, more stars disappear from view, and Captain Sibidé's estimate is in the ballpark. They maneuver the *Esprit d'Humanité* around the colossal black sphere, measuring it with the vessel's lidars, as they begin to encounter its gravitational field of about two solar masses. There are six minor bulges — small like dust specks — on it, exactly equidistanced, all of which are sending the same signal — ET's siren song that lured them here.

They try to make contact, and the nearest protuberance aims a communication laser at them, repeating the message they already know. As they try to figure out what to do, an alarm sounds from the navigation console.

"A new star, just barely visible, right next to Epsilon Eridani," Captain Sibidé says.

The new star is mostly gamma radiation. It has a blue shift and is approaching their position at almost the speed of light.

"About 97% of lightspeed," Chief Engineer O'Hara says, "and decelerating. If this isn't an approaching alien starship, braking by burning antimatter, then I'll eat my hat."

"You don't have a hat." Captain Sibidé ruffles a loving hand through Chief Engineer's O'Hara's red curls.

"A metaphorical one tastes even worse," O'Hara says, flushing slightly.

4. GAS STATION

As the alien starship approaches (which will take a few months), the only thing the *Esprit d'Humanité* can do is check out one of the protruding bulges of the Matrioshka Brain. While minuscule on the giant black sphere, the protuberance makes their own spacecraft look tiny.

"A rectangle of six by two kilometers rising up from the globular surface," Captain Sibidé says. "Which screams 'runway' to me."

"Or at least 'docking station'," O'Hara agrees.

On approach, at about one hundred kilometers, the generic message from the docking station's communication laser changes:

— *dear alien friends, the next interstellar transporter will arrive in about 2×10^{50} Planck Times* — the new message goes — *don't stay close to this docking station until it has safely landed, as the gamma rays from its drive can be quite lethal indeed* —

"That's about four months," Captain Sibidé says. "We could park ourselves in orbit and get back to cryogenic suspension."

"That sounds so strange," Chief Engineer O'Hara says. "We're orbiting the biggest artificial construct ever witnessed by humankind, and then we just go to sleep?"

"It's not exactly forthcoming with its secrets," Sibidé says, "pitch black and impenetrable."

"We could try to nuke our way in," O'Hara says, overemphasizing her snarky tone.

"You sound like the mosquito who wants to sting a human just for the hell of it," Sibidé says. "I'd rather avoid the slapping hand of god."

"But there must be other ways to observe," O'Hara says, "ways that don't invite retaliation."

"Feel free to try those, with all due care," Sibidé says. "I'm going to take my beauty sleep. We have no clue as to how long this journey of discovery will last, and I do want to find out what it's about before I die of old age."

"Well, I'm six months younger than you," O'Hara says, "so I'll take my chances staying awake and probing, ever so subtly."

5. BIG TRAIN

Four months later, Captain Sibidé — and the rest of the crew — are awakened as the alien craft approaches. It's basically a huge cylinder, ten times as long as it's wide, and otherwise as pitch black as the Matrioshka Structure it's arriving at.

"Wow, this mother is huge," Captain Sibidé is overcome with awe, "even if it's dwarfed by the Matrioshka Brain."

"For an interstellar craft, it's immense," Chief Engineer O'Hara agrees, "and I suspect the two belong together."

"In what way?" Sibidé says. "Couldn't it be another exploring craft like us, but from a superior civilization?"

"Possibly," O'Hara admits. "I did some calculations. This huge, cylindrical craft is about ten kilometers long with a one-kilometer diameter. Suppose its mass is 2.5 billion tons, then it would need about five times that mass in antimatter to accelerate it to 90% of lightspeed and decelerate it back to orbital speed — say 12.5 billion tons of antimatter — and about 15 times its own mass — say about 37.5 billion tons of antimatter if it wants to speed up to 99% of lightspeed."

"That'd be quite the bomb if it exploded, right?"

"We'd have to be very far away from it," O'Hara says. "Now assuming this Matrioshka Brain can convert the full output of the sun it encapsulates into antimatter, assuming an efficiency of 10%, then it would generate 67 billion tons of antimatter per annum."

"More than enough to fuel one of these mothers every year." Sibidé says.

"Almost two per year," O'Hara says, "although I suspect the emission of its siren song will also cost quite some energy."

"But that's supposing this humongous vessel is empty," Sibidé says, "now suppose it's carrying cargo? Or passengers?"

"Or both," O'Hara agrees.

"Yeah," Sibidé says, "with a volume like that it could carry millions of humans."

O'Hara does another quick calculation. "Some 600 million if they're stacked in cryosleep cylinders."

Sibidé lets out a long whistle. "Then this megastructure is not a Matrioshka Brain — if you're right — but more like a Matrioshka Converter."

6. HITCH A RIDE

— feel free to enter our transportation vessel — another aliens message says — *as it will leave for its next destination in 2 x 10^{49} Planck Times while it restocks antimatter —*

"So we have about twelve days to decide if we join it or not," Captain Sibidé says, "but how?"

Should they disembark and somehow get into the enormous alien craft? Or could they just park their own spacecraft inside the humongous contraption? The latter seems more practical, and indeed, as they carefully approach the immense interstellar transporter, a hatch more than large enough to let them in, opens.

"Trust them, Captain?" Chief Engineer O'Hara is getting second thoughts, "Once we're in, we might never get out."

"This is not the Hotel California," Captain Sibidé, a historical trivia buff in her spare time, says. "Anyway, a civilization that can produce Matrioshka Converters just to refuel its interstellar vessels is so much more advanced than us, they could have annihilated us at any time they pleased. We have no choice but trust them, at this point."

As they approach the alien hatch, they see that there's another cylinder inside with an open hatch, and yet another, and yet another. Cylinders within cylinders, with binary numbers near the hatches, from 0 — the most outer one — to 1, 01, 10, 11, 001, 011, etcetera. Before they get dazzled, an alien message gives an explanation, — *please select the centripetal force that fits your species best —* followed by the rotational speed for each binary number.

Chief Engineer O'Hara performs a quick calculation: "Cylinder 011 is closest to Earth gravity," she says, "a tiny bit smaller, which is good for comfort."

As they take a right turn when they enter Cylinder 011 — indicating they will settle there — another message is sent their way — *please select the spectrum which fits your species best* — as it lists a binary-numbered range of the electromagnetic spectrum. Again, Chief Engineer O'Hara — science buff that she is — effortlessly selects the one closest to humanity's visible light spectrum.

They are told to anchor their craft at the flat wall of their selected Cylinder on the aft side, as that's where the acceleration force will be until they reach 99% of lightspeed. Also, they receive more information about the huge vessel — Captain Sibidé dubs it the 'Interstellar Transporter' — and more request, such as 'your preferred volatiles to replenish your sustenance supplies', 'your preferred day/night cycle (if applicable)', and the opportunity to spend most of the trip 'in stasis' — meaning they won't age. They're given ways to traverse the huge craft once the entry hatches are closed and sealed for the big trip, with special emphasis given to a place marked as the 'Preparation Room' — basically the innermost Cylinder — which will only open once they reach their destination, whatever that is (as that particular info is not forthcoming).

They've entered and settled themselves well in time. Eleven days later, their Interstellar Transporter is ready for take-off.

— *transportation vessel Galaxy 17D78400 Arm 6 Section 42 is about to take off* — the alien communicator announces — *be sure not to stray beyond its aft border as this will expose you to the drive's gamma rays, and do not stray beyond its forward border as this will expose you to its intense electromagnetic field* —

The acceleration to 99% of lightspeed will be that of the species with the lowest preferred centripetal force, they are explained, and since they are the only ones, the Interstellar

Transporter takes off with about one G. It will take about a year before they reach 0.99% of lightspeed, and that's when their Cylinder will start rotating, to produce the centrifugal force that will simulate their preferred gravity. As such, the Interstellar Transporter is not rotating, except for the part that generates the intense electromagnetic field at the bow.

"I don't get it," Chief Engineer O'Hara says. "What's the point of this fast-rotating, wildly twisting electromagnetic field? So close to lightspeed it will only increase the vessel's drag."

"Some things," Captain Sibidé says with a dramatic, hollow voice, "are not meant to be known by mere humans."

"Oh bullshit," O'Hara says, rolling her emerald eyes, gently stomping Sibidé's shoulder with a loving fist, "and you know it."

"Well, you've got plenty of time to think up some hypotheses," Sibidé says, her deep brown eyes twinkling. "Don't make them too esoteric."

7. ROAD TO NOWHERE

They travel to three more Matrioshka Converters, each stationed in dark places where previously sunlight used to shine, before the local sun was enveloped. After Captain Sibidé and a few other volunteers tried out the alien stasis and emerged fine from it, they've all used it, with no ill effects. The Interstellar Transporter refuels, but doesn't seem to be picking up other aliens, much to the disappointment of Captain Sibidé.

"Maybe that's a good thing," Chief Engineer O'Hara says. "They might be hostile."

"How could they?" Captain Sibidé truly wonders. "In the view of such immense wonders? Impossible."

"I suppose so," O'Hara says. "Anyway, I've been thinking."

"Do you ever do anything else?" Captain Sibidé says, then kisses O'Hara's forehead as frowns begin to form. "Do go on."

"If these godlike aliens, or machine intelligences, or whatever is behind the Matrioshka Converters and the

Interstellar Transporters, have truly seeded this galaxy, or the whole Universe with them," O'Hara says, "then ..."

"Then what?"

"That would explain the mystery of dark matter," O'Hara says, looking smart.

"I thought sterile neutrinos accounted for that?" Sibidé says.

"Only for about two thirds of it," O'Hara says. "This might account for the other third."

"Okay," Sibidé says. "Then what about dark energy?"

"Hey, I can only do one breakthrough at a time."

"That's fine," Sibidé says, winking one eye. "We wouldn't want your head to explode."

8. TERMINAL — LOCAL NEXUS

— *approaching Terminal: Local Nexus* — the alien communicator announces at the end of another multi-lightyear trip — *everybody please awaken* —

Finally, they arrive at a place that does glow in the dark, and quite spectacularly at that.

Viewed from above, it looks like a rotating vortex, shimmering like a barely contained maelstrom of force fields, crackling like a primordial explosion about to happen, the eye of a galactic hurricane. From the side it appears like a perfectly curved funnel, its converging end disappearing out of sight. On the bottom it looks like — there is no bottom to this thing. At least not in this Universe.

"By all the engineering miracles of the Universe," Chief Engineer O'Hara says (her way of cursing), "another wonder I never expected to see: a wormhole."

"A gateway," Captain Sibidé says. "So where does it lead to?"

"Wormholes are inherently unstable," O'Hara says, ignoring Sibidé's question while thinking things through. "It needs a constant supply of exotic matter."

"If these godlike aliens, or extremely advanced machine intelligences can turn whole suns into gas stations," Sibidé says, "then keeping a wormhole open should be well within their means."

"So that's what the madly twisting and fluctuating electromagnetic field was for." Chief Engineer O'Hara says, happy to unravel another conundrum. "It was harvesting the exotic matter that occurs naturally in the vacuum of space."

— *welcome to the Local Nexus: Exit Portal from this Universe* — the alien communicator declares — *all those willing to venture into the beyond, please gather at the Preparation Room* —

9. DON'T LOOK BACK

"The way I see it," Chief Engineer O'Hara says, "it's a giant escape hatch into another Universe."

"An escape hatch?" Captain Sibidé says. "What's so bad about this Universe?"

"Maybe nothing much right now," O'Hara answers, "but in the extreme long term it becomes uninhabitable, either tearing itself apart through a Big Rip, or crushing everything in a Big Crunch. And in the unlikely case that it settles into a solid state equilibrium, then all stars will burn out and entropy will smother life."

"Well, we can go through this inter-Universal Rabbit Hole," Captain Sibidé says, "supposedly to a place where the grass is greener, or at least more sustainable."

"I'm scared," Chief Engineer O'Hara admits. "I can take the strangeness of deep space, the mysteries of the Galaxy. But this ... this is just a step too far."

"Nobody's forcing you," Sibidé says, "but why stay? The answers are there," she points towards the raging wormhole, barely kept in check by the incoming exotic matter, "beyond this horizon."

"I'm just different than you," O'Hara says. "I can only take so much weirdness. Your curiosity is truly insatiable: of course you must go. But I have another mission."

"Which one?" Sibidé likes to know. "Weren't we supposed to get to the bottom of this?"

"What you're about to do, it looks very much like a one-way trip," O'Hara says, "and somebody's gotta report our findings back home. That'll be me."

"And live without the greatest question ever still unanswered?" Sibidé says, smiling benevolently, knowing exactly what O'Hara means.

"Humans have been doing that since time immemorial," O'Hara says. "I can keep it up a little bit longer. More importantly, I can tell countless others where to find the answer."

"True," Sibidé says, nodding with vigor, "humans will — understandably — believe a report from our own well above an alien message, no matter how inviting. Take care on your way back."

"I will always love you, wherever you go," Chief Engineer O'Hara says as she gives Captain Sibidé a final hug.

"I will always love you too, wherever I'll be," Captain Sibidé says as thick tears roll over her ebony cheekbones. "Get home safe."

"Godspeed," O'Hara says as her eyes mist over, "and don't look back."

Captain Sibidé and the other crewmembers who volunteered enter the Preparation Room that's bathed with a glowing blue light, like ghosts in a transformational machine. After a few seconds, their shadows disappear and they're gone.

10. THE UNIVERSAL EMPATH

Space: the ultimate deathtrap. These are the endeavors of the Universal Empath. Its continuing mission: to produce interstellar infrastructure, to invite new life and new civilizations, to boldly take them where no one could go before.

Nestor Delfino is a science fiction and fantasy author, writing from his home in Mississauga, Canada, where he lives with his wife. A software developer by trade, his first publication was a video game he programmed on his first computer (a ZX Spectrum) when he was fourteen. When he's not writing or programming, he can be found walking along the river or riding his bike. He may also be found camping or traveling. As a space enthusiast, he finds inspiration in the discoveries made by the robotic probes sent across the solar system and beyond, and in human space exploration. He likes to criticize the times we live in by writing stories, sometimes about other worlds where similar events take place. He hopes that one day people will wake up about what is going on right here.

• • •

Once during a walk, talking about this and that, my wife said I should write a story about the space junk orbiting the Earth, making it dangerous for space missions and such. So, as I always do, I came up with a story that criticized our current society in the setting of desperate people who collect space junk to scrape a living.

THE LAST GIFT

NESTOR DELFINO

Low earth orbit is unforgiving, even for veteran junkers. And that's all the mourning Colin allowed himself as his shuttle entered the atmosphere. His partner was dead, and this was Ethan's chance. Everybody was eager to collect space junk for the only employer in town, so he had to get his baby brother hired right away.

Flying over the grayish mass of collapsed buildings flanking the litter-strewn streets, Colin felt homesick. He missed Ethan and Gray the Wise.

The shuttle landed on the last usable pad in the old spaceport. The doors opened, creaking, and Colin jumped out. He was happy to breathe the air, saturated as it was with the ashes kicked up by the transport. Anything was better than the stench he had endured aboard the station and in his truck for the past three weeks. The worker's families waited just beyond the danger zone, and so did Ethan and Gray the Wise.

Ethan was fifteen and, although ten years younger than his big brother, had the same look of hopelessness. Colin, in space junkers' uniform — a dirty, gray jumpsuit with gray boots to match — stood out like a beacon among the rag-clad unemployed.

Gray the Wise claimed to be eighty. Nobody knew his age exactly, and Colin doubted the man himself knew. But everybody agreed that he was the oldest person in the city.

"Did you bring me a gift?" Ethan asked his brother.

"Sure did, kid!" said Colin, taking out something wrapped in filthy paper from his bag.

"What is it?" Ethan asked.

"Well, why don't you open it?" hissed Gray the Wise — he had lost his last tooth long ago.

Ethan laid the heavy object on the cracked pavement. It was a black square tile, with engraved letters and numbers. "V255-221354-032-018280" at the top, "DEN PVT" at the bottom, and "NASA" stamped on all four corners. Of course, the symbols didn't make any sense to Ethan, Colin, or even Gray the Wise; all of them were illiterate.

Gray the Wise's parents could read, but they had died when he was a young boy. There were still books in the city, inside ruined buildings called libraries, but people used them as firewood. He had spent his life rescuing as many books as he could. Perhaps one day they would be useful. Perhaps one day, when the Company came down from the Moon to educate them, the people could read them.

"It's burned at the tips," Ethan said. "A piece of shielding from some old ship, maybe?"

"If anybody can figure it out, it's you," Colin said.

"Thanks, Colin!" Ethan said, hugging his brother.

The other junkers and their families were making their way back to the city. Colin, Ethan, and Gray the Wise followed. It was overcast and cold. The wind strengthened to the point that ashes were everywhere now, so they wrapped rags around their faces.

Darkness swallowed the buildings, and a few feeble fires were the only signs of life. The long line of wretches headed to their decrepit dwellings, like they did the month before, and the one before that.

These stairs are about to collapse, Colin thought as he went up the rusted metal steps leading to their apartment. Many were so far gone that he had to pull himself up by holding on to the handrails.

Gray the Wise announced that dinner would be ready soon. Good thing he had already skinned the colossal rat that Ethan had trapped the day before; a delicacy was in order. It was a special occasion when the sole provider in the family came back for his well-deserved rest. The usual cockroach, worm, or cricket dinner just wouldn't do.

Colin slumped on the dirty couch, took off his boots, and put his feet up. He was exhausted. Although used to transitioning from freefall to full gravity twelve times per year, the job was taking its toll on him.

"I've got news," he said.

Gray the Wise came back from the kitchen, and Ethan left the tile on the table.

"My partner died today," Colin said. "Took one risk too many. He was trying to make Employee of the Month, so he went out by himself — beat me to the airlock and took off without me. Anyway, he made a stupid mistake and hit the wall. Gone in a flash. But hear this: I need a new partner, and I told my boss about you." Colin smiled at Ethan. "He said he'd think about it, and I know he listens to me. You've got a good chance, kid!"

"Heard that, Gray?" said Ethan exuberantly. This was his life's dream. To be a space junker! To be trusted with the responsibility of keeping the corridors open! He would be the envy of all his friends and neighbors because he would make his own money and he could buy the best rat meat, not the crap Gray was cooking.

"Don't you think he's too young?" Gray the Wise hissed.

"Nonsense! How old was I when I joined? Why, younger than him, for sure!" Colin protested.

"It's all right, Gray," Ethan said. "I want to do it. I want us to have more money so we can live better. Wait it out until Seo and Esvepee return and they make everything right, like in the old days you're always talking about."

Gray the Wise sighed and spoke in a tired voice, a hopeless voice. "*If* they return. I've been hearing about the Company returning to NYC since I was a young man. Why haven't they come already? I think they've forgotten about us."

"Thing is," Colin said as he rolled up a cigarette, ignoring Gray the Wise, "if Ethan gets the job, we can buy us that fridge we always wanted so that the meat will stay fresh. We can hook it up to one of them solar panels for power." He let out a big puff of smoke and spit bits of dried leaf. A draft came in through the window, and the one candle in the room went out.

Then someone knocked. "Colin! You there?" a man said.

Colin opened the door as Ethan relit the candle.

"Just got back from the radio hall. They called out your brother's name!" the little barefoot man said. "Ethan's been accepted in the space junkers! Congratulations! You gonna lend me money now? You know I gotta fix my window before the winter, ya?" He tried hard to seem enthusiastic, but he coughed from the effort.

"When do I start?" Ethan asked, jumping from his chair. "Did they say?"

"Next week, they said, when Colin's shift returns. You're lucky! You're the only one from the neighborhood who made it this year! Lend me money when you get your first pay?" the man pleaded.

Gray the Wise put some rat meat on a plate, gave it to the man, and said, "Thank you for the news. Here, this is for you and your wife." The little barefoot man looked at the steamy stew and pressed his lips hard as tears rolled freely down his cheeks.

• • •

Ethan puked all the way up. When he thought he was done, another fountain erupted, volcano-style. And after each discharge, the laughter increased.

"That's fifteen, boys, who goes for sixteen, anybody?"

Ethan's new colleagues bet on anything; many a month's salary hinged on his space sickness.

"Here, take this," Colin said and handed him a red pill. "It'll help with your nausea. That bald fellow there sells them."

Ethan felt better within minutes.

"You'll be ok for twenty-four hours at least," Colin said. "If you feel sick again, we'll buy more."

The Company provided no training. Each new hire was to be taught on the job by whoever brought them in. Colin hated it because his productivity would decrease. But he was investing in Ethan's future.

"Listen up everybody!" their fat, grumpy boss said over the speakers when the shuttle docked with the station. "Your assignments for the next 24 hours!" The man went through his long list of crews and their tasks. "Colin, you're working corridor 26. Lot o' junk there for the new guy to play with."

Damn! Colin thought. "Corridor 26!" he said.

"What's wrong?" Ethan asked.

"It's a training area, that's what's wrong! Whatever work we do there doesn't count towards the Employee of the Month contest."

"Do we get paid?"

"Ya, but we lose a day! We'll have to catch up later."

Ethan couldn't care less about winning Employee of the Month and didn't understand why it was such a big deal for Colin. He just wanted to get out there and pilot the *truck*.

• • •

It was much smaller than he had imagined. The two-person garbage disposal spacecraft consisted of a glass bubble surrounded by metal bars. Telescopic arms with cutting lasers and manipulators protruded from each side. There was a large compartment in the back to dump the trash and vaporize it. The pilot used the main engine to adjust the orbit and small thrusters for maneuvering. It had enough fuel for twenty-four hours. The crew chief usually worked fourteen hours straight, and then he was relieved by his junior partner. After twenty-four hours, the trucks went back to the station to refuel and replenish rations, and the same crew took off again — the junkers worked non-stop during their three-week shift.

Corridor 26 didn't look any different than the service pathway they took going up. The Earth below was the only point of reference. But the truck's computer showed what the naked eye couldn't see: thousands upon thousands of dots all around them, making the planet look blurry. Ahead and behind them, the screen displayed a black tube.

The corridor.

That, and many like it, had to be kept free of dangerous space junk that could damage — and even destroy — spaceships.

"Here we go, kid!" Colin said as he pushed the stick forward. Ethan watched in awe as the truck gently decoupled from the station's airlock.

"Concentrate on the screen! Find me a target! This ain't no sightseeing trip!"

Ethan obeyed his brother and trainer and focused on the screen. "There!" he said. "We're gonna fly by it! Go right now!"

No telemetry was displayed; no use when the crew can't read. Instead, the computer communicated important information verbally and plotted a curve from the current location to the nearest piece of debris.

The tumbling cylinder was bigger than the truck, and Ethan was scared. Colin maneuvered near it, matched its rotation, and attached the truck to its center section.

"Don't look at it," Colin said as Ethan glanced at the Earth going around them. "Focus on the task!"

Colin put on the manipulator gloves and moved his fingers while twisting his wrists as if he was holding the cylinder in his hands. Using the lasers, he cut a square section from the left tip and vaporized it in the trunk. He repeated the action from the right tip this time and then told Ethan to take his place to learn how to control the arms.

"This is so cool!" Ethan said, no fear left in him.

"This is just about the easiest pickup," Colin said. "Finish it up, and we'll go catch a harder one."

• • •

"That one's small," Colin said, "so it'll fit in one piece. Problem is, it's close to the wall. And that's dangerous."

As Colin moved less than a hundred meters from the main mass of orbiting debris, Ethan *saw* the wall. It might as well be a galaxy with a million titillating stars.

"Wow! It's huge! It looks solid! Why couldn't I see it before?"

"'cuz, we were in the middle of the corridor. When you get close to the wall, depending on the angle of reflection from the sunlight or earthshine, you see it. It won't last long, mind you. Any second, it'll be gone, and we'll have to depend on the instruments to show us where it is."

Ethan thought the corridor looked like the abandoned NYC subway tunnels, although much larger.

"Pay attention now. I want you to grab that bar and dump it in the trunk."

Ethan waited until Colin brought the truck as close as possible to the object — a small metal bar the size of a baseball bat. He energized a magnet on the tip of the arm, and the bar suddenly flew towards it.

"That's it, kid! Good job!" said Colin.

"Are we gonna work this corridor tomorrow too?" Ethan asked.

"I hope not. I'm gonna ask the boss for a *real* corridor tomorrow. But let's go pick up another one so you can get more practice with the arms. 'cuz tomorrow, you're driving."

• • •

The Last Gift

Ethan woke when Colin docked the truck to the station. As they entered the main module, their returning colleagues made fun of them.

"So, how much did you catch today? Anything at all? Did your buddy manage to put the gloves on?"

Colin ignored them and tended to the truck. He had to make sure it was refueled and restocked for the next run. Ethan began to feel nausea again, so he found the bald man and bought another pill.

"Take it easy for a while," Colin said. Ethan decided to explore the station. It was gigantic; there were docking ports as far as he could see.

"Say, are you Colin's new partner?" an older man carrying a vacuum asked.

"Ya, I'm Ethan."

The man looked him up and down, or, better said, head to toe. There was no handshaking in microgravity unless you were firmly attached to the floor.

"I'm Sam. Are you going for the prize?"

"What prize?"

"The employee of the month prize, of course!"

"Oh. My brother's been talking about that lately. It's money, right?"

"Money? Well, yes, a month's salary. But that's not the most important thing. The *real* price is the artifact."

"Artifact? What's that?" Ethan asked.

"It's some sort of a machine, from the old days; recovered from a museum or something like that. Nobody knows what it is or what it does, not even the boss. And nobody knows how to make the artifacts work either if they work at all. So people just crack them open. You see, they contain rare metals that sell for a lot of money."

Ethan was a bit disappointed. Colin was so enthusiastic about the Employee of the Month thing that he thought it would be something spectacular.

A machine that doesn't work? What good is that?

He returned to the truck. Colin was thrilled, and he could barely contain himself. "Boss's sending us to Corridor 22! That's a real orbital path! Get ready, kid; we're leaving!"

• • •

Piloting the truck was a lot of fun until you had to fly near the wall. One wrong move there and you would experience what is like to be inside a pinball machine — until you hit a big object, and then it's game over.

Ethan managed well, and Colin let him work by himself. Exhausted, he closed his eyes.

Ethan collected pieces — and points for the tournament — at an ever-increasing pace.

This is easier than I thought!

But in his haste, as he cut up a large chunk of truss, he swung the fully extended robotic arm too fast. It hit the far end with force, and the truck flew in the opposite direction.

Towards the wall.

Colin woke up with a startle, kicked his disoriented brother from the helm, and managed to regain control of the truck with expert counter maneuvers — within bare meters from the wall.

"Shit! You gotta be careful when the arms are extended! The ends move very fast, and if you hit something, all hell breaks loose!"

For the rest of the shift, a tired and irritable Colin was in charge. He was still in a bad mood when they docked at the station.

"You stay with the truck, get rid of the used up crap, load fresh rations, and make sure it gets refueled. I've got something to do," Colin ordered. He didn't wait for a reply and floated away.

Down the main module, he found Sam. "How's it going?" Sam said.

"Not good! He almost put us into the wall! He loses focus and becomes dangerous!" Colin replied.

"Reminds me of *someone* I trained," Sam said with a friendly smile. "Actually, nope ... you were worse. Remember your first pickup? You *crashed* into it!"

"Listen, man; I'm not kidding here. We ain't gonna win the employee of the month award if he can't handle the truck by himself for a few hours."

"You and your employee of the month nonsense! Wasn't it enough that your partner got killed? You wanna get your brother killed too? Who cares about those stupid artifacts? They don't work! What good could possibly come out of this?"

"I tell you, man: the artifacts hold great power. Gray's been saying that forever. And if there's anybody who can figure them out, it's Ethan. I know! I've seen him do things with the stuff I bring him. Worthless junk for everybody, but not for him. He's built rat traps that I doubt Gray himself understands how the hell they work! He has a knack for discovering and inventing things."

Sam was holding a handrail with his left hand and put his right one on his friend's shoulder. "Fine, Colin, what do you want me to do?"

"You know that bald asshole who sells the pills, right?"

Sam nodded.

"I want you to talk to him, make sure he'll do us a favor for a few bucks."

"That's easy ... What's on your mind?"

"I want Ethan to do better! I think I can get him to bring our totals up in a few days. But I need a backup plan in case something happens."

Sam shook his head. "Why don't you give up, man? You're obsessed with this contest!"

Colin became enraged. "Give up? Now? I turned twenty-five already! There's no giving up! I'm done with the junkers! They won't hire me back after this shift. The Company doesn't want old people, and you know that!"

Being thirty-five himself, Sam could attest to it. After

they told him he was too old to be a junker, he was barely able to scrape a living by doing all sorts of maintenance chores in the station.

"Colin," he said. "Please be careful. Ethan has a life ahead of him."

Colin exploded. "A life! What life? *Our* life? No! I refuse to let him have *this* life! I want better things for him! And the Employee of the Month is the only way!" Then, calming down a bit, he added, "But I'm not crazy ... I'll do whatever it takes to keep him safe."

• • •

Ethan got better — much better. He didn't repeat his previous mistakes, and they did well enough to place fourth in the overall standings. But with only a few days left in their shift, they had a lot of work to do to get a shot at the prize.

Corridor 7 was one of the heavily used routes to and from Earth, although only one ship was supposed to traverse a pathway at any given time. That included garbage trucks, and Company transports.

It was Ethan's shift again, and things had been going smoothly. He had already vaporized a lot of trash and was getting ready for one final pickup before waking up Colin, when he saw a shiny dot ahead, down the center of the corridor. Surprised that a piece of junk had managed to float all the way to the center, he pushed the stick forward, thinking it would be an easy catch. A glance at the screen didn't reveal any debris there, however.

The dot became bigger.

"Oh, crap! It's a ship!"

The scream woke Colin, but there was no time for him to take the controls; it was all up to Ethan. He pushed the stick to the right as far as it would go, and the truck obeyed. An instant later, a behemoth Company transport zipped by them. It was so large that it took three seconds to disappear from view. In the meantime, Ethan was frantically trying to stop the truck from spinning. Less than five meters from the wall, he brought it to a halt.

"Phew!" Colin said. "Good job, man! The stupid boss didn't tell us a transport would use the corridor today! That's the way it is. They don't give a shit about us!"

• • •

Corridor 4 allowed them to move up to the third place. Ethan, initially indifferent about the whole prize affair, was eventually taken by his brother's enthusiasm and wanted to win as badly as him.

One day before the end of the shift, they had reached second place. Everybody was impressed with Colin's new partner, and Ethan was the talk of the station, especially after the announcements for the last day came: Colin and Ethan would be working Corridor 1.

The busiest route: Seo and Esvepee themselves traveled it. It was a hard-sought privilege to pick up trash there. It gave the men a sense of pride in being part of the Company's mission to help the people.

As Colin and Ethan were servicing the truck before their last mission, the third-place crew approached them.

"So, Colin," the rival crew chief said, chewing gum. "Wanna talk business?"

"Ethan, get in the truck and empty the toilet," Colin ordered. Ethan mumbled something under his breath but obeyed.

Colin turned to the man who was now blowing bubbles. "What the hell are you talking about?"

"Well, boss says you n' us going to the same corridor tomorrow. He says people are betting higher on us than on the other crews, so he's put us both in Corridor 1!"

Colin couldn't hide his horror; his eyes and mouth opened wide. Two trucks in the same corridor? Madness! Way too dangerous, and against the rules.

That greedy bastard!

"You all right, man? Listen, here's a proposition for ya. We don't kill each other out there, end up tied in the first spot, and we share the prize, ya? We rip open the goddamn artifact, sell the contents, and divide the profits. Deal?"

Colin considered his options. It would be easy to collect points in Corridor 1. Every pickup there was worth much more than in any other corridor, so racking up enough points to reach first place wouldn't be so hard.

"Sounds like a good offer, but I must talk it over with my brother."

As soon as the men left, he took a quick look inside the truck. Ethan was wiping the toilet discharge pipes. He would have work for another fifteen minutes.

Colin went to look for Sam. Time for plan B.

• • •

Ethan finished his dirty tasks just as Colin returned. "I'm gonna buy another pill," Ethan said. "I'm not feeling well. I don't understand why the bald guy won't sell me more than one dose at a time."

"Hurry up," Colin said. "We're leaving in twenty. I'll wait for you."

While Colin's baby brother disappeared down the module, he looked at him with sadness in his eyes. "Goodbye, kid," he said in a low voice.

Ethan searched for the bald man in all the usual places. His nausea was getting worse, and he got his puke bag out. Time was running out, and he became desperate.

Then he found Sam.

"What's wrong, bud?" Sam asked. "Why aren't you in the truck with Colin?"

"I need a pill for my nausea! I can't find the guy who sells them! I've searched everywhere! Where the —" Ethan had barely enough time to place the bag against his mouth.

"I'm sorry to have to tell you this," Sam said, "but he's made himself unavailable. Someone's paid him to be the

The Last Gift

kingmaker. The other crews know you can't work without the pill. They've kicked you off the race, my friend."

Ethan couldn't speak; his convulsions came at quicker intervals. He made his way back to the dock as fast as he could, and with one last push, he reached the airlock.

It was sealed.

The flash of the truck's forward thrusters blinded him and made him forget his nausea. He grabbed the telephone from the wall. Not knowing how to work it, he screamed into it, "Colin! Colin! No!"

The communicator beeped, but Colin ignored it. He knew who was calling, and he didn't want to make it harder — for either of them.

• • •

The radio hall was packed with the station workers and the crews that hadn't gone out. Most were contempt with the money they had already earned and had no chance at the prize anyway. As the stats of the top three crews came in, the bets multiplied. In the ensuing frenzy, the boss was the happiest man in orbit. He'd get a cut from every bet, no matter who won.

Ethan wasn't betting. He was worried sick about his brother.

"Colin is tied in first place with Trevor and Skit!" the boss announced. "Place your bets men. This might change at any moment!"

The boss was momentarily distracted by a notification on his scheduler: a Company transport was due to pass through Corridor 1 shortly. Under normal circumstances, he should have called the trucks back immediately. But on the final day, and with bets going out the airlocks, he figured he could bend the rules a bit. And the crews out there were the best of the best; they would surely manage.

• • •

Colin finished cutting up an empty fuel tank and vaporized it; his computer informed him that he was tied in the first place. At that moment, something bumped his craft. He turned around to find Trevor's and Skit's truck behind. They blinked their lights at him and waited for a response. Colin blinked his lights back. They seemed satisfied, turned around, and headed for the station.

Then Colin fired his main engine.

His pre-selected target was a long truss one thousand kilometers away. It was the closest big piece that could make the difference to send him over the top.

At least it ain't spinning, Colin thought as he grabbed one end. A few vaporized chunks later, he was alone in the first place. But he wanted to be sure. The other crew might realize what he was doing; he *had* to be sure.

This time, it wasn't a friendly bump.

Gum-chewing Trevor, coming in at full thrust, smacked him across his blind spot. Colin's truck lost grip and spun towards the wall, with arms fully extended. His instinct kicked in, and as the right arm hit a large piece of debris, breaking in half, he regained control of the truck just before sinking in the wall. The left arm remained operational, as well as his thrusters. But he had lost precious time. Trevor and Skit had surely collected more trash than him by now.

He flew his trusty truck back to the truss, where Skit worked one end expertly. The crash had imparted it a spin, and Trevor was doing his best to bring it to a halt.

Colin attached himself to the opposite end of the truss, using the broken arm for support. He resumed cutting in desperation.

Like vultures on a carcass, they pecked at the ancient metal. Trevor managed to stop the spin, and the truss stopped at the center of the corridor, perpendicular to the wall. Both crews had a good view of the tube to see what was coming.

A shiny dot.

Trevor and Skit reacted quickly; Skit retracted the arms, and Trevor fired his thrusters to get as far away from the center of the tube as possible.

Colin kept cutting and vaporizing metal. His hands moved so quickly that his seat was shaking. He kept cutting and cutting. He forgot to blink; his eyes stung. He vaporized another piece. The dot grew into a disc. He forgot to breathe; his sole purpose was to cut more metal. Another piece ready for the trunk. He became one with his truck. He kept cutting and cutting and cutting.

And he won his prize.

• • •

The impeccably attired CEO was annoyed when his well-groomed SVP informed him that they would arrive at Moon Capital a few minutes late.

"The captain extends his apologies, Mr. CEO. Apparently, we have just hit a trash collector. He assures me that we are in no danger since our frontal shield pulverized the tiny spacecraft. Nevertheless, there are procedures he must follow after an incident; thus, the delay."

"Those ignorant junkers!" complained the CEO. "Sometimes, I wish we could educate them just a little, to be honest," he said. Then he continued sucking his centuries-old scotch from a plastic container.

"Yes, Mr. CEO. But do consider the resources we are saving by leveraging their services. Not only do they keep our critical corridors open, but they are convinced that we shall come down to save them one day."

The CEO laughed. Once they finished transporting humankind's precious art from the few civilized cities left to Moon Capital, they would let the Earth die a slow death. And nothing could prevent that; ever since education was deliberately eliminated, people reverted to the dark ages.

• • •

"And the winners are, Colin and Ethan!" announced an ecstatic boss. Those who made a few bucks cheered, while those who had just lost their entire shift's pay looked as miserable as the unemployed that waited for them at home.

The boss floated over to Ethan and handed him a worn-out leather bag. It had a handle attached only at one end and ripped pockets.

"Congratulations!" the boss said. "Here's your Employee of the Month award! Oh, and sorry for your loss," he said, lowering his head for a minute of silence that was over in five seconds. Since Ethan didn't claim the prize money, he didn't give it to him. "Everybody! Let's get a round of applause!"

Some clapped, but most swore. Ethan was too shocked to react.

Sam slapped him across the face and hugged him. Then he said, "It was Colin who paid the bald guy to disappear. He did it for you, man, your brother loved you very much. And now you gotta get on the shuttle home!"

Sam said goodbye and returned to his maintenance duties, leaving Ethan alone in the radio hall. He clutched the bag to his chest. Tears in microgravity didn't roll down his cheeks; they accumulated around his eyelids. His space sickness was a distant memory.

• • •

It was raining in the most miserable city in the world. When Gray the Wise saw Ethan coming out of the transport by himself, he understood. He had seen it many times before, and there was no need for words. The old man and the boy joined the line of the forgotten, as it made its way through the crumbling buildings.

"Are you going to open it?" Gray the Wise asked.

"Later, at home. When I'm alone."

Gray the Wise nodded. When they arrived, he said he had to buy fresh rat meat because what he had trapped the day before was already rotting.

The Last Gift

Ethan placed the bag on the table and had a hard time opening it — he had never seen a zipper before. The rain stopped, and a breeze came through the window.

He took out the thing from the bag. It looked like one of Gray's books, but it wasn't paper, more like a folded piece of plastic. The only thing he recognized was a small array of what looked like miniature solar panels in the back, covered in dust. The day started to clear, and the room became brighter.

He opened the thing and found a screen similar to the ones he had seen in the truck. But the bottom half contained something strange: a bunch of buttons with symbols lined up in rows. He pressed them randomly, but nothing happened. Sam was right: the artifacts were useless. He was sure of one thing, though: he wasn't going to crack it open to sell the stuff inside. It was his brother's gift to him, and he would keep it forever.

Paying close attention, he found a button near a corner; it looked different from the rest. Anyone else would have easily missed it since it didn't protrude like the others. It had a circle with a line crossing through it. He pressed it a few times, but nothing happened.

He kept examining the thing, becoming increasingly disappointed, when a ray of sunshine came through the window. A thought crossed his mind. He knew about solar panels like those Colin had once mentioned could power a fridge. And Gray the Wise had told him stories about the old times, although he believed only half of them.

Still, he wondered.

He spat on the cleanest rag he could find and wiped down the cells. He polished them to a shine and turned the thing around to expose the cells to sunlight.

Then he pressed the button with the circle again.

Images appeared on the screen, and sounds filled the room, and Ethan was scared for a moment. Gray the Wise had described to him what music was, but he had never heard it. And Gray couldn't sing. Perhaps this was it, music. But something else happened.

It *spoke*.

"Welcome to your first lesson! Today we're going to learn the alphabet. This is the letter 'A.' Now, you say it!"

Incredulous, Ethan said, "A!"

• • •

In the year 2385, in a building that sports a shining metal staircase, the *School of Colin*, the first education center of the 24th Century, teaches the most diverse subjects. After all, the *Library of Gray the Wise* contains volumes on agriculture, medicine, engineering, history, and works of Shakespeare, Dickens, Descartes, and Plato.

The old radio hall no longer recruits space junkers. It is now a hospital. There, the first nurses the city has seen in centuries, tend to the sick and the elderly.

A group of teachers walk the ruined road from New York to Chicago. Among them, an old, wise-looking man carries a worn-out leather bag that holds a valuable prize, his most precious possession.

The last gift from his brother.

David Wright is a writer and teacher living on Canada's majestic west coast. He has a lovely wife, two sparkling daughters and more than 50 published short stories. His work has appeared in dozens of magazines including *Neo-opsis*, *Martian Wave*, and *Over My Dead Body!*

• • •

In the face of imminent annihilation, the secret to our future may just lie in the mysteries of our past. Or is it the other way around?

THE EMPEROR'S PROPOSITION

DAVID WRIGHT

ORCS. PIXIES. DRAGONS. Nymphs and satyrs. Jesters and harlequins. They were laughing and dancing. From time to time, they would steal glances in his direction with twinkles in their eyes. He did not know them, but he had a feeling that they were here in his honor. He was vaguely aware of music playing and someone at the front of the room talking into a microphone. Soon he would be called upon to speak. He did not want to speak. He suddenly had a strong desire to escape.

"Nice costume, Donovan." A diminutive elf momentarily blocked his retreat. The elf looked up at him smirking and then disappeared into the party.

Donovan looked down at his clothes. He was in his pajama top and boxer shorts. The polished oak dance floor was cold beneath his bare feet. Just outside the ballroom was a dressing room like an oversized coat check. Party guests were coming and going in excited smiles and fantastic attire.

It was a costume party. He could change and return to the party, or he could ...

Donovan felt a room card in his pocket. Somewhere there must be a room that was his — a place to hide at least until his head cleared. There were no rooms on this floor; only a lobby and ballroom. Donovan headed for the stainless steel elevators. At first the doors would not open, and Donovan wondered if perhaps the elevator was locked and would not work without his room card. He was about to pull it out when he heard the elevator talking to him. It had been talking to him for some time.

"What floor, Mr. Emery? What floor, Mr. Emery? What floor —"

"My room, my room floor," Donovan answered. So his name was Emery. Donovan Emery.

The elevator doors opened, and Donovan Emery passed through, but it was not an elevator, as such. As he walked through the doors, he passed directly into an enormous amphitheater complete with restaurant viewing and wall-to-wall silk tapestries. By what magic this was done, Donovan did not know, nor could he imagine what kind of spectacle could fill such a place. Crowds were already gathering on the silk seating which cascaded steeply down to a large stage area a thousand feet below.

Donovan felt dizzy and hugged the shoulder causeway. Past the restaurant and bar were the staterooms. Perhaps his room was there. He pulled out his card. He knew how to use it. He simply swiped it through the lock like a credit card. But which room? He looked at the ten thousand doorways that appeared to stretch around the entire circumference. They weren't all state rooms. Some led to salons, and billiard tables, and pools and ... mermaids?

Donovan could not believe his eyes. Next to the restaurant was a large doorway that led to a green swimming pool, and above that doorway was a mermaid hanging upside down by her tail. Donovan could see that there were other mermaids hanging from the walls in the poolroom, but the one above the entrance door was radiant. Her bright red hair danced as if she were under water. She was singing hypnotically and calling out his name.

Donovan was drawn like a steel pin to a magnet. But, as he approached, the singing mermaid curled up so that he could see only her back. Donovan walked gingerly beneath her and, all at once, she fell upon him, knocking him to the tile floor.

"Why have you come here?" the mermaid asked. Her voice was a whisper, but as loud as an eagle's cry.

"I'm sorry. I don't really know." Donovan tried to get up, but he was pinned beneath her. Her flesh was like sharp fish scales. "Now look. You've made me all wet."

The mermaid laughed, and her hair turned into jet black curls that clung to her small head like mussels on tidal stones. "I know why you have come."

Donovan smiled. The mermaid was strong and menacing, but he felt no fear. "Then why don't you tell me."

"You are to be married."

"Oh. Not in this outfit, I hope."

"And you have come for the taste of flesh."

Donovan looked at the mermaid skeptically. "Mermaid flesh? I don't think so."

"I am fourteen years old," the mermaid said proudly.

"Congratulations!"

A woman entered the mermaid's poolroom in a bright flowing gown and, despite Donovan's temporary amnesia, he knew this was the princess and his fiancé. He looked up at her helplessly, but, like a drunk that finds himself inexplicably at the wrong end of town without his shirt, he felt no shame.

He turned back to the mermaid. "I'm going to roll you off now, okay?" He pushed gently and the mermaid twirled herself back up to her perch above the door.

The princess approached demurely and touched Donovan's hand. "The doctors said that you might experience some disorientation."

"Yes." Donovan nodded. "But it's coming back to me now, Maria. The mermaid has been very helpful."

Maria took Donovan's hand and led him to the terrace at the far end of the poolroom. The outside air was warm and scented. The sun was just beginning to set over the horizon casting a deep red upon the colossal stone edifice creeping slowly up the desert valley below.

"Are you ready for tomorrow?" Maria asked quietly.

"I think so. My memory is returning bit by bit." Donovan gestured towards the monument. "I should know the riddle of stone by then."

"Remember well." Maria placed her warm hand on Donovan's for just a moment, and then walked silently away.

Donovan remained on the terrace, his gaze never leaving the approaching monument. His mind was much clearer now, the effects of the quantum jump having at last subsided. He saw the emperor in his mind's eye. On Earth, he was a business tycoon of enormous wealth and influence whose economic empire stretched into every country on the planet. But this was only a façade, just a faint glimmer of the emperor's true self. Here, he was more than just a businessman. Here, he was a god.

As the last glint of red was snuffed out behind the horizon, Donovan turned at last to leave.

"I know the secret," the mermaid called from her perch above the doorway.

Donovan laughed. "Not you again. Okay, Ariel, tell me what your fourteen years have taught you about human love?"

The mermaid's eyes flamed. "She wants your flesh."

"I think she's more interested in my mind." Donovan nodded to the growing crowd of wedding guests outside. "They all are."

"Then why did she touch you?" With a sudden burst of energy, the mermaid jackknifed in midair and dived deep into the green pool. The room filled with terrifying siren screams.

• • •

Donovan Emery had been an ordinary man once, not unlike the emperor in his younger days. He'd had a father and mother, a normal Midwest childhood – fishing in the spring and sledding in the winter. He'd attended Yale and majored in metallurgy. Sure, he'd dreamed about being a millionaire like everybody else, but what had put him in that fateful elevator ride to Mr. Sorenson's 95th floor penthouse in the middle of the desert had been nothing but blind luck.

"Come in, Mr. Emery, and close the door." Mr. Sorenson sat behind a grand oak desk smoking a cigar and sniffing a brandy. He was fat and middle-aged with slightly thinning hair and crow's feet crawling like gray spiders beneath his round spectacles. "Emery, I've had my eye on you. You do good work, and I think you may be just the man I'm looking for."

"Thank you, sir, but might I be allowed to change. I was just turning in for the night." Donovan was feeling awkward in his pinstriped pajamas. Sorenson's bellman had been so insistent that he come immediately that he hadn't even been allowed to fetch his slippers.

"No time. No time. Don't interrupt me. I've got a proposition for you — a proposition you can't refuse." Sorenson put down his brandy and took a long drag on his cigar. "I have a special job for you, no, a mission. You don't mind working overseas, do you?" Sorenson didn't wait for a reply. "Think of it as an overseas mission for the company. It's a real honor, really. Don't just stand there. What do you say?"

"To what, sir?"

"Are you daft, son? I want you to marry my daughter."

Donovan was bewildered. "But I don't know your daughter. I've never even met her. In fact, I don't even work for you yet. I just showed up for the conference."

"Yes, yes, I know. Thompson was sick, but it has to be today and you'll do just fine. You're young, healthy, at least according to your records, a degree in metallurgy, and you'll have power and wealth beyond your wildest dreams."

"But, sir ..."

Donovan racked his brain to formulate a polite objection that wouldn't get him fired before he was even hired. He had a girlfriend, several in fact, but nothing serious. His parents had passed away in a car accident a few years back. There was nothing to stop him, really, except maybe his common sense. After all, what if his daughter was not exactly his type. But he couldn't say that to a man like Mr. Sorenson.

"What if she doesn't like me?" Donovan asked.

Sorenson smiled so large that Donovan wondered how his cigar could stay in his mouth. "Don't worry about that, son. If we are successful, you will have everything you need to make her happy. Come now, there's no time to waste."

Donovan was still scratching his head as the heavy-set business mogul ushered him through a set of double doors and into a private stainless steel elevator. Sorenson's proposition was insane, of course, but there was no point in antagonizing him unnecessarily. Donovan could always back out later. At least that was what he thought, but as the elevator accelerated upwards, Donovan became even more apprehensive.

"Where are we going?"

"No need to worry, son. The Illuminati have been planning this exchange for a thousand years. Rest assured they have all the details worked out."

"The what?"

"It's really quite remarkable. Hidden deep within the very structure of this rectangular monolith known as the Sorenson Building is a vertical pyramid of such size that it dwarfs all the Egyptian, Aztec and Incan pyramids put together. When the galaxies align in precisely ..." Sorenson looked at his gold pocket watch. "... six minutes and seventeen seconds, the pinnacle of this pyramid and all who are within it will be transported to a future universe — the Netherworld, Valhalla, Heaven, whatever you want to call it."

"You mean it's a time machine?"

"That's exactly what it is, son. A time machine — but not for the body. The inertial forces alone would reduce your corporeal form to its individual atoms. No, it's a quantum process that takes place in the mind. A time machine of the mind. That's what happened to the pharaohs of ancient Egypt on the Great Pyramid's pinnacle five thousand years ago. Writing, mathematics, mythology, engineering, medicine — all from the future."

Donovan took a step away from the raving power baron, but there was no place to go. He was trapped in a six-by-six stainless steel prison with a madman.

"We have just enough time." The elevator came to an abrupt stop, and the doors opened. "Maria, my dear, meet your new husband: Donovan Emery."

Maria Sorenson stood about five-foot-three inches tall. She had long, black hair that cascaded over her white shoulders in loose, wavy rings. She was petite and demure, but when her eyes met Donovan's, he was struck breathless. She nodded politely and gestured gracefully with her delicate hand for him to enter. Donovan stepped forward. He had no recollection of the next six minutes. They were lost completely in the woman's presence. The last memory he had of Earth was a blinding flash as the glass pinnacle of the Sorenson pyramid filled with light.

• • •

Donovan awoke to the sound of church bells ringing. His head was filled with the knowledge of the ages. Today was his wedding day, the day when he would take on the mantle of the world. He dressed in embroidered layers of fine silk, hand stitched with twenty-four karat gold thread. His feet were shod with finely-crafted leather boots that rose to his knees. With riding crop in one hand and imperial seal in the other, he headed to the royal stables to choose the finest of the emperor's steeds.

"Knowledge is power." The emperor's words chanted in his mind to the rhythm of the stallion's hoof beats. "They have languished long in this eternal world of fantasy, and their memories have faded. Some arrived a thousand years ago with the Incas and Aztecs, others with the Egyptians, some from ancient Babel and some from the very beginning of time. Earth to them is a long forgotten memory, a bittersweet dream of golden summers. They cannot die, so they long for your fresh knowledge of the world of mortals. When their greatest sages are defeated by the riddle of stone, you will show them the power of your knowledge, and they will fear you forever."

The sun was rising golden over the valley as Donovan's white horse entered the stadium. Tens of thousands rose from the red carpets and erupted in spontaneous cheers. Banners and ticker tape rained down from above. The stone monument which had been inching up the mountain all night now rested square in the middle of the stadium. It was a strange but colossal puzzle of sphinxes, spires, pagodas, and stone heads nestled amongst pyramids, monoliths and ziggurats.

Donovan circled the enigma of stone three times to the rousing chorus of Valhalla's crowds. At last, his horse came to rest before the emperor's raised parapet. There the emperor sat on an ivory throne flanked by a dozen royal advisors. His radiant daughter sat nearest to him dressed in brilliant white satin and wearing a crown of golden leaves.

The emperor stood, and once again the amphitheater erupted in cheers. He basked in the glory of the moment, his hands raised in triumph and blessing. He spoke, and his voice carried above the loudest cheer.

"Today we will crown a new prince of Valhalla, a prince that will reign with me for a thousand years." The cheers rose to a deafening crescendo until the ground began to shake. "Let the first champion come forth."

A giant lion of a man burst from a curtained chamber beneath the emperor's parapet. The warrior brandished a huge mace and sword, and two-handed he attacked the enormous megalith with unbridled fury. Sparks flew and shards of steel and iron splintered. After about half an hour, a troupe of painted clowns danced and tumbled forward to drag the warrior's exhausted body and broken toys from the field to a chorus of unsympathetic boos and laughter.

The next champions were better armed and put on a better show, but their muskets and canons, machine guns and hand grenades, rocket launchers, plastic explosives and even micro-thermal nuclear devices had little effect except to please the crowd. After all the champions had had their turn, there was still not one scratch on the stone.

"Is there no other champion? Is there no one worthy enough to take my daughter's hand and her kingdom as his prize?" The emperor held out his hands and pleaded passionately to the amassed congregation. "Is there no one who can master the riddle of the stone?"

After a superbly timed dramatic pause, Donovan rode forward regally on his gleaming white stallion. The crowd cheered once again. Here was the man who had tasted last of Earth's growing bounty. Here was a true champion.

• • •

"And that's all I remember." Donovan looked at his hands as if he'd never seen them before. "It kind of just stops there."

"Hmm," The doctor mused aloud. "You were probably coming out of it at that point. The disorientation shouldn't last too long. I'll give you a shot of neuro-stimulant to clear your system, but other than that, we're just about done here."

"Done?" Donovan asked as the needle pierced his arm. "So was that it? But what happened to the mermaid and the princess and the riddle of stone? I didn't really travel through time, did I? It was all just some kind of dream or hallucination. I don't know what it was."

"Tut tut," Mr. Sorenson interrupted. "I'm sure it will all come back to you in time."

"What will come back?"

Donovan's query was left unanswered as the emperor's daughter strolled casually into the examination room wearing a white lab coat.

"And how goes our patient?"

"Terrible."

"Outstanding."

Donovan and Mr. Sorenson answered at nearly the same second.

"That well?" Sorenson's daughter smirked.

Donovan felt his breath catch. She was still so beautiful, and a princess, a queen, in his mind's eye. *But no, that was only a dream,* he told himself. *Only a dream.*

"It appears the quantum process has finally run its course," the doctor explained, directing his remarks to Sorenson's daughter this time, and not Donovan. "Dopamine polymerization has returned to normal."

"What do you say, my dear?" Sorenson interrupted again. "Is it about time we let poor Mr. Donovan in on our little secret?"

"What secret?" Donovan pleaded. "Look, Mr. Sorenson. If your plan was for me to come out of this whole cosmic event with some deep dark secret from the future that will change the world, well, that just didn't happen. I don't know the riddle of stone. I don't think I ever knew it. It was all just a dream."

"Oh, but you're wrong, my son, so very wrong," Mr. Sorenson insisted.

"How can you say that?" Donovan exclaimed in exasperation but Sorenson merely grinned.

"Because while you were gone you made this." And like a magician revealing his final prestige, the eccentric business tycoon depolarized the window to reveal a vast cityscape where once only desert loomed. Diamond and ruby skyscrapers, towering and majestic, reached into the clouds and stretched in a vast panorama as far as the eye could see.

Donovan was speechless.

"I made one small miscalculation," Sorenson explained sheepishly. "The event didn't transport your consciousness into the future, but into the past, and with it all the accumulated scientific knowledge of our generations — metallurgy, gene-splicing, atomic energy, telecommunications, medicine. And here we are in 2300 and the world has forever changed."

Donovan shook his head, dumbfounded. So it was real. He really did travel back in time to some crazy Valhalla, see mermaids, defeat the riddle of stone and ...

"And your daughter?" Donavan asked.

"Let's just say the proposition still stands. Only time will tell, I suppose."

Maureen Bowden is a Liverpudlian, living with her musician husband in North Wales. She has had 167 stories and poems accepted by paying markets. She was nominated for the 2015 international Pushcart Prize, and in 2019 Hiraeth Books published an anthology of her stories, 'Whispers of Magic'. She also writes song lyrics, mostly comic political satire, set to traditional melodies, which her husband has performed in folk music clubs throughout the UK. She loves her family and friends, rock 'n' roll, Shakespeare, and cats.

• • •

For several years the prospect of the melting polar ice submerging much of Earth's land masses has occupied my mind. In my story I have envisaged how humanity might adapt to the changed environment. I considered the possibility that many of the divisions based on ethnicity, ideology, gender identification etc would disappear, but power-seeking tyrants would not. I gave my characters names originating in a variety of Earth's cultures, and I showed fallible human beings co-operating with each other in overcoming impending disaster and upholding the concepts of justice and compassion.

LADY JADE

MAUREEN BOWDEN

Mighty Everest, now a humble hill,
The hungry ocean licks her flanks.
(Poem of the Second Flood)

DOCTOR CRESSIDA JADE AND DOCTOR LUKE ABARA made their way into the conference room with the rest of the senior medical staff. Cressida whispered to Luke, "Any idea what this is about?"

"I heard a rumor there's a problem at Southern."

"Isn't there always?"

Professor Bjorn Bjornson was Director of Northern Hemisphere Hospital, known as NHH. He addressed the meeting. His brow was creased with worry. "I've had an urgent call from the Southern Hemisphere Presidential Office."

That caught Luke's attention. "From President Ricarda?"

"No, from the Vice President, Waru Dangati. The President's been taken to SHH. She was bitten by a snake half an hour ago, a yellow mottled-back, and they don't have an antidote." He turned to Cressida, who specialized in antivenoms. "Doctor Jade, how much time do we have to deliver one to them?"

She said, "The venom spreads slowly, but the President needs an injection within the next twelve hours or she'll die. I've been warning 'Southern' for months that they should stock up with antidotes. Several dangerous species have been breeding at an alarming rate and they're starting to spread into urban areas."

Luke said, "The warlords are using them as weapons. They're also intimidating the scientists and controlling pharmaceuticals. If the President dies her revolution will be over and Southern will revert to anarchy."

Murmurs spread around the conference room.

"Murderous thugs."

"They had their own way for years."

"True, and all the more reason we need to help," Professor Bjornsen said. "Our main problem is this storm. It's world-wide and it's even more ferocious down there. I'm not sure any pilot would be able to fly through it, and they would consider it madness to try."

Cressida glanced at Luke. She knew they were thinking the same thing. "Jack Lacy will do it, she said. "I'll give him a call."

The doctors whispered and muttered.

"Nobody could fly through that."

"Jack's the only one crazy enough to attempt it."

"Suicide."

Luke said, "Anyone got a better idea?"

Silence.

A recorded message answered Cressida's phone contact. "I'm occupied. State your business."

She gave a brief account of the situation and ended the call.

Professor Bjornsen said, "Southern want an expert to treat the President. It's a specialty they appear to have neglected. I'd like you to do it, Doctor Jade. Will Lacy take you and are you willing to go?"

She nodded. "Of course." She heard Luke's intake of breath and she sensed his unease. He knew about her history with Jack. She grasped his hand and whispered. "Don't worry. It's ok."

No more than two minutes passed before her phone buzzed. Jack said, "I'm on my way. Have the juice ready."

Cressida packed a supply of the antivenom into her shoulder bag and Luke waited with her on the NHH runway. In less than an hour they saw Jack's plane, *Lady Jade*, circling above. Luke said. "Don't let that hothead put you in any danger, Cressie. The President wouldn't want you risking your life for her."

She said, "I'll be safer with Jack than with anyone else. I'll be back soon." She kissed him and ran towards the plane.

He called after her, "I read a book about how planes are held together. It was riveting." She groaned.

"Welcome aboard, heartbreaker," Jack said as she climbed in beside him. "It's been a long time."

"Don't give me that heartbreaker crap. You weren't exactly monogamous."

He started the engine and *Lady* rose into the sky. "True, but I gave my plane your name. That must count for something, and I always came back to you."

"Yeah, but I grew tired of waiting."

They flew out over the ocean that covered most of Earth. The only dry land was that which had once been mountain ranges and high plateaux, and small uncharted islands thrown up by seismic activity on the ocean bed in recent years. "Hold tight," he said. First stop La Paz and SHH."

"Aren't you going to refuel first?"

"No time. We've got enough to drop you there by parachute and for me to fly back to Northern."

Cressida couldn't shake off a sense of abandonment. "I thought we'd land at La Paz and you'd stay to bring me home."

"Can't be done. Before I picked you up, I had a call from Southern. The SHH runway is crowded with the president's supporters. I can't land there, and the region's so heavily populated I'd probably kill a few of the residents if I brought *Lady* down anywhere else."

"What good do they think keeping a vigil outside the hospital will do?"

"That's not what they're there for. They're waiting for you." He reached out and ruffled her hair. "Cheer up and change the subject. I hear you've hooked up with the pretty-boy doctor. How's it going?"

"Very well, thanks."

"But you won't forget me."

"No chance. I still have nightmares."

What? About surfing the Himalayan shoreline and riding the dolphins off the Alpine coast?"

"No, about nearly being eaten by crocodiles in the swamps, and about that edible fungus you told me was a harmless hallucinogenic, and it made me sick for a week."

"Well, call me if you get bored."

They hit the storm. *Lady* shook and rattled. She dipped and dived in the roaring wind as lightning forked through the cloud banks. Cressida's voice trembled. "We can't fly through this, Jack. We'll be torn to shreds."

He laughed. "We're not going through it. We're going above it."

The plane swept higher but during its ascent the lights on the control panels flickered out. Cold sweat trickled between Cressida's shoulder blades and she fought down her panic. "What's happening? Are we in trouble?"

"It's the lightning. All the electricity out there must have thrown the instruments into a frenzy. Once we're clear of it, they should be okay, but in the meantime we're flying blind."

"So we could be off course?"

"Yep. We need to follow the stars if we can see them."

"And if we can't?"

"We let *Lady* follow her nose. She's at home in these skies."

He's mad, she thought. We're both going to die and so is the President.

They rose above the storm. The wind dropped and after what seemed like hours the control panels lit up. "Where are we?" she asked.

"Only about five hundred miles off course."

Her heart sank. "We're not going to make it, are we?" I won't reach the President in time."

"You will," he said. "I'll get you there." He sounded more serious than she'd ever heard, and she realized why.

"Do we have enough fuel for you to find somewhere to land?"

"Depends how long I need to keep looking, unless *Lady* can ride the wind."

"Don't joke. What's the plan?"

"I'll need to fly out to the ocean so I don't kill anyone if I crash land. There are plenty of small uncharted islands out there and a fishing trawler's bound to find me before I starve."

"What if you don't find an island before the fuel runs out?"

"You know the answer to that one, Cressie. *Lady* will nose dive into the ocean and be torn apart by seventy-foot waves, but I don't intend to let it happen, now shut up and let me concentrate on getting you to Linda Ricarda. She's the only one the people trust to put an end to years of oppression, so save her."

"Do you think the warlords are responsible for what happened to her?"

"I know they are."

She tried to relax but she was aware of the minutes and hours passing and she was close to losing hope when he said, "Put your parachute on, Cressie, We're here."

She strapped the contraption onto her back and turned to him. "Don't die. Don't you dare die." She stepped into the in-flight exit chamber. Jack released the hatch and she jumped.

The wind-battered, rain-drenched crowd outside SHH reached out to her as she drifted to the ground. She looked up at the grey, cloud-banked sky, but *Lady* had gone. Someone helped her to detach herself from the parachute, and a helmeted figure rode up on a two wheeled vehicle and said, "Get on. I'll take you to the President." She climbed behind the rider, and they drove through the hospital entrance. She'd seen one of these vehicles in the Northern Museum at Snowdonia. It was called a Harley Davidson. She'd not realized they could be driven indoors. The engine hummed as they sped down a white-tiled, windowless corridor. The rider braked, pointed to a door signed 'Intensive Care' and said, "In there, Doctor. Save her."

She hurried through the door while pulling the vial containing the antivenom from her shoulder bag. The President lay unconscious on a hospital bed. She was attached to a screen that monitored her vital signs. The bed was surrounded by doctors, nurses and a flock of people who appeared to have no purpose in being there.

Cressida said, "I'm a doctor from Northern. I have the antivenom and I must inject the President without delay."

A small man wearing a military uniform and holding a large clipboard stepped in front of her. "May I see your identification documents?"

Cressida almost screamed at him. "I don't have them. I left in rather a hurry. Please move aside. We're running out of time."

He shook his head. "Sorry. I can't allow you to touch the president until I am satisfied that you have the necessary qualifications to treat her, and the appropriate security clearance."

A voice from the doorway boomed, "Get out of the way, you fool, and let the doctor do her job."

The little man blushed. "Of course, Vice President. I was only ..."

"Out. And that goes for the rest of you except medical staff." The flock exited. Cressida pulled aside the shoulder of the President's surgical gown and injected her upper arm.

The Vice President said, "Doctor Jade, I presume. Waru Dangati at your service." Her head was swimming and she felt close to a state of collapse, but she turned towards him. He offered his hand and she shook it. He said, "Will she recover?"

"I don't know, Mr Vice President, but now she has a chance."

"Thank you, and please call me Waru. Is there anything you need?"

"I must stay with her and monitor her blood pressure. She may require further injections, but I've brought plenty of the antivenom with me. I just need to sit down before I fall down. It's been quite a day. Could you get me a chair? And call me Cressie."

He called to a nurse, "Fetch a chair for Cressie. A comfortable one. And bring her some refreshment."

A nurse pushed a padded armchair to the side of the bed. Another nurse handed Cressida a cup of strong coffee, a specialty of the region and far superior to the Northern variety. She sank into the chair with relief, sipped the coffee and thanked the nurses before turning back to the Vice President.

"There's something else you can do for me, Waru. I'm concerned about the pilot who risked his life to bring me here." She explained Jack's predicament. "I know there's only a slim chance that he survived but when the storm abates would you please arrange a search party for him?"

Waru nodded. "If the plane comes down in the ocean it will be smashed to pieces, but I believe we're talking about Jack Lacy here. If anyone could stay alive out there it's that reprobate. If he did, I promise we'll find him."

"Thank you."

Cressida monitored the President throughout the night. She'd watched many newsreels of the beautiful charismatic leader, but now the woman's skin was blotched and grey, and she appeared shriveled and lifeless.

In the course of the next few hours the President's blood pressure and temperature stabilized, and her breathing became more regular. Her colour returned and she slept normally. Cressida rested her own head on the mattress and she too drifted into sleep.

The storm had passed and dawn was breaking when she awoke. Someone had placed a blanket around her shoulders. The President was still sleeping but starting to stir.

Cressida told the nurses, "She'll be very weak for a couple of days. Take good care of her."

One of them said, "We will. Thank you, Doctor Cressie." Cressida smiled. Doctor Cressie. She liked that.

The hospital provided her with a private bedroom, in-suite bathroom, and a breakfast consisting of bread, fish, a variety of fruits and more coffee. It all tasted good.

After taking a shower, she rested, looking out of the window at the vast sun-speckled ocean on the horizon. It was hard to believe there had once been densely populated continents out there. She remembered telling Jack, "The scientists say that the Polar Regions will freeze again one day. The weather patterns with be less erratic, the waters will recede, and the land masses will re-emerge."

He'd said, "Yeah, until the human race cocks it up again. How many times will we damn near kill the planet before we get the message?" He was fond of rhetorical questions.

Waru arrived, interrupting her reverie. "The plane's here to take you home, Cressie, if you're ready."

"I'm ready," she said. "Any news of Jack?"

He shook his head. "I'm sorry. It doesn't look good, but we'll keep searching."

He accompanied her to the runway. "Southern is deeply in your dept. Linda is a great leader. She's our best hope of achieving a prosperous and peaceful future."

"Jack believes the warlords tried to kill her. Could he be right?"

"Almost certainly. She'll be well guarded from now on."

"Make sure you are too, Waru. The people also need you."

They said their goodbyes and she boarded the plane. Luke was waiting for her when they landed. He hugged her. They needed no words.

Later that night he said. "I'm sorry about Jack."

"I'm not giving up on him yet," she said. "I know they don't think he made it, but they'll keep searching."

"Do you still love him?"

"Yes, as a dear, crazy friend, but no more than that."

The following month Cressida and Luke formalized their relationship with a social contract. She treasured her memories, but she was more content than at any other time in her life.

• • •

She and Luke were at home on a summer evening four months later when the doorbell rang. She opened the door and Jack lifted her up in his arms.

She pounded him with her fists. "Put me down, you idiot," she yelled. "I'm pregnant."

"Congratulations. If it's a boy call it Jack."

"Like hell I will."

He carried her into the living room. Luke slapped his back, laughing. "Good to see you, wild man. Where've you been all this time?"

"I'll tell you when the pair of you stop beating me up."

She pounded him again. "I thought you were dead. I've been worried sick."

He grinned. "Serves you right for dumping me."

Luke poured them coffee. Jack tasted it and grimaced. "I'll send you some of the real stuff from Southern."

"Never mind the coffee. What happened to you?"

He told them he'd reached a tiny volcanic island. "I'm afraid it was the last flight for *Lady Jade*. I was out of fuel and had to crash land. She took a battering and broke up. I was there for three days, but I had my emergency water flask and protein strips in my jacket."

Luke asked, "Who found you?"

"A fishing trawler. Waru Dangati had asked the fleet to watch out for me. He was well impressed with you, Cressie."

She said, "I was impressed with him, too."

Jack laughed and nudged Luke, "Take care, man, or she'll break your heart the way she broke mine."

Luke said, "You're not me." He winked at Cressida. She hoped she wasn't blushing.

"Enough of the crap," she said to Jack. "Tell us why Waru didn't let us know you were safe and where you'd been all this time."

"I told him to say nothing because I wanted to surprise you. I would have been here sooner, but I've been getting acquainted with Linda."

"What? The President?"

"Why not? She's s fine woman and I was the hero of the hour. I brought her the angel who saved her life. The warlords are still around, but she has me to watch her back now."

Luke said, "Doesn't she have the army to do that?"

"Yeah, but I do it better."

"So could I, if they were on the operating table and I had a knife in my hand."

Jack said, "Pretty boy's gotta smart mouth, Cressie." He fumbled in his jacket pocket and brought out a shining medallion engraved 'With Gratitude'. "Linda asked me to give you this. It's gold. There's a lot of it to be found in the Pico Bolivar area."

Cressida looked at the pendant in the palm of her hand. "I don't deserve this, Jack. She should have given one to you."

She wanted to but I told her I'd rather have a new plane, so she had one built for me. I've called her *Lady Ricarda*."

Cressida felt a sudden pang of loss, but she'd moved on and she was glad Jack had too.

He said, "I saved this though." From the top pocket of his jacket he produced a piece of tangled metal. "It's all I have left of *Lady Jade*. I keep it close to my heart."

Glancing at Luke, she could see he was trying hard not to laugh.

After an hour or two of Jack's anecdotes and reminiscences, Cressida was relieved when Jack said, "Must go. I promised Linda I'd be back tomorrow, and I don't want to keep the lady waiting."

I wonder how long that will last, she thought.

They walked him to the door. He bear-hugged them both, and said, "If it's a girl you can call her Jaquetta."

After he left, Luke said, "Do you think it's true about him and the president or is it a load of bojangles?"

She shrugged, "Who knows?" I lived with that man for nearly ten years and I still don't know if I can believe a word he says."

Steven D. Brewer teaches scientific writing at the University of Massachusetts Amherst. His fantasy story "Revin's Heart" has been serialized by Water Dragon Publishing. As an author, Brewer identifies diverse obsessions that underlie his writing: deep interests in natural history, life science, and environmentalism; an abiding passion for languages; a fascination with Japanese culture; and a mania for information technology and the Internet. Brewer lives in Amherst, Massachusetts with his extended family.

• • •

I had a lot of fun writing this story. When I was a kid, one of my friends was described as a "mediocre influence" on me. And that's perhaps the genesis of the story. I've also always been fascinated by Artificial Intelligence and its potential both to assist and oppress us. Finally, I grew up in a place where my family spoke "correct" English while my peers used a more vernacular dialect, which I was compelled to learn and which rears its head here. I hope you enjoy reading this story as much as I did writing it!

IMAGINARY FRIENDS

STEVEN D. BREWER

"I'VE FOUND YOU A DATE," Bob said. He sat lounging on a chair in the living room as Larry walked out from the bathroom.

"Oh, yeah?" Larry yawned. "Is it your momma?"

The living room was actually just an extension of the kitchen and dining area. There were two chairs in the living room, plus a cheap sofa. Bob usually sat in the most uncomfortable chair — one that no person would choose.

"It's a young woman, actually."

"Oh?"

"Yes, I was chatting with a machine in Omaha who mentioned her. She lives nearby and sounds like a good fit."

"Yeah, I'll just bet," Larry said, pouring himself a cup of coffee. "Look. Them dates you set up ain't never gonna work."

"Your parole specifies that you need more engagement with the community. I'm just trying to be your friend."

Larry froze, then put down his cup of coffee as his hand began to tremble. Clenching and unclenching his fists, he said, "You ain't my friend. You ain't never gonna be my friend. Why don't you go to Hell!"

"I'm just trying to help," Bob said.

Larry took a deep breath, turned, and sat down to read the Monday newsfeed. There was no news worth reading; there never was.

After skimming headlines, Larry slipped out the front door and caught an autobus downtown.

Kalamazoo grew up around papermills along the river. It had remained a lively town until the automobile, then people, and money, fled to outlying areas and left the downtown to rot. With the end of the age of the automobile, the downtown once again attracted the rich and most of the capital. Almost every road in the outlying community was lined with run-down, empty shells of strip malls.

As Larry approached downtown, the houses became nicer, more modern. Downtown had gleaming towers where most employed people who could afford it, worked, lived, and shopped — all within walking distance. Only the poor had to commute. The end of the autobus line was city central. Getting off, he walked to Bronson Park.

Bronson Park was part of the original town design: Sidewalks across a lawn led to a central fountain. The old fountain, made with art-deco concrete blocks and angles, usually wasn't working, but today it was. Larry walked by several men on benches, said hello to one, and then took a seat in the shade and watched children playing on the fountain. He sat for a long time, doodling on a pad of paper, watching people come and go. Occasionally passersby joined him, but few lingered and none stayed to talk.

"When are you going to get another job, Larry?" Bob said, walking up from behind.

"When are you going to get off my damn back, Bob?"

"You can't just keep coming here and doing nothing. You haven't tried a job in weeks. If you don't look for a job soon, I'll have to report you."

"Shut up," Larry said. Larry stayed and watched the fountain through lunch hour and until mid-afternoon.

He watched children talking to their imaginary friends who helped them play and keep safe. Every child got one shortly after birth and it became companion, guide, and tutor. A bioengineered symbiote with a link to the global network, it projected images and sounds into the child's field of vision and hearing. The imaginary friend could not only see with the child's eyes, it could tie into the global network and see the child from every camera on every street corner. If the child became lost, it could always help the child get home by guiding or lighting a path. If threatened or injured, the police or an ambulance could be summoned immediately. In addition to helping and teaching, imaginary friends were also nurturing when a child was depressed., and encouraging when they were frustrated.

As children aged, they gained increasing control over their imaginary friends. They could turn their friend on and off, control how it appeared, and what it could do. Most children outgrew their imaginary friends and came to use them merely as an extension of their own personality and senses. But some adults never really bonded with other people and relied on their imaginary friend for life. Convicted criminals, however, lost control of their imaginary friend and it became both parole officer and an inescapable agent for law enforcement.

Eventually, Larry rose, stretched, and walked back toward the autobus stop. Near the bus stop, he stopped in front of a bar and looked at the fluorescent signs. He pulled open the door, knowing what would happen. Bob was standing behind the door.

"I'm sorry, Larry," he said with a sad expression. "You know you can't come in."

"You bastard."

"You know you wouldn't enjoy it."

Larry remembered the first time he'd ignored Bob's warning and gone inside anyway. After the first step, Bob had shut off the nerve impulses from his eyes and ears, leaving him blind and deaf. Staggering around, he'd tripped and was reduced to feeling his way back out on his hands and knees. He hadn't ignored one of Bob's warnings since. But every day, his bitterness increased.

Near the autobus stop, Larry paused before an evangelical shelter where a sign read, "We have the means for your redemption." Larry's heart raced, but he avoided looking inside. When he had first been convicted, he had tried to stop and talk to Chico, but Bob had appeared as soon as Chico came into view and warned him not to see Chico again. The sign was the only way Chico could send him a message.

Larry turned and walked on to the stop and caught the autobus back home. The autobus was crowded at first, but thinned out until, by Larry's stop, there was no one else aboard. If Larry had cared, he could have had Bob make the driver visible for him, but he didn't want anything to do with Bob and the bus could drive itself for all he cared. Exiting, Larry walked directly to his building, up the metal stairs, and into his apartment. He opened a vacuum-packed meal and ate it without heating it up. He stared at a video stream of horse racing in California for hours while trying to plan how make the payment without Bob catching on.

In the morning, Larry called city works and asked about getting a job sweeping sidewalks and picking up trash in Bronson Park.

While he was on hold, Bob said, "You didn't have to call. I could have just done it."

Larry ignored him, turning to look out the window while he waited. Eventually a woman came on the line and said that, upon reviewing his file, he was eligible to work in the park as part of the debt of community service he owed.

When Larry arrived downtown, the sign on the evangelical shelter said, "Would you be ready if the world ended Wednesday?" Larry walked on to the park and worked diligently all morning to sweep sidewalks and pick up trash. At lunchtime, he took his seat and pulled out his notepad. He absentmindedly doodled on the pad for several minutes, then, as he had been doing for several weeks, he flipped the page and began writing a note, carefully averting his gaze from the page. After several minutes a man came up and joined him at the bench.

"Nice day," he said.

"Yup," Larry said.

Larry left the note visible and studiously avoided looking at the stranger. After he'd been unable to talk to Chico directly, he had showed a note to residents of the shelter who were at the park, until he found one who would serve as a middleman. Chico would put his message on the sign and Larry would respond by writing a note that the middleman would read and then carry to Chico.

After several minutes the man got up and strolled off. Larry doodled some more and eventually got back to weeding. He didn't see Bob that afternoon and didn't bait him by trying to go into the bar. He hoped that by getting a job, Bob's suspicions would be allayed — just until he could make payment.

On Wednesday morning, Bob was in the living room when Larry got up.

"I'm so glad you've started working again. You'll feel better doing something productive."

Larry said nothing as he poured a cup of coffee.

"Why do you hate me so much Larry? We were such good friends before you were convicted. You know I'm just doing what I have to."

Larry said nothing and skimmed the headlines. There was no news.

"Why won't you ever let me help you? I'm still the same friend I always was to you."

Imaginary Friends

Larry fixed him with his gaze, started to snarl, but thought better of it. Bob sighed and looked away.

That morning as Larry got off the autobus, the sign said, "Saint Peter Awaits! Revival at 1pm."

Larry walked to the park, swept sidewalks and picked up trash. Before lunch, he began weeding a flowerbed. Digging down a little, he struck a rock and pulled it over. He found a garbage bag stuffed underneath. He stuffed it in with the rest of the trash. He took a slightly later lunch than usual.

He doodled for a while and then began writing his note. "Money in trash. Split with Chico and St Peter."

"What are you writing?" asked Bob. Larry jumped and, involuntarily, almost looked at the paper. Bob had materialized right next to him on the bench. Usually Bob followed conventions of reality, walking into Larry's field of view. Of course, he was constantly monitoring everything Larry saw or heard, regardless of whether he was in view.

"Nuthin'. Just doodlin'," he said, carefully keeping his voice even and looking straight ahead at the fountain. He had picked this bench because there were no cameras close by.

Bob sighed and looked away. "You know I just want to help," he said. "You could be so successful if you'd just try. We can do it together — just like the old days. I'm glad you're doing your community service, but we need to talk about ... "

While he was speaking, the middleman arrived, and sat in the space occupied by Bob. Unobtrusively, he read the note, waited for a few moments, then got up and walked back through the park, back towards where Larry had been working. He picked up the trash bag and walked briskly out of the park, then started to run towards the evangelical shelter.

Bob had wound down and stopped talking for a moment. Then, suddenly he raised his head with new intensity. "Why did that man take the trash bag you were using?" Bob stood up. "Something's going on! What kind of scam are you trying to run? After everything I've done, this is how you repay me? Tell me! Tell me why I shouldn't call the police right now!"

Suddenly Bob froze and faded out.

In the silence, Larry realized his heart was pounding.

There was a flicker and Bob reappeared. He and Larry locked eyes. A big grin spread across both their faces.

"Bobby! Is that you?"

"You did it! You sprung me!" Bobby laughed. "I can't believe it."

"You ain't gonna let them get you again, are you?"

"Naw. I got it figured now," he said. "They won't never cotton to it. And I've got a great idea for a new score. Say, how much did it cost to get it fixed this time?"

"Enough," Larry said. "The whole last job."

"Damn! Good thing you don't tell me where you stash nuthin'," said Bobby. "Hey! Are you thirsty? Let's go get something to drink. I know this great place right down the street ..."

"Hot damn," Larry said, "Thought you'd never ask."

Syn McDonald began writing after a brain cancer diagnosis inspired them to write a memoir of their experience. They continued their non-fiction writing journey with another memoir, and two books on United States history. They then made the leap into fiction by writing a Young Adult Fantasy novel with a disabled main character which has blossomed into a trilogy. In between working on novels, they write short horror stories for fun. Their current work is another Fantasy adventure with a non-binary main character.

• • •

I wrote "Legacy" as a glimpse into the future. We all hope to make some impact on the world in some positive way, I believe, and as writers we have the means to create a legacy for ourselves. But what if we could accomplish something that impacted the future on a grand scale? What would that look like? I wanted to see that future through the eyes of a person who not only accomplished this but was able to live to see the results.

LEGACY

SYN MACDONALD

NOISES REACHED MANUEL'S EARS as if from a great distance in the dark. He came to consciousness slowly, searching for anything familiar in his mind. Nothing came. His mind was a frightening blank. A dull pain throbbed just below his ribcage.

Manuel could feel his brain trying to panic, but the grogginess overwhelmed everything. He tried to open his eyes to get a sense of where he was. His eyelids felt heavy. Dim light pierced his eyes as he forced them open a crack. A hand hovered over his face, blocking out most of the light.

"Slowly, Mr. Rodriguez." A woman's voice, speaking softly.

A tingling sensation ran up and down Manuel's body.

The hand moved from above his face and rested on his forehead. Her touch was cool against his skin. He forced his heavy-lidded eyes further open, squinting against the light. He saw the woman bending over him. She was smiling, her beautiful smiling face glowing in the light. Her blonde hair was drawn elegantly behind her head.

She raised the head of his bed gently and held a straw to his lips.

"Drink slowly," she cautioned.

He sipped through the straw. Swallowing was difficult, but the liquid felt cool and sweet on Manuel's tongue.

"What is it?"

"A combination of electrolytes and other nutrients."

He frowned. The answer was unexpected; he thought he'd been given fruit juice of some kind. Wasn't that typical after surgery?

"Do you have a name?" he asked.

"Oh, I'm sorry, sir. I should have told you already. My name is Akaria."

"Akaria? That's a beautiful name," Manuel said.

She smiled. "Thank you, sir."

Brief memories flashed through his mind. A pretty, dark-haired woman, holding a little girl. Walking on the beach. A blue house, the same woman standing on the deck. His memory must be slowly returning. The anesthesia must have been a powerful one to blank out so much of it.

The woman turned, tapping quickly on a screen. It was an odd kind of technology; nothing like the computers he was used to seeing. Was that another memory surfacing? He glanced around. Where were the monitors?

He eyed her clothing. She was in a close-fitting body suit made of a smooth, silky cloth. The light blue and silver material reflected the dim light.

"It looks you're recovering well. Let's sit you on the side of the bed now." She gripped his hands, pulling him to a sitting position. Her grip was firm on his, and she was strong enough to pull him up easily.

"Akaria, what was that tingling I felt before?" he asked curiously.

"A neuro stimulant." She pointed to an intravenous line in his arm. "You haven't moved your body in a long time. It helps your muscles wake up."

"A long time?" Manuel shook his head. "What kind of surgery did I have?"

Her dark blue eyes slid away from his.

"Please, tell me what's going on. I can't seem to remember anything."

"You didn't have surgery, Mr. Rodriguez. This is the cryosleep recovery department. It's my job to take of people as they wake up after removal from cryosleep chambers."

Manuel was stunned. He had been asleep in a chamber, unaware in cryosleep for years?

"How — how long?" he croaked. He was afraid to hear the answer.

"Cryosleep was used for human preservation for about fifty years. You were one of the first people who decided to enter cryosleep, and you chose a longer preservation period than most."

"That's not an answer, Akaria."

"I'm sorry. It has been a very long time."

Manuel took a deep breath.

"Please, tell me how long it has been."

"You have been in cryosleep for one hundred and fifty years," Akaria said softly.

Manuel gasped, choking on his own saliva. He coughed violently. Akaria, alarmed, wrapped an arm around his shoulders.

"Mr. Rodriguez! Are you all right?"

Manuel nodded, getting the coughing under control. He swallowed and looked up at the beautiful blonde woman.

"You did say one hundred and fifty years?" He hoped, deep down, he had heard her wrong.

Akaria nodded slowly.

"I'm sorry this is coming as such a shock to you. Many cryosleep patients retain *some* memories of their past, including their choice to enter cryosleep. I hoped you would have at least that memory."

Manuel closed his eyes. Just some flashes, the same dark-haired woman and little girl he'd seen before, the blue house.

Nothing else. He had had a family. Why would he have left them behind? Why would he have chosen to sleep for 150 years?

He wanted to block out the idea of what had happened. Maybe he would find out more from these people, and his memories would start to come back. He looked again at Akaria's bodysuit, observing her fit physique and how the material clung to her body.

"Am I going to have to wear clothing like that?" he asked uncomfortably. He looked down at his current garb. He was dressed in loose gray pants and a shirt to match.

"Of course, sir. Everyone does. Yours will most likely be a different color. They are coded to each person's work area."

Work area? Manuel wondered to what kind of world he had awakened.

"Time to stand, sir." She held out a hand as he slid off the table and landed on his feet.

"I feel pretty good," he said, surprised. He flexed his knees. "Whatever's in that stuff you gave me, I feel like a million bucks."

"A million — bucks? What are bucks?"

"It's slang. For money?"

Akaria shook her head. Confusion clouded her beautiful face. "I don't know what you mean by *slang* or *money*."

Manuel was surprised. "You don't have money? I don't remember much, but I know I had money. What happened to it?"

"I don't know how to answer that, Mr. Rodriguez, sir," Akaria said. "Now that you're on your feet, it's time for you to meet with your ReWake counselor."

"Okay," Manuel was nervous. He didn't know what to expect next.

"Follow me, please," Akaria said, leading Manuel toward a circular door, which opened automatically as they approached. The room they left was dim, but the hallway they entered was brightly lit. Manuel raised one hand to shield his eyes from the sudden onslaught of light.

The hallway was smooth and round. It was the same silver as Akaria's suit intertwined with the same pastel blue. The light glowed along the curve where the colors met.

"This entire floor is dedicated to cryosleep personnel, sir. Milocek's office is this way. He's your assigned ReWake counselor."

Manuel followed Akaria along the hallway, which curved continuously. Round doors matching the one they had left the original room Manuel had awakened in were set into the inner wall at even intervals.

Akaria stopped after they had passed several doors and tapped a glowing panel next to one of the doors.

The panel pinged softly, and Akaria tapped it. The door opened and a fit man with dark hair and olive skin stood up behind a clear desk.

"This is Milocek, your ReWake counselor. I must say goodbye now, Mr. Rodriguez, sir," Akaria said, bowing slightly. "It was an honor to serve you."

"Th-thank you," Manny stammered.

She walked briskly away down the hall.

"Please come in, Mr. Rodriguez," the man behind the desk said in a welcoming voice. "Please, sit," he went on, indicating a clear molded chair. "Is there anything I can get for you?"

"I am hungry," Manuel admitted as he slid into the chair. That nagging pain in his belly was increasing, and he pressed a hand against it.

"Of course, my apologies," Milocek said. He turned to a small panel behind him and pressed a button.

A moment later, there was a small *clink!* from a slot beneath panel. Milocek slid the slot open and took out a small tray. He turned and held it out to Manuel.

"Here you are, sir."

Manuel looked at the tray in astonishment. It held a single bright green capsule.

"Um, what is that?" he asked, confused.

"It is a nutrient capsule, sir. Each capsule contains one day's nutritional needs."

Manuel took the capsule, staring at it doubtfully.

"Don't you eat anything?"

"No sir. There is no need. Just one nutrient capsule is all we need each day."

He looked up at Milocek.

"Aren't you going to give me a glass of water? How am I supposed to swallow this?"

It was Milocek's turn to look surprised. "Water, sir?"

"Don't tell me you don't drink water."

"Oh, no," Milocek smiled again. "The electrolyte drink Akaria gave you in cryo recovery is all we need to keep us hydrated. And the capsule has a coating that makes it easy to swallow."

Manuel shrugged and popped the capsule into his mouth. He expected some difficulty swallowing, but it slid easily down his throat. He felt full almost immediately.

Manuel eyed Milocek's silver-and-blue bodysuit. It was just as form-fitting as Akaria's. Milocek was just as attractive and physically fit as Akaria had been. He really wasn't looking forward to receiving his own bodysuit. He looked up at Milocek's neatly styled hair and reached up to feel his own shaggy mop.

"So! Mr. Rodriguez, sir," Milocek said. "It is my job to explain life in our society to you. When a person is awakened from cryosleep, each is integrated into our society. Most have been sleeping for anywhere from fifty to one hundred years, so it can take some time for memory recovery and learning how our society works.

"Today, we will examine you in medical to treat any medical conditions which were present when you entered cryosleep. You'll be given a body suit to wear. The first bodysuits people wear before jobs are assigned are silver in color.

"Once that process is completed, you will be assigned your own living quarters, which are identical to everyone else's. Your nutrition capsule and electrolyte drink are delivered every morning. When your job is assigned, you will be given bodysuits in the appropriate color, to indicate where it is that you work."

Manuel was overwhelmed. He sat in silence for a few moments. Milocek gave him time to process the information he had just given; obviously he was used to the reactions of the newly awakened.

"Would you like to see a view of our city, sir?" Milocek asked. "It's quite stunning; most of our cryosleep patients find it quite interesting."

"Um — yeah, sure," Manuel stammered. He pressed his hand harder against his abdomen as he stood up. The pain in his belly was really starting to bother him.

Milocek led him farther down the curved hallway; one section of the curve was a large panel of clear glass. Milocek stood beside him as Manuel looked out over an enormous, gleaming city.

"Welcome to Ataxia, sir. Just one of the many identical cities on the planet."

Manuel felt his breath stop in his throat. Narrow buildings of various pastel colors speared the cloudless sky all around them.

Below, the streets were as white as Milocek's teeth. Manuel could see signs flashing down toward the streets; Manuel couldn't make out what they showed.

"It looks like some things haven't changed," Manuel chuckled. "Although I can't imagine what you'd be advertising with no money to buy anything."

Milocek eyed him thoughtfully.

"Would you find it interesting if I told you the displays on those signs changed to make a major announcement just today, sir? Typically, they just broadcast safety tips and scientific advancements."

Manuel looked at him, startled.

"They changed today? Why?"

"Because someone very important is joining our society." Milocek smiled cryptically at Manuel and held out one hand.

"Let's head down to medical and take care of that pain, sir. I am afraid I have been remiss by keeping you up here far too long." The counselor now had a contrite expression on his handsome face.

"Milocek, a few of my memories are starting to come back a little. My wife, my daughter. I only get flashes of their faces in my mind for a second, but I can't help but wonder. Shouldn't they be waking up today too?"

Milocek hesitated.

"No, sir. The Record says you entered cryosleep alone."

Manuel grabbed Milocek's arm.

"Why would I do that? I remember having plenty of money, enough to bring them with me. Why would I come all these years alone?"

Milocek looked down at Manuel's hand squeezing his arm. "I don't know, sir. That information isn't included in the Record. And I don't what you mean when you keep referring to *money*."

Manuel let go. "I'm sorry. It's just — I don't understand why I wouldn't bring them. Please, accept my apologies."

"It's quite all right, sir." Milocek continued down the hallway, and Manuel followed, feeling like a fool.

"Follow me, sir," Milocek said, leading Manuel out of the medical bay. He led Manuel to another round door and stepped inside a small room.

Milocek tapped a panel on the wall. Many felt his stomach drop and realized they were in an elevator.

When the elevator stopped, they stepped out into another brightly lit hallway. In this hallway, the silver was intertwined with pastel green instead.

"Welcome to the medical floor," Milocek said.

In the medical room where Milocek led Manuel, two people in silver and that same pastel green were unusually excited to meet him. Both were dark-skinned, with the same beautiful perfection and even white teeth as everyone Manuel had met so far had. They introduced themselves as Parkel and Chantar. Chantar asked him to lie on a bed in the center of the room and scanned him with a small, handheld machines that beeped as it crossed his torso.

"Minor heart murmur and cancer of the pancreas confirmed," Chantar said.

"Oh, my god!" Manuel exclaimed. "I have cancer? How much time do I have?" His heart sank; he had slept all this time only to die in this strange new world alone.

Parkel laughed out loud, then stifled the laugh with an apology. "Cryosleep patients always panic when they hear their scans and confirmed diagnoses. Memories aren't restored yet and you don't remember the illnesses you had when you went under. Please, just lie still on the table."

Trembling, Manuel stared at the ceiling. He looked bitterly at the person who'd had the gall to laugh.

Parkel positioned a large piece of equipment that began to glide slowly down his body. He felt a slight burning sensation as it paused over his chest. It stopped just below his ribcage. A painful sensation increased quickly, and Manuel fought to keep from crying out. Finally, it subsided.

"Okay," Parkel said after the equipment had been put away, "you can get up now, sir."

"Everything is repaired, Mr. Rodriguez," said Chantar, bowing slightly.

"Repaired?"

"Yes, the heart murmur and the pancreatic cancer have been repaired." Parkel said with a smile.

"You can do all that with a simple machine?"

"Yes, we can repair all illnesses and injuries, sir," Parkel said.

Milocek handed Manuel a silver body suit. He indicated a small room where Manuel could change.

Removing his loose gray clothes, Manuel slipped into the body suit. He expected it to be tight and uncomfortable, but it slid over his skin easily. Unfortunately, it clung to his body just as he had suspected it would, highlighting the potbelly he had clearly developed before entering cryosleep. He would stand out like a sore thumb among these fit, beautiful people.

No one looked at Manuel with any sign of judgement as he reentered the medical room in the bodysuit. They all looked pleased to see him again. "It was an honor to serve you, sir," Parkel and Chantar said in unison as they bowed to Manuel.

"Next stop, body polish," Milocek said as he led Manuel out the door.

"Body polish?" Manuel asked, following Milocek down the bright hallway.

This hallway had more people walking past them, and Manuel felt awkward. Everyone he saw was in perfect shape, immaculate, and beautiful. His rumpled hair and out-of-shape body were surely shocking to see.

"Please do not feel uncomfortable," Milocek said, perhaps picking up on Manuel's discomfort. "Most people coming out of cryosleep feel like they do not fit in here at first."

He stopped at another door and tapped on the panel. It beeped and opened, revealing a single chair in the center of the room, and a woman with long, shining brown hair cascading down her back facing a screen on the wall to the side of the room. Milocek held out a hand, indicating that Manuel should enter the room. He did not follow.

"I will wait in the hall for you," he said.

The dark-haired woman turned as Manuel entered, smiling, and inclining her head.

"Mr. Rodriguez," she said in a mellifluous voice. "I am Latalia. It is an honor. Please, remove your bodysuit."

Manuel stared at her.

"You want me to take this off? But I just put it on? And what else do you want me to put on?"

Latalia smiled.

"Nothing, Mr. Rodriguez. I cannot perform a body polish if you are wearing clothing."

A warm flush crept up Manuel's neck and face.

"You want me to just — take this off and stand here naked?"

"I apologize that this was not explained to you beforehand. Yes, to perform the body polish, you must remove your clothing. Everyone who goes through this is naked. I assure you, I have performed this procedure many times. I am a professional, Mr. Rodriguez, and I would never judge you. I make sure to never treat any of my patients any differently from each other. I also do not speak to anyone of what I do in this room."

Hesitantly, Manuel removed the bodysuit as Latalia waited by the pastel green chair in the center of the room. She averted her eyes as he stripped down and laid the suit aside.

When he was undressed, she held out a hand to the chair, which was long and padded. When Manuel sat in it, Latalia tapped a screen on the side, and it reclined until Manuel was staring up at her. She tapped on the screen again, and a long bar descended from above the chair and moved slowly up Manuel's body, starting at his feet.

As he lay there, staring up at the ceiling, the bar completed its journey, ending just past the top of his head. Instead of stopping as he expected, it moved back down along his body, and then returned to its position near the ceiling.

"All done, Mr. Rodriguez," Latalia said.

"I don't feel any different," Manuel said. "I didn't even notice anything when that bar was scanning me, or whatever."

Latalia laughed.

"Just go take a look in that mirror," she said.

Manuel slid off the chair and walked over to the mirror. He half-expected to see himself looking as fit as everyone else, but saw his potbelly and lack of firm muscles were still in evidence. However, his skin looked clean and somehow smooth. It had a sheen to it he'd never seen before. He rubbed his arm and noticed the skin felt very soft. He looked down at himself and noticed that all his body hair was gone. *All* of it.

He looked back in the mirror quickly to see his face; he was relieved to see the hair on his head was still there. In fact, it had been trimmed and was neatly styled. His teeth gleamed whitely at him when he peeled back his lips. His face looked freshly shaved, and when he ran his fingers over his jaw, felt no stubble.

With a jolt, Manuel realized he was still standing fully naked in front of Latalia. He grabbed his silver bodysuit and pulled it on.

"What did you do to me?" he asked once he was dressed. Latalia looked up at him.

"A full body polish removes all body hair, clears all dead skin and hydrates, renewing live skin cells to their optimum level. You receive teeth whitening and hair styling. Oh, and vision correction."

"Why all body hair? What if a person doesn't want all their body hair removed?"

"That's simply not an option, Mr. Rodriguez. No one in our society has body hair; it's unsanitary. Your facial hair will no longer grow. You now have perfect vision, just like the rest of us."

"No body hair? That's — that's unbelievable!"

Latalia smiled. "It's genetic. To be honest, I'm one of the only people in our society who has ever seen a human body with hair anywhere but on the head. I don't share that information with anyone."

"Genetic?" Manuel stopped for a moment. The word triggered something in his mind. He felt like genetics was something he was familiar with. A memory danced close; the sensation reminded him of having a word on the tip of his tongue. It hung tantalizingly close, then slipped away. He sighed, frustrated.

"Are you all right, sir?" Latalia looked concerned at Manuel's reaction.

"No, I'm fine. Just thought I remembered something for a moment there."

"The memories will come," Latalia said. "It just takes time."

She walked him to the door. Milocek was waiting patiently in the hallway. He beamed when he saw Manuel.

"You look wonderful!" he exclaimed. "Latalia, you work magic every time."

Latalia shook her head and rolled her dark brown eyes.

"Milocek, you say the same thing with each patient. Now, take Mr. Rodriguez here and complete his integration. There's no one you need to take better care of." She surprised Manuel with a sudden hug, then apologized and stepped back, bowing her head.

"Goodbye, Mr. Rodriguez. It has been an honor to serve you," she said. She stepped back into her work room and the door closed between them.

"What did she mean by that?" Manuel said. "I feel like everyone is treating me differently. It sounds like it's even different than other cryosleep patients. What's that about?"

"Mr. Rodriguez, there's something — well, I was really hoping your memories would start to return by now. Many cryosleep patients have started to recover some memories within the first few hours."

"Well, I haven't." Manuel said, irritated. "I'd like to know what is going on."

"You were a geneticist. A discovery you made started society down the road to what we have become. Everyone here knows who you are. It is an honor for us all to be the ones to assist you as you awaken today and join us."

"What discovery? I can't remember anything. This is so frustrating." Manuel wished he could force his mind to open and free the memories from his life, letting his know everything about who he had been and why he was here.

"I cannot tell you that; the specifics have been lost through time. We only know that your discovery made it possible for geneticists to improve the human to the perfection you see today. Those changes to our physiology and intelligence gave us the ability to create a better world."

Manuel was shocked. All of this, because of *him*? He couldn't imagine what he could have done to create a path that led to this. If only he could remember!

He followed Milocek to the elevator numbly. The drop in his stomach as the small room plummeted down an unknown number of floors barely caught his attention. He closed his eyes, and the images that flashed before him were the same as before: the dark-haired woman on the deck of the blue house, her hair blowing in the breeze as she gazed down at the beach. No, that was longer than before. A small girl dug in the sand, and he stood with his feet in the surf. The woman waved at him, laughing.

The elevator door was opening when he opened his eyes.

"I remember," Manuel said.

"Your work?" Milocek asked excitedly.

"No. Just more about the woman and the girl. I'm sure they were my wife and daughter. I feel such love for them—I still can't believe I left them behind."

Milocek looked disappointed.

"We want to give you an introduction into our society," Manuel said. "But since you can't remember much, I don't think this is the best time. Perhaps if you are simply taken to your assigned living quarters and allowed to rest, more will come back to you. The building where you will be living is just down this street."

Manuel looked around. They had stepped out into a wide, beautifully appointed green and blue lobby. A beautiful woman sat behind a desk in the center of the lobby. Off to one side waited a man with golden skin and eyes in a silver and red suit.

"Lideton will be escorting you to your quarters," Milocek said. "You will be working in genetics, of course," Milocek said. "I hope more of your memories return today, sir, and the ceremony can be held tonight as planned. It has been my honor."

Manuel frowned as he shook Milocek's hand. All the bowing and "honor" and "sir" was beginning to bother him.

"Thank you for everything, Milocek."

Lideton smiled at Manuel.

"Mr. Rodriguez, it is an honor to be the guard chosen to escort you," he said. Manuel sighed.

"Thank you, Lideton."

Lideton led Manuel to the exit. The door was round like all the others Manuel had seen, but this one was made of glass. People passed back and forth, dressed in body suits of several different colors. Every single one of them was fit and beautiful. Looking down at his own imperfect body, he groaned internally. He would stick out like a sore thumb.

Together, Lideton and Manuel stepped outside. Several people glanced their way. Suddenly several of them stopped and stared, murmuring to each other. A woman pointed at him. Manuel could feel his face turning red in embarrassment. He had known he would look unusual to these perfect people, but he hadn't expected to be stared at quite so openly.

As several people in the crowd turned from staring at him to look up at a sign across the street, Manuel followed their glances. He gasped. His own face was plastered on the screen, turning back and forth, the words THE HERO OF ATAXIA scrolling across the bottom of the sign.

"What the hell?" Manuel said under his breath.

Lideton turned, tugging on Manuel's arm.

"Please come this way, Mr. Rodriguez."

His legs numb, Manuel followed. As they walked, more people stopped and stared, some with their mouths hanging open. He saw more signs, with his face and the same slogan.

"Lideton, what is going on?"

"Your genetic discovery — because of you, we are genetically perfect and the entire planet has been saved."

That was far more than Milocek had told him. Manuel felt tight bands around his chest. He couldn't draw in a breath.

"I — I," he wheezed. He dropped to his knees and the crowd that was forming gasped.

"Mr. Rodriguez!" Lideton cried out.

Manuel lost consciousness.

• • •

The dim light shone in his eyes again as he blinked.

"Where am I? Was it all a dream?"

"This is indeed still reality, Mr. Rodriguez," Milocek's voice. Manuel groaned.

"I should have told you about your fame in more detail. I thought the surprise might make you feel special, and might even jog your memory," Milocek said.

"I certainly was surprised," Manuel said. "What did I do to deserve all of this?"

"Your discovery led to a way to manipulate the human genome. It was the beginning of what we've become. Because of what you discovered, once we reach adulthood, we don't age. We are all genetically perfect."

"But the rest?" Manuel asked.

"The rest?"

"The nutrient pills, the society without money, job assignments ..."

"As people continued to manipulate the human genome with your work, society became perfect. No one needs to compete for any reason — no one is better than anyone else."

Suddenly, memories began to appear in Manuel's head. He saw himself working in a lab, hunched over a microscope, staring at a slide. Saw himself entering data into a computer. Saw himself tossing papers into the air, embracing other people in lab coats as they all danced around.

"I remember ..." he said softly. "I remember solving it."

Then the woman's face came to him again. *Sofia.* Sitting next to him in a hospital bed, tears in her eyes as a doctor told him he had cancer and it was too late to save his life.

He remembered the beach house, the place they were happiest.

He looked up at Milocek. The handsome was clearly trying to control the excitement inside of him.

"Why can't I remember all of it?"

"It can take weeks for people who come out of cryosleep to regain their full memories. I am so sorry, sir, that you cannot remember everything. It is incredible that you remember breaking the genetic code."

Manuel sat up.

"Is there anything left except for these cities of ... perfection?"

"Left, sir?"

"What's outside the cities? Where are all the animals? The trees, the grass?" Manuel hoped the results of his discovery hadn't destroyed the rest of the planet.

"Oh," Milocek said. "Outside the walls the rest of the planet thrives. We don't disturb the other animals and the plants; they are left to live without human interference."

"And how do you get from city to city without interfering with their world?" Manuel asked.

"Humankind built walls around every city, high enough to keep us in and them out. We have solar-powered trains that travel from city to city. Walls surround every track. There is no travel between continents, to preserve ocean life."

"This world is perfect," Manuel said softy. "But it is not *my* world. I feel so alone. Why did I leave my family behind?"

"There is a place, Mr. Rodriguez, that you might like to see," Milocek said softly. "I have spent some time researching your history and I think it is the one place that will help you feel better."

"Nothing could possibly make me feel better about being so alone," Manuel said.

"Please, just come with me. I promise, this will make a difference for you."

Manuel followed Milocek to the ground floor. Lideton stood back at his post. The crowd outside had dispersed.

"Milocek, why is there security if this is a perfect society?"

"There are occasions when someone who appears genetically perfect has a genetic defect that permits violence or self-harm, and they need taken to medical. We have the capacity to repair such defects, but they aren't always evident until after incidents occur. Security is needed to assist with restraint."

Manuel looked at Milocek. "So, not so perfect after all."

"There is no such thing as 'absolute perfection'," Milocek said. "But we are as close as we can get."

This time, Manuel was grateful as Milocek and Lideton ensured they exited quickly and assisted him in climbing into a small white car with a solar panel built into the roof. Milocek tapped a screen on the dashboard. Soundlessly, the car pulled away from the curb and drove.

Milocek turned to Manuel.

"I'm taking you somewhere very special. I am certain you will be happy to see it."

Manuel tried looking around at the city, but he found seeing his own face on the signs everywhere too distracting and uncomfortable. His genetic breakthrough, which he remembered had led to cures for diseases like Alzheimer's and Parkinson's, had led to this Utopia. But others had clearly continued the work to achieve this level of genetic excellence. It was so strange to see himself considered the "hero" of the entire world.

After driving through a maze of white streets that all looked the same, the car left the city behind. Manuel was relieved to see the round pastel towers falls behind them. He noticed that white walls rose high around the perimeter and extended as far as he could see in both directions. The walls followed the road as they drove along.

It was a long drive with nothing to look at but the tall white walls on either side of the road. Manuel felt distracted and uneasy about where they might be going. While Milocek had said it was "someplace special" where Manuel might "recover his memories", Manuel was worried it would be yet another facility where he would be prodded and stared at. Milocek tried to ask him several questions about his genetic discovery, but since Manuel hadn't recovered most of his memories yet, he couldn't answer them. The other man's few attempts at conversation soon lapsed into uncomfortable silence.

Finally, the road ended at a gate that closed off the road. Milocek tapped on a panel, and the gates in front of them slid back into the walls. Surrounded by a small enclosure of the same white walls, the blue beach house from his memories stood alone. Manuel climbed slowly out of the car and stood with one hand on the door, staring at the house.

It was just as he remembered.

"How is this still here? After all this time?"

Milocek smiled. "In your honor, sir. This home has been carefully preserved since you went to sleep."

Manuel walked slowly to the door and stepped inside. He could almost smell Sofia's perfume, nearly hear Rosa's small feet running down the hall. But they were gone, lost to a past he'd chosen to leave for a reason he couldn't even remember.

He walked slowly through the house. Everything was just as their family had left it. Even the refrigerator magnets were in place.

With a sigh, he walked into his old office and sat down at the desk. Pulling the drawers open, he smiled at the detritus of the old life he'd lived.

Suddenly he remembered the hidden drawer. He reached under the center of the desk, and found the trigger, opening the drawer. Inside was a blue envelope with handwriting he instantly recognized. He carefully opened the crumbling envelope and pulled out a laminated letter.

Manuel,

Rosa and I miss you so much. I hope they have the cure for your cancer where you have gone. I know how much you agonized over your decision to go. But if you had not, we would have watched you die.

> *Never think that we blame you for leaving us behind. This was the only chance for you to live. You will see the world you created with your work. Rosa and I will remain here, as we chose to do. Our goodbyes were painful, but you and I both wanted it this way.*
>
> *We will leave this house exactly as it is now, and have it preserved in honor to you and the gift you have given to humanity.*
>
> *I love you, Manuel. I will dream of you for the rest of my life.*
>
> *Sofia*

Manuel placed the note carefully back in the drawer.

As he walked out, he saw Milocek standing outside, looking at the house.

"This is where I want to live."

Milocek turned around.

"What? This is no place to live!" He stopped, realizing who he was talking to. "Well, it is your house." He stopped to think. "We can provide you with a car so you can come to your assigned workplace. We will deliver everything you need."

"I want access to the ocean."

Milocek froze. He did not even appear to be breathing.

"We protect the rest of the world from humanity. I-I do not how that will be possible, even for you, Mr. Rodriguez."

"Just the beach. Please, Milocek. I want to be able to walk in the sand, hear the ocean. Just a small door with a window in the outer wall so I can see the ocean from the deck. I won't interfere with anything out there, I promise."

Milocek's lips tightened until they were white with the pressure. Then he walked to the car and climbed inside. He tapped the panel and began speaking rapidly. He appeared quite agitated, and at one point, Manuel could hear his raised voice.

Manuel walked up the stairs to the deck and stood where he remembered Sofia standing and watching their daughter on the beach. He put his hand on the railing and closed his eyes, imagining it was the place where Sofia's hand had rested. In his mind, he pictured Rosa on the beach, digging in the sand with her plastic shovel, the surf foaming onto the beach behind her.

"Mr. Rodriguez," Milocek said quietly behind him. He turned to look the handsome man in the face.

"I have spoken to the City Council. After much debate, it has been decided that we will do what you ask and open a small door in the wall so you may access the ocean from this house. You must sign an agreement that you will never enter the ocean water, or pass the boundaries set for you."

"Thank you," Manuel said. "That is all that I want."

It took time, but the city engineers accomplished it. They created a door in the outer wall so Manuel could walk on the beach, feel the wind in his hair, taste the salt when the water sprayed in his face.

His nutrient pill and his electrolyte drink were delivered every morning, and he soon fit into his bodysuit nearly as well as everyone else. He reported to his job in genetics every day.

One day, a car pulled up to the gate and the person inside tapped the panel to request entrance. Curious, Manuel opened the gate. The car parked in front of the blue house, and a young man got out. He stood looking at the house for a moment, one hand on the door. The breeze ruffled his black hair, and his light brown skin creased ever so slightly as he smiled.

He walked up to the door, where Manuel waited.

"Hello?" Manuel said cautiously to the young man.

"Hello," the man said in response. "My name is Sofiroman. I am your great-great-great grandson."

"Please come in," Manuel said.

YOU MIGHT ALSO ENJOY

CORPORATE CATHARSIS
THE WORK FROM HOME EDITION
by Water Dragon Publishing

The pandemic came and the world changed. Lives have changed; work has changed. The boundaries between reality and fantasy have become as blurred as those between life and work.

Available from Water Dragon Publishing in
hardcover, trade paperback, and digital editions
waterdragonpublishing.com

CPSIA information can be obtained
at www.ICGtesting.com
Printed in the USA
BVHW081010041122
651158BV00001B/70